William Blades

The Biography and Typography of William Caxton

England's First Printer

William Blades

The Biography and Typography of William Caxton
England's First Printer

ISBN/EAN: 9783337030865

Printed in Europe, USA, Canada, Australia, Japan

Cover: Foto ©Raphael Reischuk / pixelio.de

More available books at **www.hansebooks.com**

THE BIOGRAPHY AND TYPOGRAPHY OF WILLIAM CAXTON,

ENGLAND'S FIRST PRINTER.

BY

WILLIAM BLADES.

London:

TRÜBNER & CO., 57 & 59, LUDGATE HILL.

Strassburg:

KARL I. TRÜBNER.

1877.

PREFACE.

THE "Caxton Celebration" is in full progress, and many persons are requiring information about our first Printer, his life and works. To supply that demand the present Volume is issued. In 1861-63, two volumes quarto were published, entitled "The Life and Typography of William Caxton," in which the most full information then obtainable was afforded; but being both costly and cumbersome, it has been thought desirable to issue a new "Life" in a more handy form.

The particulars of the biographical portion have, where necessary, been re-cast; but only one additional fact of any importance has been added, viz., that Caxton was married, and left behind him a married daughter, information kindly supplied to me by Mr. Gairdner, of the Record Office.

The bibliography has been necessarily curtailed, the account of the old manuscripts of Caxton's printed books having been omitted, as well as the details under "Existing Copies" and "statistics." On the other hand, some new works, of which the "Ars moriendi," "Sex Epistolæ," and the "Officium beatæ Mariæ," are the chief, have been added to the Catalogue of Caxton's productions, and described in full. It has also been thought necessary to retain the full Collation of each work.

It is a pleasing task to acknowledge assistance, and to R. A. Graves, Esq., of the British Museum, I owe my best thanks for revising the proofs of the biographical portion, and for numerous suggestions.

The Plates, as in the former edition, are from the skilful hand of G. I. F. Tupper, Esq., of Pudding Lane, Eastcheap, whose ability in this description of work is beyond praise. To him also are due many of the remarks on the various types, both in this and the former edition.

But chiefly I am indebted to Henry Bradshaw, Esq., Librarian to the University of Cambridge, for the use of his annotated copy of "The Life and Typography of William Caxton," which has enabled me to rectify several mistakes in that work, and to assign with a greater degree of accuracy the undated books to their proper years.

Mr. J. C. C. Smith, Probate Registry, Somerset House, kindly informed me of the discovery of another portion of the Will of Robert Large, Caxton's Master.

The woodcut head-pieces, tail-pieces, and initials are from the hand of Noel Humphreys, Esq., who on this occasion kindly resumed his pencil for the subject's sake.

W. B.

CONTENTS.

PART I.

PART II.—LIST OF PRINTED BOOKS.

CHAPTER I.

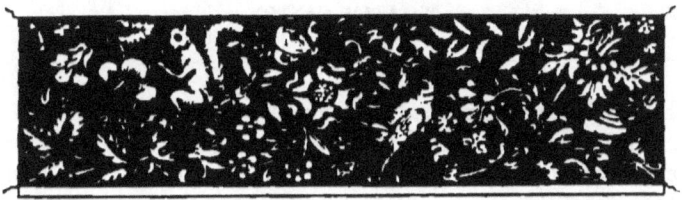

BIRTHPLACE AND PARENTAGE.

I WAS born and lerned myn englissh in Kente in the weeld where I doubte not is spoken as brode and rude englissh as is in ony place of englond." Thus briefly does William Caxton record the place of his birth and early years, and notwithstanding prolonged and careful research nothing more precise has been ascertained.

The name of "weald," rendered by Halliwell "forest," or "woody country," betokens the nature of the district, which at the time of the Conquest, and for centuries after, was covered with dense woods where thousands of wild hogs roamed and fattened. This extensive tract of country had no legally defined boundaries, and one can easily understand how Lambarde, the Kentish historian, was so puzzled when he attempted to describe it, that he declared it easier to deny altogether the existence of the weald than to define its boundaries with any accuracy. An approximate idea of its geographical position may be gained by observing that a traveller, starting from Edenbridge, and journeying through Tunbridge, Marden, Biddenden, and Tenterden to the Romney marshes, would pass through its centre.

A century before Caxton's birth a great change had commenced in the weald of Kent. Hitherto the wool for which

England was famous had been purchased by merchants and carried over to Flanders, for the purpose of being made into cloth, which was brought back for sale in England. Edward III, struck by the wealth and power which accrued to Flanders from the cloth manufacture established there, determined to try the experiment of establishing a factory in England.

The weald, covered as it then was with forests, was of little value as land; and hither, aided in his design by the sanguinary feuds at that time raging among the trade guilds of the Low Countries, the King induced about eighty respectable Flemish families to migrate and carry on the manufacture of cloth in the country which produced the wool. Exempt from taxation, and favoured by the royal patronage and many special privileges, the colony throve and grew rapidly. The Flemish settlers soon became naturalised, and increased in wealth and influence year by year; so that in the fifteenth century "their trade was of great importance, and exercised by persons who possessed most of the landed property in the weald." Thus writes Hasted in 1778, and adds, "Insomuch that almost all the antient families of these parts, now of large estates, are sprung from ancestors who have used this staple manufacture."

We read Caxton's narrative of his birth in a new light, when we bear in mind that the inhabitants of the Weald had a strong admixture of Flemish blood in their best families, and that cloth was their chief, and, probably, only manufacture. We understand why the Kentish dialect was so broad and rude, and we enter more heartily into the amusing anecdote in Caxton's preface to the "Eneydos," where he tells of the good wife of Kent who knew what the Flemish word "eyren" meant, but understood not the English word "eggs." "Certayn marchaunts," says Caxton, "were in a ship in tamyse for to have sayled over the see into zelande, and for lacke of wynde thei taryed atte forlond . and wente to lande for to refreshe them And one of theym named sheffelde a mercer cam in to an hows and axed for mete . and specyally he axed after eggys And the good wyf answerde . that she coude speke no frenshe. And the marchaunt was angry . for he also coude speke no frenshe . but wolde have hadde egges, and she understode hym not, And thenne at last a nother sayd that he wolde have eyren, then the good wyf sayd that she understod hym wel." Dr. Pegge, in his "Alphabet of Kenticisms," gives "eiren" as the equivalent of "eggs" in the Kentish dialect of old English.

Here, then, in some rural homestead, surrounded by people who spoke English "not to be understonden," was Caxton born. Kentish historians, anxious to localise the honour of having given birth to so famous a man, claim the ancient manor of Caustons, near Hadlow, in the Weald of Kent, as the original seat of the Caxton family. In the fifteenth century the name Caxton was usually pronounced *Cauxton* or *Causton*, the letter *a* having a broad sound, and the *u* being frequently inserted after it. Numerous instances are given in the "Archæologia Cantiana," Vol. V., of names of Kentish towns having this broad pronunciation. Thus Francklyn occurs in old deeds as Frauncklyn; Malling as Mauling, and Wanting as Waunting. The letters *s* and *x* were often interchanged, and so Caxton writes *Alisaunder* for *Alexander*, while to *ask* appears in the "Chess Book" as to *axe*. We may further note that *Caxton*, in Cambridgeshire, is spelt in old documents, *Causton*, and, in the records of the Mercers' Company, a certain Thomas Cacston appears as one of the liverymen appointed to welcome King Edward IV on his entry into London, and is immediately after entered as Thomas Cawston. Many years before Caxton's birth, the manor of Caustons had been alienated from the Caxton family, by whom it had long been held; and although some offshoots may have remained in the neighbourhood, the most important branch appears to have taken root in Essex, and there adopted the name of the old Kentish hundred for their new residence; for among the wills now preserved at Somerset House is that of Johannes Cawston, of Hadlow Hall, Essex, dated 1490. Nothing, however, of interest can be gleaned from it.

We therefore conclude that William Caxton probably descended from the old stock of the Caustons, who owned the manor of Caustons, near Hadlow, in the Weald of Kent. The evidence is not strong, but yet there is no other locality in the Weald in which can be traced the slightest connection, either verbal or otherwise, with the family.

Caxton's pedigree is quite unknown, no trace of any of his relatives, except a married daughter, having been discovered. The "William Caxton" who was buried in 1478, in the church of St. Margaret, Westminster, is asserted by some biographers to have been the father of our printer. This may be possible; but no relationship can be assumed from mere identity of name, for Caxtons, Caustons, or Cauxtons are to be found in many parts of England during the fourteenth and fifteenth centuries. William de Caxtone owned a house in the parish of St. Mary Abchurch, London, in 1311: a man of the same name paid his tax to the City authorities in 1441: and there was a family of Caxtons famous for centuries as merchants at Norwich, who used as their trade-mark three Cakes and a Tun.

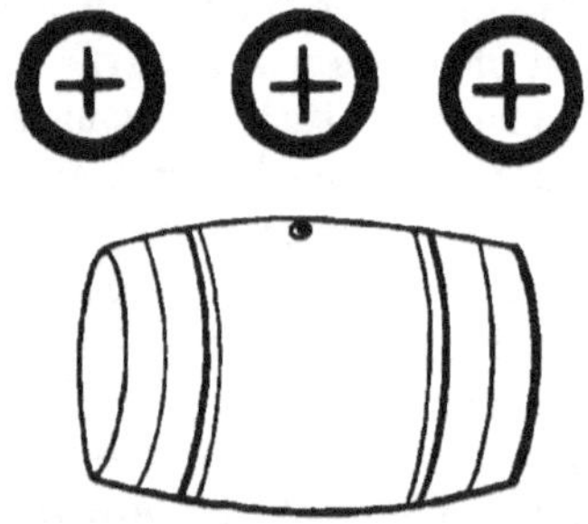

The will of Robert Caxton, alias Causton, is preserved at Canterbury; and at Sandwich, Tuxford, Newark, Beckenham, Westerham, and frequently in the early records of London does the name appear. The will of John Caxton, of Canterbury, likewise still exists: he was "of the parish of St. Alphage, Mercer," and left to the church some wooden "deskys," upon which the following device may still be seen.

When was Caxton born? To this question a more satisfactory answer can be given, for the date of his apprenticeship has fortunately been preserved in the records of the Mercers' Company. It has generally been assumed that 1412 was the date of his birth, upon the sole ground that Caxton himself complained, in 1471, that he was growing old and weak, from which the inference has been drawn that he must then have seen at least sixty years. That this date, however, must be advanced is proved by the following extract from the earliest volume of the "Wardens' Accounts" in the Archives of the Mercers' Company. The entry occurs in a list of fees for the binding and enrolment of apprentices "pur lan deūnt passe cest assauoir des Fest de Saynt John Bapte lan xvj du Roy Henr sisme;" that is, "for the year last passed that is to say from the Feast of St. John Baptist in the 16th year of King Henry VI. [June 24, 1438]," and is literally as follows:—

Entres des Appñtices.

Item	John large,	les appñtices de Robert Large	iiij s
Item	Will'm Caxston,		

We have here recorded the interesting fact that in 1438 Caxton was apprenticed to Robert Large. It is the first genuine date in his life with which we are acquainted, and affords us a starting point from which can be reckoned, with some degree of certainty, the date of his birth.

The age of twenty-one has always been considered as the period when a man arrives at his *legal* majority; but in the fifteenth century there was also what may be termed the *civic* majority, which was not attained until three years later. This custom prevailed to the end of the seventeenth century; for in 1693 an Act of Common Council was passed enjoining the Chamberlain to ascertain that every candidate for admission to the freedom of the City had "reached the full age of twenty-four." The phrase "quousque ad etatem suam xxiiij annorum peruenerit," so commonly found in old wills, refers to this custom; and in view of it the indenture of an apprentice was always so drawn that on the commencement of his twenty-fifth year he might *issue* from his apprenticeship. This necessarily caused a considerable variation in the length of servitude, which ranged according to the age of the youth, from seven years, the shortest term, to fourteen years. Taking the "entries" and "issues" in the Mercers' records as a guide, ten years appears to have been the term most usual in the fifteenth century; but if we calculate his servitude to have lasted but seven years, Caxton could not have been more than seventeen years of age when apprenticed, and would therefore have been born not later than the year 1421. That he was not much younger is evident from the position he had gained for himself at Bruges only eleven years after he entered his apprenticeship, when he was accepted as surety for a sum equal to £1500 at the present day; so that we cannot be far wrong if we assume 1422-3 as the date of his birth.

CHAPTER II.

AN APPRENTICESHIP.

CAXTON tells us, in his prologue to "Charles the Great," that, previously to his apprenticeship, he had been to school, but whether in Kent or in London he does not say. He only thanks his parents for their kind foresight in giving him a good education, by which he was enabled in after years to earn an honest living. No other particulars of his early history being known, we will pass at once to the year 1438, and imagine him, fresh from the Weald, already installed in the household of Alderman Large, and duly invested with all the rights and privileges of a London apprentice.

When we remember how many of these apprentices were young men about four-and-twenty years of age, we can readily believe that very strict rules were required to keep them within bounds, and that when they did break loose it was sometimes beyond the combined power of all the city authorities to restrain them. The Evil May Day, as it was called, in 1517, when the apprentices rose against the foreigners, especially the French, and, notwithstanding the efforts of the Lord Mayor and aldermen, ravaged the City, burning houses and killing many persons, is recorded by the old chroniclers. The day was long remembered by the masters with fear, and by the apprentices with pride—although twelve of the latter ignominiously perished by the hands of the hangman after the suppression of the riot by the King's troops.

The master's duties to his apprentice were to feed him, clothe him, and teach him well and truly his art and craft. Failing the fulfilment of these duties, the apprentice could, on complaint and proof shown before the Court of Aldermen, have his indentures cancelled, or be turned over to another master. On the other side, the apprentice made oath to serve his master well and truly, to keep all his secrets, to use no traffic on his own account, and to obey all lawful commands.

The London merchants of those days were very exclusive in their reception of apprentices, and perhaps none of them more so than the Mercers, who took precedence of all the City companies. The leading men of the great companies, as was natural, apprenticed their sons to one another, and thus the family names of Caxton's fellow-apprentices are the names also of the wardens, and the most substantial citizens of the period. The family name of "Caxton" does not, indeed, figure among those of the City magnates, but William Caxton's admission to the household of one of London's most eminent merchants, and his being apprenticed at the same time as his master's son, go far to prove the family to have been well connected. In one case only does there seem a probability of relationship. The records of the Mercers' Company contain many notices of the "entries" and "issues" of apprentices, and in 1447 it is recorded that one Richard Caxton finished his term of servitude with John Harrowe, whose son was one of the apprentices of Robert Large at the same time as William Caxton. Large and Harrowe were fellow Mercers, and evidently on friendly terms, so that it is probable the two young Caxtons were of the same family.

Robert Large, Caxton's master, was one of the richest and most influential merchants in the City. He was a Mercer, and the son of a Mercer, and a native of the City of London. In 1430 he filled the office of Sheriff, and in 1439-40 that of Lord Mayor. The Mercer's Company was then, as now, the oldest chartered company in existence, and among its members were comprised the merchants of highest standing in the City. It paid more money to the king's revenue, sent to a "riding" more well-mounted men, spent larger sums on

Plate I.

From Aggas's Map of London, showing the House of Alderman Large, Caxton's Master (marked †). The Arms of Large in right hand corner.

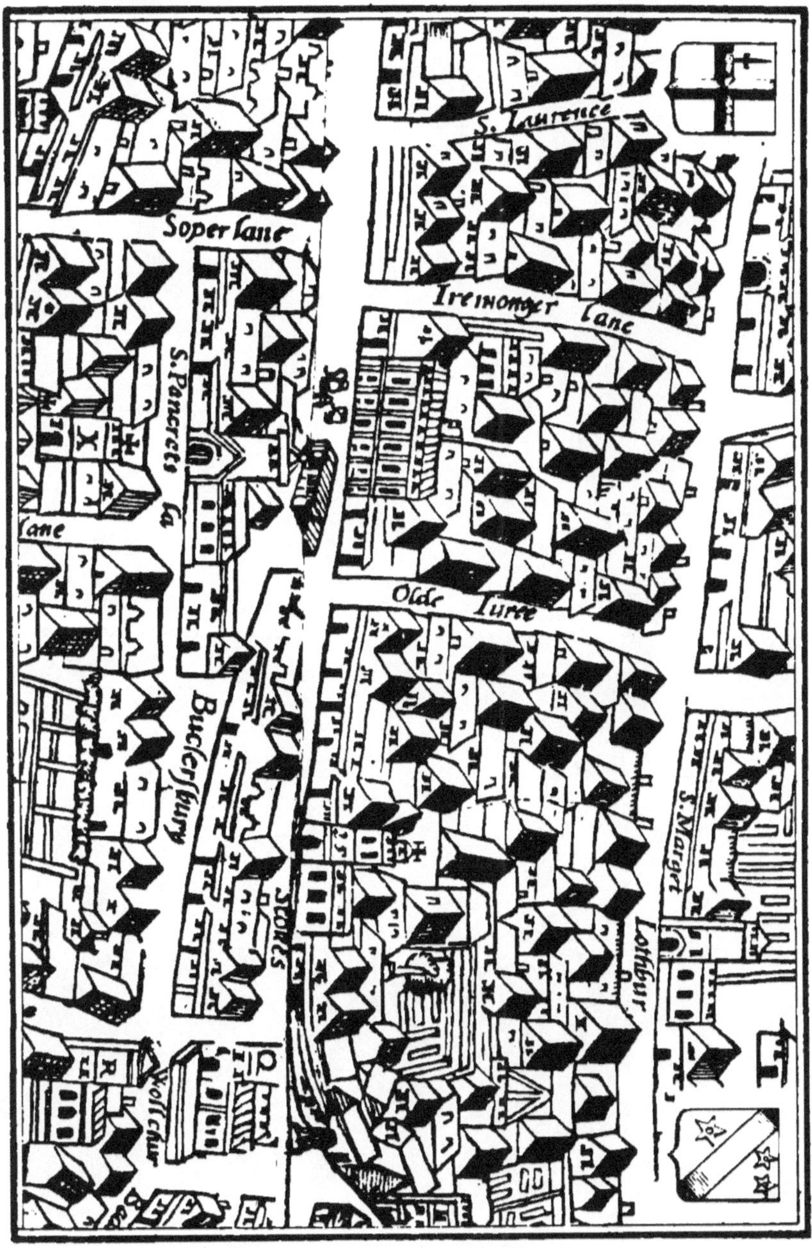

its "liveries," and yielded from its ranks more sheriffs and mayors than any two City companies besides. Large was elected "Gardein" (the old term for Warden) in 1427, and appears to have made himself very popular, if we may judge from the unusual expenditure on the Lord Mayor's Day when he succeeded to the mayoralty. Carriages not having yet come into use, the procession to Westminster was on horseback, the Mercers on that occasion riding in new robes, preceded by sixteen trumpeters, blowing silver trumpets purchased for the occasion. A few liverymen who absented themselves were heavily fined.

The house in which Alderman Large resided no doubt presented a great contrast to Caxton's home in the Weald. It stood at the north end of the Old Jewry, and appears to have been a very ancient and extensive mansion. Stow, writing in 1598, gives a curious account of its vicissitudes, and sums up its history thus:—"sometime a Jews' Synagogue, since a house of friars, then a nobleman's house, after that a merchant's house, wherein mayoralties have been kept, but now a wine tavern." Large resided there until his death.

The household of which Caxton had become a member consisted of at least, eighteen persons, exclusive of domestic servants—Alderman Robert Large and his second wife Johanna; four sons, Robert, Thomas, Richard, and John, all under age (24 years), the last being bound apprentice at the same time as Caxton; two daughters, Alice and Elizabeth, both under age (21 years); two "servants," or men who had served their apprenticeship, and eight apprentices. Large did not long survive his mayoralty. His will is dated April 11th, 1441, and he died on the 24th of the same month. He was buried in St. Olave's, Old Jewry, in the same grave as his first wife Elizabeth, and their monument, with the following inscription, existed in the time of Stow:—"Hic requiescat in Gratia et misericordia Dei, ROBERTUS LARGE, quondam Mercerus et Maior istius civitatis." An imperfect copy of Large's will is preserved in the Principal Registry of the Court of Probate at Somerset House. From it we learn that he owned the manor of Horham, in Essex, and that he left various sums to the parish churches of Shakeston, Aldestre, and Overton, where some of his relatives were buried. It would have been interesting to find that Large had a family connection with Caxton's native county; but although no trace of this can be discovered, it is remarkable that two of his apprentices should have had Kentish names, Caxton being merely another form of Causton, a manor near Hadlow, and the hundred of Strete being represented by Caxton's fellow-apprentice, Randolph Streete. He left liberal bequests to his parish church of St. Olave, Old Jewry, and for religious purposes generally, as well as considerable sums for the completion of a new aqueduct then in course of construction, for the repair of London Bridge, for cleansing the watercourse of Walbrook, for marriage portions of poor girls, for relief of domestic servants, and for the use of various hospitals of London, among which may be noticed "Bedleem," Bishopsgate Without, St. Thomas of Southwark, and the Leper Houses at "Hakeney-les-lokes." Among the many bequests in Large's will, the following are worthy of notice as showing the names and approximate ages of Caxton's fellow apprentices, of whom he appears, both by the order in which he is mentioned, and by the dates in the Mercers' records, to have been the youngest.

Richard Bonyfaunt......(issued 1440)...50 marks.
Henry Okmanton ......(entered 1434)...50 pounds.
Robert Dedes ....(   )...20 marks.
Christopher Heton ......(issued 1443)...20 pounds.
William Caxton ....(entered 1437)...20 marks.

Besides the above there were Randolph Streete, who issued in the same year as that in which Caxton was bound, Thomas Neche, who issued in 1440, and John Harrowe, who issued in 1443. These are all entered in the Mercers' books as "appñtices de Robt. Large."

Before proceeding with the account of Caxton, we may here briefly state what is known of the subsequent history of the family in which he lived. Mistress Large (whose son Richard Turnat, by her first husband, is mentioned in Large's will) was now again a widow, with a large fortune of her own and the care of two stepsons, each of whom was also well provided for. Her second bereavement appears for a time to have affected her most deeply. Over the body of her deceased husband she thus solemnly and publicly vowed to devote the remainder of her days to charity and chastity:—"I, Johanna, that was sometime the wife of Robert Large, make mine avow to God and the high blissful Trinity, to our Lady Saint Mary, and to all the blissful company of Heaven, to live in chastity and cleanness of my body from this time forward as long as my life lasteth, never to take other spoüse but only Christ Jesu." At the same time a ring was placed upon her wedding finger, and a coarse brown veil thrown over her by the priest. Her celibacy was not, however, of long duration, as in about three years she married for the third time, as we learn from the following quaint entry in the second edition of Stow's "Survey of London." Writing of John Gedney, Lord Mayor in 1427, he says, "This Godnay in the yeare 1444 wedded the widdow of Robert Large late Maior, which widdow had taken the Mantell and ring, and the vow to liue chast to God tearme of her life, for the breach whereof, the marriage done they were troubled by the Church, and put to penance, both he and she."

All the children mentioned by Large in his will were by Elizabeth, his first wife. Robert and Thomas did not long survive their father; John died soon after the expiration of his apprenticeship, which, as we have seen, was contemporaneous with that of Caxton, and his name, accordingly, does not occur in Large's will. Richard, the sole survivor, succeeded, as was his father's wish, to all the property devised to his two elder brothers, and his claims were allowed by the Court of Aldermen on his "attaining his age of 24 years" in the year 1444. Large's daughter Alice does not appear to have claimed her patrimony on arriving at her majority; she therefore, in all probability, died previously; but Elizabeth married soon after her father's death, and her husband, Thomas Eyre, son of the Lord Mayor, received her dowry in 1446.

The three years which Caxton passed as apprentice with

Large were very eventful, and, as it was during this period that he must have received his most vivid impressions of life, it may not be amiss to take a rapid glance at a few of the events which agitated the minds of the people. Caxton, no doubt, was witness of the great jousts in Smithfield in 1438, which lasted three weeks, and are so graphically described in one of the Lansdowne Manuscripts in the British Museum (No. 285), and his intense love for knightly sports may have there been first developed. But though sights of knights at tournaments were to be seen for nothing, common bread was very dear, and many deaths from starvation occurred in the same year. An old chronicle tells us that, "Men ate rye bread and barly, and bred mad of benes, peses, and fetches: and wel were hym that myghte haue ynowe thereof." In his own additions to the "Polycronicon" Caxton is more than usually minute in his record of the events which occurred during the time of his apprenticeship. Speaking of this year, he recounts that "Corne was soo skarce that in some places poure peple made hem brede of fern rotes." This makes one cease to wonder at tumults and rebellion, and possibly some chord of pity was struck in Caxton's breast when certain men from his native county of Kent, called "Risers," were beheaded, and the heads of five of them were stuck on poles and left to rot over the southern gateway of London Bridge. In 1439 Large was elected Mayor, and at his "riding" to Westminster and back, all his apprentices no doubt assisted to swell the shout in honour of their master, and to drink the wine which flowed freely from the conduits. But ere that year was ended a sad spectacle was seen on Tower Hill, when Richard Wyche, Vicar of Deptford, an old man of eighty years of age, was burnt for Lollardism. An old chronicler, at the end of his account of this martyrdom, adds, "for the which Sir Richard was made grete *mone* among the comyn peple;" and well they might moan, for his love and charity had won for him the strongest affection among the poor. He was first degraded "at Powly's," and then taken away to Tower Hill, where he was roasted over a slow fire. The excitement among the people was intense, and on the night of this event all the watches throughout the city were doubled, so great were the fears entertained of a general rising. The impression made on the mind of Caxton may be gathered from his own relation:—"This yere Syr Rychard wiche, vycary of hermettesworth was degrated of his prysthode, at powlys, and brente at toure hylle as for an heretyk on saynt Botolphus day, how wel at his deth, he deyde a good crysten man, wherefore after his dethe moche people cam to the place where he hadde ben brente, and offryd and made a heepe of stones, and sette vp a crosse of tree, and helde hym for a saynt till the mayer and shreves, by commaundement of the kynge and bisshops destroyed it, and made there a donghyll." Another grievous event appears, in the following year, to have excited the compassion of our young apprentice. On three alternate days Eleanor Chobham, the beautiful wife of Duke Humphrey, was landed on the banks of the Thames, and, accompanied by the mayor, sheriffs, and guilds of the city, walked to St. Paul's barefooted, clad in a white sheet, and holding a taper, as a penance for her presumed sorceries with the witch of Eye. Caxton has narrated this at unusual length. There were great tournaments again this year in the Tower, as well as a desperate fight between the citizens and a body of courtiers, for which the former, although first attacked, were heavily fined by the king. The old chronicler describes the fray as "a great debate by the night time, where through shots of bows there were many hurt foul and slain." But the chief event of this period, considered in its bearing upon Caxton's destiny, was the conclusion of a three years' peace between England and Flanders. This, coupled with the termination of the war which had raged furiously between Holland and Zealand and Hamburgh, was probably a material cause in determining Caxton's departure from England.

We do not know what were the exact duties which devolved upon Caxton during his apprenticeship; but as an assistant to Large, who had extensive connections, and was doubtless in frequent correspondence with Bruges, the great centre of English commerce abroad, he must have obtained considerable insight into the customs of foreign trade, and become personally known to many Flemish merchants, who, when in London, would probably stay in Large's house.

We must not forget that Caxton was not released from his indentures by the death of his master. If he wished to continue his career as a merchant, whether in England or abroad, he was obliged to serve out his apprenticeship; and that he did so we gather from his admission in after years to the livery of the Mercers' Company. Executors were bound to provide the apprentices of a deceased trader with a new home; and it would seem that the original master might appoint a new master by his will, or of his own accord assign the apprentice during his lifetime, without making the apprentice himself a party to the assignment. So far as we know, Large made no arrangement of this kind; and it appears probable that the usual course of providing a new master for the bereaved apprentice was adopted by the executors in Caxton's case. Moreover, it was not uncommon for young men in his position to be sent to some foreign town to obtain experience in trade. Wheeler says, "The Merchants Adventurers send their yong men, sonnes, and servantes or apprentices, who for the most parte are Gentlemens sonnes, to the Marte Townes beyonde the seas, there to learne good facions and knowledge in trade." Whether Caxton left England by his own desire, or at the instance of his new master, or by the invitation of a foreign friend, is unknown; but that he took up his abode in the Low Countries, and probably at Bruges, in 1441, the year in which his first master died, we gather from his own words in the prologue to "The Recuyell," where he states that he had then, in 1471, been abroad for thirty years. Thither probably he carried with him no more than the twenty marks (equal to about £150 at the present day) bequeathed to him by Alderman Large.

CHAPTER III.

CAXTON ABROAD.

THE City of Bruges had long been not only the seat of government of the Dukes of Burgundy, but also the metropolis of trade for all the neighbouring countries. Thither resorted merchants from all parts of Europe, certain of finding there the best market for their wares. English traders especially abounded, having been greatly favoured by Philip the Good, who had been almost from a child brought up in the Court of England, and who in 1446 gave great privileges to the *Merchant Adventurers* under the name of *The English Nation*, by which title they were ever after commonly known in foreign parts. So greatly were the Duke's dominions indebted to the trade in wool and cloth with England, that Philip the Good, when he instituted in 1429 a new Order of Knighthood, adopted for its title and badge "The Golden Fleece." The "Athenæum" for December 5th, 1863, gives a curious account of the choice of this name. "Philip, wearied with suggestions for the name and badge of his new Order, at last said it might be named in some reference to the season of the year in which the matter had been discussed. That season included the months of July, August, September, October and November. As the initial letters of those months (the same in French and Dutch as in English) made the word Jason, the name of the Hero of the Golden Fleece, the conclusion was hilariously arrived at that the new Order should be named accordingly."

Caxton issued out of his apprenticeship about 1446, and became a freeman of his guild, though, as this happened abroad, no notice of it occurs in the Company's books. It would appear that he immediately entered into business on his own account, and that he prospered, for in 1450 we find him in Bruges, and so far successful as to be thought sufficient security for the sum of £110 sterling, more than equal to £1,500 now. This appears from the following curious law proceedings preserved in the archives of the City of Bruges. William Craes, an English merchant, in the year 1450, sued in the Town Hall of Bruges, before the burgomasters, merchants, and councillors of the city, John Selle and William Caxton, both English merchants, for a sum of money. William Craes deposed that John Granton, of the Staple at Calais, was indebted to him in the sum of £110 sterling, for which the said John Selle and William Caxton had become sureties. and that the said John Granton having departed from the city without payment made, he, the said Craes, had caused his sureties to be arrested. The defendants admitted that they were the sureties for John Granton, but pleaded that as Granton was very rich, complainant should wait and look to him for payment, if indeed the money had not been already paid. Judgment was given by Roeland de Vos and Guerard le Groote in favour of the complainant, the defendants having to give security for the sum demanded, but it was also decreed that if John Granton on his return to Bruges should prove payment previously to his departure, the complainant should then pay a fine double in amount to that of the sum claimed.

We learn from their records that the Mercers were, at this period, engaged in a considerable trade with the Low Countries, but this soon after received a check from an edict of the Duke of Burgundy which prohibited the importation of all English cloths. The item in the Mercers' accounts—"To Richard Burgh for bearing of a letter over the sea, *6s 8d*," probably refers to this, although from the small sum paid in comparison with several similar entries, it may be inferred that he was not a special messenger, but that he took charge of the letter, having to go to Bruges on his own account.

The date when Caxton was admitted to the freedom of his Company does not appear, but it was doubtless shortly after he had issued from his apprenticeship. It must have occurred before 1453, for in that year he made a journey from Bruges to London, accompanied by Richaert Burgh and Esmond Redeknape, when all three were admitted to the Livery of the Mercers' Company, a privilege to which the admission to the freedom was a necessary step. Like Caxton, Burgh and Redeknape were probably English traders settled at Bruges: Redeknape was most likely a relative of the W. Redeknape of London, who appears farther on as a merchant trading with Bruges, and we have already noticed Burgh as the bearer of a letter to that city. We may likewise remark that the usual fees on their taking up the livery seem to have been remitted, the whole entry in the volume of accounts being erased by the pen. The Mercers' accounts of the same year show charges for sending two letters to the Duchess of Burgundy, who was not above trading in cloth on her own account, with the special privilege from her brother, Edward IV, of being freed from the payment of import and export duties. In 1453 Geoffrey Felding, Mercer, was mayor, and the names of William Caxton, Ric. Burgh, Thos. Bryce, and William Pratt appear, charged with fines of 3*s.* 4*d.* each for not attending at his riding (quils fautent de chiuachier ouesque le mair).

As an English merchant residing in Bruges, Caxton would necessarily be subject to the laws and regulations of the Chartered Company called the MERCHANT ADVENTURERS, whose Governor had control over all English and Scotch traders in those parts. All foreign trade was then carried on by means of Trading Guilds. These associations, which occupy a prominent position in the early history of European commerce, had in most cities a common place of residence, and were governed by laws and charters granted on one side by the government of their own country, and on the other side by the government of the country in which they had settled. They appear to have originated in a common necessity. The trader in a foreign country was always an object of suspicion to the inhabitants, and often found himself restricted by its laws as to the articles he should buy or sell, and to the prices he should give or receive. These laws being frequently unjust and subversive of all legitimate trade, besides being often strained to the great injury of individuals, it was found expedient for all traders in foreign lands to unite, and by combined action to secure that recognition of their rights which the individual could not obtain. Hence arose the Association of *Merchant Adventurers*, which consisted of English merchants, who ventured their goods in foreign markets. The Mercers, whose foreign trade far exceeded that of all other Companies, appear to have originated this Association in the thirteenth century, under the name of the Guild or Fraternity of St. Thomas-à-Becket, and to have retained the principal management of its affairs until their disconnection in the sixteenth century. Although Grocers, Drapers, Fishmongers, and several other trade guilds yielded their quota of members, and added their influence when support was needed, yet there were more Mercers among the Merchant Adventurers than liverymen of any other company; the meetings of the Association at their head-quarters in London were held in Mercers' Hall, and their transactions entered in the same minute-book with those of the Mercers' Company itself until 1526, when they became entirely independent, although the last link was not severed before the Great Fire of London in 1666 destroyed the office which the Merchant Adventurers held of the Mercers under their Hall. It appears, however, from the records of the Founders' Company, that the Merchant Adventurers became their tenants in 1565; that the Founders borrowed a large sum of money from them, for which, in 1647, £200 was paid for interest; and that in 1683 the Founders leased the Sising Room and the Gown Room of their new Hall in Lothbury to the Merchant Adventurers for £16 per annum. Several charters were granted by English kings to their subjects in various parts of Europe for their internal government. In 1407, Henry IV granted authority to the English merchants in Holland, Flanders, Prussia, and other States, to assemble and elect governors, with power to rule all English merchants repairing thither, and to make reasonable ordinances. Henry VI renewed these powers in 1444. On the accession of the House of York, the Mercers consulted the City Recorder and "Rigby" respecting their Corporation, and by the statute 1 Ed. IV, c. i., passed for confirming the titles of those who held under grants of any of the three preceding kings, therein described as "in fact and not in right" kings of England, all grants to the wardens of the Mercers were specially confirmed. The Merchant Adventurers now obtained a larger charter, dated April 16th, 1462, which Hakluyt calls "The Merchant Adventurers' Patent," for the better government of the English merchants residing in Brabant, Flanders, &c., and under its provisions William Obray was appointed "Governor of the English Merchants" at Bruges.

Whether Obray died about this time is not known, but he does not appear to have acted long in his new capacity, for between June 24th, 1462, and June 24th, 1463, the Mercers' books record that William Caxton was performing the official duties of governor, and was in correspondence not only with the wardens of the Mercers' Company, but also with the Lord Chancellor, writing to both about the best method of regulating the buying of ware at Bruges. The charge for boat-hire incurred by the wardens in delivering Caxton's letter to the Lord Chancellor is thus entered in the annual accounts:—

> Item for botehyre for to shewe to ye lords of ye coũsell the l're
> y[t] came from Caxton & ye felaship by yond ye See .... vjd.

When Caxton's name next appears in the Mercers' books there is no doubt of his position, as he is addressed by the title of "governor." It was one of the duties of the governor at Bruges by his "correctors" to see that all goods exported to England were of just weight and measure, and at a Court of Adventurers, held in Mercers' Hall on August 16th, 1465, William Redeknape, William Hende, and John Sutton complained that they had received both cloth and lawn deficient in breadth as well as length; whereupon it was decided that a letter should be dispatched to "WILLIAM CAXTON, *Governor beyond the Sea*," for reformation of the abuse. This being an unusually interesting entry, we quote it here as it is on folio cxl. of the original minute book:—

A^{o} xiiij^{c} lxv^{o}. Courte of aventurers holden the xvjth daye of August the yere aboue written.

ffor euell mesure of cloth & lawne.	ffor asmuche as Willm Redeknape Willm hende & John Sutton w^{t} other complayne as well for lak of mesure in all white clothe and brown clothe as in brede of the same/ and in lykewise in lawne nyvell & purpell hit is accorded that a letter shal be made to Willm Caxton goũno^{r} by yonde the see as well for refourmacion of the p'sidentes as other &c. A lettre of the same and other was sent by henry Bomsted the iiijth day of September A^{o} R^{s} E. iiij^{ti} iiij^{to}.

Whether Henry Bomsted was a special courier does not appear; but the same year another letter was sent at a cost representing more than £15 at the present day, and entered thus:—

Item to Jenyne Bakker, Currour for berying a letter to Caxton ovir ye see .... xviiij s viij d

Caxton being now established in the city of Bruges, in the influential position of Governor of the English Nation in the Low Countries, it may be as well to take a brief survey of his duties and emoluments at this period. These are expressly laid down in the charter already noticed, granted only two years before. The governor had full power to govern by himself or deputies all merchants and mariners, to make such minor regulations for the conduct of trade (not contrary to the International Treaties) as seemed needful, to decide all quarrels, and to pass sentence in a court composed of himself as governor and twelve justicers to counsel and advise him; the justicers to be chosen by the "common merchants and mariners," subject to his approval, six sergeants being allowed "to do the executions and arrests of the said court." He was to appoint at pleasure correctors and brokers to witness all bargains, as well as folders and packers to make up the packs of the merchants (who were not allowed to pack their own goods, lest any prohibited articles should be included), and he was to be present at the unpacking of goods newly arrived. No parcel was to leave the city without being sealed. The officers were paid by a fee charged on packing or unpacking every pack: the governor being paid at the rate of 2*d.* for every pack sealed for exportation, and 1*d.* for every bargain witnessed by his deputies, besides several smaller levies which are not mentioned in the charter, except under the term "accustomed dues." From all this it will be seen that the governor ruled over his countrymen with almost unlimited authority. His duties must at times have been very onerous, involving much responsibility, and requiring talents of no mean order. To him likewise would be made all communications from the Government under which they lived, and to his diplomatic skill and influence would be due to a large extent the comfort or discomfort of all the English residents.

By the charter Obray would appear to have been the nominee of the king himself, but this was only a form, as the custom seems to have been for the Court of the Adventurers to recommend "a fit person" to the king, who thereupon appointed him. The following example will show in whose hands the executive power really resided:—The name of John Pykering appears in the Mercers' books as the successor of Caxton in the office of "Governor of the English Nation." This Pykering, who was a Mercer of renown, having spoken against the wardens of his Company, was summoned before an assembly of the "Adventurers of the different Fellowships" in London. There disdaining to "stond bare hed," and speaking "alle hawty and roiall," he was by the advice of the Court of the Mercers discharged from his office of governor, and heavily fined. Shortly after, he appears to have repented his boldness, for we find him humbly asking pardon on his knees before a full Court. Nothing could more fully prove the power exercised by the Mercers' Company, which was, in fact, mainly instrumental in obtaining the new charter for the Adventurers, or, as they are usually termed, "our felawship by yond the See," for which in the year following they are charged by the Mercers' Company £47 0*s.* 10*d.*

The "English Nation," as we have already remarked, was a very important body at Bruges, and like the Esterlings, the Florentines, and other merchants, had their own "House," which existed in its original state when Sanderus, who calls it "Prætorium peramplum," wrote his "Flandria Illustrata." The engraving of the Domus Angliæ, occupied by the Merchant Adventurers, and in which William Caxton resided for many years, is taken from this work, which contains numerous illustrations of the ancient buildings of Bruges, including the residences of the various guilds.

A great similarity prevailed in the internal management of all foreign guilds, arising from the fact that foreigners were regarded by the natives with jealousy and suspicion. The laws which governed the Esterlings in London, who lived in a strongly-built enclosure, called the Steel Yard, the site of which is now occupied by the City station of the South Eastern Railway Company, were much the same as those under which the English Nation lived in Bruges and other cities. The foreign merchant had, in Caxton's time, to brave a large amount of popular dislike, and to put up with great restraints on his liberty. Not only did he trade under harassing restrictions, but he resigned all hopes of domestic ties and family life. As in a monastery, each member had his own dormitory, whilst at meal-times there was a common table. Marriage was out of the question, and concubinage was followed by expulsion. Every member was bound to sleep in the house, and to be in-doors by a fixed time in the evening, and for the sake of good order no woman of any description was allowed within the walls.

When Caxton entered upon his duties as governor, he acted under the articles of a treaty of trade between the two countries, which had been many years in force, but which would terminate on November 1st, 1465. It was highly necessary that a renewal of this treaty should be made before that date, and we accordingly find that the king issued a commission, dated October 24th, 1464, in which he showed great wisdom by joining in one mission a clever statesman and a successful merchant. These were Sir Richard Whitehill, who

Plate II.

The House in which Caxton lived at Bruges.

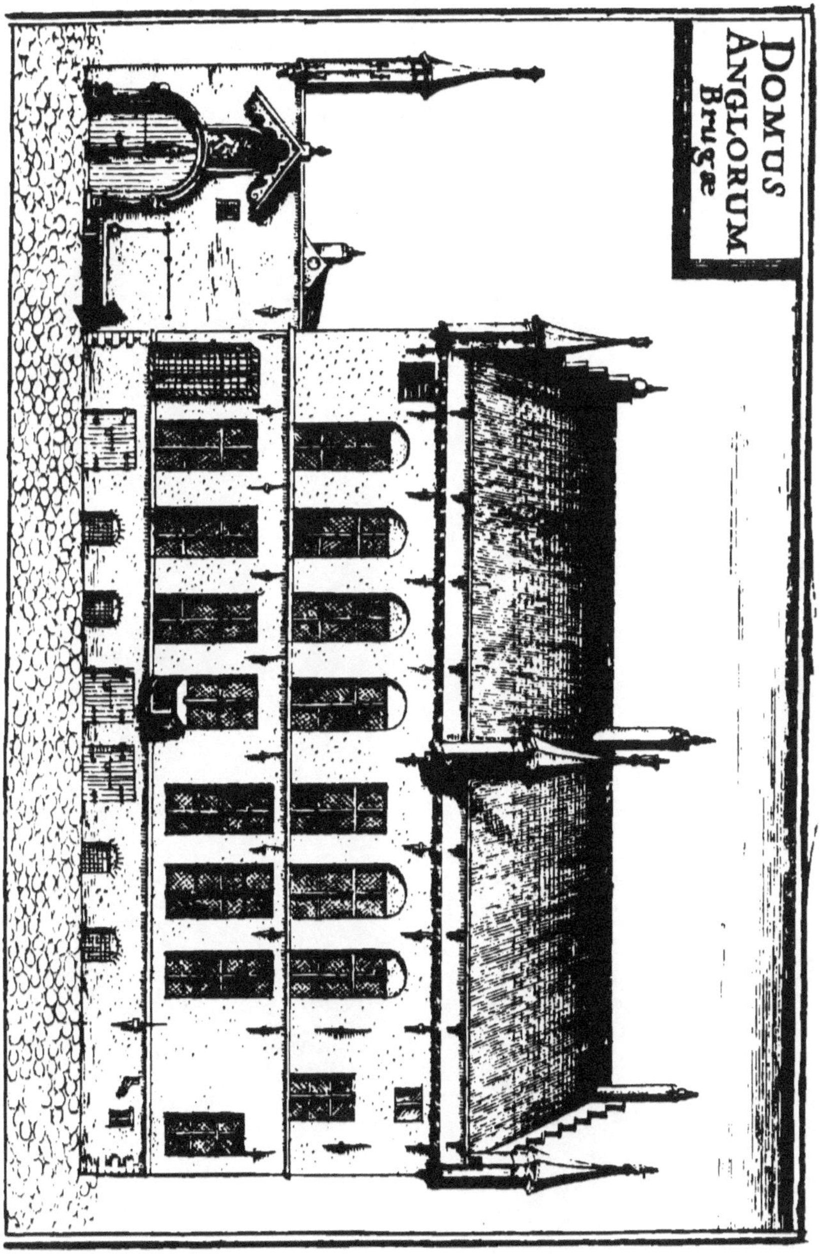

had already been employed in several important embassies, and William Caxton, who, as the chief Englishman in Bruges, and well acquainted with all trade questions was "a most fit person." They were, however, unsuccessful, although for what reason does not appear, and the treaty being still unrenewed, a "convencion of lordes" was fixed to meet at St. Omer on October 1st, 1465, to consider the matter. This convention does not appear to have taken place, for on the 14th of the same month, the wardens of the Mercers' Company wrote a long letter to Caxton, informing him that "the convention holdeth not;" that the king, taking into consideration the near approach of the term of the existing treaty, had written to the mayor of London requesting him "to provide a person" to go over to the Duke of Burgundy about the prorogation of the intercourse;" that the wardens of the Mercers with the wardens of divers Fellowships, Adventurers, considering that hitherto in similar cases the king, "with the advice of his council, had made provision in that behalf," and that it was not their part to take upon themselves a matter of such great weight, had urged the mayor to write a letter to the king in the most pleasant wise that he could, beseeching him "to provide for this matter;" and that, considering the near approach of the term of the treaty and the uncertainty of any speedy action by the king, Caxton had better consult with his fellow merchants at Bruges in as "goodly haste" as possible as to the best means of protecting their goods and persons until such time as the treaty might be renewed. This interesting letter, which appears in full in the Mercers' books, was signed by the four wardens, and addressed "a W. Caxton."

A very anxious year must this have been with Caxton, for not only was the treaty unrenewed, but the Duke of Burgundy decreed the exclusion of all English-made cloth from his dominions. This of course induced retaliation, and the importation of all Flemish goods into England was prohibited by Act of Parliament; but neither the Flemish nor the English merchants could suffer their trade to be paralyzed, and so the traffic was carried on by a more circuitous and expensive route, being smuggled through the neighbouring States. Next year the Earl of Warwick (the nobleman to whom Caxton afterwards dedicated the first edition of his "Chess Book"), wrote to Caxton, calling upon him to enforce the Act of Parliament forbidding the purchase of wares by English traders in the Duke of Burgundy's dominions. Caxton immediately communicated this order to the lord mayor and to the wardens of the Mercery at London, in a letter dated 27th May, 1466, desired to be informed what the "lordes intent" was, and whether they had received a letter which he had sent by way of St. Omer, at the same time requesting early news of any "ioperdy that shulde fall." The letter arrived in London on June 3rd, when a full court of Adventurers was instantly summoned, at which it was determined that an immediate answer should be returned. This was accordingly despatched next day by the hands of Simon Preste, addressed "a Will$^{m.}$ Caxton, Gūnor de la nac' deng$^{s.}$" and signed by the four wardens. In it Caxton was instructed that the Act of Parliament must be observed and the fines enforced in every case of infringement; that, being themselves ignorant of the intention of the Lords, they could give no information on that point; and, that as to any threatened jeopardy, it was likely to be known sooner in Bruges than in London.* Matters remained in this unsatisfactory state until the death of Philip the Good, June 15th, 1467, who was succeeded by his son, Charles the Bold.

The tide of affairs now turned in favour of England, and in the following year the Lords Hastings and Scales, John Russell, and others were sent as ambassadors to conclude a treaty of marriage between Charles the Bold, Duke of Burgundy, and the Princess Margaret, sister of King Edward IV. Lord Scales, afterwards Earl Rivers, was in later years one of Caxton's most liberal patrons, and his translation of "The Dictes and Sayings of the Philosophers" was the first book with the date of imprint which issued from Caxton's press. John Russell, "Docteur en Decret, and Arcediacre de Berk-

* Verbatim copies of all these letters may be seen in "The Life and Typography of William Caxton," Vol. I., pp. 90-92.

suir," who subsequently became Bishop of Lincoln and Lord High Chancellor, appears to have been an ancestor of the Bedford family, and his oration delivered at the investiture of the Duke of Burgundy with the Order of Garter, on February 4th, 1470, is also one of the earliest works printed by Caxton. The marriage was solemnized in Bruges on the 5th of June, 1468, with the greatest possible pomp; and long accounts of the splendour of the ceremony, and of the accompanying festivities, are given by the old chroniclers. Caxton, by reason of his position as "governor," would no doubt take part in them, and be in close intercourse with the many English nobles frequenting the Flemish court. It is not improbable that it was at this period that he attracted the notice, and gained the good-will, of the duchess herself, for he was certainly in her service two years later.

The nuptial feasts were soon followed by negociations for treaties of trade. The king having, by the advice of his counsel, determined to send an embassy to the Duke of Burgundy for the "enlarging of woollen cloth in his dominions," issued a special command to the Mercers' Company that they would present unto him certain persons of their number "to go out in embassage with diverse ambassadors into Flaunders," the Mercers thereupon nominated William Redeknape, John Pykeryng, and William Caxton. This took place on September 9th, 1468, and the three ambassadors having been approved by the king, the Court of the Mercers met again on the 28th of the same month, and voted £40 "out of the Cundith mony" for the costs and charges of Redeknape and Pykeryng in this embassy. The omission of Caxton's name from this grant leads us to infer that he was then engaged in the discharge of the duties of governor at Bruges, and would therefore not require any travelling expenses. The mission was successful, and the intercourse was renewed between the two countries in October of the same year.

The duties of Caxton's office must necessarily have occupied a great portion of his time, and obliged him, in the interests of the traders he represented, to pay visits to the various towns in which the English merchants resided. The old records of Utrecht of the years 1464, 1465, and 1467, mention free passports having been granted to Caxton, his servants and goods. Nevertheless, he seems to have found leisure for those literary pursuits to which he was so much attached. It was in March, 1468, or, as we should now say, 1469, that he began to translate the favourite romance of that age, "Le Recueil des Histoires de Troye." This, he informs us in a Prologue, he undertook to avoid sloth and idleness; and indeed the constant use of phrases in which he excuses himself for his translations by urging the duty of eschewing sloth and idleness, would almost lead one to imagine that Caxton was of an indolent nature, did not the whole of his life, and especially those few last years in which he performed such prodigies of literary labour, give a satisfactory denial. Phrases of this kind were among the conventionalities of the age, and nearly every writer in the fourteenth and fifteenth centuries seems to have considered the avoidance of sloth as the proper excuse for bringing forward any literary work. In the manuscripts of Caxton's time, these deprecatory prefaces are very common; and a comparison with the French original will show that these sentiments, although adopted by Caxton, are in reality those of the original author, and not the spontaneous avowal of the translator. This explanation is necessary in order to prevent too great weight being attached to Caxton's phraseology in the Prologue to the "Histories of Troy," for he was still "governor," an office necessarily entailing a considerable amount of responsibility and work, when he commenced that translation. Indeed, if Anderson be correct when he states in his "History of Commerce," that there were at this period sometimes more than a hundred vessels in Sluis, the port of Bruges, Caxton must have had ample work upon his hands. But whether he really had "no great charge or occupation," or whether he was too busy to devote the needful time to his translation, he himself tells us that he then proceeded no further than with five or six quires. Each quire or section consisting of eight or ten leaves, this would amount to between forty and sixty leaves of manuscript. At this point, dissatisfied with the results of his labour, he laid them aside, without any intention of ever completing his translation.

About two months later Caxton appears to have had more "occupation" than he could get through alone; for, although still acting as "governor," a judgment was delivered in his name, wherein he was styled "William Caxton marchant dangleterre maistre et gouverneur des marchans de la nation dangleterre par deca." The case in dispute being between an Englishman and a Genoese merchant, they agreed to submit it to the arbitration of William Caxton and Thomas Perrot as mutual friends; but Caxton being obliged to leave Bruges for some cause not mentioned in the document, a full court of merchants was summoned, and the judgment delivered in the names of the arbitrators. This judgment is dated May 12th, 1469, and is the latest instance, as yet discovered, in which Caxton's name appears in his official capacity.

There is, however, another notice of Caxton lately discovered in the archives at Bruges, but whether it is to be referred to a period before or after his resignation of office is uncertain. It is a document containing a list of persons who, on August 13th, 1469, were considered by the town council to be of sufficient importance to share in the gifts of the "Vins d'honneur" usually distributed on great public occasions. Caxton received four kans of wine, but whether it was presented to him as "governor," or as an official in the service of the Duchess of Burgundy, is unknown. Treaties were certainly being negociated by ambassadors from England who were at Bruges in 1469, and received, on June 11th, a present of "trois pieces de vin," but this was two months earlier than the date of the gift to Caxton.

On February 4th, 1470, an imposing ceremony took place at Ghent, ambassadors being sent by Edward IV to invest the Duke of Burgundy with the Order of the Garter, but there is no direct evidence to support the supposition that Caxton was present on this occasion. That he was at Ghent, though apparently a year later, is stated in his prologue to "The Recuyell," and he appears to have been connected with the printing of the Latin oration delivered by Dr. Russell.

In October of the same year Edward IV, accompanied by many of his nobles, took refuge in the capital of the duke's dominions from the machinations of the Earl of Warwick. Here Caxton, either as "governor" or as a servant of the duchess, had an excellent opportunity of assisting his countrymen, who were in great need, until the restoration of their sovereign. That he did so may be inferred from the royal favour extended to him in after years.

The exact date when Caxton entered the service of the duchess, as well as that when he relinquished his governorship, is uncertain. The two events may have borne the relationship of cause and effect. Caxton's own narrative shows that about two years after his first essay at translating "The Recuyell," or about March, 1471, he was in the service of the duchess, receiving a yearly salary and other benefits. He was then instructed to resume his literary work, and the "dreadful command" of his royal mistress seems to have been obeyed with wonderful alacrity; for, although he was at one time at Ghent and at another time at Cologne, the translation was not again neglected till, on the 19th of September, 1471, the whole was completed, and offered by Caxton to the duchess, by whom he was handsomely rewarded for his trouble.

The nature of the service rendered by Caxton to the duchess is very uncertain. He says of himself that he was her servant, receiving a yearly fee, and other good and great benefits. That it was an honourable office admits of no doubt, and that it was moreover one in which Caxton's knowledge and talents as a merchant would be serviceable seems very probable. We must not forget that in those days princes, nobles, and even ecclesiastics, did not consider it inconsistent with their dignity to trade on their own account, and this they frequently did under special exemptions from the taxes to which the ordinary merchant had to submit. Edward IV and many of his nobility owned ships of merchandise. In 1475 the Wardens of the Mercers' Company wrote to Antwerp concerning a ship called "The Sterre," belonging to Earl Rivers, and a document of the year 1472 throws some light on the nature of the services which a merchant like

Caxton might have rendered to his royal mistress. Edward IV in that year granted to his sister, the Duchess of Burgundy, special privileges and exemptions with regard to her own private trading in English wool. The late duchess, wife of Philip the Good, likewise engaged in similar transactions, in which, if we may judge from the following entries in the Mercers' accounts, her ladies also were apparently in some degree interested :—

1450.	Item paid to John Stubbes for perys to the Gentilwoman of the Duchesse of Burgeyn		vj d
1451.	Item paid to Hewe Wyche for a writ directe to Sandewyche for the gownys of the gentil womans of the duches of Burgeyn	ij s	vj d
1454.	Item—Pour la copie dune lettre ennoie a la duchesse de Burg^{e}	xij s	
1455.	Item—a M Gervers pour une lettre & la copie ennoi a la duchesse de Burg^{e}	xx s	

The question naturally arises—How was it that Caxton, holding the influential and lucrative position of "Governor of the English Nation" at Bruges, resigned that post to enter upon duties of a much less ambitious character? There is no reference in the Mercers' records to any disagreement between Caxton and the home authorities, nor had he at this time (1469) entertained the idea of returning to his native country. We must, however, remember that during a very eventful and anxious period he had for some years held an office of the gravest responsibility, and we may assume from his complaint of two years later, that age was daily creeping upon him and enfeebling his body, that the troubles of official life had undermined his health. We can, therefore, easily imagine that he would gladly embrace the opportunity of exchanging the cares of office for the easy service of the Duchess of Burgundy, which would allow him to indulge in the congenial pursuit of literature and the "strange meruaylous historyes" in which he so much delighted. Or perchance his complaint of "age creeping upon him" was simply one of the conventional self-depreciating remarks common to writers of his time, while the real cause of his resignation was a wish to marry and to enjoy those home joys and comforts which had hitherto been impracticable.

That Caxton was a married man, and that he could not have married much later than 1469, is a new fact in the biography of Caxton, discovered by Mr. Gairdner, of the Public Record Office, who recently came across a paper document, without seals or signatures, and therefore only a copy of the original, made for production in court in connection with some law-suit. It was found among the miscellaneous records of the Exchequer, formerly preserved in the Chapter House at Westminster, and was first printed in the "Academy" for April 4th, 1874. The tenor of the document, which is given in full in the appendix, is as follows:—A variance having arisen between Gerard Croppe, merchant tailor, of Westminster, and Elizabeth his wife, daughter of William Caxton, the matter was brought before the archdeacon and the king's chaplain, who heard the case in St. Stephen's Chapel, Westminster. It was then agreed that they should live apart, and not vex, sue, or trouble one another, each being bound under a penalty of £100 (which would represent about £1500 at the present day). Upon the signing of a deed to that effect, the said Gerard Croppe was to receive from the executors of William Caxton "twenty printed legends," valued at 13*s* 4*d* each (the sum total of which would now be equivalent to £200), and to give the executors a full acquittance of any further claim upon the estate. This document, which is dated May 20th, 1496, throws no light upon the cause of quarrel, unless it were concerning a legacy left by Caxton to his daughter.

Now, assuming that Caxton was married in 1469, which was about the period when he resigned his official position and entered the royal service, and that his daughter Elizabeth was born soon after, she would have been about twenty-one years of age at the time of her father's death in 1491, and twenty-six years of age when separated from her husband. We have already seen how John Stubbs and Hugh Wyche were in communication with the gentlewomen of the Duchess of Burgundy. Caxton, no doubt, was also in frequent attendance upon them, and may perhaps have induced one of them to become his wife. Whether this be so or not, it is now an ascertained fact that after some forty-six years of compulsory celibacy, Caxton took to himself a wife, who, it may be hoped, was truly his helpmate and solace of his declining years. It is not unlikely that the following entry in the Churchwardens' Accounts of St. Margaret, Westminster, under the year 1490, may refer to Caxton's wife:—

"Item.—Atte bureying of Mawde Caxton for torches & tapres iij s ij d."

Reverting to the "Histories of Troye," and the presentation of a manuscript copy to the duchess, no doubt can be entertained that this was the turning-point in Caxton's life. In the Prologue to Book I. he narrates in simple language the causes which led him to undertake the translation:—"Whan I remembre that euery man is bounden by the comaundement & counceyll of the wyse man to eschewe slouthe and ydelness whyche is moder and nourysshar of vyces and ought to put myself vnto vertuous occupacion and besynesse/ Than I hauynge no grete charge of ocupacion folowynge the sayd counceyll/ toke a frenche boke and redde therein many strange and meruayllous historyes where in I had grete pleasyr and delyte/ as well for the nouelte of the same as for the fayr langage of frenshe . whyche was in prose so well and compendiously sette and wreton/ whiche me thought I understood the sentence and substance of euery mater/ And for so moche as this booke was newe and late maad and drawen in to frenshe/ and neuer had seen hit in oure englissh tongue/ I thought in my self hit shold be a good besynes to translate hyt in to oure englissh/ to thende that hyt myght be had as well in the royame of Englond as in other landes/ and also for to passe therwyth the tyme . and thus concluded in my self to begynne this sayd worke."

The new "Historie" was a welcome novelty to his countrymen, who had hitherto been accustomed to read such works only in French, which still retained its pre-eminence as the language of the court and of literature, notwithstanding the great advance and improvement which had been made in English. The demand for Caxton's translation soon became greater than could possibly be supplied. His hand grew "wery and not stedfast" with much writing, as he states in the epilogue of the printed edition, and his eyes were "dimed with overmoch lokyng on the whit paper." Then it was, with Colard Mansion at hand to teach and help him, that he turned his attention to the new-born Art of Printing.

CHAPTER IV.

LITERATURE IN THE FIFTEENTH CENTURY.

THE revival of literature in Europe, commencing with the latter part of the fourteenth century, its steady growth, and its wonderful development in the succeeding age, have been dwelt upon by many writers. Nowhere was this revival more strongly marked than in France and the Low Countries.

The French kings and the princes of the royal blood had been for many generations the constant patrons of authors and of all engaged in the production of books. In 1350, John II, who has the credit of having founded the library of the Louvre, ascended the throne of France. No particulars concerning the library of this monarch have been preserved, and it was probably of no great extent; but his literary tastes descended to each of his four sons, and from the inventories which have come down to us of the libraries of these princes, we obtain very interesting information as to the number, the description, the illuminations, the bindings, and the market value of the books which they contained. Charles, the eldest son, who succeeded his father in 1364, had a highly-developed taste for every thing connected with the fine arts. He greatly increased the number of volumes in the Louvre library, so that in the ninth year of his reign, when Gilles Mallet drew up a catalogue, they amounted to 910, the greater number of which were written on fine vellum, and were magnificently bound, and enriched with gold clasps and precious stones. This library, the Duke of Bedford, when Regent of France, is supposed to have transported to England in 1429. In after years, a few of the volumes returned to France, but the famous library of the Louvre never recovered its ancient splendour. Louis, Duke of Anjou, second son of King John, shared to a great degree the love of books and works of art displayed by his elder brother. The third son, John, Duke of Berry, formed an extensive library at his château at Bicêtre, near Paris, inferior only to that of the king himself. But of all the king's sons, Philip, who soon equalled his eldest brother in power, far surpassed him in the number and splendour of his literary treasures. King John's second wife was Jane, widow of the Duke of Burgundy, and in her right he succeeded to that duchy on the death of her only son. When dividing his kingdom among his four sons, King John apportioned Burgundy to the youngest, Philip the Hardy, who, by his marriage with Margaret, only daughter and heiress of Louis, Count of Flanders, inherited, on the death of his father-in-law in 1384, a large extent of territory. Philip, who has the character of having been a generous prince, was well read in the literary lore of his age. He was passionately addicted to music and to the collection of fine books, and he spared no expense in the employment of artists, and in the purchase of their most choice productions. Nor did he rest satisfied with the encouragement of artists alone, but gathered round him some of the most learned and able authors of his time, who enriched his library with new works. This prince died in 1404, and was succeeded by his son, John the Fearless, who, although distracted by continual wars, maintained and even added somewhat to his father's library. Christine de Pisan received one hundred crowns for two books which she presented to him. But all previous patronage is eclipsed by the encouragement given to literature by Philip the Good, who succeeded to the dukedom of Burgundy upon the decease of John in 1419. At Bruges, where he kept his court, he gave continual employment to a crowd of authors, translators, copyists, and illuminators, who enriched his library with their best productions, and did not forget to sing the praises of their generous patron. David Aubert, a celebrated scribe, thus describes the duke in 1457:—"This renowned and virtuous prince has been accustomed, for many years past, to have ancient histories read to him daily. His library surpasses all others, for from his youth he has had in his service numerous translators, scholars, historians, and scribes in various countries, all diligently working, so that now there is not a prince in all Christendom who has so varied and so rich a library." In the account which M. Barrois gives of the library of this sovereign, he enumerates nearly two thousand works, the greater part being magnificent folios on vellum beautifully illuminated, and bound in velvet, satin, or damask, studded with gems, and closed by gold clasps, jewelled and chased. Many of these are still preserved in the Royal Library at Brussels.

The taste of successive rulers spread its influence among their subjects, and fashion lent its aid in multiplying libraries. No present was more acceptable than a beautifully executed manuscript, and the opulent nobles of the French and Burgundian courts offered costly books to their sovereigns and their friends. The records and inventories of this period contain numerous entries of such gifts, often with their estimated value.

Among the nobles at the court of Philip the Good, many emulated the literary taste of their sovereign, but none showed greater judgment and liberality in the formation of his library than Louis de Bruges, Seigneur de la Gruthuyse. This nobleman, who had risen by his talents to the highest position, received, at his château of Oostcamp, near Bruges, in 1470, Edward IV of England, when he sought refuge from the Lancastrians in Flanders, and was afterwards rewarded by that king with the title of Earl of Winchester. His library was scarcely inferior to that of his sovereign, and nearly the whole of the manuscripts were the production of Flemish artists at Bruges or Ghent. The large size of the volumes, thebeauty of the vellum, the elegance of the writing, the artistic merit of the illuminations and ornaments, and the luxury displayed in the bindings, are evidences of the deep interest taken by the Seigneur de la Gruthuyse in the formation of his library. On his death it passed to his son, Jean de Bruges, and was soon after added to the collection already existing at the château of Blois, belonging to the kings of France. Great pains were then taken to obliterate the armorial bearings, devices, and monograms which showed the former ownership of the manuscripts, which efforts were but partially successful, as about a hundred volumes, now among the most precious treasures of the Bibliotheque Nationale at Paris, still attest that they once belonged to this celebrated collection. As the patron of literary men and of artists, Louis de Bruges takes a high place in the annals of his country, whilst the friendly attitude he assumed towards Colard Mansion, in the early career of that unfortunate pioneer of the press, should ever endear his name to bibliographers. This passion for beautiful books was not confined to the dukedom of Burgundy, but existed equally in France, Italy, Germany, England, and other countries. Henry VI of England had a valuable library, and many of the books written and illuminated for him are still among the Royal MSS. in the British Museum. The Duke of Bedford, whose love for literature was no doubt greatly stimulated during the time he held the office of Regent of France, was surpassed by none of his countrymen in his patronage of the fine arts, and the celebrated Missal, written and illuminated for him, still remains as one of the choicest productions of his age. Humphrey, Duke of Gloucester, the protector of England during the minority of Henry VI, was also greatly attached to his library, and many manuscripts are extant, over which the antiquary pauses with respect and interest as he reads the boldly-written autograph, "Cest a moy Homfrey."

Owing to these causes, the various artists connected with bookwriting and bookbinding, as well as the trades necessary to them, received much encouragement, while, to ensure rapidity as well as excellence of workmanship, division of labour was carried out to a great extent. Indeed, so important a branch of commerce had the manufacture of books now become, and so numerous were the different classes of craftsmen thus employed in Bruges, that there sprang up in that city a guild, apparently very similar to the trade companies in London, to which, in 1454, the duke granted a formal charter and special privileges. The company is styled "der ghilde van sinte jan Ewãgz," or "The Guild of St. John the Evangelist," who was the patron saint of scribes; and the volume of receipts and expenditure of this guild, beginning with the entrance fees of the original members, exists still in a perfect state of preservation in the city archives of Bruges. Van Praet gives some interesting extracts from this volume, which show that the guild comprised members of both sexes, to whose names their respective trades are affixed, thus indicating the various branches of industry employed at that time in the manufacture of books.

Librariers et bockverkopers (*Booksellers*).
Prenter-vercoopers (*Printsellers*).
Scilders (*Painters*).
Vinghette makers (*Painters of Vignettes*).
Scrivers et bouc-scrivers (*Scriveners and copyists of books*).
Verlichters (*Illuminators*).
Prenters (*Printers, whether from blocks or types*).
Bouc-binders (*Bookbinders*).
Reimmakers (*Curriers*).
Drooch-scherrers (*Cloth shearers*).
Parkement makers et fransyn makers (*Parchment and Vellum makers*).
Guispel snyders (*Boss carvers*).
Letter sniders (*Letter engravers*).
Beelde makers (*Figure engravers*).

Similar corporations existed in other cities. Thus, at Antwerp, the Guild of St. Luke was formed before 1450, and included trades like those of the Guild of St. John at Bruges; and at Brussels there was a guild of writers called "Les Freres de la Plume." These guilds supported their own chapel and chaplain, and sometimes had considerable property. Nearly all the early printers whose names are now famous in the annals of Flemish typography were enrolled in one or other of these associations.

The object of the foregoing sketch, and its bearings on the subject of this memoir, will be evident to the reader who recalls to mind that it was while the pursuit of literature in Bruges was most ardent—that it was during the reign of the greatest bibliophile of the fifteenth century, when Bruges teemed with authors, translators, scribes, and illuminators, who resorted thither from all parts of Europe to Philip the Good as to a second Mæcenas—that it was during the time when the bibliographical treasures of Philip the Hardy, enriched by the numerous additions of his son and grandson, and the libraries of Louis de Bruges and other nobles of the Flemish court were concentrated in the same city—that William Caxton was, for thirty-three years at least, a resident in Bruges. Access to these libraries would be easy to him, and that he availed himself of the privilege seems all the more probable, since we find, without exception, that the books which he translated for his own press may be traced in the catalogues of these noble libraries. As "Governor of the English Nation," through whom all negotiations between the English and the Burgundian governments would be carried on, Caxton would be well acquainted with the nobles and officers of the court, and hence he would naturally become the agent for the literary wants of his countrymen. He would also be brought into close contact with the most clever authors, scribes, and illuminators of the time, among whom were Colard Mansion and Jean Brito, originally artistic book-writers, but afterwards the first to introduce the art of printing into the city of Bruges.

CHAPTER V.

DEVELOPMENT.

COSTUME, that sure guide of the historian and the antiquary, is perhaps nowhere more discernible than in literature, not merely in the dress of language and expression, but also in the visible exponents of that dress—writing and printing. Thus, a manuscript or a printed book may, by the character of its writing or printing alone, be ascribed to a determinate era. In other words, a careful investigation of the mode of construction will, in most cases, enable us to determine the approximate age of any book, from the early manuscript to the machine-printed volume of the present day.

In tracing the early development of printing, we are able to note those successive deviations from the form of its parent, Caligraphy, which were necessitated by the peculiarities of the new art. Commencing simply as a substitute for manuscript, it was naturally a close imitation thereof, and hence the first printers laboured under many inconveniences, which were shaken off as the capabilities of the new discovery became better understood. These changes often afford the only satisfactory evidence of the place and date of printing, as well as well as of the printer's name. We propose, therefore, as an aid to chronological arrangement, to notice the points of similarity between the earliest printed books and manuscripts, especially with reference to the productions of Colard Mansion and William Caxton, and then to trace the novelties, purely typographical, introduced by the printers.

1. There was a selection of material. The scribe naturally wrote his choicest productions on fine vellum, carefully sorted in order to secure evenness in tone and quality; and with the same idea the early printers sorted out their paper before beginning to print. This is frequently seen when two or three copies of the same book are compared together. One is found to be printed entirely on thick, while another is wholly on thin paper—one has no defects, whereas another is made up of what the modern stationer calls "outsides." The two copies of Caxton's "Knyght of the Toure" preserved in the British Museum present a remarkable instance of this plan of selection.

2. It was a common practice with the scribes, when employing paper for their books, to use parchment for the inmost sheet of every section. The object of this was to give a firm hold to the thread of the binder, and thus strengthen the volume, but the alternation of paper and parchment did not present a pleasing appearance to the eye. Caxton adopted a modification of this plan, and instead thereof pasted a strip of vellum down the centre of the section. In books which have had the good fortune to escape the modern bookbinder, the observer may still see either the slips themselves or their traces in the brown stains left by the paste.

3. When commencing a book, the scribes had a custom of passing over the first leaf, and beginning on the third page, probably with the intention of protecting the first page during the execution and binding of the work. This practice was followed in the early works which issued from the presses of Flanders and of England, but unfortunately, in most of these books, on which an expensive modern binding has been placed, the blank leaf has been rejected as too coarse for a fly-leaf, thus causing many volumes, although perfect as regards the print, to be described by bibliographers as wanting the title-page.

4. The scribe necessarily wrote but one page at a time, and, curiously enough, in this the early printers also assimi-

lated their practice. Whether from want of sufficient type to set up the requisite number of pages, or from the small size of the platen of the early presses, there is certain evidence of the first books from Caxton's press having been printed page by page. Thus, in all the books printed with type No. 1, instances are found of pages on the same side of the sheet being out of parallel, which could not occur if two pages were printed together. A positive proof of the separate printing of the pages may, however, be seen in a copy of "The Recuyell of the Histories of Troye," in the Bodleian Library; for there the ninth recto of the third quinternion has never been printed at all, while the complementary page, which falls on the same side of the sheet, has been properly printed. A variation in the colour of the ink, though often very noticeable, is not a sure proof that the two pages so differing were printed separately, as that may have occurred through imperfect beating.

5. Many bibliographers, neglecting the study of manuscripts, and confining their examination of early books to the products of the printing press, have written and argued as if "signatures" were an invention of printers. This is an erroneous idea. It was as necessary for the scribe to mark the sequence of the sheets which he wrote as for the typographer to mark the order of those which he printed; because when the sheets, whether manuscript or printed, had to be bound, it was an absolute necessity for the binder to have every sheet signed, for the signatures were his only guide in the collation of the volume. There would seem to have been, for a long time, an antipathy to these useful little signposts, which, being needed only so long as the book remained unbound, were placed by the scribe as near as possible to the bottom of the leaf, that they might disappear under the plough of the binder. This is what has happened in the great majority of cases, but in every instance of the manuscript being preserved uncut they may still be seen.

It is interesting to notice the manner in which the early printers adopted and afterwards modified this custom of the scribes. As it was very inconvenient for them to print signatures of one or two letters away from the solid page, at the extreme margin of the sheet, and as the idea of disfiguring the text by making them a part of it was objectionable, they continued the old practice for some time, and actually signed every sheet by hand with pen and ink after it was printed. The uncut copy of "The Recuyell," at Windsor Castle, is an example of a book with manuscript signatures at the extreme foot of every sheet. After some time, however, the prejudice was overcome, and the signatures were printed close up to the bottom line of the page. They were first introduced at Cologne in 1472 and adopted by Caxton in 1480.

6. The upper portion of the first written leaf of a manuscript was frequently left blank, for an illustration by the vignette-painter. Space was also left at the beginning of every chapter, and sometimes of every sentence, for an illuminated initial. For many years the early printers likewise followed this plan, every book they issued requiring the hand of the illuminator to complete it. This illumination was a distinct branch of trade, and the workmen employed in it did nothing but paint in the initials and paragraph marks. Through carelessness or ignorance a wrong initial was occasionally painted in, but as far as possible to prevent this, both scribes and printers inserted a small letter as a guide, which was usually covered over by the coloured capital.

7. When transcribing a book, it was seldom thought a matter of any importance to add the date of transcription and the writer's name, though occasional instances of this are found. It was probably a like feeling which made the early printers follow a practice which has caused the modern bibliographer much doubt on many chronological points of the greatest interest. So needless was it thought to inform the reader when, where, or by whom a book was printed, that out of twenty-one works known to have issued from the press of Colard Mansion at Bruges, not more than five have a date affixed to them, and of nearly one hundred publications assigned to Caxton's press, considerably more than two-thirds appear without any indication of the year of imprint.

8. The similarity, amounting almost to identity, between

the printed characters of the early typographers and the written ones of their contemporaries, must also be noted. It was this similarity which probably first gave rise to the now admitted fable of Fust selling his bibles at Paris as manuscripts, his impeachment before the parliament as a sorcerer, and the necessity he was under of revealing his secret to save his life.

The first printer, when he set about forming his alphabet, could not have been troubled as to the shape he should give his letters. The form which would naturally occur to him would be that to which both he and the people to whom he hoped to sell his productions had been accustomed. It is not therefore at all wonderful, that the types used in the earliest printed books should closely resemble the written characters of the period, nor that this imitation should be extended to all the combinations of letters which were then in use by the scribes. Thus the bibles and psalters which appeared in Germany, among the first productions of the press, were printed in the characters used by the scribes for ecclesiastical service-books, while the general literature was printed in the common bastard-roman. When Sweynheym and Pannartz, emigrating from Germany, took up their abode in the famous monastery of Subiaco, near Rome, they cut the punches for their new types in imitation of the Roman letters indigenous to the country. In the dominions of the Duke of Burgundy, where the labours of the scribes had been most extensively encouraged, the same plan was pursued. Colard Mansion, the first printer at Bruges, was also a celebrated caligrapher, and the close resemblance between his printed books and the best manuscripts of his time is very marked. The same character of writing was also in use in England, and Caxton's types accordingly bear the closest resemblance to the hand-writing in the Mercers' books, and to the volumes of that period in the archives at Guildhall. Nevertheless Dibdin thus censures Caxton for not adopting Roman types:—"That perfect order and symmetry of press work, so immediately striking in the pages of foreign books of this period, are in vain to be sought for among the volumes which have issued from

Caxton's press; and the uniform rejection of the Roman letter so successfully introduced by the Spiras, Jenson, and Sweynheym and Pannartz is, unquestionably, a blemish on our printer's typographical reputation."

9. The short spacing of the early printers also deserves remark.*—The uneven length of the lines, so noticeable in manuscripts, was a necessity, as the writer could not forecast the space between the words so as to make all the lines of an even length. But it certainly was no necessity with the printer; for although in this respect the time-honoured custom of the scribes was followed for a few years, the improved appearance which evenness gave to the work was soon observed, and thus a typographical step in advance was established. At Mentz and Cologne this occurred at a very early stage. The first Psalter, printed in 1457, and the Mazarine Bible of 1455 show, now and then, lines slightly deficient in length, as do some of the earliest productions of Ulric Zel; but this rudeness soon gave way to a systematic plan of spacing the lines to one even length. In the early specimens from the Bruges and Westminster presses, the practice of

* We may here observe, that bibliographers often misuse the word "justification" when referring to the practice of placing all the space at the end of lines. The printer's term "justification" does not necessarily refer to the spacing out of the words in a line. Every line in a page must be "justified" or made of the normal length, and the last line in a paragraph, containing perhaps no more than one word, must be justified equally with the full-length line. Short lines are justified with quadrats, or pieces of metal, which fill up the line, but, being lower than the type, do not print. What is called "short," or "bad," or "imperfect justification," is sure to reveal itself, to the dismay of the compositor, by allowing the faulty line to drop out when the "forme," or mass of type, is lifted. The probable reason why Colard Mansion and Caxton did not space their lines to an even length is, that at that time they had not begun to use the *setting-rule*. This useful little slip of metal enables each letter as it is picked up by the compositor, to be passed along on an even surface to its destination, instead of catching in every unevenness or burr of the previous line. Its absence would entail many obstructions to the spacing-out of lines, and render the plan of leaving all the spare space at the end, which was actually adopted, at once more easy, expeditious, and free from accident.

placing all the spare space at the end of the lines, instead of dividing it between the words, gives a very rude appearance to the page, and in these books it is carried to a greater extent than in the works of any German, Italian or French printers. Colard Mansion abandoned this practice in 1479, and Caxton in 1480.

It will be apparent, from the foregoing remarks, that the books of our first printers bore no slight resemblance to manuscripts, and indeed, until quite recently, a copy of the Mazarine Bible, in the Library of Lambeth Palace, was so regarded;* but this resemblance was soon modified, in many particulars, to suit the requirements of typography.

The execution of manuscript capitals being both tedious and expensive led to the early introduction of large letters engraved on wood, which were either printed in black at the same impression as the other portion, or in red by a subsequent operation. Colard Mansion seems never to have adopted them, although several of his books are illustrated by large and numerous woodcuts. Caxton inserted illustrations engraved on wood in two or three books before 1484, the date of "Æsop," in which woodcut initials first appear.

Title-pages, likewise, are purely typographical in their origin, the scribes having been content with heading their page with "Hic incipit" and the name of the treatise. Caxton followed the usage of the scribes in this particular; for, with one exception only, and at the very end of his career, where the title of the book is printed alone in the centre of the first page, his books appear without any title-page whatever.

Wynken de Worde adopted the use of title-pages immediately after the death of his master, but Machlinia of London, and the schoolmaster-printer of St. Alban's, never used them.

* In 1856, an old established bookseller, in one of our largest cathedral towns, marked a copy of Caxton's "Statutes of Hen. VII" as an old MS., *and sold it for 2s. 6d.!* See also the remarks on Verard's "Euryalus et Lucrece," in the Catalogue of the Harleian MSS., vol. III, No. 4392.

These minute details may appear, at first sight, to be hardly worthy of record; but when we remember that two-thirds of Caxton's books are without any date, and that, by careful examination of the workmanship, we can trace the printer gradually developing the changes from manuscript to typographical character, we appreciate the existence of a mass of technical evidence which, like the strata of the earth, or the mouldings of a cathedral arch, affords chronological data quite independent of any other source, and enables us, with a near approach to accuracy, to determine the age of any undated book. To this evidence may be added some other important signs which sometimes bear witness to the date when a book was printed. Such are the size of the printed page, its depth and width, the number of lines in a page, the number of sheets in a section, and, above all, the sequence in the use of various types. In Caxton's books this sequence is very remarkable, as will be seen by the annexed table, where only books with fixed dates are entered, so that the reader may form his own judgment as to the chronological order of the above-mentioned peculiarities.

Some interesting facts may be gathered from this table.

1. The types used by Caxton bear a definite chronological relation to one another. Type No. 1 goes out of use, and is succeeded, in 1477, by No. 2. Type No. 3 is principally employed for headlines during the use of Nos. 2 and 4. In 1480 type No. 4 makes its appearance, but not till No. 2 is about to disappear. In 1483 type No. 4* supersedes its predecessor, and, in its turn, makes way for Nos. 5 and 6, which close the list. If the books were added which give the dates of their translation, which almost always coincide with those of their printing, the result would be the same.

2. All the books printed before 1480 were with lines of an uneven length, whilst all printed subsequently were spaced out evenly.

3. Signatures and even spacing of the lines were synchronous improvements, and both, when once adopted, were never afterwards abandoned. In the signatures themselves a curious fact may be noted—that whereas the custom of Caxton

Title.	Date of Printing.	No. of Type.	Length of Line.	Lines spaced out to the end or not.	Length of Page.	Signatures.	Initials.
			Inches.		Lines.		
The Recuyell	Before 1477	1	5	not	31	none	none
The Game of Chess, 1st edition	Do.	1	5	not	31	none	none
The Life of Jason	Do.	2	5	not	29	none	none
Dictes, 1st edition	Nov. 18th, 1477	2	5	not	29	none	none
Moral Proverbs	Feb. 20th, 1478	2	In Metre.		28	none	none
Cordyale	Mar. 24th, 1479	2 & 3	5	not	29	none	none
Chronicles, 1st edition	June 10th, 1480	4	4¾	spaced out	40	rom. num.	none
Reynard, 1st edition	June 6th, 1481	2	4¾	spaced out	29	arab. figs.	none
Tullo	Aug. 12th, 1481	2	4¾	spaced out	29	arab. figs.	none
Godfrey	Nov. 20th, 1481	4	4¾	spaced out	40	arab. figs.	none
Polycronicon	July 2nd, 1482	4	4¾	spaced out	40	arab. figs.	none
Chronicles, 2nd edition	Oct. 8th, 1482	4	4¾	spaced out	40	arab. figs.	none
Pilgrimage of the Soul	June 6th, 1483	4	4¾	spaced out	40	rom. num.	none
Liber Festivalis, 1st edition	June 30th, 1483	4*	5	spaced out	38	rom. num.	none
Confessio Amantis	Sept. 2nd, 1483	4	2¾	spaced out	46	arab. figs.	none
Knight of the Tower	Jan. 31st, 1484	4*	5	spaced out	38	rom. num.	none
Æsop	Mar. 26th, 1484	4*	4¾	spaced out	38	rom. num.	wood
King Arthur	July 31st, 1485	4*	3¼	spaced out	26	rom. num.	wood
Charles the Great	Dec. 1st, 1485	4*	4¾	spaced out	38	rom. num.	wood
Paris and Vienne	Dec. 19th, 1485	4*	2¾	spaced out	39	rom. num.	wood
Book of Good Manners	May 11th, 1487	5	4¾	spaced out	34	rom. num.	wood
Directorium Sacerdotum, 2nd edition	——— 1489	6	4¾	spaced out	31	rom. num.	wood
Art and Craft	June 15th, 1490	6	4¾	spaced out	31	rom. num.	wood
Eneydos	June 22nd, 1490	6	4¾	spaced out	31	rom. num.	wood
Fayts of Arms	July 14th, 1490	6	4¾	spaced out	31	rom. num.	wood

was generally to use letters and Roman numerals, as b j, for his signatures, yet in the three years 1481 to 1483, and at no other period, he used Arabic numerals, thus b 1, or 2 1.

We may further add that the use of the paragraph mark (¶) never appears before 1483; that the great device makes no appearance, till 1487, the printed date to the third edition of the "Dictes" notwithstanding; and that initials in wood first appear in the "Æsop" in 1484.

By the application of these tests to the undated books we are enabled to assign each of them, with tolerable certainty, to a particular period.

CHAPTER VI.

COLARD MANSION.

BRUGES, the old metropolis of Flanders, offers many points of the greatest interest to the historian and the antiquary. In the fifteenth century, it was the chosen residence of the sovereigns of the House of Burgundy, and to its marts resorted the most opulent merchants of Europe. There the arts, as well as commerce, were developed to a degree of excellence unequalled since the Augustan age, and even Paris was surpassed in literary and artistic treasures. Artists and craftsmen were consequently numerous, and, as we have already seen, those of them who were connected with the production of books, were enrolled as a trade guild. And this preeminence is not immaterial to our enquiry, for William Caxton was not only for more than thirty years a constant resident in Bruges, holding for a considerable period a position of great authority, but in this city likewise took his first lessons in typography and obtained the materials necessary for the introduction of the New Art into his native country.

Colard Mansion is generally admitted to have been the first printer at Bruges, but of his history little is known. His name occurs many times in the old records still preserved in the municipal library, and always in connection either with his trade of fine-manuscript writer, or with the guild of St. John. The first time it appears it is written "Collinet," a diminutive of Collaert, from which Van Praet, his first biographer, thinks he was at that time under age. In 1450 "Colinet" received fifty-four livres from the Duke of Burgundy for a novel, entitled "Romuleon," beautifully illuminated and bound in velvet. This copy is now in the Royal Library at Brussels, and another copy, written in characters exactly like the types used twenty years later by Colard Mansion, is in the British Museum. Both the Seigneur de la Gruthuyse and the Seigneur de Crevecœur were his patrons; the former, indeed, was at one time on such friendly and familiar terms with Mansion, that he stood godfather to one of his children. It does not, however, appear that in later years, when poverty laid its heavy hand on the unfortunate printer, any of his patrons came to his assistance.

From 1454 to 1473 the name of Mansion is found, year by year, as a contributor to the guild of St. John, the formation of which has been already noticed. In 1471 he was "doyen" or dean, an office which he held for two years, at the expiration of which time he is supposed to have left Bruges for a twelvemonth in order to learn the new art of printing. This is a needless assumption, grounded solely on his subscription for 1473 having been paid through a brother of the guild. From 1476 to 1482 his name does not appear at all as a contributor, although the dates of the "Boece," the "Quadrilogue," and the "Somme rurale," show that he was still at Bruges, and pursuing his vocation. His subscription to the guild is again entered in 1483, and his name occurs in the guild records for the last time in 1484. This was a disastrous year to Colard Mansion; for, although not overtaken by death, as his early biographers have assumed, disgrace, poverty, and expatriation awaited him. He appears to have been in straitened circumstances for some years, as in 1480 he could not execute the commission of Monseigneur de Gazebeke for an illuminated copy of "Valerius Maximus," in two volumes, without several advances of money. The receipts for these instalments are still preserved, as is also a notice of Mansion's place of residence, which was in one of the poorest streets in Bruges, leading out of the Rue des Carmes. His typographical labours were carried on in one of two rooms over the porch of the church of St. Donatus, for which we may assume that he paid the same rent as the next tenant, six livres per annum. It was in this room that Colard Mansion, in May 1484, finished his beautiful edition of Ovid's "Metamorphoses," a magnificent folio of 386 leaves, full of woodcuts, printed-in separately from the text. We know nothing of the sale of this noble production; but the expenses connected with it were probably his ruin, for about three months later he left the city. The Chapter of St. Donatus, feeling uneasy about their rent, soon made inquiries as to the probability of his return, there being an opportunity of letting the room to a better tenant; but all was in vain, and in October 1484 the apartment in which Mansion had for so many years been labouring at those volumes which are now prized as among the glories of Bruges, was made over to Jean Gossin, a member of the same guild as Mansion, and, like him, engaged in the manufacture of books. The Chapter, however, took care not to lose by their tenant's flight, for the conditions upon which his room (and probably a large stock of printed sheets besides) was made over to Gossin were that the latter should pay up all arrears of rent. Nothing more is known of Mansion after this sad event; and it is mournful to contemplate the poor man turning his back upon his native city, to begin life anew at the age of nearly sixty, after so many years spent in literary labour. It has been suggested that he took refuge in Paris, as the names of Paul and Robert Mansion appear as printers in that city in 1650; but on this point there is no evidence whatever.

In examining the productions of Colard Mansion's press, it is somewhat perplexing to the lover of accuracy to find that he, like all the earliest printers, issued most of his productions without date, and many without even name or place. In this he merely followed the example of his predecessors, the scribes, who seldom affixed their names, or the date of the transcript. Van Praet enumerates twenty-one works from his press, and another has been since discovered. These, to the eye of a printer, naturally divide themselves into two classes.

1st. Those printed in a large bold Secretary type.

2nd. Those printed in a smaller semi-roman character, known as "Lettres de Somme."

No one acquainted, although but slightly, with the practical features of typography can doubt that the early books attributed to Caxton, and the early books issued by Mansion, came from the same press. Mansion employed for his first type a very bold secretary, exactly similar in character to the type first used at Westminster. In Pl. II and III they may be seen in juxtaposition. It also closely resembled in shape and size in the character in which Mansion was accustomed to execute his manuscripts. He likewise printed, at the head of each chapter, the summary in red ink; and here he displayed so curious an instance of typographical ingenuity that the reader's attention is particularly requested to it. If we closely examine into the appearance which the red ink, as used by Mansion in his "Boccace" "Bocce," "Somme rurale," and "Ovide," presents, it will be noticed that it is very dirty in colour, and moreover that the black lines, nearest the red, have their edges tipped with red, a defect which the separate printing of lines in red ink affords no opportunity for producing. The following explanation will satisfactorily show the *modus operandi*. The two colours were printed by one and the same pull of the press, all the type, both for black and red, being included in the same form. But it was impossible to beat the form with the balls, and leave a single line in the middle untouched; so the whole page was inked black, and then (a space for play being always left above and below) the black ink was carefully wiped from the intended red line, and that line re-inked with red by the finger, or by other means, after which the sheet was pulled. A two-fold inconvenience attended this clumsy process,—the black could never be removed so completely that it would not taint the ensuing red, and the utmost care would not usually prevent the black lines nearest the red receiving a slight touch from the red finger, or ball. In fact, both these defects appear in every book printed by Colard Mansion, in which the two colours were used, and to these was frequently added a third

—the loss of a portion of the black ink nearest to the red caused by the wiping process. Actual experiment shows that this mode of working both colours at once is the only solution of the appearance, and the inducement for its adoption was in all probability the perfect accuracy of "register" it secured, as there was thus no fear of the red lines not fitting exactly in their proper places—an accuracy very difficult to obtain, by separate printings, at a rudimentary press. This peculiarity of workmanship in the Bruges printer is not found in any book from the Mentz or Cologne presses; indeed all the typographical habits of the Bruges and Cologne printers were so distinct and opposite that it is difficult to believe in any connection between them.

It has been already shown that in early books uneven spacing is a sure sign that the workmanship is prior to that of books from the same press in which the lines are all of equal length. The dated books of Colard Mansion are only six in number, which fully bear this out.

Le Jardin de Dévotion	before 1476	uneven lines
Boccace du Déchiet des Nobles Hommes	1476	"
Boece de la Consolation de Philosophie	1477	"
Le Quadrilogue d'Alain Chartier	1478*	even lines
La Somme rurale	1479	"
Les Metamorphoses d'Ovide	1484	"

Taking, then, 1478 as the year in which Mansion changed his practice, we may assume, without fear of error, that all the undated books, with short-spaced lines, were anterior, and all the undated books, with their lines spaced to one length, posterior to the "Quadrilogue." On this basis his undated productions may be thus arranged.

Before 1478, having lines of an uneven length :—

Les Dits moraux des Philosophes	short-spaced
Les Invectives contre la Secte de Vauderie	"
La Controversie de Noblesse	"
Débat entre trois valeureux Princes	"

* The only date in the volume is 1477, which was the year when the Prologue was composed: the printing must have been later than this.

After 1478, having lines of an even length :—

Les Advineaux amoureux. Edit. 1	full-spaced
Le Doctrinal du temps présent	„
La Doctrine de bien vivre	„
L'Art de bien mourir	„
La Purgatoire des mauvais Maris	„
L'Abuse en court	„
Les Evangiles des Quenouilles	„
Le Donat espirituel	„
Les Adeuineaux amoreux. Edit. 2	„
Dionysii Areopagiticæ liber	„

Colard Mansion seems never to have produced works from his press with rapidity; therefore, as the "Boccace of" 1476 contained nearly 600 pages in large folio, and the "Boece" of 1477 about the same, we may fairly assume that the five other short-spaced works were anterior to the "Boccace." This hypothesis would make Mansion a printer in Bruges about the time when Caxton finished his translation of "Le Recueil des Histoires de Troyes."

In the next Chapter it is proposed to show how all the peculiarities noticeable in the printed productions of Colard Mansion may be traced in those attributed to William Caxton.

Plate III.

Type No. 1.

From "The Recuyell of the Histories of Troye."

and helpe of almyghty gode . whome I mekely supplye
to gyue me grace to accomplysshe hit to the playsir of
her that is causer therof and that she ressepue hit in gre
of me her faithfull trewe & moste humble seruant &c.
Thus endeth the seconde book .

From "Le Recueil des Histoires de Troye."

La renōmee de ces choses mōta en si hault
tres de celle tour La renōmee de ces choses mōta en si hault et ny auoit roy
son que toute grece en fut plaine de merueill et ny auoit roy
ne prince qui ne plaindist la perte de la Jennesse de danes
qui lors estoit tenue pour la plus belle de toutes les gre-
goises &c .

Plate IV.

Colard Mansion's, Gros Bâtarde Type.
Showing the hand of the same Artist that cut Caxton's No. 2.

Taken from "La Controversie de Noblesse," c. 1477.

Ja commence la controuerſie de nobleſſe
plaidoyee entre Publius Cornelius Sa-
pion dunepart. Et Gayus flaminius de
autrepart. Laquelle a eſte faicte et compo-
ſee par vn notable docteur en loix et grant
orateur nomme Surſe de piſtoye.

Plate V.

Caxton's Type No. 2.*

Taken from "Fratris Laur. Gul. de Saona," c. 1479.

Explicit liber tercius: et opus rhetorice facultatis p fra
trē laurentiū Guilelmi de Saona ordinis minoꝝ sacre pa
gine ꝓfessorē ex dictis testimonijsq3 sacratissimaꝝ scriptu
raꝝ, doctoꝝq3 ꝓbatissimoꝝ compilatū ꝛ ꝯfirmatū: quibus
ex causis censuit appellandū fore Margaritam eloquentie
castigate ad eloquendā diuina accomodatam

Compilatū autē fuit hoc opus in alma uniuersitate Can
tabrigie . Anno dñi . 1478 . die et . 6 . Julij . quo die
festum Sancte Marthe recolitē . Sub protectione Serenissi
mi regis anglorum Eduardi quarti

CHAPTER VII.

CAXTON A PRINTER.

THE evidence as to where and from whom Caxton acquired his knowledge of the Art of Printing has been considered by nearly every bibliographer as being confined entirely to the information obtained from Caxton's own Prologues and Epilogues, with the one addition of the well-known quatrain of Wynken de Worde, at the end of his "Bartholomæus de Proprietatibus Rerum." The argument from technical peculiarities in the books themselves has hitherto been almost entirely overlooked, although a mass of the truest, because unintentional evidence may be found from the attentive study of these dumb witnesses.

Mr. Bradshaw, of Cambridge, has most truly observed, in his "Classified Index," that the bibliographer should "make such an accurate and methodical study of the *types* used and *habits of printing* observable at different presses as to enable him to observe and be guided by these characteristics in settling the date of a book which bears no date upon the surface." * But the great difficulty in the way of this systematic study is the impossibility of having the books side by side, for their rarity is so great that in no one existing library can they all be found.

The books printed in Caxton's type No. 1, used only at

* A classified Index of the fifteenth-century books in the collection of M. J. de Meyer. 8vo. London, 1870.

Bruges, are five in number, although we can trace his direct connection with but two of them.

1. "The Recuyell of the Historyes of Troye," with Prologues and Epilogues.
2. "Le Recueil des Histoires de Troye."
3. "The Game and Playe of the Chesse," with Prologue by Caxton.
4. "Les Fais et Proesses du Chevalier Jason."
5. "Meditacions sur les Sept Pseaulmes penitenciaulx."

To these must be added one book printed at Bruges in type No. 2.

6. "Les Quatre Derrenniers Choses."

Before analysing the evidence supplied by Caxton's remarks and dates, it is necessary to explain how easily a mistake may be made, and an erroneous conclusion drawn, unless care be taken to remember the effect of the change of style upon the commencement of the year. In England, from the thirteenth century until 1752, the new year began on March 25th; while in Holland and Flanders it commenced on Easter Day. Neglect of this fact has led to many historical errors. Thus, one historian states that Charles I. was beheaded on January 30th, 1648, whereas others assert that the event took place on the same day in 1649; one dates the flight of James II. from his kingdom in February, 1688, whilst others date it in 1689. In these and many other instances one writer takes the old style of beginning the year, whilst others take the new style, each being right from his own stand-point. In a lately discovered tract printed by Caxton, and known as the "Sex Epistolae," we have the text of several letters which passed between the Pope and the Doge of Venice, which will be more particularly described under "Books in type No. 4." It is merely mentioned here as affording an apt illustration of the foregoing remarks. The letters commence on December 11th, 1482, and succeed one another in due order until the 7th of January, 1482, and the end of February, 1482. This was no blunder, for the old year continued until March 25th, which was New-Year's Day, 1483. Returning now to the consideration of Caxton's first lessons in the Art of Printing, we will examine each of the books attributed to him, commencing with

"The Recuyell."—This occupies the foremost place, because Caxton himself tells us that with it he began his career as a printer. Its Prologues and Epilogues contain curious and interesting gossip from Caxton's own pen, telling us how the Duchess of Burgundy, in whose service he then was, commanded him to complete the translation, which he had begun but not advanced with. He tells us that he began to translate the work at Bruges on March 1st, 1468, which, as the year in Flanders did not then commence till Easter, was really 1469, that he continued it at Ghent, and finished at Cologne on September 19th, 1471, thus making a period of two years and a half; that on its completion he presented it it to the Duchess, who rewarded him handsomely; that many persons desired copies of it, so that, finding the labour of writing too wearisome for him, and not expeditious enough for his friends, he had practised and learnt, at his great charge and expense, to ordain the book in print, to the end that every man might have them at once. As was natural to a person making practical acquaintance for the first time with the effects of typography, Caxton ends with noticing what in his eyes, accustomed to see one copy finished before another was begun, was the most wonderful feature of the new art, namely, that all the copies were begun upon one day, and were finished upon one day.

The periods of time here mentioned by Caxton require notice. He began to translate on March 1st, 1469, but soon relinquished his self-imposed task, after writing no more than five or six quires (or sections of four or five sheets each). After the lapse of two years, in March, 1471, he resumed the translation, and in the following September he presented the Duchess with the completed work. Now, six months would have been a very likely time for the translation and a fair copy thereof to take; but it would have been impossible to have accomplished the printing also in that space of time, especially as the whole translation was finished before the first sheet was printed, as will be hereafter shown. We may also notice, that the duration of Caxton's visit to Cologne must have been very short, as his absence from Bruges lasted no more than six months.

"Le Recueil" has but one date, and that evidently refers to the literary compilation alone, and affords no clue whatever to the year of printing. Indeed, the numerous copies still extant in manuscript prove that the work enjoyed considerable popularity before it came under the hands of the printer. The date of the printing of this book has been fixed, by several writers, between 1464 and 1467, from the consideration that Le Fèvre, the compiler, is spoken of in the prologue as chaplain to the Duke of Burgundy, and in such a manner as to signify that the duke was then living. But in the English version there is a material difference: Le Fèvre is not styled there as in the French, "Chappellain de montres redoubte seigneur Monseigneur le Duc Phillipe de Bourgoingne," but "chapelayn vnto the ryght noble glorious and mighty prynce, *in his tyme*, Phelip duc of Bourgoyne." Philip, therefore, was alive when "Le Recueil" was printed, but dead when "The Recuyell" went to press. The duke died in 1467; and it is therefore inferred that "Le Recueil" must date between 1464 and 1467, while "The Recuyell" must be later than 1467. That this should be considered as proving anything more than that the original French was compiled during the lifetime of Philip, and that when Caxton translated the same the duke was dead, seems unaccountable. All the copies of "Le Recueil," both manuscript and printed, followed the wording of the original, and the printer would no more think of altering it in 1476, the probable date of imprint, than the transcriber would in copying the same twenty-five years later. The National Library at Paris has a manuscript of this very book written after 1500, but reproducing exactly the clause which, in the printed edition, is considered to be a proof of its having been executed prior to 1467. Caxton altered the prologue of Le Fèvre to suit his own time, because he was translating; but, in printing from the manuscript of another (assuming his connection with "Le Recueil"), he would have been in opposition to the practice of his age had he altered the original. His translation was in its turn printed and reprinted, word for word, long after it was out of date.

There is, therefore, no reason whatever for asserting that "Le Recueil," written in 1464, was printed before "The Recuyell," translated in 1474, and sent to press about the same date. In fact, the whole tone of the epilogue to Book III. of "The Recuyell," leads unquestionably to the conclusion that *that* was the very first occasion on which Caxton had busied himself with typography. He would never have said, "I have learned to ordain *this book* in printe at my great charge and expense," if he had already printed one or two others. M. Bernard assumes that Caxton had nothing to do with the printing of "Le Recueil," and that it was executed before he turned his attention to the new art. This opinion, however, has not a single fact to support it.

"THE CHESS BOOK" affords but little evidence of value, its prologue being, for the most part, merely a translation of that written by Jehan de Vignay for the French original. It offers, indeed, one date; but that is open to question in its application. "Fynysshid the last day of marche, 1474," are the concluding words of the epilogue. But what was finished, the translation, or the printing? From the context it was probably the translation, although the printing was not many months later. This date also must be advanced a year; for, as already noticed, the new year did not commence, in Flanders, till Easter Day, which fell, in that year, on April 10th; so that March 31st, 1474, was, according to the modern reckoning, March 31st, 1475.

The prologue to the second edition throws a little light on the history of the first. Caxton there says, in reference to his connection with the book: ". . . . an excellent doctor of divinity . . . . made a book of the Chess moralised, which, *at such time as I was resident in Bruges*, came into my hands. . . . . And to the end that some which have not seen it, nor understand french nor latin, I deliberated in myself to translate into our maternal tongue; and when I had so achieved the said translation, *I did do set in imprinte*, a certain number of them which anon were depesshed and sold." He here appears to mean that upon the completion of the translation he employed some one else to print it:—"I did do set in imprinte." "Did do," according to the idiom of those days, was commonly used for doing a thing through the medium of another. The phrase was borrowed from the French—"plain pouoir de prendre et faire prendre les larrons," is the wording of an ordinance dated in the fifteenth century. "He did do be said to the messenger," for "he caused to be said," is found on folio 22 of the "History of Jason." "The Emperor did do make a gate of marble" occurs in the second edition of the "Chess Book," fol. 85. Similar examples abound, so that we may fairly conclude that Caxton did not himself print the first edition of the "Chess Book," but that both the translation and the printing were executed in Bruges.

The other books, namely, the French "Jason," the "Meditacions," and the "Quatre Derrennieres Choses," contain the bare text without remark or date of any kind, being, as bibliographers say, *sine ullâ notâ.*

The whole of the literary evidence therefore may be briefly summed up thus: "The Recuyell" was translated in 1471, and printed some time after; the "Chess Book" was printed after 1474, and probably in the latter half of 1475; and "Le Recueil" was compiled in 1464, but, like the other four, affords no evidence of date of the printing, which was probably about 1476.

We will now examine the testimony afforded by a comparison of the technical peculiarities of these six books. In collating "The Recuyell," the make-up of the sections, at the beginning of the volume, is worth noting. It was the practice of Caxton, as of other printers, to commence the printing of his books with the text, any preface which might be requisite, being added afterwards in a separate section, with a different kind of signature. When, however, the whole of the manuscript, prologue as well as text, was complete before it came into the printer's hands, there was no occasion for any such arrangement. This appears to have been the case with regard to "The Recuyell," where nothing has been added at the

Plate VI.

Type No. 1.
From "The Chess-book," 1st Edition.

The thirde chapitre of the seconde tractate treteth of
the alphyns her offices and maners .
The Alphyns ought to be made and formede in
manere of Juges syttynge in a chayer wyth a
book open to fore their eyen/ And that is be cause
that some causes ben crymynell / And some ben cyuyle
as aboute possessyons and other temporell thynges
and trespaces / And therfore ought to be two Juges

beginning, as the first section of five sheets includes all the introductory matter, as well as a portion of the text. Now the first page, which bears the date of the conclusion of the translation, being on the same sheet as a portion of the text, it is evident that the whole volume must have been in manuscript before any part was set up in type. We may infer, indeed, from his own description of the effect that so much writing had upon him, that Caxton issued several manuscript copies before he thought of using the printing-press. The copy presented to the Duchess was undoubtedly manuscript; or else how could Caxton have chronicled in the printed work her acceptance of the book and his reward for the present? And this again leads to the supposition that the portion of the epilogue relating to the printing was added by Caxton to his original manuscript when he determined to print it.

For precisely similar reasons, Caxton's prologue to the "Chess Book," which was a translation or adaptation of the original French, is also a portion of the first section of the volume. None of the other books under review having prologues, we will proceed to a comparison of some other typographical particulars.

The following table will show some of the technical features of each book, and some of what may be called the "habits" of the printer:—

No.	Title.	Size.	Type No.	No. of Sheets in a Section.	No. of Lines in a page.	Measurement of Page. — Inches.	Spacing of Lines.	Signatures.
1	The Recynell	Fol.	1	5	31	5 × 7[illegible]	uneven	none
2	Le Recueil	Fol.	1	5	31	5 × 7[illegible]	uneven	none
3	The Chess Book ...	Fol.	1	4	31	5 × 7[illegible]	uneven	none
4	Les Fais du Jason .	Fol.	1	4	31	5 × 7[illegible]	even	none
5	Meditacions	Fol.	1	4	31	5 × 7[illegible]	even	none
6	Les 4tre derrennieres choses	Fol.	2	4	28	5 × 7[illegible]	uneven	none

From this table we perceive,—

First, That the first five books are printed with the same

types, are all of the same size, and all without signatures; that all agree exactly in the size of the page; and that the even spacing of the lines in the "Meditacions" and the "Jason" proves that they were produced later than the others.

Secondly, That the five books in type No. 1 may be considered as the production of one printer.

Who, then, was this printer? When we attentively examine the shape of the letters in type No. 1, we notice a remarkable similarity between it and that of the writing of many Bruges manuscripts of the same period, which would induce us, at first sight, to attribute the design of the type to some artist of that city.

M. Bernard, whose opinion is of great weight, where his nationality is not concerned, traces the pattern of type No. 1 directly to Colard Mansion of Bruges. Speaking of a manuscript in the National Library at Paris, written by Colard Mansion's own hand, he says, "This book is written in old bâtarde, and in exactly the same character as the types of 'Le Recueil des histoires de Troyes;'" yet he attributes the cutting of the types to a French artist, and the printing to a German, Ulric Zel. The paper he also claims for a French mill, on account of the *fleurs de lis,* and the Gothic p with the quatrefoil, ignoring the fact that these are common Flemish watermarks of the fifteenth century, and found in abundance in the books from the Bruges and Westminster presses.

That any of these books in type No. 1 were printed by Ulric Zel, or any other Cologne printer, I cannot for a moment believe. It is possible, of course, that Zel, if employed to do so, could have designed and cut types of the gros-bâtarde pattern, although, as a fact, he never used such types himself; but all the Cologne printers of that period had their own peculiarities and habits, which were not at all those of the Bruges printers. Zel, from an early period, printed two pages at a time, as may be easily verified where a crooked page occurs; for the other page printed on the same side of the sheet will in every case be found crooked also. Now, the "Recuyell" was certainly printed page by page, as were likewise all the books from Mansion's press. And Caxton, when printing his smaller books, even cut the paper up and printed one page only at a time. This accounts for the entire rejection by Mansion,* and the sparing use by Caxton of the quarto size for their productions, as it necessitated twice as much press-work as the larger size. But stronger evidence is to be found in the fact that Zel, after 1467, always spaced out the lines of his books to an even length, and would have taught any one learning the art from him to do the same; yet this improvement was not adopted by either Mansion or Caxton until several years later. Whoever may have been the instructor of Mansion and Caxton, and whatever may have been the origin of their typography, the opinion that either of them, after learning the art in an advanced school such as that of Cologne, would have adopted in their first productions, without any necessity for so doing, primitive customs which they had never been taught, and returned in after years by slow degrees to the rules of their original tuition, has only to be plainly stated to render it untenable.

The printer of all these works was undoubtedly Colard Mansion, who had just before established his press at Bruges —who cast the types on his own model for Caxton, and instructed him in the art while printing *with* and *for* him "The Recuyell" and the "Chess Book"—who *certainly* printed "Les Quatre Derrennieres Choses"—who supplied Caxton with the material for the establishment of a press in England—who, about the time of Caxton's departure, used the same type for "Le Recueil"—and who, at a still later period, printed alone the "Jason" and the "Meditacions."

We will now examine "Les Quatre Derrennieres Choses," of which the only copy known is in the Old Royal collection in

* Van Praet, Brunet, and especially Campbell in his "Annales de la Typographie Néerlandaise," err in describing "Le purgatoire des mauvais Maris," printed by Colard Mansion, as a "petit in-4o." The copy described is cut a little more than usual, but the watermark which *is in the middle of the page* proves the size to be folio, whereas had it been quarto the watermark must have been in the back and partly hidden by the binding.

the British Museum. Like all Colard Mansion's books, and unlike any one of Caxton's, it is in French. It is printed in type No. 2, the type of the "Dictes" of 1477, and all the early books which issued from the Westminster press. Then the peculiar appearance of the red ink at once attracts attention. The two colours have been evidently printed at the same pull of the press, as was Colard Mansion's practice. Here the same process of wiping the black ink off lines purposely isolated, and then re-inking them with red, has been resorted to, and here, too, as in the acknowledged productions of the Bruges press, the same defects have been produced; the red ink having a tarnished appearance from the subjacent remains of the black, and the black lines nearest the red having received a red edging which, however interesting as a connecting link between two celebrated printers, by no means increases their typographical beauty. Now, as no Cologne printer is known to have resorted to this unique method of working in colours, I feel no hesitation in ascribing "Les Quatre Derennieres Choses" either to Colard Mansion or to Caxton working under his tuition; and as this peculiarity is nowhere found in Caxton's productions of the Westminster press, the former would seem the more likely conjecture.

The connection thus established between the types used by Caxton in his first attempts in England and those used by Colard Mansion is still further strengthened by the fact that the form of the &c., peculiar to type No. 1, is in several instances, by an evident mixing of the founts, used instead of the proper sort belonging to type No. 2. This furnishes positive proof that the two founts were *under one roof*, whether at Cologne or Bruges, or elsewhere. Whoever printed the five books in type No. 1 most certainly owned type No. 2 also.

Against all this, however, has to be placed the direct assertion of Wynken de Worde, who, in the proheme to his undated edition of "Bartholomæus de Proprietatibus Rerum," gives the following rhyme:—

> "And also of your charyte call to remembraunce
> The soule of William Caxton first pryntor of this boke
> In laten tonge at Coleyn hyself to auañce
> That enery well disposyd man may thereon loke."

The phraseology of this verse is very ambiguous. Are we to understand that the *editio princeps* of "Bartholomæus" proceeded from Caxton's press, or that he only printed the first Cologne edition? that he issued a *translation* of his own, which is the only way in which the production of the work could advance him in the Latin tongue? or, that he printed in Latin to advance his own interests? The last seems the most probable reading. But though the words will bear many constructions, they are evidently intended to mean that Caxton printed "Bartholomæus" at Cologne. Now this seems to be merely a careless statement of Wynken de Worde; for if Caxton did really print "Bartholomæus" in that city, it must have been with his own types and presses, as the workmanship of his early volumes proves that he had no connection with the Cologne printers, whose practices were entirely different. The time necessary for the production of so extensive a work would have been considerable; therefore, as Caxton's stay at Cologne on the occasion of his finishing the translation of "Le Recueil" was but short, the printing of this apocryphal "Bartholomæus" would have been at a subsequent visit, of which there is no record. No edition has yet been discovered which can, by any stretch of the imagination, be attributed to Caxton, although there is more than one old undated edition belonging to the German school of printing. Accuracy of information was in those days not much studied, and to a general carelessness about names and dates Wynken de Worde added a negligence peculiarly his own. We may excuse him for using Caxton's device in several books which by their dates and types are known to have been printed by himself, as well as for putting Caxton's name as printer to the edition of the "Golden Legend," printed in 1493, two years after his master's death. Such inaccuracies were at that time thought but little of. But how can we account for the blundering alteration in the 1495 edition of the "Polycronicon," where Wynken de Worde, making himself the speaker in Caxton's prologue, promises to carry the history down to 1485; or for the still greater error in the "Dictes" of 1528, in which, while adopting Caxton's epilogue, but substituting his own for Caxton's name, he makes all the transactions there related happen between Earl Rivers and himself? Wynken de Worde's blunders in statements are well matched by his blunders in workmanship, of which, however, we will quote but two. In Caxton's edition of the "Stans Puer ad Mensam," the third and fourth pages of the poem were accidentally transposed; yet Wynken de Worde, notwithstanding the break of sequence, blindly reprints the error! Again, in his edition of "The Horse, the Shepe, and the Ghoos," he actually omits a whole page without discovering his mistake! Other examples might easily be quoted, but enough has been adduced to show that Wynken de Worde was by no means careful in his statements.*

We must remember that Wynken de Worde, moreover, was too young to have had any personal knowledge of Caxton's early efforts, and that the vast importance of the art to the entire world, and the interest attaching to its origin, were ideas which would find no place in the mind of a fifteenth-century printer. We must not, therefore, regard De Worde's statement as deliberately made for the purpose of telling posterity something about Caxton. Lewis, Caxton's first biographer, was very sceptical concerning this Cologne edition of "Bartholomæus." "Its having a Latin title," he says,

* William Caxton, except in the occasional interchange of *i* and *y*, which were at that period considered as equivalents, never altered the orthography of his name, a fact the more noticeable as the name certainly varied in pronunciation: but Wynken de Worde, although mentioning his master's name but eight times, contrived to make the four variations of Caxton, Caxston, Caston, and Caxon. With regard to his own name Wynken de Worde appears to have tried how many variations he *could* invent, of which the following list is not even complete:—

Wynken de Worde.	Wynandus de Worde.
Wynden de Worde.	Wynandus de word.
Wynkyn de Worde.	winandus de worde.
Wynkyn Theworde.	Vunandus de worde.
Wynkyn the Worde.	Vuinandi de vuorde.
Wynkyn de Word.	VVinand i VVordensi.
VVinquin de VVorde.	Winandi de Wordensis.

"might possibly deceive De Worde, and make him think it was printed in Latin. However this may be, it does not appear that any edition of it, printed by Caxton or any one else, either in Latin or English, that year, is now in being."

Perhaps De Worde, who reprinted the "Recueil," had some vague recollection of Caxton having stated that he had been at Cologne, and so carelessly adopted the idea as giving point and rhyme to his verses.

The following anecdotes illustrate in a curious manner the typographical connection between Mansion and Caxton. A bookseller of Paris purchased an old volume for the moderate sum of one louis. He took it to M. de La Serna Santander, and asked him if he thought two louis too dear. "No," replied the wary bibliographer, and gave him the money. That volume is now in the National Library at Paris, and contains, bound together in the original boards, the "Quadrilogue," printed by Mansion at Bruges, and the French "Jason," printed in Caxton's type No. 1. Something similar to this happened in 1858, when Mr. Winter Jones discovered in the Library of the British Museum, "Les Quatre Derrenieres Choses," in Caxton's type No. 2, bound up with the "Meditacions," in type No. 1, and with contemporary handwriting running from the last page of one work to the first of the other, the volume being evidently in its original state, just as it was printed and bound at Bruges, in the little workshop of Colard Mansion over the church porch of St. Donatus.

Here, perhaps, I may be excused if I venture to build a brief history, founded, in the absence of sure foundation, in many parts on probability only, but which may nevertheless be welcome to some as an attempt to draw into a consistent narrative the scattered threads of Caxton's career between 1471 and his establishment at Westminster.

Caxton, having finished and been rewarded for his trouble in translating "Le Recueil" for the Duchess of Burgundy, found his book in great request. The English nobles at Bruges wished to have copies of this the most favourite romance of the age, and Caxton found himself unable to supply the demand with sufficient rapidity. This brings us to the year 1472 or 1473. Colard Mansion, a skilful caligrapher, must have been known to Caxton, and may even have been employed by him to execute commissions. Mansion, who had obtained some knowledge of the art of printing, although certainly not from Cologne, had just begun his typographical labours at Bruges, and was ready to produce copies by means of the press, if supported by the necessary patronage and funds. Caxton found the money, and Mansion the requisite knowledge, by the aid of which appeared "The Recuyell," the first book printed in the new type, and moreover the first book printed in the English language. This, probably, was not accomplished till 1474, and was succeeded, on Caxton's part, in another year, by an issue of the "Chess Book," which, as we are informed in a second edition, was "anone depesshed and solde." Mansion, finding success attended the new adventure, printed the French "Recueil," and, after Caxton's return to England, the French "Jason" and the "Meditacions." The three French works were doubtless published by Mansion alone, as Caxton is not known to have printed a single book in French, although perfectly acquainted with that language. Caxton, having thus printed at Bruges "The Recuyell" and the "Chess Book" with types either wholly or in part belonging to Mansion, now obtained a new fount of the pattern of the large bâtarde already in use by Mansion, but smaller in size, with the intention of practising the art in England. To test its capabilities, "Les Quatre Derrennieres Choses" was then produced under the immediate supervision of Mansion.

Early in 1476 Caxton appears to have taken leave of the city where he had resided for five and thirty years, and to have returned to his native land laden with a more precious freight than the most opulent merchant-adventurer ever dreamt of, to endow his country with a blessing greater than any other which had ever been bestowed, save only the introduction of Christianity.

CHAPTER VIII.

WESTMINSTER.

IN the preceding chapters Caxton's career as an Apprentice, as a Merchant, as Governor of the Merchant-Adventurers, as a Magistrate, and as an Ambassador, has been traced; the revival of literary tastes in Europe has been briefly sketched, as well as the literary influences by which Caxton was surrounded; and we have seen his translation of a romance for the Duchess of Burgundy obtain such popularity that he was forced to have recourse to the new art of printing, in order to multiply copies quickly: but we have yet to investigate the most important period of his history—those last fifteen years, to which the whole of his former life seems but the introduction—that short period which alone has caused the name of Caxton to be inscribed on the tablets of history, and the typographical relics of which form the best and only memorial which England possesses of her first printer.*

We left Caxton early in 1476 preparing to return to England, after having disposed of his printed copies of the "Chess Book" in Bruges. The next certain notice of him is after

* There is certainly the Roxburghe tablet in St. Margaret's Church, Westminster; and, better still, there is a "*Caxton Pension*" in connection with the "Printers' Corporation," by which the needs of some afflicted successors in Caxton's craft are alleviated; but a memorial worthy of our first printer and of his countrymen has never yet been attempted.

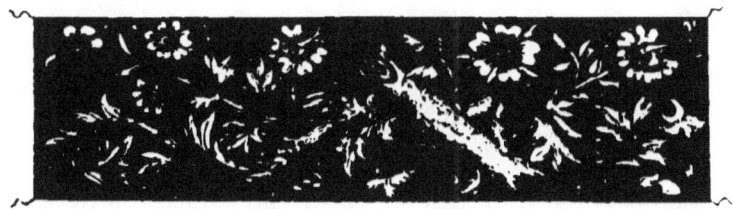

his settlement at Westminster, when, in November 1477, he had printed his first edition of the "Dictes and Sayings of the Philosophers." This book is, in fact, the earliest we have from Caxton's press with an indisputable imprint. It is evident that his arrangements for settling in England, the engagement of assistants, and all the other matters inseparable from a novel undertaking, must have occupied a considerable time. If, therefore, we assume that Caxton commenced his new career in this country about the latter half of 1476 we cannot be far wrong. A cautious man, he began to try his powers, and ascertain the probable sale for his productions, by printing small pieces. Copland, one of his workmen, who served with Wynken de Worde after his first master's death, has a curious remark upon this in the prologue to his edition of "Kynge Apolyn of Thyre," with which romance he appears to have commenced his career as a printer. "Whiche booke I, Roberte Copland, have me applyed for to translate oute of the Frenshe language into our maternal tongue, at the exhortacyon of my forsayd mayster [Wynken de Worde], gladly followynge the trace of my mayster Caxton, *begynnynge with small storyes and pamfletes, and so to other.*" That Westminster was the locality in which Caxton first settled, there is, fortunately, no room to doubt; but as the exact spot has given rise to considerable discussion, it may be useful to collect all the instances in which Caxton connects his own name with a definite locality. We therefore give the following extracts taken *verbatim et literatim* from his works:—

1477. Dictes and Sayings. First edition. Epilogue. *enprynted by me william Caxton at westmestre.*

1478. Moral Proverbs. Colophon. *I haue enprinted . . . . At westmestre.*

1480. Chronicles of England. First edition. Colophon. *enprinted by me William Caxton Jn thabbey of westmynstre by london.*

1480. Description of Britain. First edition. Prologue. *the comyn cronicles of englond ben . . . . now late enprinted at westmynstre.*

1481. MIRROUR OF THE WORLD. First edition. Prologue. *And emprised by me . . . . to translate it into our maternal tongue . . . . in thabbay of westmestre by london.*

1481. REYNARD THE FOX. First edition. Epilogue. *by me will'm Caxton translated . . . . in thabbey of westmestre.*

1481. GODFREY OF BOLOGNE. Epilogue. *sette in forme and emprynted . . . . in thabbey of westmester.*

1483. PILGRIMAGE OF THE SOUL. Colophon. *Enprynted at westmestre by william Caxton.*

1483. LIBER FESTIVALIS. First edition. Colophon. *Emprynted at Westmynster by wyllyam Caxton.*

1483. QUATUOR SERMONES. First edition. Colophon. *Enprynted by Wylliam Caxton at Westmestre.*

1483. CONFESSIO AMANTIS. Colophon. *Enprynted at westmestre by me willyam Caxton.*

1483. GOLDEN LEGEND. First edition. Epilogue. *fynysshed it at westmestre.*

1483. CATON. Colophon. *Translated . . . . by William Caxton in thabbey of Westmynstre.*

1483. KNIGHT OF THE TOWER. Colophon. *enprynted at Westmynstre.*

1484. ÆSOP. Epilogue. *enprynted by me william Caxton at westmynstre in thabbay.*

1484. THE ORDER OF CHIVALRY. Epilogue. *translated . . . . by me William Caxton dwellynge in Westmynstre besyde london.*

1485. KING ARTHUR. Colophon. *emprynted and fynysshed in thabbey westmestre.*

1485. PARIS AND VIENNE. Colophon. *translated . . . . by wylliam Caxton at Westmestre.*

[1489.] DIRECTORIUM SACERDOTUM. Colophon. *Impressum . . . . apud Westmonesterium.*

1489. DOCTRINAL OF SAPIENCE. Colophon. *translated . . . . by wyllyam Caxton at Westmestre.*

To these must be added Caxton's Advertisement, printed about 1480.

"If it plese ony man spirituel or temporel to bye ony pyes of two and thre comemoracio͞s of salisburi vse enpryntid after the forme of this prese͞t lettre whiche ben wel and truly correct, *late hym come to westmonester in to the almonesrye at the reed pale* and he shal haue them good chepe."

The following quotations are from titles or colophons of books printed by Wynken de Worde in the house of his late master, only three of which are dated.

SCALA PERFECTIONIS, 1493.
And Wynkyn de Worde this hath sett in print.
In William Caxstons hows so fyll the case.

DIRECTORIUM SACERDOTUM, 1495. *In domo Caxton Wynkyn fieri fecit.*

LYNDEWODE'S CONSTITUTIONES, 1496. *Apud Westmonasterium. In domo caxston.*

THE XII PROFYTES OF TRIBULACYON. *Enpryntted at Westmyster in Caxtons hous.*

DONATUS MINOR. *In domo Caxton in westmonasterio.*

WHITAL'S DICTIONARY. *Imprynted in the late hous of William Caxton.*

ACCEDENCE. *Prynted in Caxons house at westmynstre.*

THE CHORLE AND THE BYRDE. *Emprynted at westmestre in Caxtons house.*

DOCTRYNALLE OF DETHE. *Enprynted at westmynster Jn Caxtons hous.*

ORTUS VOCABULORUM. *prope celeberrimum monasterium quod westmynstre appellatur impressum.*

Adding to the foregoing the testimony of Stow, we shall have before us all the evidence of any authority.

"Neare vnto this house westward was an old chappel of S. Anne, ouer against the which the Lady Margaret, mother to King H. the 7. erected an Almeshouse for poore women .... the place wherein this chappell and Almeshouse standeth was called the Elemosinary or Almory, now corruptly the Ambry, for that the Almes of the Abbey were there distributed to the poore. And therin Islip, Abbot of Westmin.

erected the first Presse of booke printing that euer was in England about the yeare of Christ 1471. William Caxton, cittizen of London, mercer, brought it into England, and was the first that practised it in the sayde Abbey."

Reviewing the foregoing quotations, it will be noticed that although the precise expression, *Printed in the Abbey of Westminster*, is affixed to some books, yet the more general phrase *Printed at Westminster* is also used, and evidently refers to the same locality, for otherwise we must suppose Caxton to have carried on two separate printing-offices for many years. The word "Abbey" did not assume its modern sense, as applying only to the fabric, until after the Reformation; and the phrase "dwelling at Westminster," used in 1484, just *after* "printed in the Abbey," 1483, and *before* "printed in the Abbey," 1485, proves that Caxton himself attached to the word no very restrictive idea. We find also, from the above-mentioned advertisement, that "Westminster" in that instance meant "The Almonesrye," where Caxton occupied a tenement, called "The Red-pale." The Almonry was a space within the Abbey precincts, where alms were distributed to the poor; and here the Lady Margaret, mother of King Henry VII., and one of Caxton's patronesses, built almshouses. Other houses were also there; and we therefore conclude that by the words *in the Abbey* Caxton meant nothing more than that he resided within the Abbey precincts.

The position of St. Anne's Chapel and the Almonry, in relation to that of the Abbey Church, seems to have been misunderstood by all the biographers of Caxton. Dr. Dibdin, Charles Knight and others, place them on the site of the Chapel of Henry VII, which is the east end of the Abbey. The Almonry was considerably to the west, and the following statements, gathered from Stow, will give its exact locality. After describing the monastery and the king's palace, he proceeds to say, "now will I speake of the gate house, and of Totehill streete, stretching from the *west* part of the Close .... The gate towards the *west* is a Gaile for offenders .... On the *Southside* of this gate, king H. the 7. founded an almeshouse .... Neare vnto this house *westward* was an old chappel of S. Anne . . . . the place wherein this chappel . . . . standeth was called the Almory." The Almonry was therefore west-south-west of the western front of the Abbey.

It has been argued that Caxton was permitted by the abbot to use the "Scriptorium" of the abbey as a printing-office. Printing, even in these days of improvement, is necessarily in some parts a very unclean operation, but it was much more so in its earlier years, some of the processes employed being extremely filthy and pungent. The Abbot of Westminster would never have admitted into the scriptorium any thing so defiling, much less within the sacred walls of the church itself. There is, indeed, no evidence that any portion of the abbey was ever appropriated as a scriptorium: no mention of such a place is made by any historian, nor has any manuscript been recognised as having issued thence.

The Abbot of Westminster, at the time of Caxton's arrival in England, was John Estency, who succeeded to that office in 1474, upon the promotion of Thomas Milling to the Bishopric of Hereford. Those writers who maintain that Caxton returned to England before 1474 have mentioned Milling as his patron. George Fascet succeeded Abbot Estency in 1498, and was in turn succeeded by John Islip in 1500. Stow's chronology is very faulty in ascribing to Abbot Islip any connection with Caxton, whose death occurred about nine years before Islip's election to the abbacy.

There is nothing to lead to the supposition that Caxton and Abbot Estency were on intimate terms; indeed, the probability is that they knew but little of each other. Our printer mentions Estency but once, and that only casually, as illustrating the difficulty which even educated men experienced in deciphering documents of a bygone age. In the prologue to the "Encydos," Caxton says, "My lord abbot of Westmynster *did do shewe* to me late certayn euydences wryton in old Englisshe, for to reduce it into our Englisshe now vsid." The sense of "Did do shewe," as already noticed, would seem merely to signify "caused to be shewn;" or in other words, the abbot only *sent* the documents. Caxton always appears to have recorded, in prologue or epilogue, the names of those by whom he was employed; and if he had received any favour or patronage from the abbot, he would in all likelihood have dedicated one of his numerous translations to him, as he did to so many of his patrons, some of whom, like Hugh Bryce and William Praat, were plain "Mercers" only.

It is unlikely, therefore, that Caxton went to Westminster by invitation of the abbot, or that he occupied any place within the church itself, or that he stood in any other relation to the abbot than that of tenant. The rent-roll of the abbey was under the immediate charge of the abbot's chamberlain, and with him Caxton would have to agree as to his tenure of "The Red-pale" in the Almonry.

The reason of Caxton's preference for the Almonry is not at all evident, though his being a Mercer may, possibly, have had some connection with his choice, as the Mercers' Company held certain tenements of the abbots of Westminster. Some of these were in the parish of St. Martin Otewich (Broad Street Ward), within the city walls; and there was also a tenement called "The Pye," and another called "The Grehounde," the localities of which are not mentioned. The rents paid for these are duly entered in the "Renter Wardens' Account-books," at Mercers' Hall. But whatever induced Caxton to settle at Westminster, we may safely infer, from his own mention, not more than two or three years later, of "The Red-pale" as his house, that it was there he originally established himself, that there his translations were made and works printed, and that there, surrounded by his books and presses, and soothed by the loving attentions of his daughter, he breathed his last.

Wynken de Worde, his immediate successsor, printed several books in the same place, dating them from "Caxton's house in Westminster." This phrase was considered, by the early biographers of Caxton, as proving that he had migrated from the side chapel, where they assumed he first set up his press, and established himself in a new residence. Bagford, with his usual fertility of invention, identified the very street and house into which Caxton moved, and assigned reasons for his ejection from the abbey. For many years an old house in the Almonry was currently believed to have been that in which our first printer dwelt; but Mr. Nichols, who, as well as Knight, gives a woodcut of it, is of opinion that the house could not be older than the time of Charles I. Upon its demolition in 1846, portions of the beams were made into walking-sticks and snuff-boxes, and presented to various patrons of literature as genuine relics of the famous printer. Interesting, indeed, would it have been if we could have identified the exact spot where the first press was placed on English soil, and still more so if we could have stood in the very room where Caxton worked; but uncertainty hangs over all this part of our history.

The printers of the fifteenth century, especially in Holland and Flanders, very frequently used armorial bearings for their trade-marks, the shield being represented as hanging from the branch of a tree. A broad band down the centre of the shield is, in heraldic language, called a "pale," and this, if painted red, would be a "red pale." Doubtless this was the sign used by Caxton to designate his house. The woodcut opposite, taken from Holtrop's "Monumens Typographiques," pl. 71, shows a house of the fifteenth century, which has two tenants, both printers, each of whom has a sign. This was in Antwerp. The printers at Delff, in Holland, used a "black pale" for their marks.

We have already mentioned "The Greyhound" as being held by the Mercers' Company from the Abbots of Westminster. From the same "Account-book" it appears that in 1477 the "livelihode" made a "visitation," and "kept a dinner" at "The Greyhound," which cost them 26*s* 8*d*, besides 2*d* for washing the table-cloth. There is nothing to indicate the locality of this tenement; but from the fact that mercers, as well as drapers, dealt largely in cloth and various woollen goods, they would necessarily be much interested in the great staple of wool, held at fixed intervals, not far from the abbey walls.* They would therefore require a place in the neighbourhood for meeting during their visitation which

would, at the same time, afford them good accommodation for a dinner at its close.

And here we may remark that, although so much of his attention was devoted to translating and printing, Caxton probably still took considerable interest in his old vocation. The wool-staple at Westminster was an important mart, and many of the merchants resorting thither were fellow mercers

* Stow says the Abbots of Westminster had six wool-houses in the Staple granted them by King Henry VI.

and benefactors to St. Margaret's Church. Some of them were also fellow members with Caxton of the "Fraternity or Guild of our Blessed Lady Assumption." Several of the "Account-books" of this brotherhood are still preserved in the vestry of St. Margaret's; and although they nowhere state its objects, it seems, from the entries of salaries paid to priests, from money spent in obits, wax, and vestments, and from the granting of a few pensions, to have been somewhat like the "benefit societies" of the present day, with the additional advantage of prayers for the repose of the souls of deceased members. And yet, if only a religious guild, it is not apparent why they required certain tenements in Aldermary, which they leased of the Mercers' Company, not far from the Steel Yard of the Hanse merchants, where large quantities of raw wool were stapled. But whatever may have been the objects of this guild, their accounts, made up by their clerk every three years, show that towards the end of the fifteenth century they were in a flourishing state, with a good balance to their credit; and that, on Midsummer-day, they, too, had a "general feast," on which they spent a large portion of their income. The expenses of these lavish feasts, each time filling at least two folio pages, are entered in the accounts with great minuteness, from the amount paid to the "chief cok" as a reward (which was more than twelve guineas of modern money), down to the boat-hire for the "turbuts," and nearly £4 for "pottes broken and wasted at the same fest."* Of this guild Caxton was a member for some years before his death.

* After an entry of the payment of six priests' salaries, there occur—"Costes and peelles allowed by the hole Brotherhode toward thexpences of the geñall fest in iij^{de} yere of this accompt."

These "Costs and Parcels" occupy two folio pages, and contain the following among other items:—

"A tonn of wyne	vj li"
"Paide to John Drayton chief sok for his reward	xxv s"
"Also for the hire of xxiiij doseyn of erthen pottes for ale & wyne	iiij s"

It is pleasant to think of our printer as retaining the friendship of the city merchants after all official relationship between them had been dissolved. That this was the case is proved by his warm eulogy of the City of London, and his continuance as a member of the Mercers' Company. He, no doubt, had many personal friends and supporters; indeed, it would be hardly a stretch of the imagination to fancy that, during the holding of the great wool-staple at Westminster, Caxton would be no disinterested observer, and that at its close, when the wardens and the "livelihode" flocked to the "dener kept at the grehounde," if not there by right as a liveryman of the Mercers' Company, the printer would be always a welcome guest. Surely, before parting, in remembrance of past associations and services one of the drinking pledges would be, "The health of William Caxton, late governor of our fellowship beyond the sea."

But to return to facts. There is no doubt that Caxton was residing in his tenement in the Almonry when he printed the "Dictes" in 1477. He would, therefore, be in the parish of St. Margaret: and it is somewhat remarkable that a person bearing the same name was buried there about two years later. In 1479 the parochial records show an entry among

"Also for erthen pottes broken & wasted at the same fest	vj s viij d"
"Also to iiij players for their labour	xij s x d"
"Also to iij mynstrelles	ix s xd"
"Also for the mete of diuers strangers	xvj s"
"Also for russhes	ij s iiij d"
"Also for vj doseyn of white cuppes	iij s"
"Also for portage and botehyre of the Turbut	iiij d"
"Also for ix Turbutts	xv s ij d"

Besides scores of "Capons, chekyns, gese, conyes, and peiones (pigeons), the chief "cok" provided them with "swannys" and "herons," with all sorts of fish, including oysters and "see pranys," or prawns, with all sorts of meats and game, with jellies in "ix dosen gely dishes," and with abundance of fruits. The quantity of ale, wine, and ypocras provided by the butler is marvellous, and one cannot wonder at the heavy entries for "pottes and cuppes broken and wasted." The cook seems to have been paid much more liberally than the wardens, who had but xxx s between them "for their diligence."

the receipts of the burial fees of twenty pence for two torches and three tapers at a low mass for William Caxton. Dibdin assumes this man to have been our printer's father: possibly so, but there is no evidence of kindred. We may notice, however, that although the amount paid may to us seem trifling, yet it was more than double the average burial fees of that period, as is evidenced by the same accounts. About this time the king ordered a payment of £30 (equal to £400 or £450 now) to be made to Caxton for "certain causes or matters performed by him for the said Lord the King." Might not this have been for assistance to Edward IV and his retinue when fugitives at Bruges?

Caxton, as might be expected, held a high position in his parish; and, within a very short time of his arrival, his name appears as auditor of the parish accounts. The parish audit seems to have been a very simple affair. It was open to all the parishioners, and the accounts were probably read aloud by the clerk who was engaged by the churchwardens to keep them. The balance in cash, and the custody of the "treasures" in the church, were then handed over to the incoming wardens, and the names of the most substantial parishioners present were added by the clerk to the usual form declaring the correctness of the accounts. The business on these occasions, was fitly concluded by a good "supper." Caxton's name appears annexed to the audit for the years 1478-80, 1480-82, 1482-84; and it would have been most gratifying to have found that the signatures at the end of these and other accounts were genuine autographs. All the names, however, are in the same handwriting, which is that of the scribe or priest engaged to keep the parish books.

Caxton did not enter upon his new adventure of printing books without good and able patronage. Edward IV, as we have seen, paid him a sum of money for certain services performed; and Caxton printed "Tully" and "Godfrey" under the king's "protection." Edward's sister Margaret, Duchess of Burgundy, was his friend and supporter, and perchance may have paid a visit to her old servant at the "Red-pale," when she visited England in 1480. Margaret, Countess of Richmond, mother of King Henry VII, also favoured his designs. Earl Rivers, brother to the queen, was a fast friend, with whom Caxton seems to have enjoyed a considerable degree of intimacy, and the Earl of Warwick likewise must have had some knowledge of him, as Caxton dedicated to him the "Chess-Book." The "Order of Chivalry" was dedicated to Richard III. Henry VII personally desired Caxton to translate and print the "Fayts of Arms," and the "Eneydos" was specially presented to Arthur, Prince of Wales. Master William Daubeney, King Henry VI's treasurer, was his "good and synguler friend." William, Earl of Arundel, took great interest in his progress, and allowed him the "yearly fee" of a buck in summer and a doe in winter. Sir John Fastolf, a great lover of books, of whose library several volumes still exist; Hugh Bryce, mercer and king's ambassador; William Pratt, a rich mercer; and divers unnamed "gentylmen and ladyes," are known to have employed him. Some of these, like the "noble lady with many faire doughters," for whom he produced "The Knyght of the Toure," engaged him to translate as well as to print.

In 1486 death deprived Caxton of his old friend William Pratt, who, on his death-bed, requested him to print "The Book of Good Manners." The terms in which Caxton mentions Pratt as a fellow mercer, an honest man, and "a singular friend of old knowledge," show that a close bond of union existed between the two. It is to be hoped that their mutual object—"the amendment of manners, and the increase of virtuous living"—was promoted by the publication.

In 1490 died, and was buried at St. Margaret's, one "Mawde Caxton," of whose relationship to William Caxton there is no direct evidence. It may have been the Maude who, twenty-nine years earlier, became his wife while he was yet in Bruges: if so, it will explain, in a most interesting manner, the reason why he in that year suspended printing the "Fayts of Arms," until he had finished a new undertaking, "The Arte and Crafte to Die Well."

The history of Caxton after his settlement at Westminster is almost confined to a catalogue of the productions of his press. Fortunately many were printed from his own manuscript, and have additions which often afford the date of translation or of printing. The following table presents an arrangement of these books, from which we may obtain some

DATES.	TRANSLATION.	PRINTING.
1477—Nov. 18 ...	....	Dictes, 1st edition (*e*)
1478—Feb. 20 ...	....	Moral Proverbs (*e*)
1479—Feb. 3 ...	....	Cordyale (*b*)
Mar. 24 ...	....	Cordyale (*e*)
1480—Apr. 22 ...	Ovid, 15th Book (*e*) ...	....
June 10 ...	....	Chronicles, 1st edit. (*e*)
Aug. 18 ...	....	Description, 1st ed. (*e*)
1481—Jan. 2 ...	Mirrour, 1st edit (*b*)...	....
Mar. 8 ...	Mirrour, 1st edit. (*e*)...	....
Mar. 12 ...	Godfrey (*b*)	....
June 6 ...	Reynart, 1st edit. (*e*)...	....
June 7 ...	Godfrey (*e*)	....
Aug. 12 ...	....	Tully (*e*)
Nov. 20 ...	....	Godfrey (*e*)
1482—July 2 ...	Polycronicon (*e*)	....
Oct. 8 ...	....	Chronicles, 2nd ed. (*e*)
1483—June 1 ...	Knight of the Toure (*e*)	....
"	Æsop (*e*)	....
June 6 ...	....	Pylgremage (*e*)
June 30 ...	....	Festival (*e*)
Sept. 2 ...	....	Confessio (*e*)
Nov. 20 ...	....	Golden Legend (*e*)
Dec. 23 ...	Caton (*e*)	....
1484—Jan. 31 ...	....	Knight of the Toure (*e*)
Mar. 26 ...	....	Æsop (*e*)
"	....	Order of Chivalry (*e*)
Sept. 13 ...	Ryal Book (*e*)	....
1485—June 18 ...	Charles (*e*)...............	....
July 31 ...	....	King Arthur (*e*)
Aug. 31 ...	Paris and Vienne (*e*) .	....
Dec. 1 ...	....	Charles (*e*)
Dec. 19 ...	....	Paris and Vienne (*e*)
1486—June 8 ...	Good Manners (*e*)......	....
1487—May 11 ...	....	Good Manners (*e*)
1489—Jan. 23 ...	Fayts (*b*)	....
May 7 ...	Doctrinal (*e*)...........	....
July 8 ...	Fayts (*e*)	....
"	....	Directorium, 2nd ed. (*e*)
1490—June 15 ...	Art and Craft (*e*)......	....
June 22 ...	Eneydos (*e*)	....
July 14 ...	....	Fayts (*e*)

(*b*) means *begun*. (*e*) means *ended*.

idea of the time occupied in their translation and printing. The majority of Caxton's works, however, bear no date whatever; and here the only basis of a correct arrangement must be a careful examination and comparison of the peculiarities of the various types. In this table variations may be noticed from some of the dates as printed by Caxton; but these are merely apparent discrepancies caused by the difference between the old and new style of reckoning the commencement of the year, and also by the custom, then so common, of dating by the regnal year of the sovereign.

The same table shows that Caxton took ten weeks for the translation of the "Mirrour of the World," containing 198 pages; twelve weeks for "Godefroy of Bologne," 284 pages; and nearly six months for "Fayts of Arms," 286 pages. The period occupied in printing "Cordyale," 152 pages, was only seven weeks, whilst "Godfrey," supposing the printing immediately to follow the completion of the translation, took nearly six months. The "Knight of the Tower," 208 pages, required eight months; "Charles the Great," 188 pages, five and a half months; "Paris and Vienne," 70 pages, three and a half months; "Good Manners," 132 pages, eleven months; and "Fayts of Arms," 286 pages, more than a year.

Caxton's own translations made in this country were The Whole Life of Jason; the Mirror of the World; Reynart the Fox; Godfrey of Bulloyn; the Golden Legend; the book called Caton; the Knight of the Tower; Æsop's Fables; the Order of Chivalry; the Royal Book; the Life of Charles the Great; the History of the Knight Paris and the Fair Vienne; the Book of Good Manners; the Doctrinal of Sapience; the Fayts of Arms; the Art and Craft to Die Well; Eneydos; the Curial; the Life of St. Winifred; Blanchardin and Eglantine; the Four Sons of Aymon; and the Gouvernayle of Health. These contain more than 4,500 printed pages. The total produce of his press, excluding the books printed at Bruges, reaches to above 18,000 pages, nearly all of folio size. These figures speak more forcibly than any argument for the great industry and perseverance of Caxton; and to this list must be added the translation of the "Vitæ Patrum," which he finished only a few hours before his death, but did not live to print.

Those who have blamed Caxton for not choosing the Bible, or the works of Greece and Rome for the use and instruction of his countrymen, have quite overlooked the impossibility of making a business profitable (and Caxton tells us, in "Charles the Great," that he earned his living by it), unless it supplied the wants of the age. The demand in England in the fifteenth century was not for Bibles in the vernacular, nor for Horace, nor for Homer, whose writings very few could read in the original texts;* but the clergy wanted Service-books, and Caxton accordingly provided them with Psalters, Commemorations, and Directories; the preachers wanted Sermons, and were supplied with the "Golden Legend," and other similar books; the "prynces, lordes, barons, knyghtes & gentilmen" were craving for "joyous and pleysaunt historyes" of chivalry, and the press at the "Red-pale" produced a fresh romance nearly every year. Poetry and history require for their appreciation a more advanced mental education, and of these, therefore, the issue was more scanty. By thus bringing his commercial experience to bear upon his new vocation, and by accommodating the supply to the demand, while, at the same time, he in no slight degree directed the channel in which that demand should flow, Caxton contrived to earn an honest living by the produce of his press, and to avoid the fate of his typographical brethren at Rome, Sweynheim and Pannartz, who, having printed too many works of the

* The historian Gibbon regrets that in the choice of authors Caxton "was reduced to comply with the vicious taste of his readers; to gratify the nobles with treatises on heraldry, hawking [*Caxton printed nothing of the sort*], and the game of Chess; and to amuse the popular credulity with romances of fabulous knights and legends of some fabulous saints. The father of printing expresses a laudable desire to elucidate the history of his country; but instead of publishing the the Latin chronicle of Radulphus Higden [*which very few could have read*] he could only venture on the English version by John de Trevisa .... the world is not indebted to England for one *first* edition of a classic author!"

classic authors, about 12,000 volumes in five years, became bankrupt, and sank under the dead weight of their unsold volumes.

Thus, in the selection of books for his press, some of which he obtained "with grete instaunce, labour, and coste"—in translating and printing—in friendly communication and intercourse with the best educated men of his day—in the discharge of the social duties of his position—Caxton passed the few remaining years of his life. In 1491, when close upon seventy years of age, but still in full vigour of mind, he undertook the translation of the "Vitæ Patrum." Whether disease was at this time gradually undermining his health, or whether, as the following colophon renders more probable, he was taken off suddenly, is unknown; but it is an interesting fact that he was spared to work at his favourite task of translation till within a few hours of his death.

The following is Wynken de Worde's colophon to the "Vitæ Patrum:"—"Thus endyth the moost vertuouse hystorye of the deuoute and right renowned lyves of holy faders lyuynge in deserte, worthy of remembraunce to all wel dysposed persones which hath bē translated oute of Frenche into Englisshe by William Caxton of Westmynstre late deed and fynysshed at the laste daye of hys lyff."

The exact date of his death has not been ascertained; but the burial is entered in the parish accounts for 1490-92, and from the position of the entry would appear to have taken place towards the close of the year 1491. This date is confirmed by the following manuscript note, quoted by Ames:—"There is wrote down in a very old hand in a *Fructus Temporum* of my friend Mr. Ballard's, of Cambden, in Gloucestershire:—'Of your charitee pray for the soul of Mayster Wyllyam Caxton, that in hys time was a man of moche ornate and moche renommed wysdome and connyng, and decessed ful crystenly the yere of our Lord MCCCC LXXXXJ.'"

> "Moder of Merci shyld him fro thorribul fynd,
> And bryng hym to lyff eternall that neuyr hath ynd."

He was buried in his own parish churchyard, and in the

account-books of the churchwardens appear the following funeral charges :—

Item atte Bureyng of William Caxton for iiij torches ... vj s viij d
Item for the belle atte same bureyng .... vj d

These fees are considerably higher than those paid by the majority of the parishioners, and are equalled in but very few instances; they thus afford further evidence of the superior position held by our printer in his parish.

Caxton's property consisted probably of little more than his stock in trade. He nevertheless left a will, as fifteen copies of the "Golden Legend" are recorded in the parish accounts as having been "bequothen to the chirch behove by William Caxston." The "Golden Legend" was first printed in 1484, but the second edition, of which the bequest probably consisted, was not executed till four or five years later. By the churchwardens' account for 1496-98, it appears that by that time they had disposed of three of the fifteen copies: one for 6*s* 8*d*, and another for 6*s* 4*d*, by the agency of William Ryolle; and one for 6*s* 8*d* to the parish priest, probably for his own use. Within the next two years William Geiffe took five copies at an average of 5*s* 4*d* each; John Crosse one copy at 5*s* 8*d*; Walter Marten one at 5*s* 11*d*; and Daniel Aforge one at 5*s* 10*d*; another being sold in "Westmynster halle" for 5*s* 8*d*. This should have left remaining, in 1500, *four* copies to be accounted for, but the "Memorandum" acknowledges only *three;* probably one copy had been appropriated by the churchwardens to the use of their church. Two more copies were sold in the ensuing two years, and one left unaccounted for.

The discovery of Caxton's will would probably settle satisfactorily many questions about his family and relations, but all the registries in which it might possibly have been deposited have been searched without success.

That our knowledge of William Caxton is confined almost entirely to his public life, is much to be regretted. We can trace to some extent his career in commerce as well as in diplomacy. As a printer too, we can judge of him by an examination of his works; but when we wish to portray the man as a master, or in domestic life, or we desire to know what his neighbours thought of him, we fail for want of reliable material. From his appending a bitter satire on "women" to the "Dictes and Sayings of the Philosophers," we might have inclined to think him a bachelor, did we not know that he had a wife and daughter when he came to England; but that he was unmarried while "governor" at Bruges is almost certain, as the rules of celibacy were very strict among merchants living out of their own countries. The Steel Yard merchants had a stringent law on the subject, and the Merchant Adventurers were doubtless guided by the same policy.

We naturally turn to the prologues and epilogues attached to Caxton's translations for traits of character, but here again, we are surrounded by difficulties. There existed in those days no rights in literature. Every author took from others what best suited his purpose, and that without acknowledgment, except to give authority to his own opinions. This practice has involved many of the works of that period in considerable obscurity. Caxton was not free from this characteristic of his age, and we accordingly find him appropriating whole prologues and epilogues from the French originals, altering them only when inapplicable to himself. Such instances may be seen in the "Chess Book," the "Mirror," the "Golden Legend," "Charles," and others. Great care is therefore requisite to distinguish between Caxton's own thoughts and the mere translation of those of others. But, after making due allowance for all this, there yet remains, in Caxton's prologues and epilogues, a substratum of individuality, which must be the basis for any right appreciation of his character. His repeated eulogies of Edward IV, and the members of his family, indicate that all his political sympathies were with the House of York. This was but natural, for the development of trade consequent upon amity between England and the princes of the Low Countries, made all the English merchants staunch adherents to the White Rose. His writings also reveal that he had a deep sense of religion, and was strict in the observance of his Christian duties. Although in one sense the greatest reformer that this country has ever known, he was quite unconscious of the tendency of the art which he introduced. In the tone of his mind he was indeed eminently conservative, comparing the good old times of his apprenticeship with the degeneracy of the succeeding generations, when in the youth of London there was "no kernel nor good corn found, but chaff for the most part." Much concerned was he to note in his latter days the decline of chivalry, and he urged his Sovereign to take immediate measures for its revival, even to the extent of engaging in a new crusade against the Turks for the recovery of the "holy cyte of Jherusalem." Conservative as he was in theory, there seems reason to believe that he was no less so in practice. Caxton never gave in to the new-fangled ideas of printers about the advantage of title-pages to books, though if we may judge from the fact of Wynken de Worde using them immediately after his master's death, he was of the reverse opinion. In the adoption of signatures, initials, and lines of an even length, he was very tardy, and from the use of red ink he was evidently averse.

As a linguist, Caxton undoubtedly excelled. In his native tongue, notwithstanding his self-depreciation, he seems to have been a master. His writings, and the style of his translations, will bear comparison with Lydgate, with Gower, with Earl Rivers, the Earl of Worcester, and other contemporaneous writers. Many of his readers, indeed, thought him too "ornate" and "over curious" in his diction, and desired him to use more homely terms; but, since others found fault with him for not using polished and courtly phrases, we may fairly presume that he attained the happy medium, "ne over rude, ne over curious," at which he aimed. When excited by a favourite subject, as the "Order of Chivalry," he waxed quite eloquent; and the appeal of Caxton to the knighthood of England, has been often quoted as a remarkable specimen of fifteenth-century declamation. With the French tongue he was thoroughly conversant, although he had never been in France; but Bruges was almost French, and in the Court of Burgundy, as well as in that of England, French was the chief medium of conversation. With Flemish he was also well acquainted, as shown by his translation of "Reynart;" indeed, this language, after so long a residence in Bruges, must have become almost his mother-tongue.

Caxton's knowledge of Latin has often been denied or underrated; but as governor of the English nation in Bruges, and as ambassador, he must have been able to read the treaties he assisted to conclude, and the correspondence with the king's council. Moreover, he printed books entirely in the Latin tongue, some of which were full of contractions, and could only have been undertaken by one well acquainted with that language. These were the "Infancia Salvatoris," three editions of the "Directorium Sacerdotum," a "Psalterium," "Horæ," "Tractatus de Transfiguracione," and several "Indulgences." To "ordain in print" a Latin manuscript of the fourteenth or fifteenth century required a knowledge of the language on the part of the workman as well as of the master; for, as the letters *n* and *u* were identical in shape, and as *m* and *i* varied only in the number of strokes, the latter being without a dot, it was impossible to read some words—for instance, ııııııııııuııı (minimum), where fifteen parallel strokes distract the eye—apart from their context. We have, however, in the English translation of the "Golden Legend" positive evidence on this point; for, in the "Life of Saynt Rocke," the printer says, "which lyff is translated oute of latyn in to englysshe by me wyllyam Caxton."

As translator, editor, and author, Caxton has not received his due meed of praise. The works which he undertook at the suggestion of his patrons, as well as those selected by himself, are honestly translated, and, considering the age in which he lived, are well chosen. Romances, the favourite literature of his age, were Caxton's great delight—and that not merely for the feats of personal prowess which they narrated, although no quality was more desirable in the fifteenth century, but rather, as he himself says, for the examples of "courtesy, humanity, friendliness, hardiness, love, cowardice, murder, hate, virtue, and sin," which "inflamed the hearts of the readers and hearers to eschew and flee works vicious and dishonest." In Poetry Caxton shows to great advantage, for he printed all the works of any merit which then existed. The prologue to his second edition of the "Canterbury Tales" proves how anxious he was to be correct, and at the same time shows the difficulty he had in obtaining manuscripts free from error. The poetical reverence with which Caxton speaks of Chaucer, "the first founder of *ornate* eloquence in our English," and the pains he took to reprint the "Canterbury Tales" when a purer text than that of his first edition was offered to him, show his high appreciation of England's first great poet. In History the only available works in English were the "Chronicle of Brute" and the "Polycronicon;" the latter Caxton carried down, to the best of his ability, to nearly his own time. It was, indeed, as a writer of history that Caxton was best known to our older authors, some of whom, while including his name among those of English historians, have overlooked the far more important fact that he was also England's prototypographer.

All reference to the literary forgery of Atkyns, who, in the seventeenth century, to support his claim to certain exclusive privileges of printing under the king's patent, invented the foolish story of the abduction, by Turnour and Caxton, of one of the Haarlem workmen, and his settlement at Oxford in 1464, has here been purposely omitted. The whole account is so evidently false, so entirely at variance with the known facts in Caxton's history, and has been so often disproved in works on English typography, that it needs no further refutation.

As to Caxton's industry, it was marvellous: at an age when most men begin to take life easily, he not only embarked in an entirely new trade, but added to the duties of its general supervision and management, which could never have been light, the task of supplying his workmen with copy from his own pen. The extraordinary amount of printed matter, original, and translated, which he put forth has already been noticed; but there seems reason to believe that some of his works, both printed and manuscript, have been entirely lost. Of his translation of the "Metamorphoses of Ovid," only Book xv has been preserved; but we may be certain that Caxton never would have begun to translate at the end of a work; and it seems probable, as the manuscript is evidently intended for the press, that the whole was printed as well as translated. Moreover several of Caxton's works being unique, and others having been but recently discovered, we may conclude that time will yet reveal to us other specimens.

Great interest would attach to a veritable portrait of Caxton, but although two or three have been published, they are all apocryphal. The only one that has any appearance of probability is the small defaced illumination in the manuscript of "Dictes and Sayings" at Lambeth Palace, which has received too much praise from Horace Walpole, who engraved it for his "Royal and Noble Authors." King Edward IV is represented on his throne, with the young prince (to whom Earl Rivers was tutor) standing by his side: there are two kneeling figures, one of which, Earl Rivers, is presenting to the king a copy of his own translation, which Horace Walpole assumes to have been printed by the other, who of course would then be Caxton. If this were the case it would be very interesting; but unfortunately the second figure is evidently an ecclesiastic, as shown by his tonsure, and apparently represents "Haywarde" the scribe, who engrossed the copy, and probably executed the illumination. The portrait commonly received as that of Caxton, and which first appeared in his "Life," by Lewis, is thus accounted for by Dr. Dibdin:— "A portrait of *Burchiello*, the Italian poet, from an octavo edition of his work on Tuscan poetry, of the date of 1554, was inaccurately copied by Faithorne for Sir Hans Sloane, as the portrait of Caxton." In Lewis's "Life," this portrait was "improved" by adding a thick beard to Burchiello's chin, and otherwise altering his character; and in this form the Italian poet made his appearance, upon copper, as Caxton. Ames, Herbert, Marchand, and others, have reproduced this absurd engraving. From a note, however, written by Lewis to Ames, it appears that, although Lewis admitted the portrait, it was Bagford's creative genius that invented it, as may also be inferred from Lewis's own subscription "*inv. Bagford*," upon the plate.

As an instance of his appreciation of a higher life than can be obtained from riches alone, we will quote an anecdote which Caxton himself wrote, and added as an appendix to "Æsop's Fables."

"There were dwelling in Oxford two priests, both Masters of Art, of whom that one was quick and could put himself forth, and that other was a good simple priest. And so it happened that the master that was pert and quick was anon promoted to a benefice or two, and after to prebends, and for to be a dean. So after long time this worshipful man, this dean, came riding into a good parish with ten or twelve horses, like a prelate, and came into the church of the said parish, and found there this good simple man, sometime his fellow, which came and welcomed him lowly. And that other bade him, Good morrow, Master John, and took him slightly by the hand and axed him where he dwelled. And the good man said, In this parish. How! said he. Are ye here a soul-priest or a parish-priest? Nay, sir, said he; for lack of a better I am parson and curate of this parish. Then that other availed his bonnet and said, Master parson, I pray you be not displeased, I had supposed you not to be beneficed; but, master, said he, I pray you, what is this benefice worth to you a year? Forsooth, said the good simple man, I wot not, for I make never account thereof, although I have had it four or five years. And know you not what it is worth! it should seem a good benefice? No, forsooth, said he; but I wot well what it shall be worth to me. Why, said he, what shall it be worth? Forsooth, if I do my true diligence in the cure of my parishioners in preaching and teaching, and do the part belonging to my cure, I shall have heaven therefor. And if their souls be lost, or one of them by my default, I shall be punished therefor, and hereof am I sure. And with that word the rich dean was abashed. This was a good answer of a good priest and and honest."

No attempt has been made in the preceding sketch to exalt Caxton at the expense of historical truth. As England's first typographer, a never-dying interest will surround his name. Except as a printer, he nowhere shines forth preeminent. But although we cannot attribute to him those rare mental powers which can grasp the hidden laws of nature, nor the still more rare creative genius which endures throughout all time, we can claim for him a character which attracted the love and respect of his associates—a character on which history has chronicled no stain—a character which, although surrounded, through a long period of civil war, by the worst forms of cruelty, hypocrisy, and injustice in Church and State, retained to the last its innate simplicity and truthfulness.

CHAPTER IX.

THE MASTER PRINTER.

THE question of the exact spot upon which England's first printing press was established has already been discussed. The well-known advertisement of Caxton, which states that pies of Salisbury use were on sale at the "Red-pale," in the almonry, at Westminster, not only indicates the position of his house, but also the sign by which it was known. The precise appearance of the almonry in the fifteenth century must be to some extent imaginary, but we know that almshouses were there, and probably two or three structures besides that occupied by Caxton.

We will now ask the reader to imagine fourteen years passed since Caxton first began working at his new art. It is not difficult to picture the wooden building in the almonry occupied by his sedate but busy workmen. We can look in at yonder window, and see the venerable master printer himself "sittyng in his studye where lay many and dyuerse paunflettis and bookys." The great towers of Westminster Abbey cast their shadow across the room, for he is an early riser and already at work upon his translation of the new French romance, called "Encydos." The "fayre and ornate termes" of his author give him "grete plasyr," and he labours, almost without intermission, till the low sun, blazing from the western windows, warns him of the day's decline.

Again, we watch him pass with observant eye through the rooms where his servants are at work; we see the movements of the Compositors, who ply their rapid fingers close to the narrow windows; we hear the thud-thud of the wooden presses as the workmen "pull to" and "send home" the "bar," discussing meanwhile the latest news; and we sympathise with the binder, who, hammering away at the volume between his knees, looks in despair at the ever-increasing progeny of his master's art. Piles of books and printed "quayers" rise on all sides, and many a wise head is ominously shaken at the folly of supposing that purchasers can be found for so many books. Nevertheless Caxton pursues his busy course, ever at work with mind and body, preparing copy for the press, and guiding and instructing his workmen in the art which he had learned in Bruges at "grete charge and dispense," and the practices of which are to be explained in the following chapter.

Of all the workmen employed at the "Red-pale," the names of three only have descended to us.

WYNKEN DE WORDE, who was probably a native of the town of Worth in Belgium, appears to have been the chief man. When he entered Caxton's service is unknown; it was probably at an early age, as he was still living in the year 1535. In 1491 he succeeded to the stock in trade of his deceased master, but he did not append his own name to his books until 1493. He used many varieties of Caxton's "mark."

RICHARD PYNSON speaks respectfully of Caxton as "my worshipful master." He at first set up a press just outside Temple Bar, and used Caxton's device in his books.

WILLIAM COPLAND remained for some time after Caxton's death in the service of Wynken de Worde. He, too, in his prologue to "Kynge Apolyne of Thyre," mentions "my master Caxton." Doubtless there were many others, and some have supposed that Machlinia, Lettou, and Treveris were among the number; but there is no evidence that these printers were ever reckoned among Caxton's workmen.

We come now to the mechanical means by which, during fourteen years, Caxton carried on his business. Was the process of book-making the same as it is at the present time? What sorts of types, and how many founts were used? How were the types made, and what were their sizes? Did the compositors use upper and lower case, sticks, chases, brass rule, reglets, furniture, and the various appliances of a modern composing-room? What were the presses like, and the practices of the pressmen? And lastly, In what form were Caxton's books issued to the public? To most of these questions it would, at first sight, seem as though no definite answer could be given; but when attention is directed to the books themselves, undesigned, and therefore most trustworthy, evidence will be found in them as to many technical customs and peculiarities of the early printers.

Before the invention of printing, the art of book-making, mechanically considered, was divided into three departments: the manufacture of the material upon which to write, almost entirely parchment or vellum; the ink making and the writing, the scribe being his own ink maker; and the binding. Illuminators there were, of course, but their work was merely ornamental, and by no means necessary to the idea of a book. In monasteries famous for the diffusion of learning all these branches were carried on together. So has it been with printers, who, from the infancy of their art to the present time, have occasionally included everything necessary to a perfect book in one establishment. If all the trades which, either directly or indirectly, are called into operation by printers were to be enumerated, few indeed would be omitted; nevertheless, the absolute necessaries for the production of a book are—the material upon which to print, the types and presses with which to print, and the workmen to handle them. We will, therefore, consider Caxton's books under the following heads:—

The paper.
The types.
The compositor.
The press, the pressman, and the ink.
The bookbinder.

To these may be added, although not as necessary assistants:
The rubricator, illuminator, and wood-engraver.

THE PAPER.

Fortunately, there is no need to enter here upon the obscure origin of the manufacture of paper. The only question which concerns us is—What kind of paper did Caxton use, and whence did he obtain it? He certainly had several sizes; the largest, which was probably found too unwieldy, was used only for the first two editions of the "Golden Legend," an uncut copy of which, in the University Library at Cambridge, gives 22 × 15¾ inches for the full measurement of a whole sheet. The large size of this book was, doubtless, suited to its intended use—in the public services of the church. He likewise used several smaller sizes, which varied according to the moulds in which the sheets were made, from 18½ × 13 inches to 16 × 11 inches.

The quality of the paper varied considerably, though not to the extent apparent in the books as they now exist—chemical "doctoring" and washing, which have in many instances been resorted to for cleansing purposes, having weakened and rotted much of the paper so treated, whilst the untouched specimens remain strong and fibrous. We observe in books still in the original bindings, and apparently untouched, that the paper was rough—sometimes very rough—on the surface, with long hairs frequently imbedded in it, and marks where many more had been removed; of a strong fibrous texture, unbleached, and of a clear mellow whiteness, indicating an absence of colouring matter in the pulp.

The accompanying woodcut shows a paper-mill of this period. A water-wheel was arranged to turn a wooden shaft upon which were rows of cogs which continually lifted up to the height of a few inches a number of wooden pestles, and then let them fall upon the material, which was always in shallow water. The whole of the fibre was thus retained with its length and strength uninjured. When the pulp was ready it was taken up, in small quantities, into the hand-mould, and formed into a sheet. There would be no difficulty whatever in making paper nowadays in a similar manner, only no one in the trade would spare the time and labour, and no one out of the trade would pay for the cost and trouble of its production.

The unevenness in thickness and colour to which the manufacture was liable at this early period, appears to have necessitated a sorting of the sheets after they came from the mill; those nearest to each other in colour and weight being put together. This system of selection was adopted occasionally for single copies, economy being doubtless the inducement. When two or three examples of a book can be compared together this fact is often very evident, as in the two copies of "The Knight of the Tower" which are in the British Museum, where the variation in quality is too great to be accounted for except by this practice of selection. Several other instances show that Caxton, when preparing to print a new volume, told off the paper separately for certain copies. This custom also accounts for the astonishing variety of water-marks frequently found in one volume.

Some possessors of uncut specimens of Caxton's press have imagined them to be "large paper copies," but we have no evidence that Caxton designedly printed special copies, except, perhaps, in the instances of the vellum "Doctrinal" and

"Directorium," hereafter to be noticed, but of these the appearance is by no means that of *livres de luxe.*

Watermarks are of much less value in bibliography than some writers have imagined. In but very few instances can a limit of time be fixed for their use; and as the marks might be repeated, or the paper itself kept for any length of time, and imported to any place, they cannot be used as evidence either of the date when, or the place where, a book passed through the press. The arms of France—three *fleurs-de-lis* on a shield, surmounted by a crown—which appear as a watermark in "Le Recueil des Histoires de Troyes," have been adduced by M. Bernard as evidence of the French origin of the printed work. He was doubtless unaware that the same watermark appears in "The Recuyell," "Canterbury Tales," 1st edition, "Mirrour," 1st edition, "Jason," "Chronicles," "Polycronicon," "Speculum Vitæ Christi," "Dictes," 2nd edition, and many others, embracing the whole of Caxton's typographical career. When, however, paper bears the arms of a nation or a city, we may, in such a case, fairly conjecture, although not with certainty, the seat of its manufacture. It appears likely that all Caxton's paper was imported from the Low Countries, and it was in all probability purchased from some old connection in the great mart of Bruges. But whereever obtained, there was a great intermixture of qualities, including the make of several mills. We have never yet seen one of Caxton's books in which the same watermark runs through the whole volume, and in many cases the variety is astonishing. Thus, in a copy of the first edition of the "Canterbury Tales," now in the library of Mr. Huth, there appear no less than fifteen distinct watermarks.

A few of the marks found in Caxton's books are here given. As already remarked, they indicate the Low Countries as the land of their origin, and most of them are found also in the block-books, the works of Colard Mansion, Gerard Leeu, and other early printers.

No. 1. The Bull's Head, which appears in the earliest specimens of paper known, and was a favourite symbol with

No. 1.

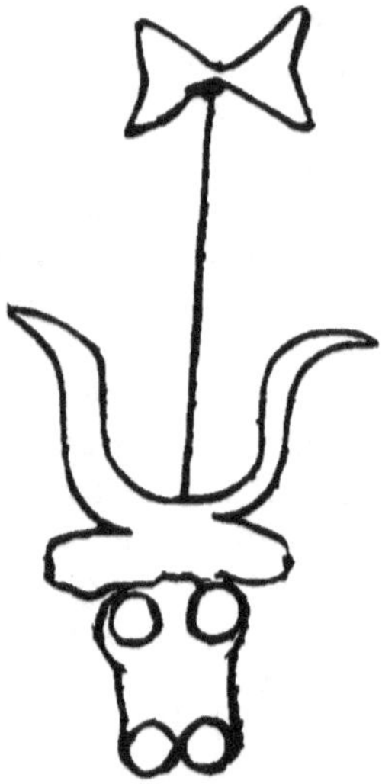

No. 2.

No. 3.

No. 4.

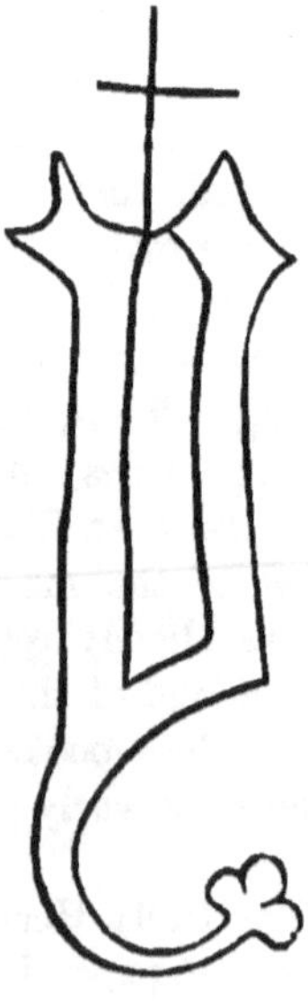

No. 5.

No. 6.

No. 7.

No. 8.

paper makers of the fourteenth and fifteenth centuries. The varieties of it are very numerous.

No. 2. The Arms of John the Fearless, son of Philip the Hardy. As eldest son the field is charged with a label: the superimposed cross referring to his crusade in 1395.

This and the six succeeding marks have a direct connection with the ruling dynasty in Flanders and the Low Countries.

No. 3. The letter p is very common in Caxton's books, and is perhaps the initial of Philip the Good; although paper bearing a p had also been made in the reign of Philip the Hardy. Its varieties are very numerous.

No. 4. The letter y is thought by Sotheby to be the initial of Ysabel, third wife of Philip the Good.

Mr. Sotheby, in his list of Caxton's watermarks, mentions the p and y combined, as occurring in the British Museum copy of "Jason." During a careful search, however, in the same copy, I was unable to detect any such mark.

No. 5. The Unicorn—a symbol of power adopted by Philip the Good, who chose two unicorns as supporters of his coat-of-arms. The same figure was used extensively as an ornament in his palace and furniture.

No. 6. The Arms of France. These were frequently used by paper-makers of the Low Countries, probably in reference to the direct descent of the House of Burgundy from the Kings of France.

No. 7. The Arms of Champagne. This province was ceded to the Duke of Burgundy in 1430 by the King of France.

No. 8. The Hand, over which is a single *fleur-de-lis*, the peculiar badge of the House of Burgundy.

In Caxton's books the p is the most common among the watermarks, the order of frequency among the others being as follows:—The Hand or Glove; the Arms of Champagne; the Bull's Head; the Arms of France; the Greyhound; the the Arms of John the Fearless; Shears; a Pot; an Anchor; an Unicorn; a Bull; a Cross; Grapes; a Pelican, &c.

The reader curious on this point may see numerous other watermarks figured by Mr. Sotheby in the third volume of his "Principia Typographica." Many of these are merely variations of the mark, the paper being made in the same mould. An accidental injury, or even the wear and tear of the mould by constant use, often caused a contortion of the wires. In rare instances the watermark occurs uninjured in shape, but quite at the edge of the paper. This has been accounted for by supposing the fine wires which held the watermark in its place on the mould to have become loosened by decay, or some accident, and so allowed the mark to slide along the face of the mould, but it is more probably caused by the use of large sheets of paper cut down to a smaller size.

Of the value of paper in Caxton's time we may form some idea from the prices paid by the directors of the Ripoli press, at Florence, between 1474 and 1483. An original "Cost book" of this establishment is still extant in the Magliabechian library at Florence. It is one of the most interesting documents connected with early typography, and has been edited and published by the Padre Vincenzio Fineschi. From this it appears that the following nine sizes or qualities of paper were then in use, the English prices given being about the present equivalent, reckoning the lira at 3*s* 9*d*.

		PER REAM.		
1.	Large paper of Bologna in common folio, about	£1	4	2
2.	Middling ditto ditto . .	0	13	2½
3.	Small ditto ditto . .	0	11	3
4.	Paper of Fabriano, with a *crossbow* for watermark	0	12	4½
5.	Ditto, with a *cross* for watermark	0	8	7½
6.	Paper of Colle	0	8	7½
7.	Paper of Prato	0	9	4½
8.	Paper of Pescia, with *spectacles* for watermark	0	10	10½
9.	The same, with a *glove* for watermark . . .	0	9	0

Zanetti quotes a document, dated 1483, which states the price of paper in Florence to have been, at that period, for "Carta reale, quaderni 10...3 lir. 6 sol. 8d;" and for "Carta da scrivere il quaderno...18 sol.;" that is, royal paper about 12s 5d per ten quires, and writing paper 3s 4½d per quire.

The first paper maker in England was John Tate. He manufactured specially for Caxton's successor, Wynken de Worde, who thus announces the fact in his edition of "Bartholomæus de Proprietatibus," printed about the year 1498:—

"And John Tate the younger,
Joye mote he broke,
Whiche late hath in Englond doo
Made this paper thynne,
That now in oure englisshe
This boke is prynted Inne."

Tate, who died in 1514, and whose will is preserved in the principal registry of the Court of Probate, left considerable property, several of his legacies being in paper.

It is somewhat remarkable that Caxton should have made so sparing a use of vellum for his books, and should have been so indifferent about the quality of the skins which he did employ. The only examples known are a copy of the "Doctrinal of Sapience," at Windsor Castle, for a long time thought to be unique, and a "Speculum vitæ Christi," now in the British Museum, to which may be added a few slips on which Indulgences are printed.

THE TYPES.

The question of the invention of moveable types, like that of the origin of paper, is one into which we have no need here to enter. The majority of writers on this subject having been unacquainted with the characteristics of type, have strayed far and wide in the discussion. M. Bernard, however, writing as a practical printer, has done much to dispel numerous misapprehensions, and especially that common error of supposing that the first moveable types were cut in wood.

We now proceed to lay before the reader the earliest notices of typefounders, and such evidence as may explain the mechanics of typefounding in the fifteenth century, especially with reference to the types of Caxton.

Perhaps no part of the Typographic Art is hidden in more utter darkness than the early manufacture of the types. Considerable secrecy no doubt accompanied all the operations of the first printers, and was maintained down to a comparatively late period. Moreover, it was but natural that the results of the new art should hold a more prominent place in men's minds than the processes by which those results were produced, and thus, although printers and printing were often mentioned, we find nothing concerning the mechanical part of typefounding anterior to that curious little book of trades, with illustrations by Jost Amman, which was issued at Frankfort in 1568 The author, in the few lines which accompany the illustration, omits all reference to the process, but, from the woodcut of the "Schrifftgiesser" and his tools, we shall further on draw some practical inferences concerning early typefounding.

Whether Caxton, whose account of his first typographical venture is contained in the prologue to the Third Book of "The Recuyell," made himself acquainted with the manufacture as well as with the use of his types there is no evidence to prove. He simply remarks, "Therefore I have practysed and lerned at my grete charge and dispense to ordeyne this said book in prynte." If he only procured types and presses, and the requisite knowledge to control their use, it no doubt cost him a considerable sum. The probability is that his first two founts were cast at Bruges according to his instructions, and that he brought the second over with him to Westminster. But, when once settled in his native country, we may well consider whether he would not, for convenience sake, have become his own typefounder. No stray hint or remark can be found to incline us to the one opinion or the other. Several generations of printers passed away before we find in any work the slightest allusion to English typefounders. The earliest appears in Archbishop Parker's preface to Asser's Chronicle of King Alfred, where, in speaking of the Saxon types with which the book was printed, the editor states that as far as he knew, Day, the printer, was the first to cut them:—"Iam verò cum Dayus typographus primus (& omnium certè quod sciam solus) has formulas æri inciderit: facilè quæ Saxonicis literis perscripta sunt, iisdem typis diuulgabuntur." This leads us to suppose that John Day was only one typefounder among others, and that therefore the art was at that time by no means a novel one in England. Seventy years later we find typefounding a distinct trade in London, and under rigid Government protection, as we learn from the following decree:—

"Decreed by the Court of Starre-Chamber, 11th July, 1637:—

"That there shall be Four Founders of letters for printing and no more.

"That the Archbishop of Canterbury or the Bishop of London, with Six other High Commissioners, shall supply the places of those four as they shall become void.

"That no master Founder shall keep above two Apprentices at one time."

Despite this restrictive care, however, the typefounders of Holland and Flanders supplied English Printers with better types than native art could produce, until the establishment of a foundry by the first Caslon.

The only English author before the rise of encyclopædias, who described the process of type manufacture was Joseph Moxon. This ingenious author, writing in 1683, gives an account of the whole Art of Printing, as practised in an improved style by himself, and devotes several chapters to the various methods of punch cutting, matrix sinking, and type founding. The process then adopted was very similar to that still in use, and differed greatly from that of Caxton, or Caxton's typefounder. The practice of Moxon, like that of modern typefounders, was to cut each letter in relief on a piece of steel to form the *punch*—to strike this punch into a small piece of copper, which made the *matrix*—and then to fit this matrix to the bottom of an iron *mould* into which the liquid metal was poured. The mould, which formed the shank of the type, was capable of a sliding adjustment, widthwise, to the width of the various letters (from an *i* to an Æ); the depth or size of the *body* always remaining the same throughout the fount. Thus, by using each matrix successively in the same mould, exactness in size of body was insured.

The want of this exactness, indicated by the uneven appearance of the lines, and other considerations, lead to the conclusion that the fifteenth-century printers did not practise this method, but is very difficult even to speculate upon that which they did employ in the production of their types. The examination of many specimens has led me to conclude that two schools of typography existed together. The ruder consisted of those printers who practised their art in Holland and the Low Countries, and who, by degrees only, adopted the better and more perfect methods of the school founded in Germany by the celebrated trio—Fust, Gutenberg, and Schœffer. None of these divulged the secrets of their art. One fact, however, we know with certainty, and that is that the German school employed the very best artists that Europe could produce to cut the patterns, or rather punches, for their types. In an interesting tract from the pen of Sir Anthony Panizzi it is proved that the celebrated Bolognese goldsmith, medallist and painter, Francia, was the artist who cut all the Aldine types, the elegance of which will for ever associate the name of Aldus with the perfection of printing. From the "Cost Book" of the Ripoli press, at Florence, we find also that steel, iron, and tin were used in the manufacture of types about 1480. But the English printers, whose practice seems to have been derived from the Flemish school, were far behind their contemporaries in the art. Their types show that a very rude process of founding was practised, and the use, as will be described presently, of old types as patterns for new, evinces more of commercial expediency than of artistic ambition.

That Caxton's types were really cast is evident from identity in the face of the same letter, where even a flaw may be noticed as recurring continuously; but the material of which the matrices were formed must be to a great extent conjectural. M. Bernard has given an interesting account of some successful efforts to cast letters in sand, but his specimen has not a single overhanging letter in it, and, from its size, was certainly much easier to produce than would have been the small types of Caxton; yet in one respect, the "bad lining," or irregular heights of the letter, it has an interesting similitude to Caxton's types. In the office of Messrs. Caslon there are still in existence some large Roman capital letters (about 3-line pica), which an old workman assured me he had himself used in by-gone years to form sand-moulds for type, a practice then by no means uncommon.

We will now turn to the little book of engravings already mentioned as giving the earliest notice of the art. We there see somewhat of the practices of the Frankfort typefounders in 1568. The woodcut shows that even a century after the invention of the art there was an important difference from the modern plan, although probably the *principle* of punch, matrix and mould, was the same. There is a small furnace, with the pan of metal sunk in the top; by the side are the bellows, basket of charcoal, and tongs. Close to the type-founder is the bowl into which he drops each type as it is cast; and the artist has correctly drawn these types with the "break" of the letter still attached. The workman holds the mould in his left hand, and is pouring in metal from a ladle. On the table at his back is what appears to be a nest of very shallow drawers, which hold the matrices in alphabetical arrangement, while upon the top of the drawers are three or four matrices for immediate use. On the wooden shelves opposite are three moulds, some sieves, and crucibles. The sieves were probably for sifting the sand in which might be cast the large types, and in which the small ingots for use in the melting pot would be run. The main interest of this woodcut lies in the type moulds, in which we notice a difference in shape from those now used; while the absence of the long wire spring which holds the matrix firm up to the mould indicates that, during its use, the matrix was a fixture in the mould. The foremost of the three moulds on the shelf shows in its side a hole which may possibly have been used for the insertion of a matrix.

As the early moulds were so dissimilar to those of modern use, let us look to the types themselves for evidence. Anticipating the result of the analysis of the various founts used by Caxton (which will follow in its proper place) we find the conclusion inevitable that hard-metal punches were not used, and that even types themselves were used either as punches, or in some analogous way for the production of new founts. The use of large types to form matrices in sand (as in the case of Messrs. Caslon's foundry, above alluded to), was not uncommon in bygone years; and that letters of a much smaller size can also be effectively employed as punches is interestingly illustrated by the shifts to which Benjamin Franklin, America's pioneer-printer, was put in the early days of the Transatlantic press. Franklin thus narrates his own practice: "Our printing-house often wanted sorts, and there was no letter-foundry in America; I had seen types cast at James's in London, but without much attention to the manner; however, *I contrived a mould, and made use of the letters we had as puncheons, struck the matrices in lead*, and thus supplied, in a pretty tolerable way the deficiencies. *I also engraved several things* on occasion."

The metal of which Caxton's types were cast can only be conjectured. The probability is that it was soft, and if even so soft as lead it would have been sufficiently durable to have performed the work for the small impression required of each book. In demonstration of this the author procured, by the kindness of Messrs. Figgins, a fount of their Caxton types in pure lead, and composed a page of Caxton's "Chess Book," working it in the usual way, at a common hand press, and numbering each impression as it came from the tympan in order to note its gradual wear. The paper was royal cartridge of the common rough quality, and was worked dry. After 500 pulls, perceiving no appreciable wear, the author stopped the experiment, being sufficiently satisfied.

Our conclusions then, in respect of the founding, are mainly negative. The moulds were *unlike* those now in use, and the punches were *not* of steel. The process, whatever it may have been, admitted of contrivances incompatible with our present mode; and we conjecture that the type-metal, if not of lead, was yet sufficiently soft to allow of it being easily trimmed up with a chisel. This trimming up, so often visible in Type No. 2*, misled the late Mr. Vincent Figgins, who, when examining the second edition of the "Game and Play of the Chess," came to the erroneous conclusion that the whole book was printed from types cut separately by hand, a conclusion which he would never have adopted had he extended his examination to other and earlier works of Caxton in the same types.

Let us now see what the founts of types really were that Caxton used.

When we look at the long list of English authors who have written upon early typography, and when we recognise among the names those of Moxon, Palmer, Smith, Bowyer, Nichols, Stower, Watson, Hansard, and Timperley, all of whom were, as printers, practically acquainted with the art which employed their pens, it is a matter of some surprise that nothing like a correct account of Caxton's types appeared. Nor is it less remarkable that the only history of English typefounding is that by Rowe Mores, a well-known antiquarian, who was brought up for the Church, and who devoted many of the later years of his life to the collection of old moulds and matrices. He purchased all the old stock of the last of the old race of letterfounders, Mr. James, of Bartholomew Close, whose extensive collection was said to date from the days of Wynken de Worde; and it is much to be regretted that, after the death of Mr. Mores, his collections were not preserved intact. His catalogues of matrices existing in his own day, or in his own possession, are probably exact enough; but his account of the types used by Caxton and Wynken de Worde is full of errors.

During Caxton's career as a printer, viz., from about 1476 to 1491-2, or a period of seventeen years, he used eight separate founts or castings of letters. These eight founts we have called, according to their chronological appearance, No. 1, No. 2, No. 2*, No. 3, No. 4, No. 4*, No. 5, and No. 6.

If we divide them into *character* of letter we find three classes :—

1st. Type No. 1 is distinct in character, and unlike any other known type. On comparison with a manuscript in the holograph of Colard Mansion, of Bruges, M. Bernard came to the conclusion that it was formed upon the handwriting of that celebrated caligrapher.

2nd. Types 2, 2*, 4, 4*, and 6, are of the same character as the early type of Colard Mansion, known as "gros bâtarde."

3rd. Types 3 and 5, were designed, like the characters of the Bible and Psalter of the early Mentz printers, upon the Church Text of the scribes, and approach nearer than any other of Caxton's types to what modern printers call "black letter."

If, however, we divide the eight founts into distinct cuttings, we find five :—

1st. Type No. 1.

2nd. Type No. 2, modified first into No. 2*, and again into No. 6.

3rd. Type No. 3.

4th. Type No. 4, modified into No. 4*.

5th. Type No. 5.

Type No. 1.

Although we believe that Caxton had less to do with this than with any of the later types, yet, as it is the first with which his name is associated—as it is that by using which he obtained a knowledge of the art of printing—and as it is the type of the first English-printed book,—it is clothed with an interest peculiarly its own.

The books printed with this fount are five :—

The Recuyell of the Histories of Troy	1472-74
The Game and Play of the Chess, 1st edition . .	1475-76
Le Recueil des Histoires de Troyes	1475-76
Les Fais du Chevalier Jason	*after* 1476
Les sept Pseaulmes penitenciaulx	*after* 1476

From the rarity of "Les Fais du Jason," only one copy being in England, and that inconvenient for prolonged examination, its peculiar features, if any, are not noticed in the following remarks.

The first thing we observe in type No. 1 is, that its general appearance is more free and manuscript-like than would be thought the case from the square-set figure of each individual letter. This is, to a considerable extent, caused by the great variety of letters, there being only five for which there were not more than one matrix, either as single letters or in combination: for, although the differences between the various matrices of the same letter may be but very slight, we have here the fundamental principle of freedom, namely, a recurrence of modified sameness. The execution of the type is good, sharp, and decided, with sufficient difference between the repetitions of the same letter to indicate independence of of tracing or mechanical contrivance; hence probably the work of one accustomed to cut letters. The body of the type, which is identical throughout the five books, is the same as the recognised Great Primer of modern printers.

The complete fount embraced at least 163 sorts, of which we remark upon the following:—

ā is not used in the English books, but often occurs in the French books.

ē is not used in "The Recuyell" or the "Chess Book," but often occurs in "Le Recueil" and "Les sept Pseaulmes."

𝔎 is often used for an 𝕶 in the French books, but always correctly in the English books.

𝔑.—This incongruous and badly-cut letter appears about twelve times, in various grades of bad casting, before the recto of folio 36 of "The Recuyell," after which it is not found.

𝕶 is only found in the English books, where it is sometimes used for a 𝔎.

Arabic numerals do not occur in this fount.

There are only three marks of punctuation, which may be called—the comma, or oblique stroke (/), the colon (:), and the full point (.). They are used arbitrarily as to power, and in numerous varieties of combination, such as, ./ ./ /' ./' '/. // :. .:. .'.:.'. &c., &c.

From the foregoing remarks it will be seen that there are certain letters peculiar to the English and others peculiar to the French books printed in this type; and as these are not in any way attributable to the fashion of the language, the fact strongly corroborates the opinion that, although from the same printer, the compositor, and perhaps the cases, were changed.

Type No. 2.

This was the first fount used in England when Caxton set up his presses at the "Red-pale" in the Almonry, and, before remarking upon its peculiarities, we will give a list of the books known to have been printed from it. Of these, as will be shown further on, there are two easily-distinguished classes; those printed first, with type No. 2, and those printed afterwards, with a re-casting of the fount, which we call type No. 2*.

TYPE No. 2.

Les quatre derrenieres choses	*ante*	1477
History of Jason	*circa*	1477
Dictes and Sayings of the Philosophers, 1st edition		1477
Horæ, 1st edition	*circa*	1477
Canterbury Tales, 1st edition	*ante*	1478
Moral Proverbs		1478
Propositio clarissimi Johannis Russell	*ante*	1479
Stans Puer ad Mensam	*ante*	1479
Parvus Catho and Magnus Catho, 1st edition	*ante*	1479
Ditto ditto 2nd edition	*ante*	1479
The Horse, the Sheep, and the Goose, 1st edition	*ante*	1479
Ditto ditto 2nd edition	*ante*	1479
Infancia Salvatoris	*ante*	1479
The Temple of Glass	*ante*	1479
The Chorle and the Bird, 1st edition	*ante*	1479
Ditto 2nd edition	*ante*	1479
The Temple of Brass	*ante*	1479
The Book of Courtesy, 1st edition	*ante*	1479

TYPE No. 2*.

This type has a more dashing, picturesque, and elaborate character than type No. 1. It is an imitation of the "gros-bâtarde" type of Colard Mansion, with same variation in the capital letters, which are extremely irregular, not only in size but also in design, some being of the simplest possible construction, whilst others have spurs, lines, and flourishes.

The general appearance of type No. 2 is very different from that of No. 2*, many letters in the earlier fount having a bolder and thicker face than in the later; and the fact of there being a perfect division of the books into two distinct classes prevents our attributing this difference to either wear of type or faulty printing—the former would be gradual, the latter irregular.

On comparing the two classes, letter by letter, we find several single and compound letters occurring in the one and not in the other. Thus **en** (not final) is peculiar to the first class, while two forms of **k** without a loop in the head, double **ll** without loops, **th**, **wa**, **we**, and **wo** are found in the second class only. Other letters are so entirely different that a single example is convincing of their not having been printed from the same founts; and the remainder, although often very nearly alike, so constantly preserve some slight characteristic peculiar to each section, that a close examination of numerous instances, after making allowance for faulty printing, leads to the conclusion that no letters of the first section are identical with those of the second.

A minute examination discloses the general fact, that the letters of Type No. 2* are somewhat thinner than those of Type No. 2, and that, in numerous instances, the tops, the descending tails, and the titles generally, have been truncated. For example, examine the letter f and its combinations in the two types; the second shows *always* a thinner-faced letter than the first. Again, notice how the tops of the various ds, the tails of en and in, and the tails generally appear in the second state. Observing that the two founts (2 and 2*) are never mixed, and that all the books dated before 1479 occur in Type No. 2, and all those dated after 1479 in No. 2*, the two types appear to indicate two distinct periods; and, taking into consideration the peculiarities just noticed, it would seem that, upon the types becoming worn, some of the best were selected, trimmed up with a graver, and used for making matrices for a new casting. If this were not the case, how should we account for the new fount being so nearly like the old? for, the two not having been used together, there was no reason for such care to make them match.

The body of Type No. 2 is the same as that of Type No. 2*, and is exactly equal to two lines of "Long Primer" (Caslon's standard), which is very near to "Paragon." A complete fount of Type No. 2 consisted of 217 sorts, and Type No. 2* of 254 sorts.

The &c of Type No. 1, which, if it occurred at all, might have been expected in the first fount used in England, is found only in books printed with Type No. 2*.

We may notice here that the sorts lʒ, cʒ, dr, and others, presume an intended French use of Type No. 2, a probability strengthened by the th, and the combinations of w, being later additions to the fount in No. 2*.

Type No. 3.

This grand type, which was in use from about 1479 to 1483, has perhaps less direct interest for us than any of the others. No English book in this type is known, and until a very recent period it was considered merely as a supplementary fount used by Caxton for headings, &c. But the discovery of a "Psalterium," fragments of a "Horæ," and a "Directorium" proves that three works at least were printed entirely with this fount. Upon these, especially the "Psalterium," and upon the headings of "Boethius," the "Golden Legend," and "Tully," the following remarks are based.

The small letters are an exact copy of those cast by the early German founders, Fust and Schœffer, and are equally well executed. The capital letters, however, are very unlike Fust's, being for the most part a modification of the Flemish "Secretary," as already presented to us in the gros-bâtarde type of Colard Mansion.

The body is identical, or very nearly so, with type No. 2, and is used with it to distinguish proper names, &c., in the "Cordial" and in "Tully," but, having a much larger face, it is never in line.

The complete fount comprised 194 sorts. The stops generally are smaller than those of type No. 2, which is remarkable, as the face of the letter is much larger.

This type was intended for Latin works, as the contractions sufficiently prove. All the books we have in it are in Latin, except headings in the first edition of the "Golden Legend," &c., and proper names, as in the "Cordial" and "Tully." Used almost entirely for Church Service books, it does not seem to have been much in favour with Caxton; but upon his death his successor, Wynken de Worde, came into possession of it, and used it continually.

Type No. 4.

Types No. 4 and 4* may be spoken of generally as *one*, there being the same intimate connection between them as between Nos. 2 and 2*; unlike them, however, there is a slight variation in the body, type No. 4 being, as compared with the re-casting of it, or type No. 4*, as 20 is to 19. In other words, the body of type No. 4 is rather smaller than that of Type No. 4*. This of course would only be possible by direct intention with modern typefounders, who use the same moulds and matrices for as many founts of the type as are required; but as is shown in the chapter on typefounding, the moulds and matrices were in those days very different.

The engraving of the types is neat, and appears to have been executed by the same hand that cut type No. 2; but there is this difference between the second states of the two founts—type No. 2* was, as already shown, cast from matrices formed by the use of old casts of type No. 2 as punches, after being trimmed by hand, but for types Nos. 4 and 4* there is the strongest evidence of the same punches having been used, and therefore the variation of body is the more remarkable, as it would have been as easy to make the re-casting agree in size with the original as to make the letters of each fount agree among themselves. The variation, however, is a fact.

The body of type No. 4 is very near indeed to modern English (Caslon's standard), and is the smallest of any used by Caxton. The re-casting, or type No. 4* (which loses 1 in 20—that is to say, 19 lines of type No. 4* take up only the same depth as 20 of type No. 4) is exactly two lines of minion. The total number of sorts in type No. 4 appears to have been 194, and in No. 4* 187, a few sorts not having been re-cast.

We will now give a list of the works for which this type, in its two states, was employed.

TYPE No. 4.

The Chronicles of England, 1st edition	1480
The Description of Britain	1480
An Indulgence	1481
Curia Sapientiæ . . . *circa*	1481
Godfrey of Boloyne	1481
The Chronicles of England, 2nd edition	1482
Polycronicon	1482
The Pilgrimage of the Soul	1483
A Vocabulary	1483
Servitium de Visitatione . . . *circa*	1483
Confessio Amantis (*mostly*)	1483

The Knight of the Tower (*partly*)		1484
Sex Epistolæ (*mostly*)		1483

TYPE No. 4*.

The Festial, 1st edition		1483
Quatuor Sermones, 1st edition		1483
Confessio Amantis (*partly*)		1483
The Knight of the Tower (*mostly*)		1484
Caton	*circa*	1484
Golden Legend	*circa*	1484
Death-Bed Prayers	*circa*	1484
Æsop		1484
Order of Chivalry	*circa*	1484
Canterbury Tales, 2nd edition	*circa*	1484
Book of Fame	*circa*	1484
The Curial	*circa*	1484
Troylus and Creside	*circa*	1484
Life of our Lady	*circa*	1484
Life of St. Winifred	*circa*	1485
Life of King Arthur		1485
Life of Charles the Great		1485
Paris and Vienne		1485

The commas have a notable chronological bearing. The short comma (/) was used alone up to the second edition of the "Chronicles," in 1482—is used occasionally with the long comma (/) in 1483—and disappears entirely after that year.

A good test by which to distinguish 4 and 4* is the shape of the lower-case w; the letter with the curled top distinguishing the book at once as belonging to type No. 4, whereas its absence is a sure sign that the type is No. 4*.

Type No. 4* makes its first appearance among Caxton's founts in a very peculiar manner. In the autumn of 1483 he was engaged in printing two works, Gower's "Confessio Amantis" and the "Knight of the Tower." At sig. y of "Confessio Amantis" we find that the inmost sheet is in type No. 4*, the three other sheets of the section being in type No. 4. Several pages in sig. z are also in No. 4*, and on sig. ꝫ iiij recto the first column is in No. 4, while the second column is in No. 4*. This mixture of founts by no means proves that the two were in use at the same time; it only shows that before the cases containing type No. 4 were finally emptied out to make room for the new fount, one compositor had worked ahead of his fellows, who had not finished their taking of copy when the new letter supplanted the old. The table, although placed at the commencement of the book, was necessarily printed last, and therefore, as a matter of course, we find type No. 4* used for it. In the "Knight of the Tower," sig. f introduces the new fount to us, all that follows, as well as the introductory matter, being type No. 4*.

TYPE No. 5.

There is much similarity of design between this and type No. 3, the likeness between some of the letters being so close as lead to the conclusion that one artist cut both.

The books printed in this letter are as follows:—

The Royal Book	*circa*	1487
The Book of Good Manners		1487
Directorium Sacerdotum, 1st edition	*circa*	1487
Speculum Vitæ Christi	*circa*	1488
Commemoratio Lamentationis	*circa*	1488
The Doctrinal of Sapience		1489
Horæ	*circa*	1490
Servitium de Transfiguratione	*circa*	1491

In the 2nd edition of the "Golden Legend" (1487?), all the headings, both of chapters and pages, are in this type.

Type No. 5 has no exact counterpart in the bodies of modern founders. The nearest would be two lines of brevier, than which it is slightly larger, losing one line in thirty-five. The total number of sorts in use appears to have been 153. The comparative scarcity of double letters is very noticeable. No Arabic numerals are used.

The large Lombardic capitals used with this fount have a bold and striking appearance. Unlike any former fount of

Caxton's) they are all cast with the largest face the body will bear, and without the least beard. They are used, more or less, in every book printed with this type, although in some books (*e.g.* "Royal" and "Speculum") they appear very seldom. They do not look at all well when used as initials to a word, on account of their size preventing them ranging with the sequent letters, and this may have been the cause why Caxton, except in the "Directorium," made a very sparing use of them, save indeed that he converted them into quadrats. For this purpose they were doubtless adapted by some shortening process, which, however, has not prevented them cropping out continually in the blank spaces of the head lines and signature lines, where they often assume a very puzzling appearance. In the latest books printed with type No. 5 these Lombardic capitals appear as *red* initials, printed at a separate operation. This use for them was, doubtless, the invention of Caxton's successor, Wynken de Worde, who appears to have inherited his master's working materials.

TYPE NO. 6.

The body of this fount is great primer (Caslon's standard) within a shade, being almost the same as type No. 1. The number of sorts in the fount is, for Caxton, very small, amounting to only 138. It may be called Caxton's last fount, for it came into use in 1489, and was used for books up to 1491, the date of Caxton's death. Indeed, there seems good reason for supposing that for some time after Caxton's death it served his successor, Wynken de Worde. With it the following works were printed:—

The Fayts of Arms		1489
Statutes of Henry VII	*circa*	1489
The Gouvernal of Health	*circa*	1489
Reynard the Fox, 2nd edition	*circa*	1489
Blanchardin and Eglantine	*circa*	1489
The Four Sons of Aymon	*circa*	1489
Directorium Sacerdotum, 2nd edition	*circa*	1489
Eneydos	*circa*	1490

The Fifteen Oes, &c. . . . . *circa* 1490
The Dictes and Sayings of the Philosophers 3rd edition . . . . *circa* 1490
The Mirrour of the World, 2nd edition . . . *circa* 1490
Divers Ghostly Matters . . . . *circa* 1490
The Art and Craft to know well to Die . . . *circa* 1491
The Book of Courtesy, 2nd edition . . . . *circa* 4491
The Festial, 2nd edition . . . . *circa* 1491
Quatuor Sermones, 2nd edition . . . . . . *circa* 1491
The Chastising of God's Children . . . . . *circa* 1491
A Treatise of Love . . . . *circa* 1491

We have in this fount another remarkable instance of the contrivances employed by the early typefounders. A new fount was required, but whether Caxton gave the founders instructions concerning its size, or whether the fount was cast first, and then sold to our printer, there seems no possibility of discovering; but this we can prove from the pages themselves, that the greater portion of type No. 6 was made from the punches, or from old letters of Caxton's Nos. 2 and 2*. The body is rather smaller, nine lines occupying the same depth as eight lines of No. 2; and it is amusing to observe the shifts and contrivances resorted to for reducing those letters which, in type No. 2, occupied the full body. For instance, the 𝔄, 𝔐, and 𝔑 have the flourish which passes under the letter brought close up to the letter itself. The ℜ was also treated in the same way, but the violence used has damaged the flourish so much that, in most instances, it broke away; in some cases, however, it remains in a most pitiable and crippled condition. The corresponding flourish in the 𝔅 has been boldly cropped off. 𝔉 and 𝔍 are strangely transformed, evidently by a blow on the soft metal, lengthwise. A few characters altogether new appear, and a few interpolations from other founts, besides a quaint set of Lombardic capitals, among which occurs now and then a letter from the Lombardic fount used with type No. 5. The total number of sorts was 141.

But here the question may very naturally be asked, How do we know that the books in the foregoing lists which are without date, without place, and without printer's name, although printed with the same types as those of Caxton, are not really from the workshop of another printer, who had obtained his material from the same source as our printer? The evidence is entirely negative, but it is nevertheless very strong.

When a new branch of industry becomes sufficiently developed, one of the immediate consequences is a division of labour. Thus typefounders became separated from printers, as soon as the latter became sufficiently numerous to keep the former in constant employment. The earliest printers were almost of necessity their own typefounders, and it appears that they each made or otherwise exclusively possessed those patterns of types which they used. There is certainly no evidence that prior to the end of the 15th century the types of one printer were at the same time in use by another. This exclusive use of types has been accepted as a fact by the best authorities, and has been of great use to the bibliographer in identifying the printer of books *sine ullâ notâ*, for a printer may thus be recognised at once by his types, just as a man may be distinguished by his handwriting.

THE COMPOSITOR.

We will now suppose a fount of type delivered over to the compositors to be laid in the cases, an operation requiring much more care than in the present day, on account of the numerous double letters and combinations. One effect of the combinations would be to equalise the size of the boxes, as the letter "e" for instance, which now requires the largest box, would then most frequently occur in combination with one of the consonants, and not be used alone oftener than many other letters. Counting the respective numbers used of each sort throughout many pages of different books, the fact is ascertained that single vowels and single consonants were more often required than any one particular combination. Arranging a case on the basis that the sorts most in use should be placed before the compositor in the position most accessible to his fingers, and remembering that in all the old representations of a "case" there is no division into upper and lower as now, we arrive at the accompanying plan, which is doubtless a tolerably exact representation of a compositor's case as used by Caxton. There are 209 boxes, which would lead to some little difficulty in keeping "clean cases;" and one need feel no surprise at finding wrong letters so often making their appearance in Caxton's pages. The combinations of *in, ni, un, nu, nn, im, mi* were often found in the wrong boxes, and have brought down to the present day the strongest evidence against the usefulness of logotypes.

In the earliest representation of a printing office the press is always made the most prominent object; very often, however, as in Plate VII, with a compartment for the compositor. Figure 1 is the earliest instance, and we there see a compositor at work. Before him is the case divided into even boxes, and raised on a cleft stick is the copy. The composing-stick is in his *right* hand, doubtless owing to the engraver not having reversed the drawing from which he copied: it is held correctly by the man in Pl. VIII. We have already noticed the use of a composing-stick and setting-rule, and the evenness of lines consequent thereon. It was not adopted at Westminster until 1480, although Caxton must often have seen the improved appearance which lines of an even length gave to the page in the numerous works previously issued from all the Continental presses. He would, doubtless, have imitated them had his mechanical appliances permitted; but we do not find evenness of page until the arrival of type No. 4, in the year 1480; and then, probably for the first time, composing-sticks, setting-rules, and chases were seen in the Westminster printing office. Before this the types were no doubt, as M. Bernard has shown to be the case in the later block books and the early examples of Dutch printing, taken straight from their boxes, and placed side by side in a sort of coffin, made of hard wood, with a stout bottom, and screws at the foot to tighten the page when completed. The width of the page could not be extended beyond the internal measurement of the "coffin," but might be reduced at pleasure by placing down either side a straight piece of wood.

The depth would be regulated in a similar manner, by varying the thickness of the foot-block against which the screws worked.

Let us, then, imagine the workman with his wooden box before him. The further end would be slightly raised, to keep the types from falling forward. He begins at the left-hand corner, and adding, from the case, letter to letter, soon gets to the end of the first line, and, not having room for the next word, makes it quite tight with quadrats or spaces. Then comes the second line, and this, as well as all the rest, would not be so easy. Placing rough types *upon* rough types admits of very little shifting or adjustment, and to this fact, I imagine, we must attribute the practice of leaving the lines of an uneven length in early books. Any attempt to push along the words of a line in order to introduce more space between them, without some plan of easing the friction, would be certain to break up the line altogether—and so the lines were left just as they happened to fall, whether full length or short. Sometimes, when a word would come into the line with a little reduction of the space between the last two words, the space was reduced accordingly; but more often a syllable at the end of the line was contracted, such as "men" into "mē," or "vertuous" into "vertuo᷒." Most often the compositor, knowing the practice to be understood by his readers, would finish his line with just so many letters as his measure would take, and accordingly it is common to find words divided thus:—why-|che th|at w|ymen w|iche m|an. But when once the "setting-rule" was brought into use all that was altered, and the various words of a line could be pushed about, and the spaces between them augmented or reduced with ease. Having completed his proper number of lines, the foot-piece would be placed after the last line for the foot-screws to work upon, and the "form" would be ready for press. There being a bottom to the box, nothing could fall out, and, although doubtless not very tight in some parts, the sloppy ink then used would not, like modern stiff ink, draw up any loose letters.

If the sides of these coffins, or wooden boxes, were equal

in height with the types they enclosed they would, like them, leave their mark on the paper. This was the case in some of the early Dutch block-books, where the sides of the chase appear occasionally printed in the margin. I have searched in vain for any marks of the chase in the margins of Caxton's books. But whatever method he used—whether he screwed up the types in wooden boxes, or whether he used iron chases, —one thing is very plain in nearly every book he issued either the "justification" was bad, or the pages were "locked up" very loosely, for quadrats and spaces are continually "working up" and showing themselves.

The composing-sticks were originally of hard wood, without any sliding adjustment; one set, all the same, were for folio pages, another for quarto, another for octavo.

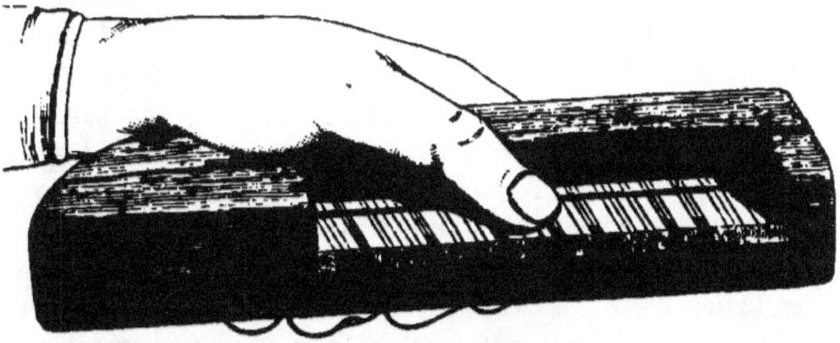

"Reglets," or thin pieces of hard wood the length of a line, appear never to have been used. When a "white" line was wanted under a chapter head or over a colophon, em quadrats were ranged side by side for the purpose, and very often capital letters which had been reduced in height for the purpose, although often not sufficiently. These low capitals would often work up while at press, and make undesirable appearances in very conspicuous places. For examples the reader may examine the "Royal Book," and "Speculum vitæ Christi," in the British Museum.

The "balls" with which the page was inked before taking an impression appear to have undergone no change in shape or make from the earliest times until the very beginning of the present century. When, however, the flexible composition now in use was invented it soon superseded entirely the old plan, and now it is a matter of great difficulty to find an old pair of balls. These balls were hollow hemispheres of wood with a handle. Wool was fitted into the hollow, upon which the skin, or "pelt," was nailed on the side more than half-way round; then more wool was pushed in till the skin was extended and tight: the last nails were then hammered in, and the balls fit for use.

The page having been completed by the compositor, it went to press in its chase or wooden box without any further operation. The business of "reader" as yet was not. All the workmen's blunders and errors, the turned letters, the wrong sorts, and the numerous literal mistakes were left uncorrected. Even whole lines were occasionally omitted by the workman, and the omission remained throughout the edition, affording indisputable evidence that "proof sheets" after composition were quite unknown. At page 125 of Lewis's "Life of Caxton," we read concerning our printer—"As he printed long before the present Method of adding the *Errata* at the End of Books was in Use and Practice, so his extraordinary Exactness obliged him to take a great deal more Pains than can easily be imagined; for, after a Book was printed off, his way was to revise it, and correct the Faults in it with red Ink, as they then used to correct their written Books. This being done to one Copy, he caused one of his Servants to run through the whole Impression, and correct the Faults he had noted with a Stancsil or Red-lead Pencil, which he himself afterwards compared with his own corrected Copy, to see that none of the Corrections he had made were omitted." A most laborious task indeed, had so foolish an idea ever entered the mind of so practical a man as Caxton, but the whole assertion is a mere fiction, started by Bagford, adopted by Lewis, and repeated by every subsequent writer, without a shadow of evidence to support it. The only books in which manuscript additions were made at the time of publication were the "Polycronicon" and "Mirrour of the World." The former, in the majority of copies, has the year of the world and the regnal year engrossed in red ink on the

Plate VII.

The oldest known representation of a Printing Press. Paris, 1507.

Luther's Press. Augsburg, 1522.

Plate VIII.

The "Prelum Ascensianum." *Paris*, 1520.

Plate IX.

From a German Book of Trades, A.D. 1568.

Plate X.

Scheme of Caxton's Type Case.

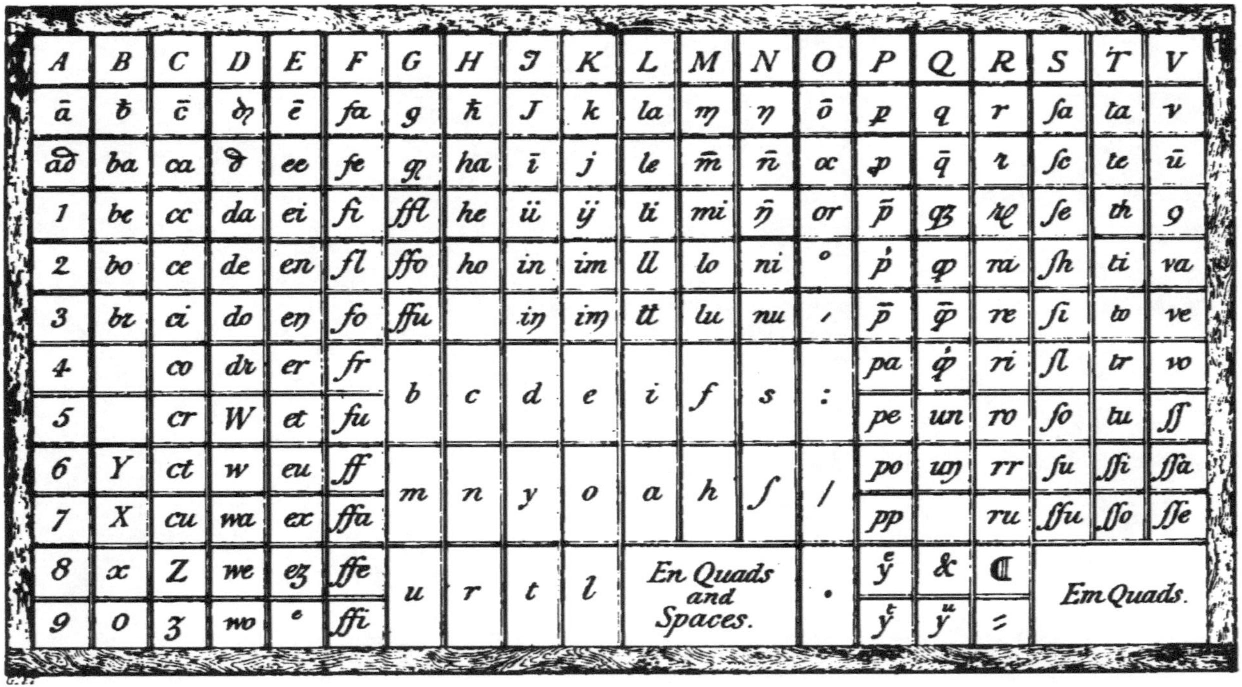

side margins; and the latter, in the woodcut of the seven concentric circles which represent the astronomical heavens, has the names of the celestial spheres written in black ink between each circle. But although I have examined about five hundred of Caxton's books, I have never seen anything approaching to a grammatical correction coëval with the date of the book.

PRESSES, PRESSMEN, AND PRINTING INK.

The method adopted by the earliest printers to obtain impressions from their blocks was to lay the sheet to be printed on the already inked block, and to rub it carefully. Wood-engravers of the present day take proofs in the same manner. The plan was continued for block printing many years after the invention of moveable types. The method of obtaining an impression by a direct pressure downwards is generally supposed to have been synchronous with the use of moveable types. Mr. Ottley, however, describes several of the earliest wood-blocks, which he had no doubt were printed by means of a press. Of one he states, "I am in possession of a specimen of wood engraving, printed in black oil colour on both sides the paper by a downright pressure, which I consider to have been, without doubt, printed in or before the year 1445." There can be no question, therefore, that the earliest type printers found a press ready to their hands; but as we have no description of the mechanism of the early presses, we must, as in the instance of type founding, have recourse to the first dated engravings. The earliest representations of a printing-press are found in the works of Jodocus Badius Ascensius, the celebrated printer of Paris. Two of these are delineated in Plates VII and VIII, whereof the earlier is found as a printer's device in the title of a work dated 1507. The large press, Plate IX, having upon its basement the date 1520, was taken from the Bagford collection, and has hitherto been generally considered as the earliest representation of a printing-press. The small press was taken from a tract of Luther's dated 1522. The other comes also from the Bagford fragments, and appears to be about the middle of the sixteenth century, as the mechanism of the spindle is evidently improved. It is represented here, however, principally on account of the figure of a type-founder seen through a door in the background, a feature very rarely pourtrayed: I have not been able to trace the work for which this woodcut was designed. In all these presses the principle is the same. There is a simple worm screw, with a long pin for a lever; the head of the press and the table bear the pressure, and the "hose," as the transverse piece between the screw and the platen was called, served to steady the downward pressure. The girths, drum, and handle served to run the table out and in, and the tympans and frisket were identical in principle, if not in appearance, with those now used. In Plate IX we see some of the pressman's appliances exposed to view. There is the shears for cutting out his tympan-sheet, and for general purposes; next to it is a pick-brush for cleaning out picks in the type; a pair of compasses for accurately testing the "furniture" between the pages; and, lastly, a screw point for making "register."

To each press is assigned two workmen; one is pulling lustily at the bar, while the other is distributing ink upon the balls previously to beating the form. The two heaps of printed and white paper, in Fig. 2, appear to our modern notions very awkwardly placed, being both on the *off* side of the press, so that the workman had to reach over the form whenever he took up or laid down a fresh sheet of paper. As however this peculiarity is represented continually, and so late as the seventeenth century, it was doubtless a common custom.

No doubt the ink was better and the impression harder in the time of these presses than in Caxton's time. His ink was of the weakest description, and the amount of power required for a "pull" of the press proportionately weak, the one necessitating the other. His presses, in the earlier part of his printing career, did not take more than a post folio page; and, with a very sloppy ink, the pull, if strong, would have made a confused mass of black instead of a legible impression. As it is, the ink has been almost invariably squeezed over the edge of the letters, and has contorted their shape. Few indeed although practical men, would imagine the deceptive nature of an impression taken from new types with weak ink and light pressure. In such a case the type appears at one time much thicker than it is, from the "spuing" of the ink—at another time battered, with some portion of it broken—and again, to use a technical term, as if it were all "off its feet."

The representation of the "Printer" in the "Book of Trades," 1569, shows that the presses then were fitted with both "tympans" and "frisket;" and many signs lead to the belief that similar appliances were used by Caxton's workmen. In short pages we often find a few lines of matter put at the bottom, which was blocked out by the frisket, and answered the purpose of a "bearer." Several instances occur in the "Godfrey," at the Public Library, Cambridge; also in the "Life of Our Lady," at the British Museum. In "Speculum vitæ Christi" we actually find "a bite," half of the bottom line remaining unprinted.

We have already noticed that only one page at a time was worked in the earlier part of Caxton's career, although later, at the probable introduction of Wynken de Worde, two pages were managed. This necessitated great care in getting the unsigned pages in their right places, and that such care was needed is proved by several instances of transposition.

Before leaving this portion of our subject, a peculiarity probably connected with the mechanism of the press must be noticed. A small hole at the four corners of each sheet appears in every book printed with type No. 1. Such holes (first noticed by Mr. Tupper), have not been observed in any books printed with the later types, except "Quatre derrennieres choses." The employment of points by modern pressmen to obtain accuracy of register, and the punctures (called "point holes") in the paper, consequent upon the use of them, are well known. The holes under notice certainly suggest a similar practice.

After due time allowed for the ink to dry upon the paper, the printed sheets passed into the hands of the binder, whose operations come next under consideration.

THE BOOKBINDER.

The art of bookbinding had not in England, in the fifteenth century, reached the perfection seen in the beautiful Continental specimens of the same period. Nor indeed was any uncommon binding required for the cheap productions of Caxton's press. His sheets were not, as in modern practice, pressed between glazed boards after being printed, but went, without further process, from the press side to the hands of the binder. The few specimens which have reached us in a pristine state show the indentation, more or less distinct, made by the types. The edition of "Eneydos," 1490, was hurried through the binder's hands so soon after the first section (which, containing the prologue and table, necessarily went to press last) was printed, that all the leaves of that section, in every copy I have seen, show a very bad "set-off" from the type on the opposite pages.

To enable the binder to collate the sheets of each section correctly, it was the custom, as well with the scribes as with the printers, to place distinguishing marks on the first page of each sheet; these were called signatures, and as Caxton used only 4os for his books, the binder (as a rule) was sure that when he had got sheets a j, a ij, a iij, a iiij together his section was complete. Some printers, who were irregular as to the number of sheets in a section, adopted the plan of signing the centre sheet of every section upon the third as well as the first page, so that the binder by this distinguishing mark might directly see the number of sheets intended for each section, however great the irregularity. In such cases the 4° would be signed on the first five rectos, leaving only three unsigned. Caxton, however, never adopted this plan, his sections always containing the same number of unsigned as of signed leaves. The sheets having been collected into sections, the signatures served again to collate the sections into volumes, the only use for which they are now retained. All the early books from Caxton's press are described as unsigned, because the signatures were not printed, but inserted in manuscript at the extreme bottom of the page.

The modern binder begins by folding all his sheets into quarto, octavo, &c., according to the size of the book, each folded sheet making a section; they are then collated and bound. In Caxton's books the collation of the sheets preceded the folding. It has been already observed that the quarto sizes were treated, both in printing and binding, as folio, the paper being cut in half before going to press. The type was so arranged that when three, four, or five sheets were folded one inside another, quirewise, the pages should be in their proper sequence. The open sheets of each section being gathered were knocked even, and folded in the middle. This adoption of one plan for books of all sizes was in accordance with the old usage of the scribes, who necessarily cut their vellum sheets to the intended size before the manuscript was commenced, and varied their sections from three sheets, if very thick, to six or seven, if very thin. The section of three sheets was called "ternio"—of four sheets "quaternus"—of five sheets "quinternus"—and so on. Caxton adopted the "quaternus" or "quaternion" for all his books, using a larger or smaller section only if the beginning or end required it. Wynken de Worde, however, made frequent use of the ternion.

From the foregoing remarks we see that the ternion and quaternion must necessarily be arranged in the order of the following diagrams, by consulting which the reader may easily know the pages belonging to any given sheet.

A Ternion—Three sheets of paper folded in half, quirewise, or one inside another. This gives six leaves, or twelve pages.

A Quaternion—Four sheets of paper folded in half, quirewise, or one inside another. This gives eight leaves, or sixteen pages.

If this arrangement be kept in mind it will be found very useful in many ways. For instance, it is often important to know whether a leaf preceded the first printed page, and, if so, whether the blank leaf found in many volumes is that leaf. It is plain that if a quaternion was adopted for the first section, then the first and the eighth leaf would belong to the same sheet of paper; and therefore if sig. a 8 had a watermark sig. a j should not have any; if a ij had a watermark, a 7 should be without, and so on with a iij and a 6, and with a iiij and a 5, where we arrive at the middle sheet of the section, and where a careful examination in the fold will certainly show the thread of the binder, always a true sign of the centre. These indications are often the only decisive evidence of the completeness or incompleteness of a volume, and enable us to decide, even where printed signatures are wanting, the true collation of a book.

Catchwords are not found in any of Caxton's books, although here and there a word by itself at the foot of a page may look very like one; but in every instance this word will be found to form an integral part of the text, and therefore in no sense a catchword, which by its very nature must be treated as the first word of the next page.

In paper manuscripts of the fifteenth century it is not uncommon to find vellum used for the inmost sheet of each section, or to find a slip of parchment pasted down the centre of each section. This was to give an increase of strength to the back where the binder's thread would be likely to tear through the paper. Instances where these slips are used are common in "unwashed" specimens from Caxton's press. The manuscript volume at Althorp, containing "Propositio," is treated so throughout, and in the quarto poems at

Cambridge the marks of the paste, where the slip was torn away at the rebinding of the volume, are very visible.

The earliest pictorial representation of a binder at work is displayed in the little "Book of Trades," to which reference has already been made; but as there is nothing in it peculiar to the age we will pass on to the material of the covers. This was very frequently only a stiff piece of parchment, with the edges turned in, and a blank leaf pasted down inside as a lining. A few books still remain in this state, just as issued from the "Red-pale" by Caxton. Such are the copies of "Tully de Senectute" in Queen's College, Oxford; the "Art and Craft," "Directorium," and the "Game and Play of the Chess," in the Bodleian; and the "Godfrey of Boloyne" in the library of Mr. Holford. If intended to be more durable, Caxton used "boards" sometimes made of oak, or beech, and sometimes (fortunately for bibliographers) of waste sheets from the press pasted together. These were covered with brown sheepskin, upon which was a simple pattern of circles, or crosses, or dragons, &c. Instances may still be seen in the 2nd edition of the "Festial" at the British Museum; in the "Servitium de Transfiguratione," lately purchased for the same library; in the 2nd edition of the "Mirrour of the World," at Bristol; and at other libraries. In the last-mentioned volume four leaves of the unique "Fifteen Oes" were used as linings for the inside of the boards. An account of a "Boethius," of which the interior of the covers was composed entirely of "waste sheets," is given in the description of that work.

When bound, we may consider that the book was generally ready for delivery to the purchaser. It was so with all Caxton's later publications, but the earlier books still required the services of the rubrisher.

THE ILLUMINATOR, THE RUBRISHER, AND THE WOOD-ENGRAVER.

It has already been noticed that, in the latter half of the fifteenth century, the great development of book manufacture led to a corresponding division of labour. Thus in Bruges we find there were *Scrivers*, or persons who wrote the text only of books, *Verlichters*, or Rubrishers, who probably confined their attention to illuminated capitals, and *Vinghette makers* (miniatores), who were artists capable of designing and painting subjects. In only one instance do the books of Caxton suggest the idea that the services of the *Vinghette maker* were to have been employed. At the commencement of his edition of Gower's "Confessio Amantis" (sig. 1, 4), the prologue of the author is begun more than half-way down the page. The blank was evidently intended for a design of some sort, possibly for a large woodcut, after the fashion of Colard Mansion, who printed all the great cuts to his "Ovid" by a separate working. As a rule, however, Caxton's books required no help from the vinghette maker, although he certainly employed, so late as 1485, the services of a rubrisher, to insert the initial letters at the beginning of chapters, and to make paragraph marks in appropriate places. For this purpose a vermilion ink was nearly always used, although occasionally a light blue alternated. For the initial of the first chapter a square space was left equal to the depth of four or five lines of type: for succeeding chapters a space of two lines was generally considered sufficient.

The first use of woodcut initials was in 1484, after which year they were never (except on rare occasions when a sort ran short) omitted. Caxton had only two or three of each letter, and sometimes only one, as may easily be seen by the recurrence of a particular initial. Some of them have their heavy blackness relieved by a few white dots punctured in the face of the letter, a practice frequently adopted by the German school to lighten the groundwork of early woodcuts. Caxton's initials are varied in shape, and often elegant in design, but with the exception of the floriated 𝔄 at the beginning of the "Order of Chivalry," and "Æsop," and perhaps the 𝔅 in "Eneydos," they demand no especial notice. A few of them are given here.

The woodcut illustrations to Caxton's books have not received much attention from the writers on the early history of wood engraving. Strutt, Singer, and Ottley in his "Enquiry" have omitted to notice them. Dibdin and Jackson have devoted a few pages to their consideration; and Ottley, in the posthumous work on the "Invention of Printing," has some interesting remarks on the early use of the art in England. His opinions are enforced by a facsimile of some rude woodcuts in his own possession, which he believed to have been executed as early as the celebrated S. Christopher of 1423. From his arguments we may conclude that although no great amount of vitality can be attributed to the art of wood engraving in England in the early part of the fifteenth century, it nevertheless was known and practised by native artists; and that the use of native talent for Caxton's books was therefore possible.

At the same time it requires no artistic education to see that there is a great similarity in general appearance between the illustrations in some of the early Dutch books, and the woodcuts of Caxton's "Chess Book," "Golden Legend," and others. In the "Troy Book," folio, printed at Augsburg in 1483, and the French-printed "Æsop," 1476, the broad outline and heavy black feet of the figures at once suggest a similarity of style if not identity of artist. But whether Caxton's cuts be native or foreign there can be little doubt of the origin of the designs. His artist merely copied the outlines found in the manuscript from which the book was being (or to be) printed. At that period there were a certain number of standard works always in demand, and for each of these the illuminators had a conventional treatment, which appears repeated over and over again in different books. To those who have examined the illuminated manuscripts of the fifteenth century, executed in the Low Countries (of which there are numerous examples in the Royal Collection of the British Museum), the identity of design and treatment in Caxton's engravings will be evident.

It is somewhat remarkable that woodcut illustrations preceded the use of woodcut initials in Caxton's books by about four years. In the "Fables of Æsop," 1484, we meet with printed initials for the first time, while woodcuts, illustrative of the text, had been used in great abundance for the "Golden Legend," the "Chess Book," the "Mirrour of the World," 1st edition, and "Parvus et Magnus Catho," the last dating about 1481.

The following is a list of all the books printed by Caxton with woodcut illustrations:—

Parvus et Magnus Catho, 3rd edit.	1481 ?	Two designs.
Mirrour of the World, 1st edit.	1481	Numerous designs.
The Game and Play of the Chess, 2nd edit.	1481 ?	Sixteen designs.
Golden Legend	1484	Very numerous designs.
Canterbury Tales, 2nd edit.	1484	Very numerous designs.
Æsop	1484	Very numerous designs. Initials first used.
Order of Chivalry	1484	Large floriated A.
Royal Book	1487 ?	Seven small designs.
Speculum vitæ Christi	1488 ?	Numerous designs.
Doctrinal of Sapience	1489	Two designs.
Horæ, 3rd edit.	1490 ?	A fragment, with one design.
Servitium Transfiguratione	1490 ?	One small design.
The Fifteen Oes	1490 ?	The Crucifixion cut and borders.
Mirrour of the World, 2nd edit.	1490 ?	Old cuts reprinted.
Divers Ghostly Matters	1490 ?	One small design.

Had Caxton's opportunities allowed, he would probably have used the wood-engraver's art to a much greater extent. The above table shows that in 1481, when he first employed woodcuts, he also discontinued them: that in 1484 he again, for one year only, used them; and that in 1487 they took a permanent position in his typography. This seeming capriciousness was probably owing to the difficulty experienced in obtaining the services of a wood engraver.

The engravings in 1481, 1484, and partly in 1487-8, appear to have come from the hand of the same artist. In the last year, however, we find considerable improvement, as shown in the illustrations to the "Royal Book," and "Speculum Vitæ Christi;" but Caxton's best specimen of the wood-engraver's art, and one which has been much praised by Dibdin, and especially Jackson, for its composition and feeling, is the well-known "Crucifixion." This design is frequently seen in the books of Wynken de Worde, who received great credit for it until its earlier use was discovered as a frontispiece to Caxton's "Fifteen Oes."

The largest woodcut known to have been used in Caxton's books is the Assembly of Saints, at the beginning of all the editions of the "Golden Legend," and the smallest, of which there are four, are found in illustrations to the text in the "Speculum vitæ Christi."

This portion must not, however, be dismissed without a few words upon that most interesting of all Caxton's woodcuts, the large device. Caxton used but one; the small device, of a similar design, which is commonly attributed to him, and which is first seen in the "Chastising of God's Children," being certainly not earlier than 1491.

The interpretation of the device offers a question by no means of easy solution. The common reading W. C. 74, meaning William Caxton, 1474, is, I think, correct, and we may dismiss, as unworthy of serious notice, the suggestions that the figures should be reversed to read 1447, or that the 74 or 47 refer to Caxton's age and not to a particular year. The problem to be solved is, does the design mean 74, and if if so, why did Caxton use the year 1474 on his device? Bibliographers have hitherto assumed that it must be in reference to the introduction of printing into England, and quote the colophon to the 1st edition of the "Chess Book" in support of the argument. But, as already shown, the date of the "Chess Book" refers to the translation of the work, the printing having been certainly accomplished at Bruges, and probably in 1476, Caxton's settlement at Westminster not having occurred until late in that year, or in 1477.

On the whole it seems most natural that a date used in that manner would refer to some turning point in Caxton's typographical career; and I therefore believe that the old reading of 1474 is correct, and that the reference is to the date of printing "The Recuyell," which, although translated in 1471, was circulated for a considerable time in manuscript only. Caxton certainly learnt the art while assisting to print this book: it appears also from his description that it was the first-fruit of his authorship, and at the same time the first book printed in his native language—all which circumstances might lead him to look back upon 1474 as an epoch to be commemorated.

The theory has been started that the so-called figures are not meant as such, but are only a fanciful interlacement of lines, such as may often be seen in fifteenth-century merchants' marks; that Caxton did not make his figures like these, nor would he have used Arabic figures but full Roman numerals for any date he wished to note. In fact that this design is simply Caxton's trade mark, which he used as a merchant, revived with ornamentations. The reader must judge for himself: certainly, in the form adopted by Wynken de Worde, who used them all his life, the 74 are much less like Arabic figures than in Caxton's device.

The opinion that the interlacement is a trade mark only is much strengthened by the discovery of its original use. In 1487, Caxton wishing to print a Sarum Missal, and not having the types proper for the purpose, sent to Paris, where it was printed for him by W. Maynyal, who in the colophon states plainly that he printed it at the expense of William Caxton, of London. When the printed sheets reached Westminster, Caxton wishing to make it quite plain that he was the publisher, engraved his design and printed it on the last page, which happened to be blank. This is the first occasion on which it is known to have been used. The unique copy of this Missal is in the possession of Stephen Legh, Esq., M.P.

The following list of books in which the device is found shows that it was not until the end of Caxton's typographical life that he adopted this distinguishing mark.

Missale ad Usum Sarum		1487
Speculum vitæ Christi	*circa*	1488
Doctrinal of Sapience		1489

The History of Reynard the Fox, 2nd edition	*circa*	1489
Directorium Sacerdotum, 2nd edition	*circa*	1489
Eneydos		1490
The Dictes and Sayings of the Philosophers, 3rd edition	*circa*	1490
The Mirrour of the World, 2nd edition	*circa*	1490
Divers Ghostly Matters	*circa*	1490
The Festial, 2nd edition	*circa*	1490
Four Sermons, 2nd edition	*circa*	1490
St. Katherine of Senis	*circa*	1491

The *magnum opus* of Caxton was undoubtedly the edition of "The Golden Legend," 1484. The translation alone of this great work must have been no slight task, while, as to number of leaves and size of both paper and printed page, it far exceeded his edition of "King Arthur," which was the next largest. The smallest pieces of his printing now extant are "The Advertisement" and the "Indulgences."

The commercial results of Caxton's trade as a printer are unknown; but as the fees paid at his burial were far above the average, and as he evidently held a respectable position in his parish, we must conclude that his business was profitable. The preservation of the "Cost Book" of the Ripoli press has already been noticed, and some extracts of interest translated therefrom. We may presume that Caxton also kept exact accounts of his trade receipts and expenditure, and if such were extant the many doubts which now surround the operations of his printing-office would be definitely solved. We should then know the price at which he sold his books, how many pence he asked for his small quarto "quayers" of poetry, or his pocket editions of the "Horæ" and "Psalter," how many shillings were required to purchase the thick folio volumes, such as "Canterbury Tales," "King Arthur," &c. That the price was not much dearer than that paid for good editions now, we may infer from the rate at which fifteen copies of the "Golden Legend" sold between 1496 and 1500. These realised an average price of 6*s*. 8*d*. each, or about £2 13*s*. 4*d*. of modern money, a sum by no means too great for a large illustrated work. This, however, would depend on the number of copies considered necessary for an edition, which probably varied according to the nature of the work. On a blank leaf in the 1st edition of "Dictes," at Althorp, is written, apparently by Bagford, "N.B.—Caxton printed 44 books, 25 of which were with Dates, and 19 without." One would imagine that so definite a statement must have had some foundation, but it appears to rest entirely on the writer's bare assertion. Some foreign printers issued so many as 275 or 300 copies of editions of the "Classics," but it is not probable that Caxton ventured upon so large an impression, as the demand for his publications must have been much more restricted.

APPENDIX TO BIOGRAPHY.

ORIGINAL DOCUMENTS ILLUSTRATIVE OF THE LIFE AND TIMES OF WILLIAM CAXTON.

APPENDIX.

MERCERS' RECORDS.—WARDENS' ACCOUNTS.

(Mercers' Hall, London.)

A FOLIO Volume in the Archives of the Mercers' Company, written on parchment by various scribes in the 14th and 15th Centuries, extending from 1344 to 1464. The contents of the volume include —a rent-roll—the oath of householders—of linen cloth meters—of liverymen—of brethren—of brokers —of apprentices on their entry and issue—of freemen—an almanack—and the balance-sheets of the whole Company.

The accounts of the receipts and disbursements of the Company are annual, and reckoned by the regnal year of the King. These accounts are generally made up under the following heads:—The annual fee of every liveryman—fees paid on the entries of apprentices—fees paid on the issues of apprentices—fines—quit-rents—general expenses—and foreign expenses. The last head comprises all payments made for goods and service not included in the legitimate business of the Company.

Oath taken by Caxton on "issuing" from his apprenticeship.

Ye shall swere that ye shal be true vnto oure liege lorde the kyng and to his heires kynges/ ye shall also be obedient & Redy to come at all leffull Sumonns & Warnyng of the Wardenis of the mercery whan and as often as ye be duly monysshed & warned by them/ or by any of them/ by their Bedell/ or by ony other in their name/ leffull excuse alwey except/ All Ordynaunces & Rules by the ffeliship of the merceri Ordeyned made and stablished and here after for the wele worship & profitt of the seid feliship to be made/ ye shall holde and kepe/ All coicacons necessarij Ordynaunces and Cowncels for the welfare of the seid ffeliship and the secrets therof to you shewed/ ye shall kepe secrete

& holde for councell/ and them ne ony of theym to discover or shew by ony meane or collour vnto ony persoone or persoones of ony other ffeliship. Ye shall also be contributory to all charges to you putt by the wardeins & ffeliship & to bere & pay yor parte of charge sett for yor degre like as other of the same ffeliship shall do for their degre. Moreou ye shall not departe oute of the seid ffeliship for to serve ne ye shall not accompany you w^t^ ony persoone or persoones of ony other felиship wherthrough preiudice & hurte may in ony wise growe vnto the seid ffeliship of the mercery And on this ye shall swere that during the tyme of your seruyce ye shall neither bey ne sell for yor owne self ne for ony other persone ne that ye shall Receive ony goodes or marchandise by ony collour belonging vnto ony other p'soon than oonly to yor maist whiche that ye now serue or shall serue w^t^ynne the ffeliship of ye mercerie except by his speciall license & will And also that ye shall not take ony shop hous ch'mbre seller ne warehous by ony collo^r^ for to ocupie byeing and sellyng vnto suche tyme as that ye have ben w^t^ the wardeins of the mercery for the tyme beyng and by oon of hem for shopholder amytted sworn and entred Ne that ye shall take ne haue ony apprentice or ony sẽ for to ocupye vnto that he by you vnto oon the seid Ward. for apprentice first presented & by the seid Wardein so amytted All which poynts & eny of hem to y^r^ power wele & truly ye shall hold & kepe so help you god &c.

The oath administered to Caxton upon taking up his freedom.

Ye shall swere that ye shal be good and trew vnto o^r^ liege Lord kyng of Englond and to his Eyres kyngs/ obeisaunt & obedyent to the Mayor & to the minysters of this Cite/ The ffrunchises and Custumes thereof ye shal maynteyne and the cite kepe harmles in that that in you is/ ye shall be contributary to al man^r^ charges w^t^ in this cite as somons watches contribucions taskes tallays lotte and skotte and all other charges bere yor parte as ony other frema shall/ ye shall colo^r^ no foreyns good wherby the kyng might lose his custume or his auauntage/ Ye shall know no foreyn to bey sell nor merchundise w^t^ another fforeyn within this Cite nor the fraunches therof but ye warne the Chaumberleyn therof or some mynysters of the chamber/ ye shall emplede no frema out of this Cite while ye mow have right & lawe here within/ ye shall take none apprentice but if he be fre borne and for no lesse time than for vij yers/ within the first yere ye shall do hym be enrolled and at the termes end ye shall make hym fre if he have wele and truly served you/ ye shall also kepe the peace/ in yor owne persone/ ye shall know no gaderyngs conventicles nor conspiracies made ayenst the peace but ye warne the Maier thereof & let it to yor power All these poyntes ye shall wele and truly kepe accordyng to all the Lawes & Custumes of this Cite to yor power so help you god and holidame & by this Boke/

1348.

The Fellowship in the 22nd year of Edward III numbered 4 Wardens and 101 Liverymen, and in this year among those who paid their fees appear—

Richard de Causton	Theobald de Causton
Michael de Causton	Nichol de Causton
William de Causton	Roger de Causton
Henry de Causton	

Also in the 2nd year of Henry VI.—Stevyn Causton.

1401.

Under the 2nd year of Henry IV, among the "Entrees des Apprentices," is—William Causton/ Appr. de Thos. Gedeney . . . ij s

1427—1428.

Under the 6th year of Henry VI the name of Robert Large appears for the first time.

Cest la compte de John Whatley, Robert Large, Thomas Bataill, et John Pidinyll fait alffeste de Seint John Baptist lan vj^{me} aps. le conquest en quils ils estoient gardeins de la mistere del mercerie come piert apres.

Under the same year, among "Entrees des Apprentices,"—

Robert Halle, Randolf Streete } Appñtys de Robert Large . . . iiij s

1430—1431.

Under the 9th year of Henry VI, among the "Entrees des Apprentices,"—

Item ress. de Thoms Nyche appñt de Robt Large . ij s

Item ress. de Rich Bonifaunt appnt de Robt Large, Item de James heton appnt de dit Robt . . . . } iiij s

1431—1432.

The following item is from the Warden's Receipts in the 10th year of Henry VI.—

Item. Ils soy chargent qilz ount ressu de Thos. Staunton ffrere et Attone de Robert Large de monye quil ad ressu outre mere en ptie de paiement de les xli prestres a John Wavyn ples gardenis de lan passe.

1435—1436.

Among the Entries of Apprentices in the 14th year of Henry VI.—

It de Henr. Onkmanton le aprentice de Robert Large ij s

1437—1438.

Among the Issues of Apprentices in the 16th year of Henry VI.—

It Randolffe Streete lappñtice de Robert Large . . ij s

Among the entries for the same year—

It John large } les appñtices de Robert Large . iiij s
It Willm' Caxston }

1438—1439.

Among the Wardens' Receipts in the 17th year of Henry VI.—

It Ils soy chargeont pour argent ressu p^r fynes de dius persones en lo^r temps p^r ces qils fautent de chiuachier ouesqz le mair Robert large.

In the same account, under "fforein expenses."

Item paie a xvi trumpetts le xxix i^r doctobre lan xviij^me du dit Roy Hen vj^me pour le chiuachee de Robert large maij v li vi s viij d

1440—1441.

From the Warden's Receipts in the 19th year of Henry VI.—

It ils soy chargeont pour argent rescue des Executos Robert large del legace du dit Robert xx li

In the same year under the Issue of Apprentices—

It Thomas Neche qui fuist appñtice de Robt large . . ij s

In the next year, under the Issue of Apprentices—

It Rich Bonefant q fuist appñtice de Robt large . . ij s

1442—1443.

Among the Issues of Apprentices in 21 Henry VI.—

Xrofer Heton appñtice de Robt large . . . . ij s

Among the Entries—

Richard large appñtice de Geffrey Felding . . . . ij s

Among the Issues of Apprentices in 22 Henry VI.—

John Harrowe appñtice de Robert large . . . . . . ij s

Among the Issues of Apprentices in 25 Henry VI.—

Richard Caxton* s'unt de John Harrowe . . . . . . ij s

1448—1449.

In Foreign Expenses for the 27th year of Henry VI.—

To Richard Burgh for berynge of a l're our the See vj s viij d

1450—1451.

Under Foreign Expenses in the 29th year of Henry VI.—

Item. Paid to John Stubbes for Perys to the Gentilwoman of the Duchesse of Burgeyn vj d

Item paid to Hewe Wyche for a writ directe to Sandewyche for the Gownys of the Gentil womans of the duches of Burgeyn ij s vj d

1453.

Lan du grace m cccc liij Et del Roy Herry sizme puis le conqueste xxxj^e

Under the heading "Entre en la lyvere pm' An"—

It Emond Redeknape	vj s	viij d
It^m Richaert Burgh	vj s	viij d
It^m William Caxton	vj s	viij d

These names have been erased with the pen, and the following memorandum added beneath—"qz int' debitores in fine copot9."

In the list of persons fined "qils fautent de chiuachier ouesque le mair Geffrey Felding" in the same year are the names of—

William Caxton	iij s	iiij d	Thomas Bryce	iij s	iiij d
Richard Burgh	iij s	iiij d	William Pratt	iij s	iiij d

1462—1463.

Under Foreign Expenses in the 2nd year of Edward IV.—

Item for botehyre for to shewe to ye lords of ye cousell the l're y^t came from Caxton & ye felaship by yonde ye See vj d

1464—1465.

At the end of the Wardens' Account for the 4th year of Edward IV.—

Dettours.

Item. Ye ffelaship by yende ye see for yeir patents xlvij li x d

Among the Foreign Expenses for the same year—

Item to Jenyne Bakker, Currour, for berying of a letter to Caxton ovir ye see xxviij s viij d

1465.

[Folio c xlj recto.] Anno xiiij^c lxv^o.

Courte holden of the hole felyshipp the xvij^th daye of octobr' the yere aboue written.

* * * * * *

A lettre sent ou the see. — Welboloued we grete you well certifiyng youe that as towchyng the convencion of the lordes that was appoynted to begyn at sent Omers the first daye of the p'sent moneth of october/ the whiche we trusted vppon/ it is so that it holdith not/ Neu the lesse oure sonaign lorde the kyng Remembryng that thentrecourse expired the ffirst day of Nouembre next comyng/ hath written a letter to the maire of london/ whereof ye shall receyue a copye closed in this letter/ And where as the kyng by his lettre willeth that suche a p'sone as shulde go in message for the brogacion of thentrecours shulde be p'vided in suche fourme as ye may conceyve by the lettre it is thougth here that it is not oure parte here in the Citie to take vppon vs a mater of so grete weyght where that all tymes here to fore the kyng by thavise of his lords of his Councell have made the p'vision in that behalfe and vppon this we have labored to the mayre w[t] the wardens of dius felyshippes aventerers that he will write an aunsware to the kyng of his lettre in the most plesunt wise that he can that it will pleas his highnes by thavise of his Councell to p'vide for this mater for the weall of all his subietts/ wherfore consideryng that the day comyth nygh vppon and how that the kyngs wrytyng and his message shalbe spedde from hens we are not certen/ wherfor we pray youe for the welle of alle the kyngs subietts by thavise of the felishipp there in as goodly hast as ye can labo[r] for a meane by the whiche yo[r] p'sones & goods may be in suretie for a reasonable tyme/ and in the mene whyle there com wrytyng from the kyng to the duke/ or eles from the duke to the kyng if it will so happen for p'rogacion of the same/ and suche costs as ye do vppon the suytt we will that they be generally levied there in suche mañ and fourme as ye seme most expedient/ written &c.

a W. Caxton. John lambert John Warde / John Baker John Alburgh } Custoses.

1466.

[Folio C xliiij.]

Courte of adventerers holden the iij[th] (*sic*) day of June A[o] xiiij[c] lxvj.

ffor a lettre send from Caxton Gouerno[r].

IIit is accorded by the said felishipp for by cause of a lettre send from William Caxton and theryn a Copye of a lettre sent to the said William by therle of Warwike for thabstinens of bying Wares forboden in the dukes londes of Burgoyne by acte of p'lement that a lettre shalbe made and sent to the said William by the Custoses and Adventerers whiche is made and sent in the fourme following &c.

A lettre send on to Caxton gouno[r].

Right trusty Sir We grete youe well/ lettyng youe witt the daye of makyng of this We receyved a lettre from you directed to the mayre and vs written at Brudgs the xxvij[th] daye of maye last past and theryn closed a copye of a letter directed to youe from oure good lorde therle of Warwik whiche we haue well vnderstonde & conceyved/ and oppened it to our felishipp for whiche we desire and praye youe/ in that youe is to consider and fulfill thentent made by acte of p'lement and the speciall desire of oure forsaid lorde for the publique weall of this lande and that due inqueraunce be made there in that youe is for the complyshment of the same/ as right requyreth/ we willyng in no kynde the saide acte to be broken nor hurte by non of oure felyshipp in that vs is and that the p'sones founde quyely yf any suche be as god forbede that ye do correcion after th ordenauce there made and thentent of yo[r] lettre and as for yo[r] desire of aunsware of the lordes intent here as yitt we can not vnderstonde their disposicion but as sone as we have knowlege ye shall haue wittyng and as for the lettres that ye write ye shulde sent from seint Omers we receyued non as yitt and as for any ioperdy that shulde fall ye shall vnderstonde it ther soner than we here/ and if we knowe of any ye shall have wrytyng &c.

Writ at london the iijth day of June/

J. Tate/ J. Marshall/ Ed. Betts & J. Broun Custoses of the mercery & thaventerers of the same.

a Willm Caxton Gunor de la nac deng.
Envoye p' symond preste le iiij th ior de June.

1468.

[Folio xij recto.] Anno xiiijo lxviijo.

Parsones assiged to go in ambassate by the kynges commaundment.

Courte holden the ix daye of Septembr the yere aboue writtē hit was accorded and agreede thot for asmoche as the kyng & his Counsell desyred of the felisshipp to haue certen p'sones of the same to go ou in Ambassatt wt dius Enbassatos into ffaunders as for the enlargyng of Wollen clothe that theis persones vnderwritten shulde be p'sented to the kynges highnes & his Councell/ they to do as shall pleas them/

William Redeknape
John Pykeryng
William Caxton

[Same Folio and year.]

Mony assigned to the said ambassatos for theire Costs.

Courte holden the xxviij daye of Septebr' the yere aboue said
hit is accorded that William Redenape and John Pykeryng shall haue in honde xl li st'ling towarde thoire costs & charges for thambassatt of thenlargyng of Wollen clothe in the Duke of Burguñ londes whiche shalbe leyde oute of the cundith mony at this tyme receyued vnto the tyme another Courte be had for the p'vision of the same by the advise of the Aldermen of oure felyshipp.

MERCERS' RECORDS.—RENTER WARDEN'S ACCOUNTS.

(*Mercers' Hall, London.*)

A folio Volume on paper, in the Archives of the Mercers' Company, written in the 15th Century, being a continuation, on a different plan, of the "Wardens' Accounts."

It appears that about 1463-4 the wealth of the Mercers, especially in houses and lands, had so much increased, that it was found convenient to appoint one out of the four Wardens, whose business it should be to keep an account of the Company's estate. Accordingly every year a "Renter Warden" was chosen; and from this period the Rent-roll is the main feature in the books, the sum total only of the Fees and Expenses of the Company appearing under their separate heads.

1463—1464.

Under "Qwyterents."—3rd Edward IV.

Item paid to ye Chamberleyn of Westm^r for ye pye at S Martyns Otewich for iiij t'm^s at Est' A^o iij^c^e xx s

1464—1465.

4th Edward IV.

Item to ye m' of S Giles in ye ffeld for tent^s at S Martyns Oteswich vj s viij d

Item to ye Chamberleyn of yabbey of Westm^r fer ye same xx s

1467—1468.

7th Edward IV.

Item paid for Rep'ac^s done at S Martyns Oteswich as ap'ith by ye pap' of yacopts/ as in tyleng and oy^r yings xx s vj d ob9.

1475.

A^o xiiij c lxxv. Under the head "Discharge by Qwyterents of the mercery."

Paid to the Chambleyn of West^r for the pye xx s

Same year. Under "Qwyterents of Whet'" (Whittington).

The Ward^s of O^r lady brethered of seint Margaret at Westm^r v s

1477.

A^o xiiij c lxxvij. Under "Qwyterents of Whetyngton."

It' of the Wardeyns of O^r lady brethered of Seint Margarets at Westminster v s

1484.

Under "Qwyterents."

Itm to the Chawmburleyn of west^r for the grehound iiij s vj d

Under "Other paiements."

For a dener kept at the grehound at the visitacion of the lynelod xxvj s viij d

Itm for wesshyng of a tabyll cloth ij d

A^o xiiij c lxxxiiij Under the same.

It of the ward^s of o^r lady brethered of seint marg'ets at Westemest^r for their tent9 in Aldermare v s

THE WILL OF ROBERT LARGE,

Citizen of London and Mercer—dated 11th April, 1441—translated from the original copy in the book, called "Rouse," formerly deposited in the Prerogative Court, Doctors' Commons, and now in the Probate Registry of the High Court of Justice.

TRANSLATION.

In the Name of GOD Amen. On the eleventh Day of the month of April in the Year of our Lord One Thousand CCCC and forty one in the nineteenth Year of King Henry the Sixth after the conquest I Robert Large Citizen and Mercer of the City of London being in perfect health and memory do hereby make execute and ordain my Will in this manner First I bequeath and commend my Soul to Almighty GOD my Creator and Saviour to the Blessed Virgin Mary His Mother and to all the Saints and my body to be buried in the parish Church of St. Olave in the Old Jewry London to wit in the same place in which the body of Elizabeth my late wife lies buried which my body being buried I will and bequeathe first and principally that all and singular my debts shall be faithfully and entirely paid in full And afterwards I bequeath to the High Altar of the said Church of St. Olave that the Vicar of the same shall specially pray for the good of my soul Cs Also I bequeath for the use of the structure of the same church to be applied wherever it shall be most requisite according to the sound discretion of the parishioners twenty marcs Also I leave twenty pounds for my executors to buy one set of vestments to be chosen according to the judgment of the aforesaid parishioners and such set of vestments I will to remain in the said church of St. Olave to serve for the glory of GOD so long as they shall last Also I bequeath two hundred marcs for the purpose of providing a Chaplain fit and honest and well instructed in those things which pertain to the holy offices to celebrate mass at the altar of the blessed Mary in the said church of St. Olave daily when it shall be appointed or otherwise according to the discretion of my wife and to be present at divine service at each hour appointed for prayer to officiate to pray and to minister according to the discretion of four approved most profitable for the salvation of my soul Also I bequeath to Alice my daughter one hundred pounds to be paid to her when she shall arrive at the age of twenty-one years to be spent in the purchase of furniture and utensils most necessary for her house according to sound advice and counsel Also I bequeath to Elizabeth my daughter five hundred marcs sterling and I will that the said Elizabeth my daughter together with the aforesaid five hundred marcs left by me as above to the said Elizabeth my daughter be and remain in the governance of the aforesaid Stephen Tychemerssh until the said Elizabeth my daughter shall arrive at the age of twenty years or be married he the said Stephen finding sufficient security in the chamber of Guildhall in the City of

London according to the custom and usage of the said City to deliver up to the said Elizabeth my daughter the aforesaid five hundred marks sterling when the said Elizabeth my daughter shall arrive at the aforesaid age of twenty years or be married without rendering any other interest therefor only and except the reasonable support of the said Elizabeth my daughter And if the said Elizabeth my daughter shall happen to die unmarried or before the age of twenty years then I will that two hundred and fifty marks of the aforesaid five hundred marks left by me as above to the said Elizabeth my daughter revert to the said Alice my daughter if she shall survive and if she be dead then the said two hundred and fifty marks together with the other said two hundred and fifty marks remaining be at the disposal of and distributed by my executors in pious uses and works of charity for the good of my soul and the souls above mentioned in manner as afore is set forth Also I bequeath to the common box of the Mystery of Mercers of the City of London for the support of the poor of the said mystery twenty pounds. Also I bequeath ten pounds to be disposed of according to the discretion of my executors in the purchase of a vestment to serve in the Mercers' chapel in the church of St. Thomas of Acan London so long as it will last Also I bequeath to each convent of the four orders of mendicant friars in the City of London to pray for my soul forty shillings Also I bequeath to the convent of friars of the order of St. Cross near the Tower of London twenty shillings. Also I bequeath one hundred shillings for the purchase of bedding linen and flannel according to the discretion of my executors to serve in the Hospital of St. Bartholomew in West Smithfield so long as they will last Also I bequeath one hundred shillings wherewith to purchase in like manner bedding for the new hospital called St. Mary Spital without the aforesaid thousand pounds left by me to him the said Thomas my son be and remain in the safe charge and government of the aforesaid Johanna my wife until the said Thomas my son shall arrive at the age of twenty-four years she the said Johanna my wife finding sufficient security in the Guildhall chamber of the city of London according to the manner and custom of the said City to deliver up to the said Thomas my son the aforesaid thousand pounds when he Thomas my son shall arrive at his aforesaid age of twenty-four years without rendering any interest therefor only and except the reasonable support of my said son Thomas Also I bequeath to Robert my son one thousand pounds sterling and I will that the said Robert my son together with the aforesaid thousand pounds so left by me as above to the said Robert my son be and remain in the safe charge and governance of the aforesaid Thomas Staunton my brother until the said Robert my son shall arrive at the age of twenty-four years the said Thomas Staunton finding sufficient security in the Guildhall chamber of the City of London according to the manner and custom of the said City to deliver up to the said Robert my son the aforesaid thousand pounds so left by me as aforesaid when the said Robert my son shall arrive at his aforesaid age of twenty-four years without rendering any interest therefor only and except the proper support of my said son Robert Also I bequeath to Richard my son one thousand pounds sterling and will that the said Richard my son together with the said thousand pounds so bequeathed by me to him as above shall be and remain in the safe custody and governance of the aforesaid Johanna my wife until Richard my said son shall arrive at the age of twenty-four years the said Johanna my wife finding sufficient security for the said thousand pounds in the same way as above specified And in case one or more of my said sons Thomas Robert or Richard shall die before reaching the said age of twenty-four years then I will and bequeath that the portion or portions of that my son or those my sons so dying before the age of twenty-four years shall revert to that one or those of my said sons surviving And if all my said sons shall die before arriving at the age of twenty-four years then I will and bequeath that the said three thousand pounds shall be disposed of and distributed by my executors in pious uses and works of charity for the good of my own soul and the souls of my parents my wives and my children also of my friends and benefactors for the souls of all I hold in esteem and of all the faithful departed this life in such way as my executors may consider to be better for the pleasing of GOD and among poor unmarried men and women desirous of marriage Also I bequeath to the parish church of Shakeston where my father lies buried a vestment of the value of ten pounds to serve in the same church to the glory of GOD so long as it will last Also I bequeath to the parish church of Aldester where my ancestors are buried a vestment of the value of ten pounds Also I leave to the parish church of Overton where some of my relatives are buried a vestment of the value of ten pounds Also I bequeath to Thomas Nyche my servant l marks Also to Richard Bonyfaunt my apprentice l marks Also I bequeath to Henry Onkmonton my apprentice l pounds Also I bequeath to Robert Dedes my apprentice xx marks Also I bequeath to Christopher my apprentice xx pounds Also I bequeath to William Caxton my apprentice xx marks Also I bequeath to John Gode my servant x pounds Also I bequeath to William Brydde my servant x marks Also I bequeath to William my kitchen servant xl shillings Also I bequeath to Katherine my servant x marks and to Isabella Lynde xl shillings Also I leave to William Sampson my servant at my manor of Horham five marks Also I bequeath to Peter my servant at the same place xl shillings and to Thomas my servant at the same place xxvj shillings and viij pence Also I bequeath to John de Ramsey servant of Isabella Boteley x marks on his marriage Also I bequeath to Richard Turnat the son of Johanna my wife xx pounds Also I bequeath C marks to be divided by my executors among the children of John Chirch Citizen and Mercer of the City of London who shall be living at the age of xxiiij years Also I bequeath to Thomas Staunton my brother if he will undertake the charge of executing this my will and will act with good diligence in this office C pounds Also I bequeath to Arnulph Strete Mercer on the same condition C marks and to Stephen Tychemerrsh on the same condition C marks Also I leave to Katherine my mother C marks Also I bequeath to Johanna my wife by way of gift and instead of her portion of all and singular my moveable goods and chattels by law belonging to her four thousand marks And in case that she Johanna my wife shall be dissatisfied with this my said legacy then I will that this my legacy to the said Johanna do cease and become void in law and that then the said Johanna my wife do have of my moveable goods and chattles only that portion to which she is entitied by law without any addition or advantage whatsoever Also I bequeath to Thomas my son one thousand pounds sterling and I will that the said Thomas my son together with parishioners of the aforesaid church for twenty years next after my decease the said chaplain taking for his annual salary ten marks to be paid and administered at the hands of my executors in order that he the said Chaplain may specially commend to GOD my soul and also the souls of Elizabeth and Johanna my wives Richard Herry my late master and the souls of all those whom I esteem and the souls of all the faithful departed Also I bequeath to the high altar of St. Margaret in Lothbury London C s Also I bequeath xx Pounds to be paid by my executors for the purchase of one set of vestments according to the expressed choice of the aforesaid parishioners which set of vestments I wish to remain in the said Church of Saint Margaret to serve for the worship of GOD so long as they shall last. Also I leave xx pounds to be disposed of and divided by my executors among the more indigent poor men and women of the ward of Coleman Street Also four pounds to be divided by my executors among the Chaplains and Clerks in the Churches of St. Olave and St. Margaret aforesaid within two years next after my decease that is to say xl s each year in order that the aforesaid Chaplains and Clerks may pray for my soul Also I bequeath for the new making and construction of an aqueduct lately begun in the City of London CCCC marks to be paid within four years according to the discretion of my executors on condition however that the aforesaid aqueduct be completed within four years next after my decease and not otherwise Also I bequeath for the work of making and repairing London Bridge C marks to be paid within four years according to the discretion of my executors Also I bequeath for the cleansing of the Watercourse called Walbrook near the church of St. Margaret Lothbury and for the enlargement and upholding of the same church to be disposed of according to the wise discretion of my executors and four approved parishioners of that Church CC marks or more if necessary so that it do not exceed CCC marks Also I bequeath C marks to be disposed of according to the wise discretion of my executors for the marriage of ten poor girls of good character namely to each of these ten girls at her marriage ten marks whether in the country or in the City of London Also I bequeath C pounds to be divided by my executors among poor domestic servants in the counties of Lancashire and Warwickshire that is to say one poor manservant ten shillings and to another twenty shillings and to another forty shillings as occasion may require so long as the said C pounds shall suffice Also I bequeath xx pounds to be distributed by my executors where it may be most needed Bishopsgate London so long as it will last. Also I leave five marks wherewith in like manner to purchase bedding for the hospital of the Blessed Saint Mary of Bethlehem without Bishopsgate aforesaid. Also I bequeath forty shillings wherewith in like manner to purchase bedding for the hospital of St. Thomas of Southwark near London. Also I bequeath six pounds wherewith in like manner to purchase bedding for the Lepershouses at Hakeney les lokes without the barriers of St George Southwark and of St Egidius beyond Holborn London namely to each of the said houses forty shillings Also I bequeath one hundred shillings wherewith to provide and purchase food and other things most necessary for the poor prisoners in Newgate London to be distributed according to the sound discretion of my executors Also I bequeath one hundred shillings to be distributed in like manner among the prisoners in Ludgate London Also I bequeath for repairs in the nave of the church of Thakstede five marks Also I bequeath for repairs in the body of the church of Chawrey in the county of Essex forty shillings Also I bequeath to Richard Foliet mercer twenty marks Also I bequeath to William Halle mercer lately my servant twenty pounds Also I bequeath to Agnes lately my servant forty shillings Also I bequeath to each of my two said daughters Alice and Elizabeth three cups with covers from among my cups called standing cups of silver-gilt whichever of such cups with the covers shall weigh twenty-four ounces and * * * *

[*one leaf of the original is here missing*]

the s^d^ Richard Turnat dying without male heirs lawfully begotten, then I will that all the above lands and tenements with their appurtenances shall revert to the male heirs of my before-mentioned son Robert Large. Provided nevertheless that if the s^d^ Richard Turnat shall take possession of all the aforesaid lands and tenements in Newton that then he shall be excluded entirely from the manor of Horham in the county of Essex with the lands and tenements and appurtenances belonging thereto.

Then follows the Probate, dated May 6th, 1441, and proved before Zanobio Mulakyn, Dean of the Church of St. Mary-le-Bow, London.

BRUGES RECORDS.—CIVIL JUDGMENTS.

(*The Archives, Bruges.*)

The following document is found in one of the many volumes of Records preserved in the Archives of the City of Bruges. Like the other volumes of this interesting series it is in manuscript coeval with the history it elucidates. The title at the beginning of the book is as follows:—

"Registre van alle zaken ghehandelt by Scepen van Brugghe, in huerl. camore daer zy daghelicx vergaderen. Beghint in Septembre in 'tjaer dunst vierhondert xlvij."; or, "A register of all matters brought under the notice of the Councillors of Bruges, in their daily session assembled. Begun in the month of September, in the year one thousand four hundred xlvij."

(TRANSLATION.)

To all who see or hear these Presents—the Burgomasters, Sheriffs, and Council of the Town of Bruges send greeting. Be it known that William Craes, an English Merchant, Complainant, of the one part, and John Selle and William Caxton, English Merchants also, Defendants, of the other part, have this day appealed for justice before Roland de Vos and Guerard le Groote our Fellows, Sheriffs. The said Complainant says, that John Granton, Merchant, of the Staple at Calais, was bound and indebted to him in certain sums of money; that is to say, firstly in £60 sterling for and because of a certain obligation, and further, in the sum of £50 sterling on account of a certain exchange which had taken place between them, as well as for expenses and costs incurred in that matter, amounting on the whole to £110 sterling. For this sum he had caused the said John Granton to be arrested in the Town of Bruges, and that the said John being arrested, the said John Selle and William Caxton became sureties for him, in equity and law.

And because the said John had departed the Town of Bruges without having paid and satisfied him, or appealed for justice, he demanded that the said Defendants should be compelled and adjudged, as Sureties of the said John, to pay the said claim,

The said Defendants, in answer, acknowledged that in the manner aforesaid they had become Sureties to the said William Craes for the said John Granton, but submitted that the said John was quite solvent, rich enough, and would certainly pay the amount; requiring therefore that the said Complainant might seek his debt of the said John, who was the real debtor, and that they might be discharged from their said suretyship: disputing also the sum demanded by the Defendant on account of the said exchange, for certain reasons thereupon alleged; the aforesaid Plaintiff holding the validity of the said suretyship, and demanding as aforesaid; together with many other reasons submitted by the said parties. And after hearing the said parties on the said questions, with their arguments, as well as certain Merchants, that the said dispute had been determined by our Fellows, Sheriffs, who had adjudged and decided: That the said Defendants should, as the Sureties of the said John Granton, pay and satisfy the said William Craes, firstly in the said sum of £60, of which the said obligation made mention, and furthermore in the sum of £35 sterling on account of the said exchange and costs. And that, upon the surrender of the said obligation, good and sufficient security amounting to the two said sums of £60 and £35 sterling should be given; that in case at some future time the said John Granton should deny the debt of the said sums, or allege payment, that then, on the other hand, the said Plaintiff should be sentenced to render and repay the said two sums and more. Right of action being reserved to the said Defendants against the said John Granton, the original debtor, as law and equity direct.

In witness whereof, &c., 2 January (1449).

BRUGES RECORDS.—TOWN REGISTERS.

(*The Archives, Bruges.*)

A Register written on paper in the fifteenth century, and containing Civil Judgments, given in the Town of Bruges during the years 1465-9.

(TRANSLATION.)

Whereas Daniel, son of Adrien, called Sheriff Daniel, Plaintiff of the one part, and Jeroneme Vento, for and in the name of Jaques Doric,* Merchant of Genoa, Defendant of the other part, have promised and agreed to leave all the differences between them to the judgment and arbitration of William Caxton, Merchant of England, and Master and Governor of the English Nation in these parts; and of Thomas Perrot, as Arbitrators, and amicable Umpires and common friends, the said parties, and each of them, promising well and legally to abide by, observe and perform all that the said Arbitrators shall decide and adjudicate on the said differences, without opposition of any kind. And that the said Arbitrators having heard the pleas of the said parties, and formed thereon their sentence and judgment which they have reported to the full chamber of the Sheriffs of Bruges, it has been notified to the said parties, that, because the said William Caxton was unavoidably absent from the said City of Bruges, the said parties have been summoned before the said full chamber of the Sheriffs of Bruges, and have appeared. To whom has been signified the arbitration and judgment by the said Arbitrators, which was and is as follows; that is to say—That the said Jeroneme Vento, for and in the name of the said Jaques Dorie, shall pay to the said Scepheer Daniel promptly and in current money the sum of £4 gross; and that the said Jeroneme abovenamed shall advance to the said Sheriff Daniel another £4 gross, the said Scepheer Daniel, however, giving good surety to the said Jeroneme that he will repay the said sum of £4 gross which he had advanced, within the first four voyages, in whatever country it may be, that Sheriff Daniel may make with his vessel, that is to say, on each voyage £1 gross.

* Perhaps one of the celebrated Doria family of Genoa.

Provided always, that in case the said Daniel shall not make a voyage with his said ship within the next six months, and that the said Daniel, or his sureties, shall be bound to pay and restore to the said Jeroneme Vento (without the said Jeroneme agree to a postponement) the other payments above-named. The observance of which judgment and arbitration by the said parties, and each of them, has been decreed in the said full chamber of Sheriffs of Bruges.

Done the 12th of May, 1469.

ISSUE ROLL OF THE EXCHEQUER.

Under the date of "Easter. 19 Edward IV, 15th June," is the following:—

To William Caxton. In money paid to his own hands in discharge of 20 *l.* which the Lord the King commanded to be paid to the same William for certain causes and matters performed by him for the said Lord the King.

By writ of privy seal amongst the mandates of this term 20 *l.*

ST. MARGARET'S RECORDS.—CHURCHWARDENS' ACCOUNTS.

(*In the Vestry of St. Margaret's Church Westminster.*)

A Volume of biennial Accounts of the Churchwardens, audited by the chief Parishioners. Each Account is written on a quire of parchment, complete in itself: they vary considerably in size, but have been carefully bound in one Volume, and are in beautiful condition. The period included in this Volume is 1464 to 1503. The contents consist of —Receipts of Fees for Burials, Obits, &c.—Rents—Legacies, and Gifts —Payments for Repairs—Salaries—Pew-rents—Collections—and other expenses.

1474.

"Compus Thome Frampton & Willī Stafford custod' bonorꝰ & ornamentorꝰ ecclie p'ochial' scē margarete Westm' videl't a xvij° die Maij A° regis Edwardi quarti post conq'm Angl' quarto vsqu xxij diem eiusdem" * * *

In the List of Fees for Burial is—

"Itm recd de Oliver Cawston die sepult' p' iiij tapr' viij d"

Among the Miscellaneous Receipts for 1476—

"Itm of a rewarde for a boke & a Chales lent to Sir Ric' Widenyle xx d"

1478.

"Here folowith Thaccompt of John Wycam and of Nicholas Wollescroft Wardeins of the parisshe Churche of seynt margarete of Westm' * * from the vijth day of the moneth of may in the yere of our lord god Me CCCC lxxviij * * * vnto the xviijth day of may in the yere of our lord god M^{l} CCCC lxxx" * * *

In the List of Fees for Burial in the first year—

"It^{m} the day of burying of William Caxton for ij torchis and iiij tapirs at a lowe masse xx d"

The amount paid does not appear large; but in a very long list of burial fees there are only four equal in amount, the common rate of fees being ij d, iiij d, or vj d.

1480.

The same Account. In the List of Fees for burial in the second year—

"It^{m} the day of bureying of Jone large for ij tapirs iiij d"

1481.

The Audit at the end of the same Account is as follows:—

"The whiche some of xxiij li. x s v d ob. q^{a} the forsaide wardeyns haue paid and delyued in the fulle Audite vnto william Garard and William Hachet their Successours togeder w^{t} the tresoures of and in the chirche aforeseid to them delyued in the begynnyng of this accompte * * in the presence of John Randolf squyer Richard Vmfrey gentilman Thomas Burgeys John Kendall notary William Caxton * * with other paryshyns" * *

1490–92.

In the Account for the years 1490-2, among the Burial Fees for the first year—

"Item atte Bureyng of Mawde Caxston for torches and tapres iij s ijd"

In the second year—

"Item atte Bureying of William Caxton for iiij torches vj s viij d"

"Item for the belle atte same bureyng vj d"

Here we remark again that in both these cases the fees paid are considerably larger than usual.

In the Accounts for 1496-8 among thr Legacies, and their produce—

"It^{m} receyued by the handes of William Ryolle for oone of thoo printed bokes that were bequothen to the Churche behove by William Caxston vj s viijd"

"It^{m} receyued by the handes of the said William for a nother of the same printed Bokes called a legend vj s iiij d"

"Itm by the hands of the parisshe prest for a nother of the same legendes vj s viij d"

At the end of the Account—

"Memornnd' there remayneth in store to the said Chirch"

"Itm in bokes called legendes of the bequest of William Caxton xiij d"

Among the Payments at the end of the same Account—

"Itm paide for a supper gevyn vnto the Auditours heryngo and determenyng this accompt and to the newe Chirchwardeyns as it hath ben vsed and accustumed here tofore xx s"

In the Accounts for 1498-1500—

"The Receites of Bookes called Legendes in the first yere of this accompte"—

"Fyrst Receyued of John Crosse for a prainted legende v s viij d"

"Item Receiued for a nother legende solde in Westmynster halle v s viij d"

"Item Receiued of Willm geyfe for a nother of the same legendes v s viij d"

"Itm receiued of the said Willm Geyfe for a nother Legende v s viij d"

"Item R of Walter Marten for a nother legende v s xj d"

In the second year of the same account—

"Item R. of William Geiffe for ij legendes printed x s iiij d"

"Itm R of Daniell aforge for a printed legende v s x d"

"Item R of William Geiffe for a printed legende v s"

"Memorand' ther remayneth in store to the saide chirch" * * *

"Itm in bokes called Legendes of the bequest of William Caxton iij"

In the Accounts for 1500-2 there are not entered any sales of "Legends."

"Ther remayneth in store to the saide chirche" * * *

"Item a prynted legende booke of the bequeste of Will'm Caxton."

ST. MARGARET'S RECORDS.

GUILD OF OUR LADY; WARDENS' ACCOUNTS.

(In the Vestry of St. Margaret's Church, Westminster).

A Volume of triennial Accounts of the Fraternity of our Blessed Lady Assumption, beautifully written on vellum, and in excellent preservation. It includes the period between 1474 and 1522, and is of very great interest in illustrating the customs of that period. The earlier as well as the later Volumes are not known to exist. The following are the principal headings of the various Accounts:—Arrears of Members—Rents received—Bequests and Gifts—Receipts for Obits of Members—

Fees of new Members—Rents paid—Payments of Salaries—Wages—Annuities to Almsmen and Women—House-repairs—Wax Candles, and other expenses, for the Shrine of our Lady in St. Margaret's Church—and Miscellaneous expenses.

(24th June, 1474, to 24th June, 1477).

The first Account is headed—

"This is thaccompte of maister William Thirleby henry marble gentilman and James Fytt maistres or Wardeyns chosen of the Frat'ñte or gylde of oure blessed lady seint mary the virgyn wtin the p'issh chirch of seint margaret of the towne of Westm in the shire of midd' founded, that is to say from the fest of Natiuite of seint John Baptist in the yere of ye reigne of kyng Edward the iiijth after the conquest xiiij vnto the said fest of the Natiuite of seint John the xvijth yere of the reigne of the same kyng by three hole yeres as it p'ticulerly appiereth in p'cellez here folowyng that is to wete."

Under Payments of Rent in the same Account—

"Also the said late maistres charge themsilf wt a certeyn quite rent due by John Randolff of london mercer for a licence of Fre entre of comyng in and going out for his teñntes thurgh the gate and an Alley called our lady Alley in the kynges Strete of the towne of westmr."

In the same Account, under "thentre of diũes p'sones of new to the said frat'nite is "John Caxston vj s viij d."

Also among the Payments—

"Diũers payments by the said late maisters for the said Fraternite * * * of the which thay axe to be allowed in this accompt."

"Of the money by them paid to the wardeins of the Craft of mercery of london for certain quite rent going out of the teñ't in the p'isshe of Aldermarie Chirche of london at v s by the yere."

The Fraternity appear also to have held tenements in King Street, Westminster, at Kensington, and at Stroud.

In the same Account, after the payment of six priests' salaries—

"Costes and p'celles allowed by the hole Brotherhode toward thexpences of the geñall fest in iijde yere of this accompt."

These "Costs and Parcels" occupy two full folio pages, and have yielded the following items:—

"A tonn of wyne	vj li"
"Paide to John Drayton chief cok for his reward	xxv s"
"Also for the hire of xxiiij doseyn of erthen pottes for ale & wyne	iiij s"
"Also for erthen pottes broken & wasted at the same fest	vj s viij d"
"Also to iiij players for their labour	xij s xd"

"Also to iij mynstrelles	ix s x d"
"Also for the mete of diũes of strangers	xvj s"
"Also for russhes	ij s iiij d"
"Also for vj doseyn of white cuppes	iij s"

* * * * * *

"Also for portage and botehyre of the Turbut	iiij d"
"Also for ix Turbutts	xv s ij d"

In addition to scores of "Capons, chekyns, gese, conyes, and peiones," (pigeons), the chief "cok" provided them with "swannys" and "herons," with all sorts of fish, including oysters and "see pranys," or prawns, with all kinds of meats and game, with jellies in "ix dosen gely disshes," and with abundance of fruits. The quantity of ale, wine, and ypocras provided by the butler is marvellous, and one cannot wonder at the heavy entries for "pottes and cuppes broken, and wasted." The Cook seems to have been paid much more liberally than the Wardens, who had but xxx s between them "for their dilligence."

In the Accounts for 1490-3 are the Receipts of Rent from tenements, known as "The Maidenhead," "The Sonne," "The Rose," and "The Wolstaple."

Also, under payment of Rent—

"For a certayn Quit rent paid out of a litell tent̃ in the wolstaple to the mair of the staple at xxd by the yere."

"Also for a certain Quit rent paid out of the Rents in
Alderm'ay p'isshe to John More Renter of the Mercers xv s"

From "Rymer's Foedera." Folio. London. 1710. Vol. XI. 536.

(TRANSLATION.)

CONCERNING THE TREATY OF BURGUNDY.

The King to all whom it may concern, &c. Greeting.

Be it known that

Inasmuch as determinate arrangements concerning the intercourse of merchandise between our subjects and the subjects of our well-beloved Cousin the Duke of Burgundy have in a sure form and manner been accorded and agreed to in times past and since that time often renewed,

We,

Wishing on our part to hold good and observe such arrangements, and being well assured of the faithfulness and discretion of our well-beloved subjects Richard Whetehill, Knight, and William Caxton,

Do make, ordain and constitute, by these presents, the said Richard and William our true and accredited Ambassadors, Agents, Nuncios, and several Deputies;

Giving and Granting to our said Ambassadors, Agents, Nuncios, and Deputies, and to either of them, full power and authority and general as well as special commandment to meet, to enter into treaty and to communicate with our aforesaid Cousin or his Ambassadors, Agents, Nuncios, and Deputies delegated with sufficient powers for this purpose by our said Cousin, concerning and upon the continuation and renewal of the aforesaid Intercourse, and, should occasion require, to make and conclude new arrangements,

And to do and exercise all and singular other deeds which may be fit or necessary.

Promising, in good faith and on our kingly word, always to hold as ratified, acceptable, and binding, all and any the Acts and Deeds of our said Ambassadors, Agents, Nuncios, and Deputies, or either of them, as aforesaid, which may be done, performed, or done by procuration, in the foregoing matters, or any portion thereof.

As witness our hand at Wycombe, this 20th day of October (1464).

A SHEET OF PAPER IN THE NATIONAL RECORD OFFICE.

The manuscript is—

"To tharchedeacon of Westm' that nowe is and for the tyme shalbe. We, Richard FitzJames, Almoner and Counsaillor unto oure souverain lord the King, and Richard Hatton, chaplayne and counsaillor vnto our said souverain lord, greting in our Lord God euerlasting. And whereas we, the said Richard and Richard, were appoynted, lymytted and assigned by our said souverain lord and the lordes of his most noble counsaill to examine, determyne and pacific a certain variaunce depending betwene Gerard Croppe of Westminster, taillour, of the oone partie, and Elizabeth, the doughter of William Caxton, wif to the said Gerard, of the othre partie; We, the vijth daie of May, the xjth yere of our said souverain lord, had the said parties before us in the Kinges Chapell within his palois of Westminster at this appoyntement and conclusion by theire both assentes and aggrementes:—That noon of theim, ne any othre for theim, shall fromhensforth vexe, sue or trouble othre for any maner matier or cause theim concernying for matrimony betwix theim before had; and every of theim to lyve sole from othre, except that the said Gerard shall mowe fynde the meanes to have the love and favour of the seid Elizabeth. For thaccomplisshment of which aggrement eithre of theim of their owne voluntarie willes bound theim self unto us by their faithes and trouthes, and never to varie from their said promyses. And therupon the said Gerard to have of the bequest of William Caxton, the fadre of the said Elizabeth, xx^{ti} prynted legendes at xiij s iiij d a legend. And the said Gerard to delyver a generall acquitaunce unto thexecutours of William Caxton, her said fadre, for their discharge in that behalf. And besides thies premisses both the said parties were aggreed before us to be bound, eche to othre, in C.li. by their dedes obligatorie with the condicions above wreten to performe alle the premisses. In wittenesse whereof I, the said Richard FitzJames, have to thies presentes sette the seale of myn office. And I, the said Richard Hatton, have sette my seal, and eithre of us subscribed our names with oure owne handes, the xx^{ti} daie of May the xjth yere of the reigne of our said souverain Lord."

A

DESCRIPTION OF BOOKS PRINTED

IN

TYPE No. 1.

EXPLANATION OF TERMS.

5n, or QUINTERNION, means a section of five sheets folded together in half = 10 leaves = 20 pages.

4n, or QUATERNION = 8 leaves = 16 pages.

3n, or TERNION = 6 leaves = 12 pages.

RECTO is the right-hand page of an open book.

VERSO is the reverse, or the left-hand page.

A DIRECTOR is the name given to the small letter placed where the Illuminator was intended to paint in a large initial.

LIST OF BOOKS IN TYPE No. 1.

1. The Recuyell of the Histories of Troye .	1474 ?
2. Le Recueil des Histoires de Troyes . . .	1476 ?
3. The Game and Play of the Chess Moralised .	1475–76 ?
4. Les fais et prouesses du noble et vaillant Chevalier Jason .	147– ?
5. Meditacions sur les Sept Pseaulmes penitenciaulx .	1478 ?

No. 1.—THE RECUYELL OF THE HISTORIES OF TROY. *Translated* 1469-71. *Folio. Without Place or Date.* (1474?).

COLLATION.—*Book I* has fourteen 5^{ns} and one 4^{n}=148 leaves, of which the first is blank. *Book II* has nine 5^{ns}, one 4^{n}, and one 3^{n}=104 leaves. *Book III* has ten 5^{ns}=100 leaves. *Total* 351 printed leaves and one blank.

TYPOGRAPHICAL PARTICULARS.—Type No. 1 only. Lines of very uneven length; full lines measure 5 inches, but vary in different parts from 4¾ to 5¼ inches. 31 lines to a full page. Without signatures, catchwords, or numerals. Space is left, with a director, for 3 to 7-line initials. As may be seen by the collation, each book begins a fresh gathering, probably for the convenience of binding in three separate volumes.

Commencing the work with a blank leaf, Caxton's preface follows, printed in red ink, and occupying the second recto.

The Text begins thus:—

Ere begynneth the volume intituled and named
h the recuyell of the historyes of Troye/ composed
and drawen out of dyuerce bookes of latyn in
to frensshe by the ryght venerable persone and wor=
shipfull man . Raoul le ffeure . preest and chapelayn
vnto the ryght noble gloryous and myghty prynce in
his tyme Phelip duc of Bourgoyne of Braband &c
In the yere of the Incarnacion of our lord god a thou=
sand foure honderd sixty and foure / And translated
and drawen out of frenshe in to englisshe by Willyam
Caxton mercer of y^e cyte of London / at the comaudemet

of the right hye myghty and vertuouse Pryncesse hys redoubtyd lady . Margarete by the grace of god . Duchesse of Bourgoyne of Lotryk of Braband &c/ Whiche sayd translacion and werke was begonne in Brugis in the Countee of Flaundres the fyrst day of marche the yere of the Incarnacion of our said lord god a thousand foure honderd sixty and eyghte / And ended and fynysshid in the holy cyte of Colen the . xix . day of septembre the yere of our sayd lord god a thousand foure honderd sixty and eleuen &c.

And on that other side of this leef foloweth the prologe

Caxton's Prologue begins on the verso of the same leaf, with space for a 4-line initial W.

Han I remembre that euery man is bounden

The first book commences on the fifth recto, with space for a 7-line initial W. The second begins on the 149th, and the third on the 253rd recto, the whole ending with some Latin rhymes on the 352nd recto, the verso being blank.

Remarks.—No one speaking the English language can look at this patriarchal volume with indifference. Here, for the first time, our forefathers saw their language in print; and, could our interest in any way have been heightened, it would have been by knowing it to have been printed in our own instead of a foreign land. The history of its origin is shortly this. In the original French it was a favourite novel of the English and Burgundian courtiers, for, although nominally an account of the Trojan wars, it is really a series of love scenes mixed with mythology and knight-errantry. The manuscript translation made by Caxton for the Duchess of Burgundy, whose court was at Bruges, having excited great interest, a demand arose for copies quicker than Caxton could supply them. The printing-press having been just established in that city by Colard Mansion, Caxton, whose thoughts were now homewards, determined to use it as a means of multiplying his translation, and of learning at the same time a new trade which would support him on his return to England. This he did at a great charge and expense, and then, having procured a new fount of types and all the necessary material, came over to England and erected his press at Westminster.

Fortunately this work cannot be reckoned among the rarities of Caxton's press, as there are copies in the British Museum, Sion College, College of Physicians, London, at Oxford, Cambridge, Paris, and fourteen other libraries. The Duke of Devonshire gave £1060 10*s*. for a copy in 1812, the same copy having been purchased by the Duke of Roxburgh a few years previously for £50.

No. 2.—Le Recueil des Histoires de Troyes. *Composé en l'an de grace* 1464. *Folio. Without Printer's Name, Place, or Date.* (1476?).

Collation.—*Book I*, twelve 5ns=120 leaves, of which the first and last are blank. *Book II*, eight 5ns and one 3n= 86 leaves. *Book III*, eight 5ns = 80 leaves. *Total*, 284 printed and two blank leaves.

Typographical Particulars.—Type No. 1 only is used. The lines for the greater part are spaced out to one length, being more even in this particular than the two English books in this type. A full page has 31 lines, without signatures, numerals, headlines, or catchwords. A space two to four lines in depth has been left at the commencement of each chapter for the insertion of an illuminated initial, a director being sometimes inserted.

The Text, 31 lines to a page, which is divided into three books, begins thus on the second recto, after a blank leaf:—

Cy commence le volume Intitule le recueil des histoires de troyes Compose par venerable homme raoul le feure prestre chappellain de mon tresredoubte seigneur Monsei= gneur le Duc Phelippe de bourgoingne En lan de grace. mil.cccc.lxiiii. : .

and ends on the 286th verso.

antipho' le roy estori' le roy prothenor et le roy obtome'.
· : · Explicit · : ·

Remarks.—The history of the Trojan War, a favourite subject for several centuries with European writers, was the foundation of numerous romances. Of these the chief were the apocryphal history by Dares Phrygius, a Trojan priest, celebrated by Homer; the account of the same war by Dictys Cretensis, a supposititious historian; and the History of the Siege of Troy by Guido of Colonna, a native of Messina in Sicily, who wrote in the thirteenth century. The rise of these histories, their growth under the editorial care of successive scribes, the incorporation of incidents from other romances, and their final development in the compilation of "Le Recueil des Histoires de Troye," form a curious and typical example of this class of literature. According to the unanimous testimony of all printed editions and all manuscripts of the complete work, "Le Recueil" was the composition of Raoul Lefevre, chaplain and secretary to Philippe le Bon, Duke of Burgundy: but in a manuscript copy of this work in the National Library, Paris, the first two books are attributed to Guillaume Fillastre. And this is remarkable—that Lefevre succeeded Fillastre (who was a voluminous author) in the office of secretary to the duke. Probably, finding his predecessor's history unfinished, he took it up, and, after adding Book III, issued the whole under his own name. In that age a similar course was by no means uncommon, nor was it an infringement of any recognised literary right; we can hardly, therefore, with M. Paris, call it (even if true) "une grande fraude literaire." On the other hand, several copies were issued with the name of Lefevre while Fillastre was yet living, and Caxton, who was contemporary with both writers, ascribes the whole work to Lefevre. Nor is there any noticeable variation in style between the two portions, as might be expected if composed by two authors; indeed the style of "Le Recueil" is the same as that of "Les fais du Jason," an acknowledged work of Lefevre.

Steevens asserts that Shakspere derived the greater portion of his materials for the play of "Troilus and Cressida" from Lydgate's metrical composition, "The last destruction of Troy;" but Douce, in his "Illustrations," is far nearer the truth in tracing the incidents employed by our great poet to Caxton's translation of "Le Recueil des Histoires de Troye." The latter was popular, and frequently reprinted long after Lydgate's laboured metre had become antiquated.

There is a perfect copy in the British Museum, besides a large fragment. The National Library, Paris, has a copy, and four others are in private libraries. A fragment of eight leaves was purchased some years ago by a bookseller, and made into four thick volumes, each volume having two printed leaves with a hundred blank leaves on each side. These were all disposed of as specimens to lie open in the show-cases of museums.

No. 3.—THE GAME AND PLAY OF THE CHESS MORALISED. (*Translated* 1475). *First Edition. Folio. Without Printer's Name, Place, or Date.* (1475–76?)

COLLATION.—Eight 4^{ns} and one $5^{n}=74$ leaves, of which the 1st and 74th are blank.

TYPOGRAPHICAL PARTICULARS.—There is only one type, No. 1, used throughout the work. The lines are not spaced out; the longest measure 5 inches; a full page has 31 lines. Without title-page, signatures, numerals, or catchwords.

The volume commences with a blank leaf, and on the second recto is Caxton's prologue, space being left for a 2-line initial, without director.

The Text begins thus:—

O the right noble/ right excellent & vertuous prince
George duc of Clarence Erl of Warwyk and of
salisburye/ grete chamberlayn of Englond & leutenant
of Irelond oldest broder of kynge Edward by the grace
of god kynge of England and of fraunce / your most
humble seruant william Caxton amonge other of your
seruantes sendes unto yow peas . helthe . Ioye and victo=
rye upon your Enemyes / Right highe puyssant and

The Text ends on the 73rd recto,

And sende yow thaccomplisshement of your hye noble.

Joyous and vertuous desirs Amen :/: Fynysshid the last day of marche the yer of our lord god . a . thousand foure honderd and lxxiiii.·.:.:.·.

The 74th leaf is blank.

Remarks.—"Fynysshid the last day of Marche the yer of oure lord god a thousand foure honderd and lxxiiii." The word "fynysshed" has doubtless the same signification here as in the epilogue to the second book of Caxton's translation of the Histories of Troy, "begonne in Brugis, contynued in Gaunt, and *finysshed* in Coleyn," which evidently refers to the translation only. The date, 1476–76, has been affixed, because in the Low Countries at that time the year commenced on Easter-day; this in 1474 fell on April 10th, thus giving, as the day of the conclusion of the translation, 31st March, 1475, the same year being the earliest possible period of its appearance as a printed book.

The literary history of the "Game and Play of the Chess" does not appear to have hitherto received that attention which is its due. Before 1285, Ægidius Colonna had composed his renowned work entitled "De regimine principum," which treats of self-government, domestic government, and national government. The "Liber de ludo Scachorum" of J. de Cessolis appears to have been based upon this work, its chief originality being the representation of the several stations and duties of life by the pieces used in chess. About the middle of the fifteenth century two distinct French versions were made. The earlier was probably that by Jean Faron, in 1347, who translated it literally from the original Latin. About the same time appeared the favourite and standard work of Jehan de Vignay, who took great liberties with the text, and added many stories and fables. Both these men were of the order of Preaching Friars, and seem to have worked quite independently of one another. Caxton's edition was principally from the version of Jehan de Vignay, to whom he gives the title of "an excellent Doctor of Divinity, of the Order of the Hospital of St. John's of Jerusalem," which is remarkable, as in his preface Jean de Vignay styles himself "hospitaller de l'ordre de haut pas," and he is so termed in all the manuscripts. On comparing the English and the two French versions, it is evident that Caxton must have been well acquainted with both. His prologue addressed to the Duke of Clarence contains, nominis mutatis, the whole of Jean de Vignay's dedication to Prince John of France; while Chapters I and III are taken entirely from the translation of Jean Faron. The remainder of the book is from the version of Jehan de Vignay, with one or two special insertions evidently from the pen of Caxton himself.

To show the curious way in which Caxton adopted and adapted while translating, the dedication to the Duke of Clarence, hitherto considered as his own composition, is here given side by side with its French original.

CAXTON'S PROLOGUE TO "THE GAME AND PLAY OF THE CHESS."

TO the right noble / right excellent & vertuous prince George duc of Clarence Erle of warwyk and of / salisburye / grete chamberlayn of Englond & leutenant of Irelond oldest broder of kynge Edward by the grace of god kynge of England and of frañce / your most humble seruant william Caxton amonge other of your seruantes sendes vnto yow peas . helthe . Ioye and victorye vpon your Enemyes / Right highe puyssant and redoubted pryñce / For as moche as I haue vnderstand and knowe / that ye are enclined vnto the comyn wele of the kynge our said

PROLOGUE OF JEAN DE VIGNAY TO HIS FRENCH TRANSLATION (A.D. 1360) OF THE "LUDUS SACCORUM" OF J. DE CESSOLIS.

A Tres noble & excellent prince Jehan de france duc de normendie & auisne filz de philipe par la grace de dieu Roy de france . Frere Jehan de vignay vostre petit Religieux entre les autres de vostre seignoire / paix sante Joie & victoire sur vos en-

saueryn lord . his nobles lordes and comyn peple of his noble royame of Englond / and that ye sawe gladly the Inhabitans of the same euformed in good . vertuous . prouffitable and honeste maners . Jn whiche your noble persone wyth guydyng of your hows haboundeth / gyuyng light and ensample vnto all other / Therfore I haue put me in deuour to translate a lityll book late comen in to myn handes out of frensh in to englisshe / Jn which I fynde thauctorites . dictees . and stories of auncient Doctours philosophes poetes and of other wyse men whiche been recounted & applied vnto the moralite of the publique wele as well of the nobles as of the comyn peple after the game and playe of the chesse / whiche booke right puyssant and redoubtid lord I haue made in the name and vnder the shadewe of your noble protection / not presumyng to correcte or empoigne ony thynge ayenst your noblesse / For god be thankyd your excellent renome shyneth as well in strange regions as with in the royame of england gloriously vnto your honour and lande / whiche god mul-

nemis . Treschier & redoubte seignr / pour ce que Jay entendu et scay que vous veez & ouez volentiers choses prouffitables & honestes et qui tendent alinformacion de bonnes meurs ay Je mis vn petit liuret de latin en francois le quel mest venuz a la main nouuellement / ou quel plussieurs auctoritez et dis de docteurs & de philosophes & de poetes & des anciens sages / sont Racontez & sont appliquiez a la moralite des nobles hommes et des gens de peuple selon le gieu des eschez le quel liure Tres puissant et tres redoubte seigneur jay fait ou nom & soubz vmbre de vous pour laquelle chose treschr seignr Je vous suppli

teplye and encrece But to thentent that other of what estate or degre he or they stande in . may see in this sayd lityll book / yf they gouerned them self as they ought to doo / wherfor my right dere redoubted lord I requyre & supplye your good grace not to desdaygne to resseyue this lityll sayd book in gree and thanke / as well of me your humble and vnknowen seruant as of a better and gretter man than I am / For the right good wylle that I haue had to make this lityll werk in the best wyse I can / ought to be reputed for the sayte and dede / And for more clerely to procede in this sayd book I haue ordeyned that the chapitres ben sette in the begynnynge to thende that ye may see more playnly the mater wherof the book treteth &c.

& requier de bonne voulente de cuer que il vo⁹ daigne plaire a receuoir ce liure en gre aussi bien que de vn greignʳ maistre de moy / car la tres bonne voulente que Jay de mielx faire se je pouoie me doit estre reputee pour le fait / Et poʳ plus clerement proceder en ceste ouure / Jay ordene que les chappitres du liure soient escrīps & mis au commencement afin de veoir plus plainement la maticre de quoy le dit liure p'ole.

Before concluding this article we must give an interpolation of the text which has real interest as showing Caxton's feelings towards "men of law." His author is regretting the conduct of some lawyers of Rome and Italy, and Caxton adds with a natural burst of indignation, which suggests that personal experience had something to do with it :—

"Alas ! and in England what hurt do the advocates, men of law, and attorneys of court to the common people of the royaume, as well in the spiritual law as in the temporal : how turn they the law and statutes at their pleasure ; how eat they the people, how impoverish they the community. I suppose that in all Christendom are not so many pleaders, attorneys, and men of the law as be in England only, for if they were numbered all that long to the courts of the Chancery, King's Bench, Common Pleas, Exchequer, Receipt and Hall, and the bag-bearers of the same, it should amount to a great multitude. And how all these live and of whom, if it should not be uttered and told it should not be believed. For they extend to their singular weal and profit and not to the common."

There are ten copies known of this book, of which two are in the British Museum, one at Oxford, one at Cambridge, and six in private libraries.

No. 4.—LES FAIS ET PROUESSES DU NOBLE ET VAILLANT CHEVALIER JASON. *Folio. Without Printer's Name, Place, or Date.* (147-?

COLLATION.—Sixteen 4^{ns} and one $3^{n} = 134$ leaves, of which the first and last two are blank.

TYPOGRAPHICAL PARTICULARS.—There is no title-page nor colophon. The type used is No. 1 only. The great majority of the lines are fully spaced out, agreeing in this respect more with the French editions of "Le Recueil" and the "Psaulmes" than the English "Recuyell" and the "Chess Book." Full lines measure 5 and $5\frac{3}{16}$ inches; 31 lines to a page. Without signatures, numerals, head-lines, or catchwords.

A blank leaf commences the book; at the head of the succeeding recto, with space for a 4-line initial, and director. The Text begins thus:—

l A gallee de mon engin flotant na pas long
temps en la parfondeur des mers du pluseurs
anciennes histoires ainsi comme Je vouloie me=
ner mon esperit en port de repos / soudainement
sapparu au pres de moy vne nef conduitte par vng homme

The text ends on the verso of the 131st printed leaf:—

ant a mon deuant dit tresredoubte seigneur / Et atous ceulx

qui le contenu de ce present volume liront . ou orront lire . quil leur plaise de grace excuser autant que mon petit et ru de engin na sceu touchier ne peu comprendre &c · : .

Explicit

The existence of this edition was first made known in England by a letter from M. Van Praet to Dr. Dibdin, who sent an account of it to the "Gentleman's Magazine" for July, 1812.

REMARKS.—All the books printed with these types are traced to Mansion, either alone or assisted by Caxton. In this work and the "Meditacions," the even length of the lines proves them to be later productions than those in which the lines are more uneven; and this is plain evidence that if these two works were printed by Mansion (as doubtless they were) it must have been after 1478, the year in which he adopted the plan of even lines; but if we attribute them to Caxton, we must suppose him to have forsaken his own establishment at the Red-pale, in or after the year 1480 (being the period when he first adopted the practice of making his lines of an even length) for the purpose of printing abroad what he had every facility for printing at home.

Only three copies of this scarce book have been as yet discovered. A magnificent one is at Eton College, another in the National Library, Paris, which, when purchased in 1808, was bound up with "Le Quadrilogue," a work printed by Colard Mansion in 1478, and a third in the Library of the Arsenal, Paris.

No. 5.—MEDITACIONS SUR LES SEPT PSEAULMES PENITENCIAULX. *Folio. Without Printer's Name, Place, or Date.* (1478 ?)

COLLATION.—Three 4^{ns} and one 5^{n}=34 leaves, of which the last only is blank.

TYPOGRAPHICAL PARTICULARS.—There is no title-page. The only type used is No. 1. The lines are for the most part fully spaced out, though now and then there is a deficiency in this respect, which only occurs, however, on the verso of the folios, the recto throughout being fully spaced. This peculiarity is observable to a greater or less extent in all the French books printed in this type. The full lines measure 5 inches, and 31 lines make a full page. There are no signatures, folios, nor catchwords.

The text begins on the first recto,—

A vraye penitance est comme aucune eschielle
l par laquelle lomme pecheur qui selon la parabole
de leuuangille descendy de Iherusalem en Iherico
monta de rechief de Iherico en Iherusalem / cest avision de

And ends on the 33rd verso, with a full page, followed by a blank leaf,—

exultacion de leesse espirituelle / Puis encores sil te plaist
me donne que par ce septenuaire der pseaulmes de peniten=
ce lesquelz correspondent aux sept affectz de lomme prins
pour les sept degrez de leschielle de penitence Je puisse mo=
ter et paruenir atoy en cette tant glorieuse cite de Iherusa=
lem en laquelle tu habites et te offrir auec les sains et be=
neurez le sacrifice de loenge sans fin /: AMEN

REMARKS.—This work is a translation from the original Latin of Cardinal Pierre d'Ailly, entitled "Meditacions Circa Septem Psalmos Penitentiales." It was composed about the end of the fourteenth century, and translated shortly after into French, but by whom is uncertain, although from the style it is supposed by several of his biographers to have been from the pen of the Cardinal himself. The Commentary on the Penitential Psalms, printed by Wynken de Worde was composed by Bishop Alcock, and has nothing in common with this.

In all typographical particulars this work agrees with the French edition of "Jason," already described, and there is little doubt was printed by Colard Mansion at Bruges, about 1478.

The only EXISTING COPY at present known was discovered in the General Library of the British Museum, in 1841, by Mr. J. Winter Jones, bound up with "Les Quatre Derrenieres

Choses." It is *perfect*, in an excellent state of preservation, clean, and free from all disfigurements. It has the final blank leaf, the verso of which is covered with quotations in the handwriting of the fifteenth century. These quotations are extended over the first recto (which is also a blank) of the book mentioned above as being bound up with it, proving that they were bound together soon after printing. For an article on both works, from the pen of Mr. Jones, see "Archælogia," vol. xxxi, page 412.

A

DESCRIPTION OF BOOKS PRINTED

IN

TYPE No. 2.

BOOKS PRINTED IN TYPE No. 2.

6.	Les Quatre Derrenieres Choses	1475 ?
7.	The History of Jason . . .	1477 ?
8.	The Dictes and Sayings. First Edition .	1477
9.	Horæ	1478 ?
10.	The Canterbury Tales. First Edition	1478 ?
11.	The Moral Proverbs of Christine .	1478
12.	Propositio Johannis Russell .	1478 ?
13.	Stans puer ad Mensam . . .	*ante* 1479
14.	Parvus Catho. First Edition . .	*ante* 1479
15.	Ditto Second Edition	*ante* 1479
16.	The Horse, the Sheep, and the Ghoos. First Edition	*ante* 1479
17.	Ditto ditto Second Edition	*ante* 1479
18.	Infancia Salvatoris	*ante* 1479
19.	The Temple of Glass	*ante* 1479
20.	The Chorle and the Bird. First Edition	*ante* 1479
21.	Ditto ditto Second Edition . .	*ante* 1479
22.	The Temple of Brass, or the Parliament of Fowls	*ante* 1477
23.	The Book of Courtesy. First Edition . .	*ante* 1479
24.	Queen Anelida	*ante* 1479
25.	Boethius . .	*ante* 1479
26.	Corydale	1479
27.	Fratris Laur. Gulielmi de Saona Margarita	1479-10 ?
28.	The Dictes and Sayings. Second Edition .	1480 ?
29.	Indulgence	1480
30.	Parvus et Magnus Chato. Third Edition	1481 ?
31.	The Mirrour of the World. First Edition	1481 ?
32.	Reynard the Fox. First Edition . .	1431
33.	Tully of Old Age	1481
34.	The Game and Playe of the Chesse. Second Edition .	1481 ?

No. 6.—LES QUATRE DERRENIERES CHOSES ADVENIR. *Folio. Without Printer's Name, Date, or Place.* (1476?)

COLLATION.—Nine 4^{ns}=72 leaves, of which the first only is blank.

TYPOGRAPHICAL PARTICULARS.—Type No. 2 only is used. The lines are of very irregular length, 28 to a page. Without signatures, folios, or catchwords. Commencing with a blank leaf, the table follows on the second recto, the first three lines being in red ink.

The text begins:—

Ce present traictie est diuise en quatre parties principa les : Desquelles chascune contient trois autres singuli / res parties en la fourme qui sensuit :

and ends on 72nd verso:—

quilz pourueissent aux choses derrenieres / dont la frequete memoire et recordacion Rapelle des pechiez a culpe aux der tus et conferme en bounes oeuures / par quoy on paruient a la gloire eternelle :Amen

Explicit liber de
quatour Nouissimis

An important typographical peculiarity in this work is the mode in which the printer has employed red ink for the title-lines or chapters. The *modus operandi* and how the red ink overlies the black, is explained at p. 52, *ante*. This curious and primitive practice is not seen in any books except that under notice, and those printed by Colard Mansion of Bruges. Another typographical characteristic which intimately connects this book with those printed in Type No. 1 is the existence of two small holes on the outer margin of each leaf, made by points in use by the pressman. These, it should be noticed, occur in all the works for which type No. 1 was used, but none, except the present, printed with type No. 2, nor indeed in any English printed books. Again, we find among the undoubted first issues of the press at Westminster that the books in folio, such as "The Life of Jason," "Dictes," "Canterbury Tales," "Cordyale," &c., have all 29 lines to the page, while "Les quatre derrenieres choses" has but 28. On taking, however, the actual measurement, it will be seen that the depth of the page is exactly the same as in the type No. 1 books. Evidence has been already produced to show that the five books in type No. 1 were printed in Bruges by Colard Mansion alone, or assisted by Caxton; and to the same source we have no hesitation in ascribing "Les quatre derrenieres choses."

Remarks.—The title, "De quatuor novissimis," was applied to many religious treatises of the fourteenth and fifteenth centuries; and so many Latin manuscripts of distinct works have come down to us that it is difficult to distinguish between them: nor were the early printed editions less numerous, Hain, in his "Repertorium Bibliographicum," giving the titles of twenty-one editions printed in the fifteenth century. They all agree, however, in one particular, viz.—that no copy gives the name of its author. The Latin original of one work on this subject is attributed to "Denis de Leewis, natif de Rikel," who died in 1471: it was printed at Antwerp about 1486. But the Latin original of this particular version is given to Gerardus à Vliedenhoven, of which Mr. Holtrop gives an account of three editions. There is a fourth in the University Library, Cambridge, besides which there are four Dutch editions. Early French anonymous versions were also very numerous, and it is fortunate that a manuscript in the Royal Library, Brussels, has preserved the name of the author to whom we are indebted for the present translation. It bears the following colophon: "Cy fine le traittie des quatre dernieres choses, translaté de latin en francois par Jo. Mielot l'an de grace mil cccc liij."

Philippe le Bon, as is well known, employed many secretaries for the purpose of adding to the treasures of his library by translations, collations, commentaries, &c. In this way were employed Guy d'Angers, David Aubert, de Hesdin, Droïn Ducret, de Dijon, and others. They brought into use that peculiar style of writing termed "grosse bâtarde," which, at a later date, Colard Mansion took as a pattern for his types. Among the duke's secretaries, one of the most indefatigable was Jean Mielot. He united in himself the qualifications of author, translator, and scribe, as he lets us know in the manuscript, "Traité de vieillesse et de jeunesse," now in the Royal Library, Copenhagen.

The only EXISTING COPY known of this edition was discovered by Mr. J. Winter Jones while re-cataloguing a portion of the old royal library in the British Museum. It was bound in the same volume as the "Meditacions," already described at page 177, to which the reader in referred for further particulars.

No. 7.—THE HISTORY OF JASON. *Folio. Without Printer's Name, Place, or Date.* (1477?).

COLLATION.—Eighteen 4^{ns} and one 3^{n} = 150 leaves, of which the first is blank.

TYPOGRAPHICAL PARTICULARS.—There is no title. The only type used is No. 2. The lines are very uneven in length, the longest measuring 5 inches. A full page has 29 lines. Without signatures, folios, or catchwords. Space is left at the commencement of chapters for the insertion of a 2-line initial, with director.

The Text begins thus, on the second recto, the first leaf being blank:—

f Or asmoche as late by the comaudement of the right
hye & noble princesse my right redoubted lady / My
lady Margarete by the grace of god Duchesse of Bour=

and ends on the 149th verso,

among the most worthy · And after this present life eu=
lasting life in heuen who grant him & vs that boughte vs
with his bloode blessyd Jhus Amen

REMARKS.—As already noticed when treating of the original French version of "Jason," its compiler was Raoul Lefevre, secretary to the Duke of Burgundy, and while in the service of the duchess, it seems most probable that Caxton became possessed of a copy. The date of imprint has been generally attributed by bibliographers to the year 1475, but this is, I think, too early. The features of Caxton's history about that time seem to point to 1476-77 as the date of his settlement in England; and November 18th, 1477, is, as we know, the day on which the printing of "Dictes" was finished. Now the typographical appearance of "Jason" proves it to have been one of the very earliest products of the Westminster press; and Caxton's remarks in the prologue to "Golden Legend," show the translation to have followed "The Recuyell" and "Chess Book." The evidence, therefore, seems to point to a date immediately preceding "Dictes" or the early part of 1477, when the young prince, to whom it was dedicated, would be six years old, and much more likely to make use of the work than if presented to him two years earlier.

Gerard Leeu, at Antwerp, reprinted this English text in 1492, a fact noticed thus by Gerard Legh in "The Accidence of Armory," 1576—"The History of Jason, which was translated out of Frenche, and printed at Andwarpe by one of my name."

Of the six known copies there is one in the British Museum, one in the Bodleian, and four in private libraries.

No. 8.—THE DICTES AND SAYINGS OF THE PHILOSOPHERS. *Folio.* "*Enprynted by me William Caxton at Westmestre.*" 1477. *First Edition; without Colophon.*

COLLATION.—Nine 4^{ns} and one 3^{n}=78 leaves, of which the first and two last are blank.

TYPOGRAPHICAL PARTICULARS.—There is no title-page. Only type No. 2 is used. The lines are of very uneven length, the longest measuring 5 inches; 29 lines to a full page. Without folios, catchwords, or signatures. Space is left at the beginning of chapters for the insertion of 3-line initials, with director.

Commencing with a blank leaf, Earl Rivers's prologue follows.

The Text begins thus, on the second recto:—

Here it is so that euery humayn Creature by the
w suffrance of our lord god is born & ordeigned to
be subgette and thral vnto the stormes of fortune
And so in diuerse & many sondry wyses man is perplex=

The work concludes on the verso of the 73rd folio at foot, and is followed on the 74th recto by Caxton's epilogue and additions, commencing with space for 3-line initial.

Ere endeth the book named the dictes or sayengis
h of the philosophres enprynted /by me william
Caxton at westmestre the yere of our lord · M ·
CCCC · Lxxvij · Whiche book is late translated out of

The Text ends on the 76th verso, with a short page of sixteen lines—

posicion in this world / And after thys lyf to lyue euer=
lastyngly in heuen Amen

Et sic est finis . · . ·

Remarks.—This book is remarkable as being the first which bears a plain statement of the place and time of its execution. It is thought by some to be really the first book printed in England. A few of the quarto pieces may perhaps have preceded it, but there is none that can be proved of earlier workmanship; and if, as there seems good reason for supposing, Caxton did not settle at Westminster before 1476-77, he would not have had time to produce much.

The history of the English translation of this work is interesting. It appears that Earl Rivers, moved thereto by a remembrance of relief from many worldly adversities, determined to pay his vows at the shrine of St. James of Compostella. In the British Museum (C. 18. e. 2) is "An Abbreviation of the graces and indulgences which Alexãder vj granteth to all true believing people of every sexe or communitie of the grete hospytall of Saynt James of Cōpostella." This shrine had been for many years the favourite resort of those who intended a short pilgrimage. Many ships, and those of the largest burthen, were engaged in this passenger traffic, the chief port of embarkation being Southampton. Thence in the year 1473 the earl sailed, and while on the voyage Lewis de Bretaylles, a Gascon knight celebrated for his great prowess, at the court of Edward IV, showed the earl a copy, in French, of "Les dits moraux des philosophes," with which Lord Rivers was greatly delighted, retaining it for more intimate perusal. On his return to England, in the same year, the king appointed him one of the governors of the Prince of Wales; and now, having more leisure, the earl began a translation of the work into English, which, however, notwithstanding the assistance of an earlier translation by Scrope, occupied him some years, supposing it to be completed only a short time previously to its being printed in 1477. Earl Rivers evidently had a good opinion of Caxton's literary abilities, for he requested him "to oversee" his translation before printing it, and the result was the addition of a chapter "towching wymmen," introduced by a very characteristic prologue from Caxton's own pen. This prologue is replete with a quiet humour, which reveals to us more of Caxton's real disposition than all his other writings. It proves also the intimate terms which must have existed between Lord Rivers and himself.

We may infer from this, the first edition, had a rapid sale, as about 1481 a second edition (described further on) was produced in the same type, and page for page, the same as the original.

There is an oft-quoted but much overrated manuscript of this translation in the Archiepiscopal Palace, Lambeth. It is on vellum, and has one inconsiderable illumination, famous only on account of giving the sole representation known of Edward V. Earl Rivers is presenting a copy on bended knee (probably this very one) to the prince, who is seated on his throne. By the earl's side is pourtrayed an ecclesiastic with shaven crown, probably "Haywarde," whose name appears at the end of the volume as the writer. We may suppose the earl to be in the act of reciting the metrical prologue which appears at the commencement, and the first five lines of which are—

> This boke late translate here in sight
> By Anthony Earl (*erasure*) that vertueux knyght
> Please it to accepte to youre noble grace
> And at youre conueniens leysoure and space
> It to see reede and vnderstonde

The writing is the usual secretary hand of the fifteenth century, and the date of transcription, as given in the colophon, is December 29th, 1477, or about six weeks after the publication of Caxton's printed edition, of which it is a verbatim copy, with the addition of the metrical prologue already noticed, and the following paragraph which precedes Caxton's prologue to the chapter on women—"And suffice you with the translation of the sayinges of thes Philosophres, And one William Caxton atte desire of my lorde Ryuers / emprinted many bokes after the tonour and forme of this boke / whiche Willm saide as foloweth:" then comes Caxton's chapter.

A different and somewhat earlier translation is in the Ms. department of the British Museum (Harl. 2266), "late translatyd out of frensh tung in to englysh the yer of our lord M cccc l to John Fostalf knyght for his contemplacion and solas by Stevyn Scrope squyer sonne in law to the seide Fostalle." Literary taste is not often associated with the name of Sir John Falstaff.

Thirteen copies of this edition are known—Two in the British Museum, one at Cambridge, and the remainder in private libraries. The Rev. T. Corser's copy, sold in 1868, wanting three leaves, sold for £110.

No. 9.—Fragment of a "Horæ." *Octavo. Without Printer's Name, Place, or Date.* (1478?)

Four leaves only. Type No. 2. Lines very uneven in length, the longest measuring 2¼ inches; twelve lines to a full page. Without signatures, catchwords, or numerals.

From the small portion remaining of the original work, it is impossible to state with accuracy under what particular class of service-books it should be ranged. To all appearance it is part of a primer, or "Horæ secundum consuetudinem Angliæ;" though its diminutive size renders it improbable that it contained, as well as the Hours, the Litany, the Vigils of the Dead, and all the miscellaneous prayers usually found in this class of books. The above fragment will be found to include the following portions of Suffragia at Lauds:—St. Thomas of Canterbury (the last few words only), St. Nicholas, St. Mary Magdalene, St. Katharine, St. Margaret; after which, in the four leaves that are wanting, there is room for All Saints, the Prayer for Peace, the Versicle and Response, Benedicamus domino, Deo gracias, and the commencement of the Suffragia of the Three Kings, the rest thereof occupying, as above, the head of the second portion of the fragment. Then follow the Suffragia of St. Barbara and the concluding verse Benedicam⁹ dño Deo gs, with which the service ends. On comparing this with the Horæ of the same period it will be seen that these prayers always occur at the end of Lauds, and are peculiar in their order to the English Church, with the exception of the Three Kings and St. Barbara, which, in this sequence, are peculiar to this fragment. Suffragia of the Three Kings, and of St. Barbara, are found amongst the miscellaneous commemorations in most of the English primers; but those of St. Barbara, as found in this fragment, differ altogether from those which occur elsewhere. The evidence which a perfect volume might afford being wanting, the following suggestion, by Mr. Bradshaw, of Cambridge, is offered:—It is well known that the Esterlings were a thriving and influential corporation in Caxton's time, consisting of German merchants from the City of Cologne and the other towns in the Hanseatic League, and occupying the Steel Yard in Cannon Street as their London residence, with All Hallows the Great as their parish church, and St. Barbara as their patron saint. Now in their accustomed service, comprising Matins and Lauds, the Suffrages of the Three Kings of Cologne, which, as already remarked, do not commonly occur at those hours, would be most appropriate, not on account of the name so much as the subject of the prayer, which is for success in trade, and for peace and health in travelling;—"concede propitius . . . . ut itinere quo ituri sumus, celebritate, letitiâ, gratiâ et pace, ad loca destinata in pace et salute et negotio bene peracto cum omne prosperitate, salvi et sani redire valeamus." This alone proves very little; but when we find that the next suffrages are those of St. Barbara, whose name never occurs in the English Lands, but to whom the Esterlings prayed as their patron saint, it becomes probable that the fragment before us was part of an Anglican primer (or Horæ), with additional prayers, for their especial use. And if these German merchants, in whose country the typographic art had made great progress, wished to have this, their daily service, printed, to whom could they go but to Caxton, the only printer then in England.

Should this view be correct it considerably increases the bibliographical value of the fragment, which is otherwise of great interest as being, in all probability, the earliest English-printed service in existence, and which, from the unevenness in the printing and the early types, must have been one of the first products of the Westminster press.

The fragment on which the foregoing remarks have been founded is in the Bodleian Library (Douce Fragments). When originally extracted from an old book-cover it formed a half-sheet, but now two quarters.

No. 10.—Chaucer's Canterbury Tales. *Folio. Sine ullâ notâ. First Edition.* (1478?)

Collation.—Forty 4^{ns}, one 3^{n}, one 5^{n}, one 3^{n}, one 5^{n}, one 3^{n}, one 5^{n}, and one 2^{n}, making together 372 leaves, of which the first only is blank.

Typographical Particulars.—There is no title-page. The only type used is No. 2. The lines in the prose portions are very unevenly spaced, but the longest measure 5 inches; 29 lines to a full page. Without folios, signatures, or catchwords. The book commences with a blank leaf, after which the Text begins thus:—

Han that Apprill with his shouris sote
w And the droughte of marche hath peid ye rote
And badid euery veyne in suche licour
Of whiche vertu engendrid is the flour

On the 372nd leaf recto are the following lines, being the conclusion of the Parson's tale:—

tificacion of synne / To that lyf he vs brynge that bought with his precyous blood Amen.

Explicit Tractatus Galfrydi Chaucer de
Penitencia vt dicitur pro fabula Rectoris.

The reverse is occupied by what is called Chaucer's retraction, commencing—

n Ow pray I to hem alle that herkene this litil treatyse

and ending—

deus . Per omnia secula seculos Amen.

which concludes the volume.

Nine copies are known, of which two are in the British Museum, one at the Bodleian, one at Merton College, Oxford, and the others in private libraries.

No. 11.—THE MORAL PROVERBS OF CRISTYNE. *Folio.*
"*Enprinted by Caxton At Westmestre,*" 1478.

COLLATION.—Two sheets, or four leaves, all printed.

TYPOGRAPHICAL PARTICULARS.—The only type used is No. 2. 28 lines to a page. Without signatures, catchwords, or folios.

The Text begins, with a head-line on the first recto, thus:—

The morale prouerbes of Cristyne

t He grete vertus of oure elders notable
Ofte to remembre is thing profitable
An happy hous is . where dwelleth prudence

and ends on the fourth verso,

> At westmestre . of feuerer the . xx . daye
> And of kyng Edward / the . xvij . yere vraye

Enprinted by Caxton
In feuerer the colde season

REMARKS.—Cristyne de Pise was, with the single exception of Joan of Arc, the most famous woman of her age. She was born A.D. 1363, in Italy, and, at the early age of fifteen, married Etienne Castel. After a few happy years her husband was taken from her by death; and now, although, to quote her own words, "nourri en delices et mignottemens," she found herself almost in destitution, with aged parents and three young children dependent upon her. Fortunately her father, who had been physician to Charles V of France, had taken great pains in her education, by which she had well profited. Urged on by necessity, she devoted herself to a literary life, and soon became famous. Her writings, which show a vast amount of reading, were ever on the side of virtue, morality, and peace. Her unimpeachable life assisted the tendency of her writings, and both were an honour to the age in which she lived. For many years her labours were incessant. After a last song of rejoicing on the victories of the French arms under "La Pucelle" she retired to a convent for the remainder of her days. The date of her death is unknown. The biographers of Cristyne vie with one another in her praises. There is a charming monograph upon her, by M. Raimond Thomassy, entitled "Essai sur les Ecrits Politiques de Christine de Pisan." 8vo. Paris, 1838. See also "Les Msc. Franc.," vol. iv, p. 186; and "Mém. de l'Acad. des Insc.," vol. ii, p. 762.

"Les prouerbes moraulx" were originally composed as a supplement to "Les enseignemens moraux," written by Cristyne for the instruction of her son, Jean Castel, who passed a part of his youthful days in the service of the Earl of Salisbury, in England.

The translation of these proverbs into English by Earl

Rivers appears to have taken place about the same period as his longer effort the "Dictes of the Philosophers." And here we may notice that the earl has been credited by Horace Walpole and Dr. Dibdin with the pedantic design of making nearly all the lines of his translation end with the letter "e." A very cursory examination of the poetry of the fifteenth century would have shown that the terminal e was common in all writings of that period.

In the "Fayttes of Arms," translated and printed by Caxton at a later period, we meet with another production of the same authoress. The only copies known are in the libraries of Earl Spencer, Earl of Jersey, and Mr. Christie-Miller.

No. 12.—PROPOSITIO JOHANNIS RUSSELL. *Quarto. Without Printer's Name, Date, or Place.* (147–?)

COLLATION.—Four printed leaves, the recto of the first and the verso of the last being blank.

TYPOGRAPHICAL PARTICULARS.—There is no title-page. Only one type, No. 2, is used. The lines are very irregular in length, a full line measuring 4 inches. A full page has 22 lines, without signatures or catchwords. The speech, which is all in one paragraph, bears evidence of having been printed a page at a time. It commences with a 2-line space for the insertion of an initial, with a small director, and has been reprinted in full by Dr. Dibdin.

The Text begins on the first verso:—

> Propositio Clarissimi Oratoris . Magistri Jo
> hannis Russell decretorum doctoris ac adtunc
> Ambassiatoris xpianissimi Regis Edwardi

and ends with twelve lines on the fourth recto, of which the last three are—

> phare ad dei laudem / et exaltationem fidei xpia
> ne / nostri q; seremissimi regis robur . solacium re
> uelationem q; / et gloriam plebis sue . amen

In the eighth volume of the "Censura Literaria," page 351, appeared the first public notice of this tract, which till then had been mistaken for a manuscript. Whether printed at Bruges, which is not unlikely, or at Westminster is difficult to decide.

John Russell, "Orator clarissimus," Bishop of Lincoln and Lord Chancellor, held many offices of trust under three sovereigns. He was born in the parish of St. Peter's, Winchester, in the beginning of the reign of Henry VI, and commenced his education there. At an early age he went to the University of Oxford, where he obtained the degree of Doctor of Decrees. In 1449 he was made fellow of New College; was afterwards appointed to a prebendal stall in Salisbury, and in 1466 to the Archdeaconry of Berkshire. On the latter appointment he removed to court, where he was much noticed by Edward IV. In September, 1467, he was commissioned by the king, together with Lord Hastings, Lord Scales, and others, to conclude a treaty of marriage between the king's sister Margaret and the Duke of Burgundy. A few months later he was engaged in arranging the trade relationship between this country and Flanders. It was probably then, if not at an earlier period, that he became acquainted with our printer. His name appears often after this as assisting in the negotiation of various treaties. In February, 1469-70, "Messire Galiard, chevalier; Thomas Vaghan, Escuier et Tresorier de la Chambre; et Jehan Russell, Docteur en Decret, Arcediacre de Berksuir," accompanied by Garter King at Arms, were commissioned by King Edward IV to invest the Duke of Burgundy with the order of the Garter. On this occasion the oration which forms the foundation of the present article was delivered. The investiture took place at Ghent, and here, if Caxton were present, of which however there is no positive evidence, he would again make acquaint-with John Russell. In 1476 the Archdeacon was raised to the bishopric of Rochester, and in 1480 translated to Lincoln. In March, 1483, he appeared as "Orator" before Pope Sixtus IV (see *Harleian MS.* No. 433), and was probably in Rome when his Sovereign, Edward IV, who had appointed him one of his executors, breathed his last. In the short reign of Edward V he was appointed Lord Chancellor, to which office he was re-appointed by Richard III. In 1485 he retired to private life, and died in January 1494. He was interred in Lincoln Cathedral, under an altar tomb in the Chantry Chapel, founded by him on the south side of the Lady Chapel.

He was the first Chancellor of Oxford appointed for life, in which university he was very popular. England also should keep his name in memory if only for the great change he iniated in promulgating the statutes of the realm in the vulgar tongue, instead of Latin or French, a practice continued ever after. Sir Thomas More thus draws his character: "A wyse man and a good, and of much experyence; and one of the best learned menne undoubtedly that Englande had in hys time."

An interesting autograph, as showing the Archdeacon at Bruges in 1467, when Caxton was governor, occurs in a volume of "Cicero de Officiis," in the Public Library of Cambridge:—"Empt' p Jo. Ruscel . archidiaconū berkshyrie apud oppidū bruggense flandric a° 1467 mens' Ap'l' 17° die."

A fine uncut copy is in the magnificent library of Earl Spencer. It appears to have been bound up by mistake in a volume of blank paper intended for manuscript alone, being in the original binding, and the whole volume otherwise consisting of the common manuscript hand of the fifteenth century, which afford no indication of local execution. It was discovered in cataloguing the library of John Brand, which was sold in 1807, and where it appeared among the manuscripts (Part I, Lot 30) "A work on Theology and Religion, with five leaves at the end, a very great curiosity, very early printed on wooden blocks or type." The Marquis of Blandford bought it at the reasonable price of £2 5*s.* At the sale of his library in 1819 (Lot 5752), Earl Spencer was obliged to give £126 for it. It was for many years considered as unique, until another copy was discovered in the library at Holkham.

No. 13.—Stans Puer ad Mensam—Moral Distichs—Salve Regina. *Quarto. Sine ullâ notâ.* (*Ante* 1479).

Collation.—Four leaves, all printed.

There is no title-page. Type No. 2 only is used. There are 23 lines to a page, or three stanzas in "Balad Royal,"[1] with a blank line between the stanzas. Long lines measure 4 inches. Without signatures or catchwards.

The Text begins, on the first recto, thus:—

· Stans puer ad mensam .
m I dere childe first thy selfe enable
With all thin herte to vertuo' disciplíne
Afore thy souerayn stondyng at the table

The poem concludes with two stanzas on the third recto, the latter of which is:—

Go litill bylle bareyn of eloquence
Pray yong children that the shal see or rede
Though thou be not compendious of sentence
Of the clawses for to take hede
Whiche to alle vertue shal thy yougth lede
Of the wrytyng though ther be no date
Yf ought be amys put the faute in lidgate
. Explicit .

Moral Distichs immediately follow the above, and fill up the page. The whole is here given.

Aryse erly	And aryse temperatly
Serue god deuoutly	And to thy soup soberly
The world besily	And to thy bed merily
Goo thy way sadly	And be there iocondly
Answere demurely	And slepe sewrly
Go to thy mete appetently	· Explicit .

(1) "Ballad Royal" was the title of a particular rythm, each stanza of which, consisting of seven lines, rhymed as follows:—*a—b—a—b—b—c—c*.

The SALVE REGINA begins on the verso of the preceding, at the head of the page.

. An holy Salue regina in englissh .

Alue with all obeisance to god i humblesse
Regina to regne euyr more in blysse
Mater to crist as we byleue expresse

The "Salue" ends at the foot of the 4th recto,

Mater of lyf and eterne creacion
Salue euer as feir as we can suffyse . Amen.

The reverse of this leaf gives the following:—

Wytte hath wonder and kynde ne can
How mayden is moder and god is man
Leue thyn askyng and beleue that wonder
For myght hath maistry & skyll goth vnder
. Deo laus &c .

This is followed by six proverbial couplets, the last being—

Knowe er thou knytte & than thou maist slake
Yf thou knyt er thou knowe than it is to late

This finishes the Text as it stands in the only two copies known.

From the absence of the word **Explicit**, or any other similar ending which Caxton made a rule of placing at the end of his works, great and small, it is not unlikely that this piece is imperfect. This is rendered more probable by the absence of the blank leaf at the beginning, which, supposing a printed leaf wanting at the end, would be its counterpart. At the same time it should be noticed that the only two known copies agree in this deficiency, and that Wynken de Worde, who reprinted from Caxton's edition, concludes in the same abrupt way; though it is not impossible that he printed from an imperfect copy, and did not know it, as in this very tract he has reproduced, with his usual carelessness, an accidental error of Caxton's edition. Caxton, in printing, had transposed the two pages of the second leaf, proving that, even in the quarto size, he had not arrived at the art of printing more than one page a time, and Wynken de Worde blindly repeats the mistake.

Among the many pieces which make up the catalogue of Lydgate's works must be included "Stans Puer ad Mensam," as the two concluding lines prove:—

> "Of the writing, though there be no date,
> If ought be amiss put the fault in lydgate."

Dan John Lydgate, who knew Chaucer in his old age, and may have been acquainted with Caxton in his youth, was an indefatigable rhymester. Ritson gives a list of 251 pieces attributed to his pen. The dates of his birth and death are equally obscure, and the only fact concerning him, of any certainty, is that he was born at Lidgate, near Bury St. Edmunds, whence he doubtless derived his name. (*Harl. MS.* 2251, folio 283).

The "Stans Puer" is a translation of the "Carmen juvenile de moribus puerorum" of Sulpitius, of which the first edition was probably printed at Aquila in 1483." But the type used for Caxton's tract (the last dated use of which in its first state was in 1479), proves it to have been printed at least some years previous to the impression at Aquila; so that we may fairly consider this as the "editio princeps" of the tract. It was reprinted by Wynken de Worde three times early in the succeeding century.

The "Salve Regina," in its style and metre, closely resembles the acknowledged pieces of Lydgate, and was also, in all probability, from his pen.

The copy in the University Library of Cambridge is the only one known, and though now in a separate binding, was formerly in a volume of poems all printed by Caxton, of which an account is here appended.

Bishop Moore's library, rich in old black-letter poems, contained, among its other treasures, one priceless little volume, in quarto, bound in plain brown calf, and lettered on the back "Old poetry printed by Caxton." The collection appears to have been made before it came into the bishop's possession; but the fact of the poems being bound together led Middleton and all succeeding writers to describe them as one work. Mr.

Bradshaw's careful examination, however, showed that the volume contained eight distinct publications, which have since been bound separately. Some of these are unique, and some are found alone in other collections. Before re-binding, the volume contained the following pieces in the following order:—

I. Stans Puer ad Mensam; Moral Distichs; The Salve Regina. II. Parvus Catho and Magnus Catho. III. The Chorle and the Bird. IV. The Horse the Goose and the Sheep; Stanzas; The proper use of certain nouns; The proper use of certain verbs. V. The Temple of Glass. VI. The Temple of Brass; A treatise which John Skogan sent unto the lords and gentlemen . . . . exhorting them to use virtues in their youth; The good counsel of Chaucer; Balad of the village without painting. VII. The Book of Courtesy. VIII. Anelida and Arcyte and The Complaint of Chaucer to his purse.

There is nothing to show in what order these tracts were printed. Being all in verse we can draw no conclusions from irregularity of spacing, and even where two editions were printed it is sometimes impossible to say which had precedence. That they were *all* printed before February 2nd, 1479, we may safely assume, as they are, without exception, in the early state of type No. 2, which then made its last dated appearance in "Cordyale;" and that many were among Caxton's first essays seems probable from their popular nature, and the small amount of labour required in their production. For these reasons they are treated consecutively, together with three other editions, in Nos. 14 to 25, those pieces whose longest lines all measure 4 inches being placed before those measuring 3¾ inches.

No. 14.—Parvus Catho.—Magnus Catho. *Quarto. First Edition. Sine ullâ notâ.* (*Ante* 1479).

Collation.—Three 4^{ns} and one $5^{n}=34$ leaves, of which the first was doubtless blank, though wanting in the only known copy.

There is no title-page. The type is No. 2 only. Full lines measure 4 inches, and each page contains 23 lines, counting the blank line between the stanzas. Without signatures or catchwords.

The Text commences with title-line on the second recto, a blank leaf having originally preceded it—

. Hic Incipit paruus Catho .

Cu aiadutere qua plurimos hoies guiter errare
Whan I aduerte to my remembrance
And see how fele folkes erren greuously

"Parvus Catho" terminates in the middle of the third recto,

Whan ye it rede let not your hert be thense
But doth as this saith with al your hole entente

. Hic finis parui cathonis .

making in all seven stanzas, in "Balad Royal."

"Magnus Catho" immediately follows on the verso, with space left for the insertion of a 2-line initial S, with director.

. Hic Incipit magnus Catho .

s I deus est aimus nobis ut carmina dicut
Hic tibi precipue sit pura mente colendus
For thy that god is inwardly the wit

The Text ends on the 34th verso,

Here haue I fonde that shal you gyyde & lede
Streight to gode fame & leue you in hir hous
. Explicit Catho .

The work is in four books, containing 42, 39, 27, and 52 stanzas of "Balad Royal," each of which is headed by a couplet from the original Latin.

The "distichs" of Cato were very popular for many centuries. Their author, and even the origin of their title, is entirely lost, though some of their stanzas are traced as far back as the second or third century of the Christian era. In the middle ages they were used as a school-book, to teach Latin, as well as to inculcate moral maxims; so that to be unacquainted with "Cato" was synonymous with general ignorance. Chaucer continually mentions the work. "He knew not Catoun, for his wyt was rude," says the miller of the rich "Gnof." These remarks apply to "Magnus Cato" only. About 1180 Daniel Churche, an ecclesiastic attached to the court of Henry II, added a few Latin precepts as introductory to the original, and from that period the two were mostly transcribed together, being distinguished as "Parvus Cato" and "Magnus Cato." Of the English version of these "distichs" we cannot have a better account than that given us by Caxton himself in his preface to "Cathon" glossed; "which book," he says, "hath been translated out of Latin into English by Master Benet Burgh, ... which full craftily hath made it in Balad Royal for the erudition of my Lord Boucher son and heir at that time to my Lord the Earl of Essex." This translation of Benet Burgh is the text printed by Caxton, twice in quarto, and once in folio with woodcuts, before he undertook the translation of the extensive French Gloss, which will be brought to the reader's notice under the year 1484.

"Maister Benet Burgh" was Vicar of Maldon, in Essex, when he translated "Cato," as we learn from the colophon in *Harl. MS.*, No. 271. He afterwards filled the offices of Archdeacon of Colchester, 1464; Prebendary of St. Paul's, 1472; and soon after High Canon of St. Stephen's, Westminster. He appears to have been an author as well as a translator. The following is the title of a poem in *Harl. MS.* 7333, folio 149 *b*—"A cristemasse game made by Maister Benet: howe god almyghty seyde to his apostelys and echeñ off them were baptiste and none knew of othir, &c." He also appears to have written a considerable portion of the poetical translation of "De regimine principum" attributed to Lydgate, as we infer from *Harl. MS.* 2251, folio 236, in which occurs this side-note, in the same handwriting as the body of the poem—"Here deyde the translato[r] a noble Poet Dane John Lydgate And his folower gan his prolog in this wise p' Benedictũ

Burgh." He or Lydgate also wrote an original fourth book to "Catho Magnus," which, although not printed by Caxton, may be seen in several manuscripts. Ritson, indeed (*Bib. Poet.*, page 66), ascribes the whole to Lydgate.

It does not seem improbable that the printing of "Parvus et Magnus Catho" was undertaken by desire of "High Canon Burgh," who, holding a canonry in Westminster, was likely to have become acquainted with Caxton.

The only EXISTING COPY is in the Public Library, Cambridge (AB. 8. 48. 2). It is *perfect,* but without the original blank leaf, and measures $8\frac{1}{4} \times 5\frac{1}{2}$ inches. For an account of the volume which contained it, see page 200 *ante*.

No. 15.—PARVUS CATHO.—MAGNUS CATHO. *Quarto. Second Edition. Sine ullâ notâ.* (*Ante* 1479).

COLLATION.—Three 4^{ns} and one $5^{n} = 34$ leaves, of which the first was doubtless blank, although wanting in the only known copy.

TYPOGRAPHICAL PARTICULARS.—The variation in this edition is only typographical. The poem is reprinted page for page, and line for line, yet the composition of the type is different throughout.

The only EXISTING COPY known is in the library of the Duke of Devonshire, at Chatsworth, where it is bound with the quarto edition of "Stans Puer," already described. It came from the old library at Hardwicke Hall. In the *Harleian Catalogue* (III. 6202) the above two tracts appear together—probably this very copy.

No. 16.—THE HORSE, THE SHEEP, AND THE GOOSE.—VARIOUS STANZAS.—THE PROPER APPLICATION OF CERTAIN NOUNS SUBSTANTIVE, AND VERBS. *First Edition. Quarto. Sine ullâ notâ.* (*Ante* 1479).

COLLATION.—One 4^{n} and one $5^{n} = 18$ leaves, of which the first was doubtless blank, although wanting in the only known copy.

TYPOGRAPHICAL PARTICULARS.—There is no title-page. The type is all No. 2. Full lines measure 4 inches, and each page contains 23 lines, inclusive of the blank line between the stanzas. Without signatures or catchwords.

THE HORSE, THE SHEEP, AND THE GOOSE commences on the second recto, the first leaf being blank.

The Text begins, with space for a 2-line initial, with director,

> c Ontreversies / plees and discordes
> Bitwene persones were two or thre
> Sought out the groundes be recordes
> This was the custom of antiquite

On the fourteenth leaf verso,

> Alle in one vessell to speke in wordes pleyn
> That noman sholde of other haue disdayn
>
> . Thus endeth the horse the ghoos & the sheep .

There are in this poem 77 stanzas of seven lines each.

VARIOUS STANZAS follow, ending on the sixteenth recto, the verso being occupied with short sentences, as "An herde of Hertes. A murther of crowes. A byldyng of rooks," &c. The whole ends on the eighteenth verso—

> a Cony vnlaced — Yf he take the londe he
> a Heron dismembrid — fleeth. Explicit.

The only EXISTING COPY is in the Public Library, Cambridge (AB. 8. 48. 4), and was formerly bound, with other pieces in a volume already described at page 51.

The whole of these fugitive pieces are attributed to the prolific pen of Dan John Lydgate.

NO. 17.—THE HORSE, THE SHEEP, AND THE GOOSE.—VARIOUS STANZAS.—THE PROPER APPLICATION OF CERTAIN NOUNS SUBSTANTIVE AND VERBS. *Quarto. Second Edition.* (*Ante* 1479.)

COLLATION.—One 4^n and one 5^n = 18 leaves, of which the first is blank.

TYPOGRAPHICAL PARTICULARS.—These are the same as in the first edition, with the exception of the orthography and the use of a title-line, which in the other edition is altogether wanting, a sufficient reason for attributing this to a later period; for, had the first edition been printed with a head-line, we may certainly assume that the improved appearance would not have been omitted by Caxton in the reprint. In this edition we find the sixth leaf, noticed as wanting in the only known copy of the first edition.

The text begins on the second recto,

The hors . the shepe & the ghoos.

Ontreversies . plees and discordes
Bitwene persones were two or thre
Sought out the groundes be recordes
This was the custom of antiquite

and ends with **Explicit** on the eighteenth recto.

There is a fragment of six leaves in the University Library, Cambridge, and a perfect copy, with the original leaf, in the Cathedral Library, York, a reprint of which was presented by Sir M. M. Sykes to the members of the Roxburgh Club.

No. 18.—INFANCIA SALVATORIS. *Quarto. Without Printer's Name, Date, or Place.* (147-?).

COLLATION.—Eighteen printed leaves, unsigned, with a blank both at beginning and end.

The type is all No. 2. There are 22 lines of uneven length to a full page, and a long line measures 3¾ inches. Without signatures, folios, or catchwords.

The Text begins thus on the recto of the first printed leaf:—

Hic Incipit Tractatus qui Intitulatur
Infancia saluatoris .
Xijt edictu a Cesare Augusto vt de
e scriberetur vniusus orbis Hec autem
descripcio prima facta est a preside .
Sirie Cirino . Et ibant oms ut pfiterentur
singuli in ciuitatem sua Ascendit et Joseph

and ends with a full page on the eighteenth recto.

| Ecclesiastici vijo. Si filii tibi sint. erudi illos et curua illos a puericia illos. Si filie tibi sint / serua corpus illas et non ostendant hilarem faciem tuam ad illas. Gregorius. Quauis q's iustus sit. tu in hac vita no debet esse secur⁹ q; nescit quo fine sit terminandus.

This printed tract differs entirely from the MS. in the British Museum, *Royal* 13 A XIV, "De Xti infantia," but agrees partially with the "Evangelium Infantiæ" attributed to St. James, and printed in vol. i of the "Codex apocryphus Novi Testamenti," by Fabricius.

The only EXISTING COPY known is in the Royal University Library, Göttingen. It is in good condition, and was purchased in 1746 of Osborne, for this library, at 15*s* (?). Ames described this very copy when in the library of Lord Oxford, but neither Herbert nor Dibdin could hear of its existence, nor discover it in the Harleian Catalogue. It is there nevertheless, among the "Libri Latini. Quarto," and thus described, "Infantia Salvatoris Tractatus, *corio turcico, deaurat. Lond. apud Caxton, sine Loco.*" (See *Catalogus Bibliothecæ Harleianæ*, vol. v, page 252, No. 7008).

No. 19.—THE TEMPLE OF GLASS. *Quarto. Sine ullâ notâ.* (*Ante* 1479.)

COLLATION.—Three 4^{ns} and one 5^{n}, unsigned, or 34 leaves, of which the 1st is (?) blank.

TYPOGRAPHICAL PARTICULARS.—There is no title-page. The type is No. 2 only. Full lines measure 4 inches, and each page contains 23 lines. Without signatures or catchwords.

After the blank the poem commences on the 2nd recto, with space for a 2-line initial, with director:—

. The temple of glas .

f Or thought constreynt & greuous heuynes
For pensifhed and high distres
To bed I went now this other nyght

The Text ends at the foot of the 34th recto,

> I mene that benygne and goodly of face
> Now go thy way and put the in her grace
>
> . Explicit the temple of glas .

There seems no doubt that this was one of the less favoured compositions of Dan John, although by some writers it has been attributed to Hawes. It was reprinted by Wynken de Worde.

The only EXISTING COPY is in the Public Library, Cambridge (AB. 8. 48. 5). It is *perfect*, excepting the blank (?) leaf, and was formerly bound with other pieces in a volume already described at page 51. Measurement 8¼ × 5½ inches.

No. 20.—THE CHORLE AND THE BIRD. *Quarto. First Edition. Sine ullâ notâ.* (*Ante* 1479.)

COLLATION.—One 5ⁿ, or 10 leaves, of which the 1st is blank.

TYPOGRAPHICAL PARTICULARS.—There is no title-page. The type used is No. 2 only. Full lines measure 4 inches, and each page contains three verses of "Balad Royal," or 23 lines, including a blank line between the stanzas. Without signatures or catchwords.

After the blank the poem commences on the 2nd recto, space being left, with a director, for the insertion of a 2-line initial.

The text begins thus :—

> p Roblemes of olde liknes and figures
> Whiche prouyd ben fructuo' of sentence

The Text ends on the 10th verso,

> Goo litell quayer and recomande me
> Unto my maister with humble affection
> Beseke hym lowly of mercy and pyte
> Of thy rude makyng to haue compassion

And as touching thy translacion
Out of frenssh / how that hit englisshid be
Alle thing is said under correction
With supportacion of his benygnyte

. Explicit the chorle and the birde .

This fable is always included among the compositions of Lydgate. It was reprinted by Pynson, and a copy in the Grenville library (11226), has the following autograph note—"The same story is told by Alphonsus in his fable of the labourer and the nightingale, and in Gesta Romanorum, cap. 169." A perfect copy is at Cambridge, taken from the volume of poems already described at p. 200, and a fragment is in the British Museum.

No. 21.—The Chorle and the Bird. *Quarto. Second Edition. Sine ullâ notâ.* (*Ante* 1479.)

The similarity of these two editions is exact so far as the number of stanzas, number of lines to a page, and the general state of the text; but there is an evident variation in the typographical minutiæ, such as the omission of the director, the use of full-points and colons as ornamentation, and above all the constant variation in orthography. Take the 1st line as an example:—

Ed. 1. p Robleмes of olde liknes and figures
Ed. 2. roblemes of olde liknes and figures

and the last line,

Ed. 1. . Explicit the chorle and the birde .
Ed. 2. Explicit the Chorle and the birde . : .

The only known Existing Copy is in the Chapter Library at York. It is *perfect*, with the original blank. A reprint from this copy was presented to the Roxburghe Club by Sir M. M. Sykes.

No. 22.—THE TEMPLE OF BRASS, OR THE PARLIAMENT OF FOWLS. SOME BALADS. ENVOY OF CHAUCER TO SKOGAN. *Quarto. Sine ullâ notâ.* (*Ante* 1479).

TYPOGRAPHICAL PARTICULARS.—There is no title-page. The type used is No. 2 only. Full lines measure 3¾ inches, instead of 4 inches, as in the former pieces, and each page contains 23 lines. Without signatures or catchwords.

The Text begins on the first recto, without a blank leaf,—

he lyf so short the craft so loge to lerne
Thassaye so hard so sharp the conqueryng

On the 17th recto,

Explicit the temple of bras

The Tract ends on 24th verso,

Was neuer erst scogan blamed for his toge

Doubtless the poem did not end here, but the copy at Cambridge is imperfect, having only 24 leaves, besides which there are a few leaves at the British Museum, but no perfect copy has yet been discovered.

No. 23.—THE BOOK OF COURTESY. *Quarto. First Edition. Sine ullâ notâ.* (*Ante* 1479).

COLLATION.—One 4^{n} and one 3^{n}=14 leaves, of which the last is blank.

TYPOGRAPHICAL PARTICULARS.—There is no title-page. The type is all No. 2. Full lines measure 3¾ inches. 23 lines to a page, including a blank line between the stanzas. Without signatures or catchwords.

The Text begins thus:—

l ytyl John syth your tendre enfancye
Stondeth as yet vnder / in difference
To vice or vertu to meuyn or applye

The Text ends on the 13th recto,

And how to hurte / lyeth euer in a wayte
Kepe your quayer / that it be not ther bayte

Explicit the book of curtesye.

The 13th verso, and the 14th leaf are blank.

The only EXISTING COPY is in the Public Library, Cambridge (AB. 8. 48. 7), and was formerly in the volume of tracts described at page 51.

No. 24.—QUEEN ANELIDA AND FALSE ARCYTE.—THE COMPLAINT OF CHAUCER TO HIS PURSE. *Quarto. Sine ullâ notâ.* (*Ante* 1479).

COLLATION.—One 5^{n} or 10 leaves, all printed.

TYPOGRAPHICAL PARTICULARS.—There is no title-page. The type is No. 2 only. Full lines measure $3\frac{3}{4}$ inches, 23 lines to a page. Without signatures or catchwords. Space is left at the commencement for a 2-line initial.

The Text begins:—

t hou fiers god of armes / mars the rede
That in the frosty contre called trace
Within thy grysly temple ful of drede

The Text ends on the 9th recto,

How that arcite / anelida so sore
Hath thirled with the peynt of remebrace

Thus endeth the compleynt of anelida

On the same page is Chaucer's "Complaint to his Purse," in three stanzas of "Balad Royal," the tract ending with

Et sic est finis. · . ·

on the 10th recto.

The only EXISTING COPY known is in the Public Library, Cambridge, and was formerly in the volume of tracts described at page 51.

No. 25.—BOETHIUS DE CONSOLACIONE PHILOSOPHIÆ, TRANSLATED INTO ENGLISH BY GEOFFREY CHAUCER. *Folio.* *"I William Caxton have done my devoir to enprinte it."* *Without Place or Date.* (*Ante* 1479).

COLLATION.—Eleven 4^ns and one 3^n = 94 leaves, of which the first is blank.

TYPOGRAPHICAL PARTICULARS.—Without title-page, signatures, catchwords, or folios. Two types No. 2 for the body and No. 3 for the Latin quotations, are used. The lines are not spaced to one length. Full lines measure 5 inches, and there are 29 to a page. Space has been left at the commencement of chapters for the insertion of 2-line initials.

After a blank leaf the Text commences with the title in Latin in type No. 3, on the 2nd recto, the English translation being uniformly in type No. 2:—

Boecius de consolacione philosophie

Carmina qui quondam studio florente peregi
Flebilis heu mestos cogor inire modos

a Llas I wepying am constrained to begynne vers
of sorowfull matere. That whylom in flourisshing
studye made delitable ditees / For lo rendyng muses of

On the 93rd recto, third line,

eyen of the Jugge that seeth and also that demeth alle
thynges / Deo gracias

Explicit boecius de
consolacione philosophie

Caxton has added an interesting epilogue, which occupies the remainder of the recto and the whole of the verso, being followed, on the 94th recto, by the "Epitaphiū Galfridi Chaucer," printed in type No. 3, which concludes on the verso, and the last few lines of which are:—

Post obitum Caxton voluit te viuere cura
Willelmi. Chaucer clare poeta tuj
Nam tua non solum compressit opuscula formis
Has quoq; s; laudes. iussit hic esse tuas

This epitaph was written by a brother poet, Stephen Surigo, Lic. Decr., of Milan, and is most interesting as showing, in connection with the previous epilogue (given in Vol. I, page 149), that not only did Caxton perpetuate the memory of the great poet by printing his works, but that he also raised a public monument to his memory before St. Benet's Chapel, in Westminster Abbey, in the shape of a pillar supporting a tablet upon which the above "Epitaphye" was written.

There are few ancient authors, whose works received greater attention in the fifteen century than those of Boethius. M. Paris gives an account of five different translations of the "De Consolatione" into French verse, all of that age, and contained in the Bib. Imp., Paris.

Every library of the fourteenth and fifteenth centuries, of which we have any account, appears to have contained a copy: many had several. In the Ducal Library, Bruges, 1467, was a manuscript with this title, "Boece de Consolacion en englois," which is not unlikely to have been the translation of Chaucer.

Some writers, and among them Dibdin ("Typ. Ant." Vol. I, page 306), have doubted whether Chaucer was the real translator of the version under review, but none of the manuscripts attribute it to any other writer; and, not to quote the express mention of it in the "Retractation," Chaucer himself includes it among his works in the following couplet (line 425) from the "Legend of Good Women,"—

> And for to speke of other holynesse
> He hath in prose translated Boece.

In this translation Chaucer appears to have chosen the original Latin for his text. He certainly did not take it from any of the French versions noticed above, nor from those described by M. Paris; nor is it, as Dibdin suggests, from the anonymous translation, printed by Colard Mansion in 1477. But from whatever source derived, it was, if we may judge from the many copies extant, very favourably received. Our printer especially took great delight in what he terms the "ornate and fayr" language of the poet, and in the epilogue to his edition he has left us a most interesting tribute of his admiration.

There are three copies of this book in the British Museum, one at Cambridge two at the Bodleian, one at Exeter, and one at Magdalen College, Oxford; one at Ripon Minster, one at Sion College, London, and six in private hands. The copy discovered at the St. Alban's Grammar School was sold to the British Museum, and was remarkable for the largest "find" of printed fragments in the boards with which the book was bound, ever recorded.*

* An account of this discovery may be found interesting, showing strongly the importance of examining the covers of old books before rejecting them. In the summer of 1858 I inspected the old library in the Grammar School attached to the Abbey of St. Albans. I found a few valuable books all contained in an old deal cupboard, upon which the leakage from the roof had dripped, apparently for years. It must have been long since any one had touched a book there, and the amount of dust and decay was certainly enough to deter even a bibliomaniac from so doing. After examining a few interesting books I pulled out one which was lying flat upon the top of others. It was in a most deplorable state, covered thickly with a damp sticky dust, and with a considerable portion of the back rotted away by wet. The white decay fell in lumps on the floor as the unappreciated volume was opened. It proved to be Geoffrey Chaucer's English translation of "Boecius de Consolatione Philosophiæ," printed by Caxton, in the original binding, as issued from Caxton's workshop, and uncut!! On examining the amount of damage it had sustained, I found that the wet, which had injured the book, had also, by separating the layers of paper of which the covers were composed, revealed the interesting fact that several fragments, on which Caxton's types appeared, had been used in their manufacture. After vexatious opposition and repeated delays the Acting Trustees were induced to allow the book, which they now prized highly, to be deposited in the care of Mr. J. Winter Jones, of the British Museum, for the purpose of rebinding. On dissecting the covers they were found to be composed entirely of waste sheets from Caxton's press, two or three being printed on one side only. The two covers yielded no less than fifty-six half-sheets of printed paper, proving the existence of three works from Caxton's press quite unknown before. The following is the list of the fragments, all genuine specimens of England's first printer, though unfortunately mostly in very poor condition:—

No. 26.—CORDYALE, OR THE FOUR LAST THINGS. *Folio. With Printer's Name, but without Place. March 24th,* 1479.

COLLATION.—Nine 4^{n} and one 3^{n} = 78 leaves, of which the 1st and last are blank.

TYPOGRAPHICAL PARTICULARS.—There is no title-page. Two types are used, Nos. 2* and 3, the latter for proper names and Latin only. The lines are not spaced out to one length. A full line measures 5 inches. Mostly 29 lines to a page, but sometimes 28. Without signatures, catchwords, or folios. Space left for the insertion of 3 and 4-line initials, with director. Commencing with a blank leaf the prologue of the translator follows on the 2nd recto, space being left for a 4-line A.

The Text begins thus:—

Prologue of the Translator.

a L Ingratitude utterly settyng apart / we owe
to calle to our myndes the manyfolde gyftes
of grace / with the benefaittis . that our lorde
of his moost plentiueuse bonte hath ymen vs
wretches in this present transitoire lif . Whiche Remem

The text ends with twenty lines on the 77th verso, the last eight of which are—

---

1. The English "Jason," ten leaves.
2. "Dictes," three leaves.
3. "Chronicles," six leaves.
4. "Description of Britain," eight leaves.
5. "Works of Sapience," (extremely rare), two leaves.
6. "Tulle," seven leaves.
7. Lydgate's "Life of onr Lady," two leaves.
8. "Assembly of Fowls," fourteen leaves.
9. "The Chorle and the Bird," two leaves.
10. "The Horse, the Sheep, and the Goose," four leaves.
11. "Horæ beata Virginis" (unique), four leaves.
12. "Pica Sarum" (unique), eight leaves.
13. "An Indulgence of Pope Sixtus V," (?) two slips of parchment (unique).

lasting permanence in heuen Amen . Whiche werke present I began the morn after the saide Purificacionof our blissid Lady . Whiche was the the daye of Seint Blase Bisshop and Martir . And finisshed on the euen of than nunciacion of our said bilissid Lady fallyng on the wednesday the xxiiij daye of Marche . In the xix yeer of Kyng Edwarde the fourthe

The 78th leaf, which closes the volume, is blank.

The French edition of this work (see page 183, *ante*) was, if similarity of workmanship in all points may justify the conclusion, before the printer while at work upon this the English edition.

Dr. Dibdin, to whom the French edition was unknown, says that Earl Rivers translated from the Latin; but as all the other productions of the Earl's pen, printed by Caxton, were from the French, there would be strong grounds for supposing that this had come through the same channel, were not the fact established by its not being a literal translation of any Latin edition, while it is an accurate reproduction, line for line and almost word for word, of the French edition.

About the date also there has been some confusion. Maittaire and Panzer attribute the printing to 1478, Lewis to 1479, Dibdin to 1480; and Lord Orford thinks Caxton, unless he was two years employed upon it, has made a typographical error in the date. The dates in reality are very plain. Caxton says that Lord Rivers delivered the English translation to him to be printed, upon the day of "The Purification," which is further stated to have been the 2nd day of February, 1478; but as the year did not then begin until the 25th of March, it would, according to the present reckoning, be February, 1479. The printing was begun the very next day, on the "morning after the said Purification," and completed upon the 24th day of March, in the nineteenth year of Edward IV. This regnal year was comprised between March 4th, 1479, and March 3rd, 1480, thus again giving the year 1479 for the completion of the book. From this it is evident that instead of taking over two years for the printing it occupied Caxton just seven weeks. In Vol. I, page

149, may be seen the entire epilogue, as written and printed by Caxton.

For the literary history of "Cordyale," see the remarks on "Les Quatre Derrenieres Choses," already noticed.

Copies are in the British Museum, Cambridge, Bodleian, and Hunterian Museum, Glasgow. Five are in private libraries.

No. 27.—Fratris Laurentii Gulielmi de Saona Margarita Eloquentiæ castigatæ ad eloquendum divina accommodata. *Folio. Sine ullâ notâ.* (1479–80?)

Collation.—One 3^{n}, one sheet, eleven 5^{ns}, and one 8^{n} = 124 leaves.

Typographical Particulars.—There is no title-page. Type No. 2* only is used. The lines, of which there are 29 to a page, are in most cases of uneven length, although in some pages they are spaced out very regularly. Long lines measure 5 inches. Without signatures or catchwords. Space is left, with a director, for the insertion of initials 3 or 4 lines in depth. The hyphen is in this volume not unfrequently used instead of the / or / , as a mark of punctuation. Chapters generally commence with a line, or two or three words, in capital letters; and the ends of paragraphs are often ornamented with an array of points; for instance, .:·:.:·:.

The Text begins on the 1st recto, with the prohemium,—

Fratris laurencij guilelmi de saona ordinis
mio fac^e theo^e doctois phemiu i noua rthoica
c
Ogitanti michi sepenumero-ac diligenci9 con-
templati q)tu comoditatis q)tuq; splendoris & glorie afferre

On the 5th verso,

EXPLICIT PROHEMIUM .:.

On the 53rd recto,

INCIPIT SECUNDUS LIBER rhe-
torice facultatis : In quo specialiter auctor agit de hijs que

The Second Book ends and the Third begins on the 83rd recto,

INCIPIT LIBER tercius rhetorice facultà

On the 135th recto is a concluding chapter, the Text ending, on the verso of the 136th leaf, thus:—

in trinitate perfecta uiuit et regnat per infinita secula seculorum . AMEN .

Explicit liber tercius : et opus rhetorice facultatis p fra tre laurentiu Guilelmi de Saona ordinis minor sacre pa gine pfessore ex dictis testimonijsq; sacratissimar scriptu-rar / doctorq; pbatissimor compilatu et ꝯfirmatu : quibus ex causis censuit appellandu fore Margaritam eloquentie castigate ad eloquendu diuina accomodatam

Compitatu ant' fuit hoc opus in alma uniuersitate Can tabrigie . Anno dni . 14^8 . die et . 6 . Julii . quo die festum Sancte Marthe recolitr. Sub protectione Senissi mi regis anglorum Eduardi quarti

Remarks.—There can be no doubt in the mind of any one acquainted with the Westminster books that this issued from Caxton's press. It agrees with them not only in character of type, but in length of line, depth of page, and other typographical peculiarities. Nor is there much uncertainty about the date. It was not written till July, 1478, and the first dated book in the types with which it is printed (Type No. 2*) made its first appearance in March, 1479, the latest dated book in the preceding Type (No. 2) being February, 1478. In 1480 Caxton discontinued entirely the practice of leaving his lines of an uneven length, but the majority of pages in this volume have their lines uneven. The book was therefore printed after July, 1478, and before or very early in 1480.

It is worthy of notice, that about the same time that Caxton, at Westminster, was engaged upon this work, the printer-schoolmaster at St. Alban's was also making it one of the first essays of his press. There certainly was not a longer period than two years and a half between the two editions, which, so far as the text goes, agree very closely, the St. Alban's printer having apparently reprinted from the edition by Caxton.

It is also very remarkable that this work should have been known and described for more than 150 years, yet never till October, 1861, recognised as the production of Caxton's press. In the Public Library, Cambridge, is a volume of documents relating to Corpus Christi College, which was used by Strype for his Life of Archbishop Parker; and among them is a catalogue of the books bequeathed by the Archbishop to the library of that College. At folio 255 is the following entry under the general head of "Books in parchment closures as they lye on heaps on the upmost shelves:"—"*Rethorica nova impressa Canteb. fo.* 1478." Strype, in his Life of Parker, misled by this entry, attributed the book to an early press at Cambridge; and Bagford, writing to Tanner in 1707, says, "I cannot but impart unto you, that very lately good Mr. Strype hath gave me an account of a booke which archbishop Parker gave to the Publick library of Benet college, and is a piece of rethorick, by one Gul. de Saona, a minorit, printed at Cambridge, 1478." Ames, who only knew the book from these accounts, and a facsimile of the beginning and end sent him by Mr. North, placed this work at the head of the list of Cambridge books in his Typographical Antiquities, 1749, and gave an engraving of North's facsimile; which led him to state that "the types were much like Caxton's largest." Herbert merely repeated the account of Ames; and thus it was reserved for Mr. Bradshaw in consulting the library of Corpus Christi College for another purpose, to examine the volume and to recognise the interesting fact that, although compiled at Cambridge in the year 1478, it was printed with the unmistakeable types of Caxton, and agreed in typographical particulars with the books issued from the Westminster press between 1479–80.

Laurentius Gulielmi de Traversanis, of Saona (or Savona, as it is more commonly called), was born about 1414. His native city, not very far from Genoa, is better known as the birthplace of Christopher Columbus. He entered the Franciscan Convent there under Francesco di Rovere, afterwards Pope Sixtus IV. He studied at the universities of Padua, Bologna, Cambridge, and Paris, and seems finally to have retired to his own convent at Savona, where he died, and to which he was a great benefactor. Wadding (*Scriptores Ord. Min.* folio, Romæ, 1650) mentions several of his works.

Besides the copy mentioned above, there is one at the University Library, Upsala, both being in perfect condition.

No. 28.—The Dictes and Sayings of the Philosophers. "*Emprynted by me William Caxton at Westmestre.*" *Folio. Second Edition. Dated* 1477, *but printed about* 1480. *With Colophon.*

Collation.—Eight 4^{ns}, and two 3^{ns} = 76 leaves, of which the 1st is blank.

Typographical Particulars.—There is no title-page. Type No. 2* only is used. The lines are nearly always spaced out to an even length, and measure 5 inches; 29 lines to a full page. Without signatures, folios, or catchwords. Space is left at the beginning of chapters for the insertion of 3-line initials.

The difference between this and the 1st edition (see page 186, *ante*) is considerable. *That* was printed from the original fount of type No. 2; *this* from a re-casting of the same fount, showing many alterations in the punches. (See the preliminary chapter to this volume). *That* has the pages throughout the volume very uneven as to the length of the line; *this* nearly always even. *That*, with the unique exception of the Althorpe copy, is without the colophon; *this* has the colophon, of which a facsimile is given in the annexed plate, in every copy. Lastly, the orthography varies throughout the whole volume.

We must here notice the first instance of a practice common among the early printers, and doubtless inherited from the scribes, namely, that of reprinting in subsequent editions the colophons and dates strictly applicable to the 1st edition only. Thus the three editions of "Dictes and Sayings," which issued from Caxton's printing office, all bear the same date of imprint, November, 1477, while we know that type

No. 2*, in which the 2nd edition is printed, was not used till after February, 1478, and type No. 6, in which the 3rd edition is printed, was not in use till about 1488.

The literary history of "Dictes and Sayings" has been already recounted at page 188, *ante*.

Copies are in the British Museum, Trinity College, Dublin, and the library of the Duke of Devonshire.

No. 29.—LETTERS OF INDULGENCE ISSUED BY JOHN KENDAL IN 1480, BY AUTHORITY OF POPE SIXTUS IV, FOR ASSISTANCE AT THE SIEGE OF RHODES. *On parchment.*

TYPOGRAPHICAL PARTICULARS.—The type is No. 2* only, but from the warping of the skin assumes in many parts a very deceptive appearance. The lines, which are considerably extended, but all of one length, measure 9¼ inches. The large 4-line wooden initial is to be noticed as being in all probability the earliest instance of printed initials in this country; they certainly do not appear in any book for which this type was used. The whole of the document occupies 19 long lines, of which the following are the beginning and end:—

F Rater Johannes kendale Turcipelerius Rhodi ac commissarius A sanctissimo in xpristo patre | et domino nostro domino Sixto diuina prouidencia papa quarto et vigore litterarum suarum pro expe= | ditione contra perfidos turchos xpristiani nominis hostes . in defensionem insule Rhodi & fidei catholi= | ce facta et facienda concessarum ad infrascipta p vniuersum orbem deputatus . Dilect' nobis in xpo | *Symoni Mountfort et Emme vxori ei'* **Salute in dno sempiterna Prouenit ex tue deuotionis affectu quo romana |**

In quor' fidem has l'ras nostras Sigilli nostri ap | pensione munitas fieri iussimus atq; mandauimus . Dat' *ultimo die Mesis marcij* **Anno domini | Millesimo quad= ringentesimo octogesimo**

REMARKS.—The following particulars concerning John Kendal are gathered from an article in *Archæologia*, vol. xxvii, page 172, written by Sir F. Madden, and entitled "Documents relating to Perkin Warbeck."

In a deposition made by one Bernard de Vignoles, at Rouen in 1495, concerning a plot against the king's life, one of the persons implicated was John Kendal, Grand Prior of the Order of St. John of Jerusalem in England. He is also remarkable as having been the subject of the earliest contemporary English medal in existence, which is dated 1480, the period of the Siege of Rhodes. On this he is styled "Turcopolier," or General of the Infantry of the Order, the office of which was annexed to that of Grand Prior of England. Yet although the medal so designates him, it is not probable that he was actually present at the siege, as in that very year (*Rymer*, April, 1480) Edward IV ordered all persons to assist John Kendal, in Ireland, in procuring aid and money against the Turks. In this proclamation he is styled "Turcopolier of Rhodes, and *locum tenens* of the Grand Master in Italy, England, Flanders, and Ireland." In Browne-Willis (Mit. Abb.) Kendal appears in 1491 and 1501 as Prior of the Hospital of St. John of Jerusalem in London. He was lieutenant of the Grand Master in Italy, England, Flanders, and Ireland, and was amply furnished with indulgences and pardons for all who give personal service. In this office of recruiting he was occupied at the time of the celebrated Siege of Rhodes in 1480. His arms, impaled with those of England, may still be seen on the walls of an hotel at Rhodes.

In the Numismatic department of the British Museum is a medal connected with John Kendal. *Obv.* Bust of Kendal in armour marked with the cross of the Knights of St. John; head bare; hair straight and long; legend, IO. KENDAL RHODI TVRCVPELARIVS. *Rev.* Arms of Kendal. Cross of St. John in Chief. Legend, ✠ TEMPORE OBSIDIONIS TVRCHORVM MCCCCLXXX.

There are probably two EXISTING COPIES, although but one is a present known. This is in the British Museum (C. 18, e. 2), and was purchased in 1845. The blank space for the name is filled in with "*Symoni Mountfort et Emme vxori ei*", and it is dated the last day of March, 1480.

The Rev. Joseph Hunter noticed the existence of this "Indulgence," and wrote to Herbert about it, but it was not then recognised as a production of Caxton's press; and, although the same document, must have been another copy, as the blanks were filled in with the names of Richard Cattlyn and John Cattlyn, April 16th, 1480.

No. 30.—Parvus et Magnus Chato. *Folio. Sine ullâ notâ. With Woodcuts. Third Edition.* (1481 ?)

Collation.—a b c 4^ns, d 2^n = 28 leaves, of which a j is blank.

Typographical Particulars.—There is no title-page. Two sizes of type occur. No. 2* and No. 3, the latter being used for the Latin couplets as well as the "Incipit" and "Explicit" lines. Length of long lines 4¾ inches; 29 lines to a page. Signatures are met here for the first time, lower-case letters and Roman numerals being used. Without folios or catchwords.

Commencing with a blank leaf the title-line follows, on a ij recto, in type No. 3. The Text begins thus:—

Hic incipit paruus Chato

(Woodcut of Four Pupils, one of whom wears a fool's cap, kneeling before a Tutor, who, rod in hand, sits in a high-backed chair).

Cum aia aduertere quam hoies grauiter errare
Whan I aduerte in my remembraunce
And see how fele folkes erren greuously

On sig. a iiij recto,

Whan ye it rede let not your herte be thence
But doth as this sayth with al your entente
Hic finis parui cathonis

(Woodcut of Five Pupils kneeling before their Tutor, who, seated in a chair, is teaching them from a book upon a lectern before him).

"Parvus Chato" contains 7 stanzas, and is followed, on sig. a iii verso, by

Hic incipit magnus Chato

The Text ends, on 4th recto of sig. d—

> Here haue I fond that shal ye gyyde and lede
> Streyght to good fame & leue you in hyr hous

Explicit Chato

Remarks.—The Text is evidently a reprint from one of the early editions in quarto (see pages 200 and 203, *ante*), and was by no means intended as a kind of supplement" to the "Cathon glossed," printed a year or two later by Caxton, as supposed by Dr. Dibdin in *Typ. Ant.*, vol. i, page 201.

Two woodcuts add to the interest of this volume; one being at the beginning and one at the end of the "Parvus Chato." (See Plate 27.) The same cuts also appear in the "Mirrour of the World," which raises the question of precedency. Here, at first sight, one would give priority to the "Mirrour," as the cuts appear newer and cleaner; but this is very deceptive, depending more upon the amount of ink and pressure used than on the condition of the cuts. The breakage of some of the lines in the "Mirrour" is a much more sure sign, and this tells strongly in favour of "Parvus Chato." The greater appropriateness of the designs to the "Parvus Chato," a boy's book, than to the illustration of grammar and logic as in the "Mirrour," leads to the same conclusion. It is therefore considered that these two cuts were designed originally for the "Parvus Chato," which in that case must have been printed previously to the "Mirrour," 1481.

There is nothing to induce us to attribute to foreign artists the production of these woodcuts, which show no amount of skill either in design or execution, which is not far surpassed in the undoubted productions of English scribes and miniature painters of the same period. They may, therefore, be considered as probably the earliest specimens of wood-engraving in England.

Two perfect copies are known : one in St. John's College, Oxford, and the other at Althorpe.

No. 31.—The Mirrour of the World. *Folio. First Edition. Translated* 1481. *Woodcuts. Without Printer's Name, Date or Place, but in* 1481.

Collation.—a b c d e f g h i k l m are 4^ns^, n is a 2^n^ = 100 leaves, of which a 1 and the verso of n 4 are blank.

Typographical Particulars.—There is no title-page. The only type used is No. 2*. A full page contains 29 lines, which are fully spaced out and measure 4¾ inches. Without folios or catchwords. Signatures in lower-case letters and Arabic numerals. The number of woodcuts is 34. After the first (blank) leaf the "Table" commences on sig a 2 recto.

The Text begins thus:—

Here begynneth the table of the rubrices of this presen te volume named the Mirrour of the world or thymage of the same

ends on the 4th recto of sig. n, the verso being blank,

helthe / And after this short & transitorye lyf he brynge hym and vs in to his celestyal blysse in heuene Amen /

Remarks.—The origin of this work cannot be traced very satisfactorily; but as showing a much better acquaintance with the cosmology of the world than any previous composition, it may be interesting to examine the evidence of its authorship.

Vincent de Beauvais, of the Order of Preaching Friars, who, from the dedication attached to several of his productions, appears to have flourished in the reign of St. Louis, composed an extensive work in Latin, consisting of four parts—"Speculum Naturale," "Speculum Doctrinale," "Speculum Historiale," and "Speculum Morale." The whole was entitled "Speculum majus," for the following reason, given in the third chapter of the First Book, "*Majus* autem, ad differentiam parvi libelli jamdudum editi, cujus titulus Speculum vel Imago mundi, in quo scilicet hujus mundi sensibilis dispositio et ornatus paucis verbis describitur. M. Daunou thinks that the "parvus libellus" here referred to was the "Imago

Mundi" from which "Lymage du Monde" was translated, and that it was a previous composition of Vincent de Beauvais; and Montfaucon quotes a manuscript in the St. Germain collection (Fonds Latin, 926) in support of the same view, in which we read "Iste liber intitulatus Speculum vel Imago Mundi editus a fre. Vincentio ordinis fratrum predicatorum." But Vincent's reference to a Speculum Mundi, "jamdudum editus," by no means suggests that he wrote that as well as his own; and unfortunately as no copy is known, the fact even of its agreement with "Lymage du Monde" cannot be verified. The manuscript quoted by Montfaucon is no evidence at all, as M. Paris, on examination, found it to be identical with the "Speculum Historiale," or the Third Part of Vincent's "Speculum Majus," which is by no means "a rational description of the world and its products shortly described." The compilation of "Speculum Mundi," from Vincent's "Speculum Naturale," as suggested by Greswell, is equally far from the truth. Although no copy of the Latin "Speculum vel Imago Mundi," referred to by Vincent, is known, there appears little reason to doubt that it existed in the thirteenth century. Perhaps an earlier copy of the Latin manuscript in the Cotton Library, already described, may have formed the foundation of the French version, although in that case, as in Vignay's translation of the "Chess Book," considerable additions have been made. The history of the "Mirrour of the World" may be summed up thus:—Before the middle of the thirteenth century an unknown author wrote in Latin "Speculum vel Imago Mundi;" of this no copy has yet been recognised (*Cotton, Vesp.* E III?) In 1245 this was turned into French metre for the Duke of Berry, of which manuscripts in several libraries attest the popularity (*Sloane* 2435; *Royal* 20, A III). Shortly afterwards the French metre was turned into French prose, probably by "Maistre Gossouin." (*Royal* 19, A. ix; *Bib. Imp., Paris*, No. 7070). Here we find the Text used by Caxton for his translation, who even adopted a considerable portion of the French prologue (see *ante* Vol. I, page 153). Who this "Gossouin" or "Gossevin" was, and whether he was the author or only the scribe is quite unknown.

The celebrated Cardinal Pierre d'Ailly compiled, in 1409, a work entitled "Tractatus de ymagine mundi" (*Harl. MS.* 637), which, however, is principally astronomical, having a portion of the same as the work under review.

The publishing of this book was not a speculation on Caxton's part. He was employed, as we learn from the prologue (printed *verbatim* in Vol. I), to translate and probably to print it by Hugh Brice, citizen and alderman of London, who wished to make a present to Lord Hastings. To adorn, as well as illustrate the pages, the art of the wood-engraver was employed, and we may consider the figures here displayed as some of the earliest specimens of that art in England. The designs were borrowed from the manuscript copy, the illuminations in the French manuscripts showing the same treatment. All the copies issued from Caxton's press have the words necessary for the explanation of the diagrams inserted with the pen, instead of being engraved on the wood, which may perhaps be an argument for their home execution, as the Flemish artists were certainly well skilled in engraving words in their blocks. They all appear to have been perfected by the same scribe, which probably induced Oldys to assert that they are in Caxton's autograph. Of this there is no evidence.

Hugh Brice, of the same county as Caxton, where he held the manor of Jenkins (*Lysons*, vol. iv, page 75), was also of the Mercers' Company, although Stow calls him a goldsmith (*Thoms's Stow*, page 77). He was knighted about 1472; and in that year accompanied John Russell and others on a trade embassy to Bruges. John Russell was the orator whose celebrated speech, upon the reception of the Order of the Garter by the Duke of Burgundy, is one of the earliest pieces attributed to the press of Caxton. In 1473, Hugh Brice, who is called "Clericus in officio Contrarotulatoris Monetæ nostræ," was sent on a similar embassy, "De difficultatibus super intercursu Burgundiæ removendis;" and on both occasions would necessarily become personally acquainted with Caxton, who at that time was in the service of the Duchess of Burgundy at Bruges (*Rymer*, edit. 1727, vol. xi, page 738, &c. &c.) He also held the offices of Keeper of the King's Exchange,

London; Governor of the King's Mint in the Tower, under Lord Hastings; and Mayor of London, 1494. He died in 1496.

Fifteen copies are known: British Museum (2), Cambridge, Bodleian, St. George's, Windsor, and ten in private libraries.

No. 32.—THE HISTORY OF REYNARD, THE FOX. *First Edition. Folio. Translated in the Abbey of Westminster by William Caxton,* 1481, *but without Printer's Name, Place, or Date.*

COLLATION.—a b c d e f g h i are 4^{ns}, k and l are 3^{ns}, a 1 and l 6 being blank. Between the leaves h 8 and i 1 is inserted a leaf half printed on both sides. This was probably owing to the accidental omission of a page by the compositor. Total, 84½ leaves, of which the first and last are blank.

TYPOGRAPHICAL PARTICULARS.—There is no title-page. The type is No. 2*, none other being used throughout the volume. The lines are spaced out to one length, and measure 4¾ inches. A full page has 29 lines. Without folios or catchwords. Arabic figures are used in the signatures. Spaces 2 lines deep are left for the insertion of initials.

The Text begins, on sig. a 2 recto, thus:—

This is the table of the historye of reynart the foxe

ending half-way down sig. a 3 recto,

How the foxe with his frendes departed nobly fro the kynge & wente to his castel maleperduys / capitulo xliii

On the verso begins the story—

Hyer begynneth thystorye of renard the foxe

ending half-way down the verso of the 5th folio of sig. l,

Where they shal fynde faute / For I haue not added ne mynusshed but haue folowed as nyghe as I can my copye whiche was in dutche / and by me willm Caxton translated in to this rude & symple englyssh in thabbey of west=

mestre . fynysshed the vj daye of Juyn the yere of our lord · M . CCCC . Lxxxj . & the xxj yere of the regne of kynge Edward the iiijth /

Here endeth the historye of Reynard the foxe &c

REMARKS.—The date of printing this book is nowhere stated, though it was probably put to press directly after if not during the translation, which was finished on the 6th of June, 1481. The literary history of this fable is very obscure. It appears to have had great popularity for some centuries previous to Caxton's time, as quotations from it appear so early as the twelfth century. Caxton's translation was made from "Die Historie van Reinaert die Vos, gheprent ter goude in hollant by mi gheraert leeu Jnt iaer Mcccc en lxxix," or perhaps from the still earlier edition in Dutch, discovered in 1854, and described in K. Gödike's Deutsche Wochenschrift for that year, Heft 8, page 256.

Copies are in the British Museum, Eton College, and two private libraries.

No. 33.—TULLY OF OLD AGE; TULLY OF FRIENDSHIP; THE DECLAMATION OF NOBLESSE. *Folio.* "*Emprynted by me symple persone William Caxton.*" *No Place.* 1481.

COLLATION.—*Old Age:* sigs. 1 and a are 8^ns^, with 1 1, and a 6 blank—b c d e f g h are 4^ns^—i is a 2^n^, with i 4 blank. *Friendship* and the *Declamation:* a b c d e f are 4^ns^, with no blanks. The first section in the "De Senectute" is signed in Arabic numerals only, thus: 1 2—1 3—1 4, the rest of the work being signed in letters and Arabic numerals. The three tracts together have 117 printed and three blank leaves.

TYPOGRAPHICAL PARTICULARS.—There is no title-page to any of the three treatises. The type is all No. 2*, except where Latin quotations or proper names are introduced, when Caxton's largest type, No. 3, is used. The lines are fully spaced out, and the long lines measure 4¾ inches; 29 lines make a full page. Without folios or catchwords. Space is left at the beginning of the chapters with a director, for the insertion of 2 to 5-line initials. The peculiar &c belonging to type No. 1 is used in this book.

After a blank leaf the Text begins on sig. 1 2, space being left for a 2-line initial H with director,

h Ere begynneth the prohemye upon the reducinge / both out of latyn as of frensshe in to our englyssh tongue / of the polytyque book named Tullius de senectute . whiche that Tullius wrote upon the disputacons &c

The treatise "De Senectute" ends, with the following colophon, at the head of the 3rd recto of sig. i,

Thus endeth the boke of Tulle of olde age translated out of latyn into frenshe by laurence de primo facto at the comaundement of the noble prynce Lowys Duc of Burbon / and enprynted by me symple persone William Caxton into Englysshe at the playsir solace and reuerence of men growyng in to olde age the xij day of August the yere of our lord . M . CCCC . lxxxj :

A blank leaf, and then the "De Senectute" begins with a new series of signatures on a j, the whole work ending on the 8th verso of sig. f,

that we at our departyng maye departe in suche wyse / that it maye please our lord god to receyue vs in to his euirlastyng blysse . Amen :

Explicit Per Caxton

Although in three distinct treatises, Caxton intended them to form but one volume, as is plainly stated in the epilogue, which renders it difficult to imagine a reason for his printing the volume with two sets of signatures.

We learn from Caxton's own pen, that the translation of Cicero's "De Senectute" and "De Amicitiâ" into French was made by the command of Louis Duke of Bourbon, in 1405, by Laurence de Premierfait. This learned priest was a native of the city of Troyes, and obtained great celebrity by his numerous translations.

To Jean Mielot we must attribute the French version of "The Declamation," in which he styles the author "Surse Pistoie, Docteur en Loix, et grand Orateur." This was one of the first books that issued from the press of Colard Mansion at Bruges.

The English translation of the "De Senectute" was accomplished, as we learn from the first prologue, at the ordinance and desire of Sir John Fastolfe. It has been ascribed by Leland to the Earl of Worcester, and by Anstis to Wyllyam de Wyrcestre; in both cases without evidence. We have seen already that the "Dictes and Sayings of the Philosophers" had been translated in 1450 for Sir John Fastolfe, by Stephen Scrope, his son-in-law (see page 189, *ante*), and this possibly came from the same pen. Whoever the translator may have been he took for his text the work of Laurence Premierfait, of which this version is a most literal translation, notwithstanding his assurance (see the end of the first prologue) that "this book is more amply expounded and more sweeter to the reader, *keeping the just sentence of the Latin.*" The English version of "De Amicitiā" and the "Declamation" are attributed by Caxton to the Earl of Worcester, a great traveller, a great collector of books, and a great orator. The Earl's history and acquirements have been described by Fuller, Dr. Henry, and many others; Caxton's admiration for him is expressed in the most touching and characteristic terms. Probably their love of literature was a friendly bond. The Earl also translated, at a later period, Cæsar's Commentaries, which Rastell printed.

Of 22 copies extant, twelve are in the chief corporate libraries in England, and ten in private hands.

No. 34.—THE GAME AND PLAY OF THE CHESS. *Second Edition. Folio. Woodcuts. "Explicit per Caxton." Without Place or Date.* (1481 ?)

COLLATION.—a b c d e f g h i are 4^{ins}, k l are 3^{ns} = 84 leaves, of which the first is blank.

TYPOGRAPHICAL PARTICULARS.—There is no title-page. The only type used is No. 2*. The lines are spaced out to an even length, and signatures are used. A full page has 29 lines, and a full line measures 4⅞ inches. Space left for the insertion of 2 or 3-line initials, with director. Without folios or catchwords.

After the blank leaf the prologue of Caxton commences on sig. a iij.

The text begins thus:—

t He holy appostle and doctour of the peple saynt
Poule sayth in his epystle . Alle that is wryten
is wryten vnto our doctryne and for our ler=
nyng . Wherefore many noble clerkes haue endeuoyred

The table of chapters follows on the verso, and ends on a iij recto, the verso being blank. On a iiij recto, the first chapter commences, and is illustrated with a woodcut representing King Evilmerodach, son of Nebuchadnezzar, "a jolly man without justice who did do hew his father his body into three hundred pieces."

The Text ends on l 6 recto, the verso being blank—

man but as a beste . Thenne late euery man of what
condycion he be that redyth or herith this litel book redde·
take therby ensaumple to amende hym·

Explicit per Caxton.

The woodcuts in this volume number only sixteen, not twenty-four, as Dibdin and other writers say, eight of them being impressions from blocks used for previous chapters. As already noticed, there seems a probability that the two cuts for "Parvus Chato," third edition, were the earliest used by Caxton. These were soon after printed again, with the addition of many others in the "Mirrour of the World." The present cuts were perhaps the third essay of Caxton in this department, and for these, judging by the general style, and greater breadth of treatment, he appears to have employed another artist.

The literary history of the work has been given under the first edition, but we must notice that the original prologue

"EVILMERODACH, A JOLLY MAN WITHOUT JUSTICE WHO DID DO HEW HIS FATHER IN PIECES."

dedicated to the Duke of Clarence, the major portion of which was a translation from the French, has been superseded in this edition by a prologue from Caxton's own pen, the ideas in which, with the exception of the first few lines, and almost the very words, are often met with in manuscripts of that age.

The year in which this edition is generally considered to have been issued seems to me very incorrect. Ames assigns no date to it, but Dibdin, probably misled by Bagford's observations, thinks it one of Caxton's earliest efforts, while in some remarks attached to a reprint of this edition by Mr. Figgins, it is considered as the *earliest* specimen of the Westminster press, and to have been printed from *cut* metal types. An examination of the work, however, with a typographical eye does not afford a single evidence of very early workmanship. All Caxton's early books were uneven in the length of their lines—this is quite even. Not one of the early works had any signatures—this is signed throughout. These two features alone are quite sufficient to fix its date of impression at least as late as 1480, when Caxton first began the use of signatures.

Copies are in the British Museum; the Pepysian and Trinity, Cambridge; Bodleian and St. John's, Oxford; Imperial Library, Vienna; and six in private hands.

A

DESCRIPTION OF BOOKS PRINTED

IN

TYPE No. 3.

BOOKS PRINTED IN TYPE No. 3.

35. An Advertisement .	. 1477-78?
36. Directorium. First Version	1477-78?
37. Horæ. Second Edition .	1480?
38. Psalterium, &c.	1480-83?

No. 35. An Advertisement. *Octavo. Westminster. No Date.* (*About* 1477–78.)

Typographical Particulars.—The type is all No. 3, the whole advertisement being in one paragraph of seven lines, unevenly spaced, the longest measuring five inches. The verso is blank.

If it plese ony man spirituel or temporel to bye ony pyes of two and thre comemoracios of salisburi vse enpryntid after the forme of this preset lettre whiche ben wel and truly correct / late hym come to westmonester in to the almonesrye at the reed pale and he shal haue them good chepe . ˙ .

Supplico stet cedula

Remarks.—This is an interesting relic, not only as giving us the name of the house inhabited by our first printer—the Red-pale ("reed" was commonly used by Caxton for "red") —but also as a specimen of advertisements in the fifteenth century. Although small in size it may also be considered as the earliest instance known of a "broadside" printed in this country.

Our printer was not alone in advertising his books, although, from the fugitive nature of such productions, specimens are very rarely to be found. An interesting list of books printed by Coburger, at Nuremberg, in the fifteenth century, is in the British Museum (C. 18. e. 2. 27), to which is attached the following heading:—" Cupientes emere libros infra notatos venient ad hospicium subnotatum Venditorem habituri largissimum," &c.

The "Pye"* was a collection of rules to show the priest how to deal (under every possible variation in Easter) with the concurrence of more than one office on the same day. In reading Caxton's Advertisement the question arises, "In what respect did the "pyes of two and three commemorations of Salisbury use" differ from the ordinary pyes of Salisbury use? The very Reverend Canon Rock, D.D., has kindly placed at my disposal for an explanation which confines the "pye of two commemorations" to the rules for Easter and Whitsuntide, and the "pye of three commemorations" to the rules for Easter, Whitsuntide, and Trinity.† Caxton's Advertisement, therefore, refers to separately published portions of the common "Directorium seu Pica Sarum," applicable, perhaps, to the current year only. In the succeeding article is described a "Pica," which, in some particulars, agrees entirely with Caxton's description.

* The *Pica* type of printers is commonly supposed to derive its name from having been used for printing the early "Pica seu Directorium." I have searched in vain among the earliest editions of the Directorium for a copy printed in types approaching the size of *Pica*. They are mostly the size of modern Brevier.

† "Easter being a moveable feast, and ruling the time for Septuagesima, Sexagesima, and Quinquagesima Sundays, and the beginning of Lent, as well as the Sundays for Whitsuntide and the beginning of Trinity, makes great and ever-recurring alterations in the Service of the Calendar on Saints' days. Hence was it to show the Cleric at a glance how to commemorate the Saints' days that came in the ever-changing times of Lent, Easter, Whitsuntide; and the Octave of the Trinity, the *Pica* began by giving a table of the Dominical letters, which make the keys of all the rest of the *Pica;* and after such a way no matter what month or week Easter might fall on, the manner of commemorating the Saints' days happening then, or of putting them off till another time, was accurately described for all variations. But as the chief variations in keeping the Saints' days happened at Easter and its following week—at Whitsuntide and its week or Octave—and at Trinity and its Octave; and, as during these three great feasts, with their Octaves, the occurring feast itself was chiefly celebrated with mere mention, or Collect, or Commemoration; and as people in Caxton's

A poor copy is among the Doucé fragments in the Bodleian; and a good one, formerly in Dr. Farmer's library, at Althorpe.

It has been suggested that the first line being very short, the syllable *co* has accidentally dropped out, and that the text should read "to buy any *co*pies," &c.; but the word "copy," in that sense, was unknown in the fifteenth century.

No. 36.—DIRECTORIUM, SEU PICA SARUM. *First Version. Quarto. Sine ullâ notâ.* (*About* 1477–8.)

No perfect copy of this book being known, the COLLATION is necessarily omitted. The four fragments from the covers of the St. Alban's "Boethius" are from separate half sheets in quarto, making a total of sixteen pages.

TYPOGRAPHICAL PARTICULARS.—Only one type, No. 3, is used in these fragments. The lines are not spaced out to one length. The longest measure 3⅝ inches. A full page has 22 lines. Without signatures, or catchwords, or printed folios to the leaves. There are no initial letters, nor is there any space left for them. The whole is in very contracted Latin.

REMARKS.—There can be no doubt that this was the product of Caxton's press, as all the circumstances connected with it tend to prove. It was extracted from the covers of a book which was evidently bound in Caxton's workshop, and for the binding of which he had used waste sheets from the press (see *ante*, page 214). The fragments belonging to known books were all printed by Caxton before 1481; while the "Advertisement" and "Directorium," reasoning from the

---

days had not printed but handwritten Breviaries without the *Pica* or *Pye* in them, Caxton printed, to supply their want, "pyes of two and three commemorations,"—that is to say, directions for saying the whole office of *two* Octaves or Commemorations, say of Easter and Whitsuntide, and of *three* Octaves, Easter, Whitsuntide, and Trinity. It should be borne in mind, as I have pointed out in *t.* 4, *p.* 139 of "The Church of our Fathers" that the Laity as well as the Clergy used to say the Breviary. Hence Caxton's invitation to buy his "pyes" to the Laity too.—*Extract from a letter to J. F. Goulding, Esq., from the Very Rev. Canon Rock, D.D. February*, 1862.

measurement of the lines and their uneven length, were certainly printed before 1480, and probably about the same time as the later set of quarto poetic pieces, *i. e.* about 1478.

This "Directorium" is not the same version as that printed by Caxton, about 1486, in type No. 5, and a second edition of which was issued a few years later in type No. 6. These last are the text revised for Bishop Rotherham, founded upon an earlier version, of which latter the leaves under notice appear to be a portion.

Formerly in the library of the St. Alban's Grammar School; they are now in the British Museum.

No. 37.—HORÆ AD USUM SARUM. *Second Edition. Quarto.* (1480–83.)

No perfect copy being known, the COLLATION is of necessity omitted, and the following remarks are made from three fragments rescued from the St. Alban's "Boethius," already noticed.

TYPOGRAPHICAL PARTICULARS.—The only type used, judging from these fragments, was No. 3. The lines are spaced out, and measure $3\frac{3}{8}$ inches. A full page has 20 lines. The initials and paragraph marks are not inserted.

The first fragment, a quarto leaf printed on both sides, but very defective, contains part of the "Suffragia of the Three Kings," which are among the additions to the first part of the "Primer;" and in an early edition by Wynken de Worde, immediately precede the Latin "Fifteen Oes."

The second fragment is also but one leaf, and contains the commencement of Part II of the "Horæ," the "Ne Reminiscaris" being the anthem belonging to the Seven Penitential Psalms.

The third fragment consists of two pages of prayers, containing the first of the "Fifteen Oes" in Latin, and some prayers near the end of the Litany.

REMARKS.—As all the "Fifteen Oes" and the Litany, as well as other prayers, intervene between the two pages of the third fragment, it is evident they were not intended to be printed on one sheet; this, added to the fact that the paper is printed only on one side, makes it clear that these are proof pages.

This edition of "Horæ" is entirely unknown to any of our bibliographers, and was doubtless a second edition of that already noticed at p. 189.

These fragments, now in the British Museum, were purchased in 1874. They were formerly in the library of King Edward VI Grammar School, St. Alban's.

No. 38.—PSALTERIUM, ETC. *Quarto. Sine ullâ notâ.* (1480–83?)

COLLATION.—a b c d e f g h i k l m n o p q r s t u x y are 4^ns^, with a 1 blank; but as only one copy is known to be in existence, and that imperfect, no complete collation can be given.

TYPOGRAPHICAL PARTICULARS.—There is only one type, No. 3, used throughout the work, excepting for the signatures, where the Arabic numerals belong to type No. 2. The lines, which are spaced out, measure 3⅝ inches, and a full page has 20. Without printed folios or catchwords. Space for the insertion of 2 to 4-line initials, generally without director, is left at the beginning of paragraphs. The signatures are in letters and Arabic numerals, a mode of signing used by Caxton only between the years 1480 and 1483.

The book doubtless commenced with a blank leaf for a 1, which is wanting in this copy.

The Text begins at the head of a 2 recto, thus:—

Jheronimus de laude dei supe.
psalterium
Ichil enim est in hac vita
n mortali in quo possumus fa=
miliarius inherere deo q) di=
uinis laudibus. Nullus e'm mor=

"Jheronimus super Psalterium" ends on a 6 recto, and is followed by two prayers and a metrical hymn.

The Psalter finishes on sig. t 3 recto, and is followed by the Canticles, Te Deum, Athanasian Creed, a general Litany, including most of the prayers now in use, and ends imperfectly on sig. y 7 verso. There is an eighth leaf, which at first sight is very defective, seeming to be y 8; in fact it is an intercallary leaf, consisting of two pages accidentally omitted between x 7 and x 8, and bound up wrongly after y 7, the real y 8 being absent.

The only copy at present known is in the British Museum, having formed a portion of the old Royal Library. It was recognised as being printed with Caxton's types by Mr. Bullen, through whose hands it passed for re-cataloguing.

A

DESCRIPTION OF BOOKS PRINTED

IN

TYPE No. 4.

BOOKS PRINTED IN TYPES No. 4 AND 4.*

39.	Chronicles. First Edition	Type 4	1480
40.	Description of Britain	Type 4	1480
41.	Curia Sapientiæ	Type 4	1481 ?
42.	Godfrey of Bologne	Type 4	1481
43.	Indulgence. First Edition	Type 4	1481
44.	Ditto Second Edition	Type 4	1481
45.	Chronicles. Second Edition	Type 4	1482
46.	Polychronicon	Type 4	1482
47.	Pilgrimage of the Soul	Type 4	1483
48.	A Vocabulary	Type 4	1483 ?
49.	The Festial	Type 4*	1483
50.	Four Sermons	Type 4*	1483 ?
51.	Servitium de Visitatione	Type 4	1483 ?
52.	Sex Epistolæ	Type 4 and 4*	1483 ?
53.	Confessio Amantis	Type 4 and 4*	1484
54.	The Knight of the Tower	Type 4 and 4*	1484 ?
55.	Caton	Type 4*	1484
56.	Golden Legend	Type 4 and 4*	1484
57.	Death-bed Prayers	Type 4*	1484 ?
58.	Æsop	Type 4*	1484
59.	Order of Chivalrye	Type 4*	1483-85
60.	Canterbury Tales. Second Edition	Type 4*	1484 ?
61.	Book of Fame	Type 4*	1484 ?
62.	The Curial	Type 4*	1484 ?
63.	Troilez and Cresside	Type 4*	1484 ?
64.	Life of our Lady	Type 4*	1484 ?
65.	St. Winifred	Type 4*	1485 ?
66.	King Arthur	Type 4*	1485
67.	Charles the Great	Type 4*	1485
68.	Paris and Vienne	Type 4*	1485
69.	The Golden Legend. Second Edition	Type 4*	1487

No. 39.—THE CHRONICLES OF ENGLAND. *Folio.* "*Emprynted by me William Caxton in thabbey of Westmynstre.*" *June* 10*th*, 1480. *First Edition, with short commas.*

COLLATION.—Prologue and table a 4^n^, signed j, iij, and iiij, the first leaf being blank. a (a j blank) b c d e f g h i k l m n o p q r s t u x are 4^ns^; y is a 3^n^. Total 182 leaves, of which two are blank.

TYPOGRAPICAL PARTICULARS.—There is no title-page. Type No. 4 only is used. There are forty lines to a full page. The lines are spaced out to an even length, and measure 4¾ inches. The signatures are in lower-case letters and Arabic numerals. Spaces left for the insertion of initials. Without folios or catchwords.

Commencing with a blank leaf, the prologue follows on sig. ij recto, the Text beginning, with a space for a 5-line initial,

I N the yere of thyncarnacion of our lord Jhu crist M. CCCC. lxxx. And in the xx. yere of the Regne of kyng Edward the fourthe / Atte requeste of dyuerce gentilmen I haue endeuourd me to enprinte the cronicles of Englond as in this booke shall by the suffraunce of god folowe / And to thende that euery mon may see and

The Chronicle ends on the sixth recto of sig. y, the verso being blank,

Thus endeth this present booke of the cronicles of englond / enpn | ted by me william Caxton In thabbey of westmynstre by london | Fynysshid and accomplisshid the x . day of Juyn the yere of thin= | carnacion of our lord god M . CCCC . lxxx . And in the xx . yere of | the regne of kyng Edward the fourth

Remarks.—The use of short commas, which characterises the early state of this type, would induce us to give priority to this edition over the other, in which the long commas are used, independently of any printed date.

The history here printed by Caxton differs but little from the "Cronicle of Brute," one of the most popular of the fifteenth and sixteenth century books. It is, however, carried further than any manuscript chronicle I have seen, and it appears probable that, as any writer who felt competent made his own additions in transcribing, so Caxton added more or less to his copy, and brought the history down, as he acknowledges having done in "Polycronicon," to the battle of Towton. The old "Cronicle of Brute" was so called from the opening chapter which describes the settlement of Brutus, the descendant of the Æneas in Britain. The respective parts due to Nennius, Douglas of Glastonbury, and Geoffrey of Monmouth, are probably too obscure to determine. The St. Alban's Chronicle, printed two or three years later, and in types somewhat resembling those of Caxton, is the same text, interpolated throughout with a history of the Popes and ecclesiastical matters. This, and the edition of Machlinia (Caxton's text), about the same date, are not unfrequently catalogued erroneously as from Caxton's press.

This work is often called "Caxton's Chronicle" by old writers, probably from the publicity he gave it both as editor and printer, and he is often blamed for its inaccuracies, although, with the exception of the last few pages, he had nothing to do with its compilation; nor indeed does he in any way lay claim to it.

Of this edition with the short commas there are copies at Cambridge, Bodleian (2), St. John's, Oxford, Hunterian Museum, Glasgow, and Lambeth Palace. Six are in private hands.

No. 40.—THE DESCRIPTION OF BRITAIN. *Folio.* "*Fynyshed by me William Caxton.*" *No Place.* 18*th August*, 1840.

COLLATION.—Three 4^ns and one 3^n, unsigned. Thirty leaves, the last being blank.

TYPOGRAPHICAL PARTICULARS.—There is no title-page. Type No. 4 only is used. There are forty lines to a full page. The lines are spaced out to an even length, and measure 4¾ inches. Spaces left for the insertion of initials. Without signatures, folios, or catchwords. The signatures were probably omitted on account of the limited extent of the work.

The text begins, on the verso of the first leaf, thus:—

Hit is so that in many and diuerse places the comyn cronicles of englond ben had and also now late enprinted at westmynstre

and ends on the 29th recto,

lated the book of Policronicon into englissh / Fynysshed by me william Caxton the xviij . day of August the yere of our lord god M . CCCC . lxxx . and the xx . yere of the regne of kyng Edward the fourthe .

REMARKS.—"The Description of Britain" is one of the chapters out of Ralph Higden's "Polycronicon." Caxton printed it as a supplement to the Chronicles, and evidently intended it to follow on after the termination of that work. The blank leaf at the end instead of the beginning favours this idea.

It is improbable that a second edition of "The Description of Britain" was issued, as no copy with the long commas (/) has yet been found.

Copies are in British Museum, Cambridge, Oxford (3), St. John's, Oxford, Lambeth, Glasgow, and four in private libraries.

No. 41.—CURA SAPIENTIÆ; OR THE COURT OF SAPIENCE.
Folio. Without Printer's Name, Place, or Date. (1481?)

COLLATION.—a b c d are 4^{ns}, e is a 3^{n} = 38 leaves, of which the first is blank.

TYPOGRAPHICAL PARTICULARS.—There is no title-page. The type is No. 4 throughout. The whole work is in "Balad Royal," or stanzas of seven lines, of which there are five to each page. Without folios or catchwords. Space is left for the insertion of 3-line initials.

After a blank the Text begins on a ij recto, with space for a 3-line initial, with director,

Me labero⁹ & yᵉ most merueylo⁹ werkes
Of sapience syn firste regned nature
t My purpos is to tell as writen clerkes
And specyally her moost notable cure

The Text ends half-way down the second column, on the sixth verso of the same signature,

lyuyng / nedeful werkes / and
dredeful dedes of ioye and of
peyne

REMARKS.—The only manuscript copy of this poem is preserved in the library of Trinity College, Cambridge. It belonged formerly to John Stow, who has noted several omissions in the text, as compared with some other copy, probably the printed edition; and who has written over the top, "By John Lydgate." The poem itself is headed "Here beginneth a brief compiled treatise called by the Author thereof *Curia Sapientiæ.*"

The following description by Oldys is taken from *Bib. Harl.* Vol. III, No. 3313: "Though neither the author's nor printer's name appears to this poem, it was visibly enough printed by Caxton and composed by Lidgate, had we not the authority of John Stowe for it, in the catalogue of his writings. The author tells us it was written at the command of his Sovereign (perhaps King Hen. V), and it seems to be one of the scarcest of his pieces extant. There seems to be more invention in it and variety of matter than in most other poems of his composition, displaying, after a copious debate between Mercy and Truth, Justice and Peace, a distinct survey throughout the palace and domains of Sapience, of all the products of nature, in distinct chapters, and of arts and sciences; with his further reference, at the end of each, to the authors who have written on them." Ames says (*Typ. Ant.*, page 67), after quoting the whole of the "Prohemium," "I take Caxton to be the poet or author, by the above verses." This opinion was perhaps too readily adopted. Although there is a curious parallel between the poet's statement of his rude and corrupt speech, and the apology of Caxton in his additions to "The Recuyell" for his "vnperfightness" in English, owing to his having been educated where was "spoken as brode and rude englissh as is in ony place of englond;" and although we know that Caxton could put together a few verses, as in the instance of the last two stanzas of "Moral Proverbs;" yet, judging from the literary ability of his known works and translations, we should hardly be justified in ascribing the authorship of "Curia Sapientiæ" to him. The plan of this work, in which theology, geography, natural history, horticulture, grammar, rhetoric, arithmetic, geometry, music, and astronomy are all in turn described, was certainly too high a flight for our printer.

The titles given to this book, "The werke of Sapience" and "Tractatus de Fide et Cantus famule sue," adopted by Ames and other bibliographers, were taken from the first and last lines of the poem. The proper title, "Curia Sapientiæ," appears at the end of "Liber Primus."

Caxton's edition is very scarce. St. John's, Oxford, and Earl Spencer, have copies, and fragments are in the Bodleian and the British Museum.

No. 42.—THE HISTORY OF GODFREY OF BOLOYNE; OR THE CONQUEST OF JERUSALEM. *Folio. Printed the 20th November, in the Abbey of Westminster, by William Caxton*, 1481.

COLLATION.—𝔞 is a 3^n, with 𝔞 j blank; 𝔟 a 2^n, 𝔟 1 being blank; 1, 2, 3, 4, 5, 6, 7, 8, 9, 10, 11, 12, 13, 14, 15, and

16 are all 4^{ns}, 17 is a 3^{n} = 144 leaves, of which two are blank. Excepting the first two gatherings, the signatures are entirely in Arabic numerals. Dibdin corrects Ames, and says he counted 146 leaves, but Ames was right.

TYPOGRAPHICAL PARTICULARS.—There is no title-page. The type is entirely No. 4. A full page has forty lines, which are of an even length, and measure 4¾ inches. Without folios or catchwords. Space at the commencement of chapters is left for the insertion of 3 to 7-line initials.

The volume commences with a blank leaf, after which follows the prologue, the Text beginning on a 2, with a space for a 4-line initial,

He hye courageous faytes / And valyaunt actes of
t noble Illustrous and vertuous personnes ben digne
to be recounted / put in memorye/ and wreton. to thende
that ther may be gyuen to them name Inmortal by so=
uerayn laude and preysyng. And also for to moeue and
tenflaw |

ending half-way down the recto of the sixth folio of sig. 17, the verso being blank,

myng . whiche boook I began in marche the xij daye and
fynys= | shyd the vij day of Juyn / the yere of our lord ·
M . CCCC · lxxxj | & the the xxj yere of the regne of our
sayd sauerayn lord kyng Ed | ward the fourth . & in this
maner sette in forme & enprynted the | xx day of nouem=
bre the yere a forsayd in thabbay of westmester | by the
said wylliam Caxton

In the British Museum is a splendid manuscript of this work, a large folio, on vellum, fifteenth century, with numerous illuminations. The character of the writing is very similar to the large type of Colard Mansion, and it begins "Les anciennes histoires dīet que eracles fut moult bon x'pien et gouuerneur de lempire de romme." The text is without doubt the original of Caxton's translation, with which it agrees chapter for chapter, but is carried much further than the death of Godfrey, with which Caxton concludes. The author appears to be unknown.

An edition was printed at Paris, in 1500, with the title "Les faits et Gestes de preux Godefroy de Bovillon et de ses chevalereux freres Baudouin et Eustache."

Copies are in the British Museum, Cambridge (2), Imperial Library, Vienna, Hunterian College, Glasgow, Baptist College, Bristol, with four in private libraries. The copy belonging to S. Holford, Esq., is specially interesting; it is in its original vellum cover, and contains the following interesting notice:—"This was king Edw. y[e] fourth Booke." Also the autographs, "p'tinet Rogero Thorney," and "Rob[t] Wellborne." The former of these names is worth a comment, because it throws some doubt upon the accuracy of the previous notice. Roger Thorney, like other literary mercers of his time, was probably a friend and supporter of Caxton: he certainly patronised his successor, Wynken de Worde, as the following lines from the "Polychronicon" of 1495, show:—

> " ———— this boke of Policronicon
> " Whiche Roger Thorney Mercer hath exhorted
> " Wynken de Worde of vertuous entent
> " Well to correcte, and gretely hym comforted,
> " This specyal boke to make and sette in prente."

How then did Roger Thorney become possessed of the copy of "The History of Godefroy of Bulloyn," belonging to his king? On the inside cover is also the book-plate of Sir John Dolben, Bart., of Finedon, in Northamptonshire. This volume was sold among the books of Secondary Smyth, in 1682, and passed into the library of the Earl of Peterborough. It was afterwards in the Vernon collection, which is now included in that of Mr. Holford.

No. 43.—Letters of Indulgence from Johannes de Leigliis, alias De Liliis, issued in 1481 on the authority of Pope Sixtus IV, for assistance against the Turks. *On Parchment.*

This Indulgence is represented by two slips of parchment, extracted from the St. Alban's "Boethius." (See *ante*, page 214).

Originally in one, the document was cut in two pieces by Caxton's binder, who used them for strengthening the back of the book. They were pasted, one at the beginning and one at the end, down the whole length, inside the boards. When the volume was dissected they were, unfortunately, subjected to the usual soaking in water. This has entirely changed their original appearance, as the print has necessarily participated in the shrinking of the parchment. From personal examination, while the volume was in its original state, the following particulars are obtained:—

Typographical Particulars.—The Type is all No. 4. The lines, which are spaced to an even length, measured nine inches. The complete document, apparently, contained 13 lines.

The second slip containing the date, is as follows:—

mutare libere et licite . . . . . | . et singuloru fide pre-
sentes sigilli ꝯmissionis indulgenciaru et dispensacionu
sancte cruciate qu . . | mus et fecimus appensione com
. . iri / Datum die mensis |
CCCC . lxxxj . Ac pontificatus prefati sanctissimi domini
nostri do . ini Sixti pape . .

The two slips, now measuring each 7¼ × 1 inches, were originally about 11 × 2 inches. They are now in the British Museum.

No. 44.—Letters of Indulgence issued in 1481, on the authority of Pope Sixtus IV, for assistance against the Turks. *Second Edition. On parchment.* 1481.

The type is all No. 4. The lines are spaced to an even length. The whole document is printed on one side of a slip of paper.

The only two copies known are pasted inside the "Royal Book" printed by Caxton, and now in the Bedford Library, Bedford. They measure 8 × 6 inches. A slip of parchment containing four lines was discovered by Mr. Bradshaw in the Library of King's College, Cambridge.

No. 45.—THE CHRONICLES OF ENGLAND. *Folio.* "*Emprynted by me william Caxton In thabbey of westmestre,*" *October 8th*, 1482. *Second Edition, with long commas.*

COLLATION.—Prologue and title a 4^{n}, signed ij, iij, and iiij, the first leaf being blank. a (a j blank) b c d e f g h i k l m n o p q r s t u x are 4^{ns}; y is a 3^{n}. Total 182 leaves, of which two are blank.

TYPOGRAPHICAL PARTICULARS.—There is no title-page. Type No. 4 only is used. There are forty lines to a full page. The lines are spaced out to an even length, and measure $4\frac{3}{4}$ inches. The signatures are in lower-case letters and Arabic numerals. Spaces left for the insertion of initials. Without folios or catchwords.

The above collation and particulars are identical with those of the first edition, described at page 245, *ante*.

Commencing with a blank leaf, the prologue follows on sig. ij recto, the Text beginning with space for a 4-line initial,

N the yere of thyncarnacyon of our lord Jhu crist M
CCCC / lxxx / And in the xx yere of the Regne of
i kyng Edward the fourth / Atte request of dyuerse gen
tylmen I haue endeuyryd me to enprynte the Cro=
nycles of Englond/as in this book shal by the suffraunce
of god

The Text ends on the sixth recto of sig. y, the verso being blank,

Thus endeth this present book of the Cronycles of Englond/Enprynted by me William Caxton In thabbey of westmestre by london / Fynysshed / and accomplysshyd the / viij / day of Octobre / The yere of the Incarnacyon of our lord God / M / CCCC / lxxxij And in the xxij yere of the regne of kyng Edward the fourth

Copies are in the British Museum (2) and Oxford, with three in private libraries.

No. 46.—POLYCRONICON. *Folio.* "*Imprinted and set in forme by me William Caxton.*" *Without place or Date. Translation ended* 2nd *July*, 1482.

COLLATION.—a b are 4^ns^, with the first leaf of a blank; C is a 2^n^; sigs. 1 to 28 are 4^ns^, the first and 5th leaves of sig. 1 being blank; sig. 28 is followed by an unsigned single sheet, of which but one leaf is printed, the other being blank; 29 to 48 are 4^ns^; 49 a 2^n^; 50 to 55 are 4^ns^, with the last leaf of 55 blank; sig. 50 is followed by 52, sig. 51 being accidentally omitted=450 leaves, of which five are blank.

TYPOGRAPHICAL PARTICULARS.—There is no title-page. The type is all No. 4. The lines, which measure 4¾ inches, are fully spaced out, and forty make a full page. Space is left at the beginning of the chapters for the insertion of initials. The first gatherings have the signatures in Roman numerals, but all the rest are signed with Arabic numerals. After the introductory matter folios are introduced, although with many errors.

The Text, preceded by a blank, begins on sig. a 2 recto, with space for a 4-line initial,

Prohemye

g Rete thankynges lawde & honoure we merytoryously ben bounde to yelde and offre vnto wryters of hystoryes / whiche gretely haue prouffyted oure mortal lyf / that shewe vnto the reders and herers by the ensamples of thynges passyd / what thynge is to be desyred/

The Text ends on the recto of 55-7; the verso and 55-8 being blank.

wrytynge / Ended the second day of Juyll the xxij yere of the regne of kynge Edwardthe fourth & of the Incarnacion of oure lord a thousand four honderd foure score and tweyne/

Fynysshed per Caxton

REMARKS.—Few of Caxton's books have excited more interest and research than the "Polycronicon." It appears to have had its origin with Roger, Monk of St. Werberg, in Chester, who, about the beginning of the fourteenth century, made an extensive compilation in Latin from several of the old chronicles and works on natural history then in existence. Ralph Higden, of the same monastery, who died before 1360, amplified this compilation, entitling his work, "Polycronicon;" and this, judging from the numerous copies still extant, had a very extended popularity. In 1387 Trevisa, chaplain to the Earl of Berkeley, translated the Latin of Higden into English prose. An account of Trevisa, with a history of his works, is given by Dr. Dibdin, in *Typ. Ant.* vol. i, page 140, who, however, has not included in his list Trevisa's English translation of the Gospel of Nicodemus (*Addit. MS.* 16165). Trevisa's translation of the Bible is expressly mentioned by Caxton in his prologue. Nearly a century later, Caxton revised the antiquated text of Trevisa, which, together with a continuation of the history to the year 1460, was finished on July 2nd, 1482, and printed soon after. Caxton entitled his continuation "Liber ultimus," and it is most interesting as being the only original work of any magnitude from our printer's pen.

Caxton tells us very little of the sources of his information. He mentions two little works, "Fasciculus temporum" and "Aureus de Vniverso," from which, however, he certainly obtained but little material for his "Liber ultimus," which treats almost entirely of English matters.

As a specimen or the alteration made by our printer, when he "a lytyl embellyshed" the text as rendered by Trevisa, the following quotation is given, in which the consequences of Man's fall are graphically described. The embellishment chiefly consists in modernising the old English, although here and there Caxton added sentences to the text.

TREVISA'S TEXT, 1387.
(Harleian MS., No. 1900, fol. 94*b*).

From that day forthward ye body y[t] is corrupt by syne

CAXTON'S TEXT, 1483.
(Sig. 10 4 verso).

Fro that day forth the body that is corrupt by synne greu-

greuey ye soule / Ye flesche couetiy azen^9 ye soule / and mãnes wittes torney & assentith liztlich to euel A mãnes owne meynal wittes bey his owne enemyes ¶ So y^t al a mãnes lif is temptacion while he lyuey here in erye Also man is eũ failynge and aweyward. he may nouzt stidfastlich abide he falliy liztliche bot he may nouzt lightlich arise. P'fite is of birye sorowe & care ĩ lyuyng/ and man mot nedes deye And thouz alle oy^e yat bey made haue schelles · ryndes · skynnes · wolle. heer. bristels · fethers · wynges other skales · man is y bore wiyout eny helyng / naked & bar. anone at his birye he gyney forto wepe atte bygynyng liche to a best. but his lymes failey hym & may nouzt help hymself. But he is febler yan any oy^r beste · he kan noon helpe · he may nouzt do of hymself but wepe wiy al his myzte. No best hay lif more brutel and vnsiker Noon hay sekenesse more greuous · noon more likynge to do oy^{r}wise than he sholde / noon is more cruwel Also oy^r bestes louey eũeche oye of ye same kynde & woney to gedres & bey nouzt cruwel but to bestes

eth the soule The flesshe coueyteth ayenste the soule and mannes wyttes torne and assente lightly to euyl A mannes oune meynal wyttes / be his owne enemyes / so that al mannes lyf is in temptacion whyle he lyueth here in erthe. & the disposipon of the soule ruleth meynteneth / helpeth and conforteth the body / But ayeinward the wretched disposicion of the bodye distourbeth the soule · Also man is euer fayllyng and wayward he may not stydfastly abyde / he falleth lightly but he may not lightly aryse / Profyt of byrth is sorow and care in lyuyng and man must nedes dye And thaugh oll other that be made haue shelles ryndes skynnes. wolle heer bristels feders wynges owther skals / Man is born withoute ony helyng or keueryng nakede and bare / anone at his birth. he gynneth for to wepe atte begynnyng lyke a beest but his lymmes fayllen hym and maye not helpe hym self · but he is febler than ony other beeste / he can noon helpe / he may nought doo of hym self but wepe with al his myght No beest hath lyf more brutyl & vnseker / None hath sekenesse more greuous of other kynde y[t] ben contrairie to hem But man torney y[t] maner doyng vpsodoū & is contr'ie to hym self & cruel to oy[r] men

noon more lykyng to do otherwyse than he shuld . none is more cruel Also other bestes loue eueryche other of the same kynde . and dwell to gyder and be not cruel / but to beestes of other kynde that be contrary to hem / But man torneth that maner doyng vp so downe and is contrary to hymself and cruel to other men /

This is one of the most common of Caxton's works, at least thirty copies being known, of which half are in various public libraries.

No. 47.—The Pilgrimage of the Soul. "*Emprynted at westmestre by william Caxton, and fynysshed the sixth day of June,*" 1483.

Collation.—An unsigned 2[n], with the first leaf blank; a b c d e f g h i k l m n are 4[ns], with a j blank; o is a 3[n], with the last two leaves blank. Total 114 leaves, of which four are blank.

Typographical Particulars.—There is no title-page. The type throughout is No. 4. The lines are of an equal length, and measure 4¼ inches. A full page has forty lines. There is a running head to the pages, and the leaves have printed folios, numbered very carelessly. Space has been left for the insertion of 2, 3, and 6-line initials. Commencing with a blank, the title and table follow on folio ij, which is unsigned.

The Text begins, on the second leaf, thus:—

Folio ij

This book is intytled the pylgremage of the sowle / translatid ‖ oute of Frensshe in to Englysshe / whiche book is ful of deuoute ‖ maters touchyng the sowle / and many ques=

tyons assoyled to ca || use a man to lyue the better in this world / And it conteyneth fyue || bookes / as it appereth her= after by Chappytres

The text ends on the fourth leaf of sig. o, and the verso of folio **Cx**,

Here endeth the dreme of pylgremage of the soule trans= latid || oute of Frensshe in to Englysshe with somwhat of addicions / the yere of our lord / M.CCCC / & thyrten / and endeth in the Uigy || le of seynt Bartholomew

Emprynted at westmestre by William Caxton / And fynysshed || the sixth day of Juyn / the yere of our lord / M.CCCC / lxxxiij || And the first yere of the regne of kynge Edward the fyfthe / ||

This is the only book from the press of Caxton having the name of Edward V in the colophon.

Remarks.—The common custom among preachers of the Middle Ages of engaging the attention of their hearers by *spiritualising* tales and even jests current among the people is well known. This practice seems to have suggested to a monk named Guillaume de Deguilleville the idea of *moralising* the celebrated "Roman de la Rose." His poem was divided into three parts, and completed about 1335. It contains more than 36,000 lines, and its title is "Le Romant des trois Pelerinages." These three pilgrimages are "Le pelerinage de la vie humaine;" "Le pelerinage de l'Ame;" and "Le pelerinage du Jesus Christ." Brit. Mus. *Addit. MS.* 22937 contains the three parts complete. None of these appear to have been printed. Not satisfied, however, with the result of his labours, Guillaume again set to work and recast the whole poem, with many amplifications and additional verses. This, which was finished about 1350, and of which a manuscript copy is in the *Bib. Imp. Paris*, 6988², is the text of which several editions were issued from the early French press.

Nearly a century passed when another monk, Jehan de Gallopes, transposed the rhymes of Deguilleville into French prose. This was with the object of modernising the old language, or, as he says, "pour esclaircir et entendre la matiere la contenue." Gallopes, however, apparently extended his labours no further than "The Pelerinage de l'Ame," and here we find the text used by the translator of "The Pylgremage of the Sowle," printed in 1483 by our William Caxton. Manuscripts of the prose "Pelerinage de l'Ame" are very scarce, but a perfect copy is in *Bib. Imp. Paris*, No. 7086.

Of the author and translators mentioned above, but little can be said. Guillaume de Deguilleville was monk, and afterwards prior, of the Abbey of Chalis; and this seems all that is known of him. His name appears in the later manuscripts as Guillaume de Guilleville, and is mostly so printed, but is spelt correctly in some of the early French printed editions. In a fourteenth century manuscript, already noticed, the name appears "de Deguilleville," and that this is the true orthography is placed beyond question by an acrostic, consisting of two "chansons" in the French text. Here the author has veiled himself in the initial letters of each line, and by putting these together we obtain his real name, "Guillaume de Deguilleville."

"Jean de Gallopes, dit le Galoys," as we learn from the prologue to his French prose version, was the "humble chapellain" to John, Duke of Bedford and Regent of France, for whom the translation was undertaken. It was, therefore, executed before the death of the Regent, in 1435, and there seems reason to suppose that its author was an Englishman. In the Imperial Library, Paris, is a manuscript, mentioned by M. Paris (*Les Msc. Franç.*, vol. v, page 132), entitled "Vie de Jesus Christ," which is attributed also to Gallopes, but which appears to be a different work from the third "Pilgrimage" of Deguilleville.

To John Lydgate, monk, of Bury, is generally attributed the English version of "The Pylgremage of the Sowle," and probably with truth, as some of the additional poems found here form a part also of Lydgate's well-known poem "The Life of our lady." He is also supposed, from internal evidence of style, to be the author of "The Pilgrimage of man" (*Cotton MSS.*, Vitel. C. XII), an English metrical translation of Deguilleville's "Pelerinage de la vie humaine."

The numerous copies of the "Pilgrimages" still extant in our old libraries prove that they must have attained a considerable amount of popularity. In France there were several printed editions; but in England, probably owing to the growth of the Reformation, "The Pylgremage of the Sowle," printed by Caxton, is the only known edition.

Copies are in the British Museum, St. John's, Oxford, and Sion College, London; also in the Althorpe and Britwell Libraries.

There is no connection whatever between this work and Bunyan's "Pilgrim's Progress." Caxton's book treats of the journey and trial of the soul *after* death, the only point in common being that both are supposed to happen in a dream. "The Pilgrimage of man" is nearer in idea, but equally distinct in treatment.

No. 48.—A VOCABULARY IN FRENCH AND ENGLISH. *Folio. Sine ullâ notâ.* 1483?

COLLATION.—Two 4^ns^ and one 5^n^, unsigned = 26 leaves, the first being, doubtless, blank.

TYPOGRAPHICAL PARTICULARS.—There is no title of any sort. The type is No. 4 throughout. 42 lines in double column (84 lines) make a full page, and the long lines measure $2\frac{7}{8}$ inches. The words "Frensshe" and "Englissh" appear as head-lines to every page. Without folios, catchwords, or initials.

The Text begins, in double column, on the 2nd recto, thus:—

Frensshe	Englissh
Cy commence la table	Hier begynneth the table
De cest prouffytable doctrine	Of this prouffytable lernynge
Pour trouuer tout par ordene	For to fynde all by ordre
Ce que on vouldra aprendre	That whiche wen wylle lerne

The Text ends, with seven lines on the 26th recto, thus:—

Frensshe	Englissh
La Grace de sainct esperit	The grace of the holy ghoost
Ueul enluminer les cures	Wylle enlyghte the hertes
De ceulx qui le aprendront	Of them that shall lerne it
Et nous doinst perseuerance	And vs gyue perseueraunce
En bonnes operacions	In good werkes
Et apres ceste vie transitorie	And after this lyf transitorie
La pardurable ioye & glorie	The euerlastyng ioye and glorie

"A Book for Travellers" is the title given to this work in *Typ. Ant.* vol. i, page 315, but as there is no especial suitability in it for the use of travellers, and as from its composition it appears to have been formed with a scholastic aim, it has been thought advisable to change so evident a misnomer.

No manuscript of this compilation in French or English is known to exist, nor is there any clue to the author.

A copy is in each of the four following libraries—Ripon Cathedral, Bamborough Castle, Earl Spencer, and Duke of Devonshire.

No. 49.—THE FESTIAL (LIBER FESTIALIS). *First Edition. Folio.* "*Enprynted at Westmynster by Wyllyam Caxton the laste day of Juyn,* 1483."

COLLATION.—a b c d e f g h i k l m n are 4^ns, a j being blank; o and p are 3^ns=116 leaves, of which one is blank.

TYPOGRAPHICAL PARTICULARS.—There is no title of any sort. The type is entirely No. 4*, which here appears for the first time. The lines, which are fully spaced out, measure 5 inches. A full page has 38 lines. Without folios or catchwords. Space left for the insertion of 3 to 5-line initials, with director.

Commencing with a blank leaf, the sermon for the First Sunday in Advent follows on sig. a ij, space being left for the insertion of a 5-line initial.

The Text begins thus:—

His day is callyd the first sonday of aduent / that is the sonday in cristys comyng / Therfore holy t chirche this day maketh mencion of ij comynges The first comyng was to bye mankynde out of bondage of the deuyll and to brynge mannys sowle to blysse / And this other comyng shal be at the day of dome

The Text ends on the sixth recto of sig. p,

vs that for vs deyed on the rood tree / Qui cum deo patre & spu || sancto viuit et regnat deus AMEN /

Explicit

Enprynted at Westmynster by wyllyam Caxton the laste day of Juyn Anno domini M CCCC Lxxxiij

The compiler of "The Festial," John Mirkus, was a canon of the Monastery of Lilleshul, an old foundation in Shropshire, as we learn from a MS. copy of his work in the Cottonian Library. He says that, finding many priests, from incapacity, were, like himself, unable to teach their parishioners properly, he had taken pains to compile sermons for all the principal feasts of the year, which he had extracted chiefly from the "Golden Legend." The omission of the prologue, by Caxton, as well as the sermons on Burial and Paternoster, mentioned above, makes us suspect that our printer had a copy imperfect at beginning and end. The subject of nearly every chapter in "The Festial" may also be found in the "Golden Legend;" but, taking the two books, as printed by Caxton, for comparison, it will be seen that the sermons for the Moveable Feasts, with which each work commences, have nothing in common but their subject, and that the histories of the saints are treated very differently, and often disagree even in their supposed historical facts. The "Gesta Romanorum" furnished many stories for the "Golden Legends," but in "The Festial" that mine of anecdotes has contributed still more largely to the illustration and enforcement of the preacher's remarks. "The Festial" is yet further removed from our Book of Common Prayer, with which it has been associated. With the exception of the names in the calendar there is nothing in common between them.

Although in Caxton's edition of this work it is entirely without a name, there seems no reason for giving it the Latin title by which it is generally known, "Liber Festivalis." John Mirkus, its compiler, who wrote it in English, says, "I will and pray that it be called a Festial;" and, accordingly, it was so called by Wynken de Worde in several editions, by Rood of Oxford, and by other early printers.

Copies are at the British Museum, Bodleian, Lambeth, and Althorpe.

No. 50.—FOUR SERMONS, ETC. (QUATUOR SERMONES, ETC.) *First Edition. Folio.* "*Enpryuted by Wylliam Caxton at Westmestre.*" *Without Date.* (1483?)

COLLATION.—a b c are 4^{ns}, d a 3^{n}=30 leaves. No blanks.

TYPOGRAPHICAL PARTICULARS.—There is no title. The type is entirely No. 4*. The lines are fully spaced out, and measure 5 inches. A full page has 38 lines. Without folios or catchwords. In this book we find, for the first time, the paragraph mark ¶ used—a mark which never appears in the early state of this type.

The Text begins on sig. a j, with space for a 3-line initial, without director,

He maystec of sentence in the second booc and the
first dystynction / sayth that the souerayn cause /
why god made al creatures in heuen erthe or water /
was his oune good ‖ nes / by the whiche he wold that some of

On sig. d iij recto,

¶ The Generalle Sentence

God men and wymmen I do you to understonde that
g We that haue cure of your sowlys be commaundyd of
our ordenaries and by the constytucions and the laWe
of holy chirche to shewe to you foure tymes by the yere
in eche a quarter of the yere ones when the peple is most

The Text ends on the sixth verso of sig. d,

resurrectionis gloria inter sanctos et electos tuos resussitati respi ‖ rent / per xpristum dominm nostrum Amen /

Enprynted by wylliam Caxton at westmestre /

Remarks.—The name of the writer of these homilies is not known, nor do they appear attached to any of the manuscripts of the Festial above noticed. That they were, however, printed by Caxton at the same time as the Festial appears evident from the identity of their typographical arrangements, strengthened by the fact of their being, in several instances, under the same cover. That Caxton also intended to allow their separate use may, nevertheless, be deduced from the first gathering having a for its signature, and from the existence of some copies unaccompanied by the Festial. In the Lambeth copy the sermons precede the Festial.

The four sermons are thus apportioned:—

1. On the Paternoster, the Creed, and the Ten Commandments.

2. The Seven Sacraments, the Seven Deeds of Mercy, and the Seven Deadly Sins.

3. A continuation of the subject of Deadly Sins.

4. On Contrition, Confession, and Satisfaction.

After the sermons are "The General Sentence or Comminacion," and two forms of bidding prayer, called "The Bedes on Sondaye."

Every priest was obliged by the Canon Law to read the "Modus Fulminandi," or Commination, and to preach at least one sermon every three months, and these were probably compiled for that purpose.

Nine copies are known, of which two only are in private hands.

No. 51.—Servitium de Visitatione B. Mariæ Virginis. *Quarto. Sine ullâ notâ.* (1481-3).

Collation.—One 4^{n}=8 leaves, of which the last is blank.

TYPOGRAPHICAL PARTICULARS.—The type is entirely No. 4. The lines, which are fully spaced out, measure 3¼ inches in length; there are 26 lines to a full page. Without signatures, folios, or catchwords.

The first leaf is wanting in the only copy known. The second recto commences with space for a 2-line initial, with director,

p Rima aut mihi tunc aurora refulsit &
horridis polo fugientib; umbris celo ru
bescente die utrunq; a nocte distinxi . tuc quo

followed, on the same page, by—

Lectio sexta

On the verso is—

Lectioties de Omel' . p octauas prima die

giving the lessons for the week. On the fourth recto is—

Ad missam Introitus

The sixth verso, which is given entire in the accompanying plate, begins—

Oratio sanctissimi . d . n . Sixti pape quarti

The Text ends on the seventh verso, two lines short of a full page,

et exultatioe ppetua renascamur . Per xpm
dominu nostru

The only EXISTING COPY is in the British Museum (C. 21. c), and, although wanting the first leaf, has the final blank. Measurement, 8⅝ × 5⅝ inches.

No. 52.—SEX PERELEGANTISSIMÆ EPISTOLÆ PER PETRUM CARMELIANUM EMENDATÆ. *Quarto. Per Willelmum Caxton. In Westmonasterio.* (1483).

COLLATION.—a b c are 4^{ns} = 24 leaves, of which a j is blank.

TYPOGRAPHICAL PARTICULARS.—There is no title-page. The types used are Nos. 4 and 4*. The lines, which are spaced to an even length, measure 3¼ inches, and there are 26 to a page. Without catchwords or folios. The whole appearance of the print is like the "Servitium de Visitatione" and the "Order of Chivalry."

The use of types 4 and 4* together points unmistakably to 1483 as the period of issue; and this date, gathered from the typographical particulars only, is completely verified by the letters themselves, the dates of which range from December 11th, 1482, to February, 1483.

The Text begins on a ij recto, with an introduction which occupies three pages.

> h Erculez dux Ferrarie in eo ducatu venetoru armis constitutus paulo post vetustissimus eorum violat immunitates / init foedus cum Therdinando Rege Neapolitano Mediolanensium duce / et florentinorum repu / quod per veneta foedor' no licebat / Ueneti propria reposcunt / ille tergiuersari / Xystus pontifex quartus / relic Therdinadi foed &c.

The six letters begin on sig. a iij verso. On c 8 recto is the following colophon:—

> Finiunt sex p'elegantissime epistole / quarum tris a summo Pontifice Sixto Quarto et Sacro Cardinalium Collegio ad Illustrissimum Uenetiarum ducem Joannem Mocenigum totidemq; ab ipso Duce ad eundem Pontificem et Cardinales / ob Ferrariense bellum susceptum / conscripte sunt / Impresse per willelmum Caxton / et diligenter emendate per Petrum Carmelianu Poetar' Laureatum in Westmonasterio

Beneath this is a Latin quatrain, beginning

Eloquii cultor,

followed by

Interpretatio magnarum litterarum punctatarum paruarumque.

The text ends with 23 lines on the verso of the same leaf.

REMARKS.—These six letters passed between the Sacred College of Cardinals on one side and the Doge of Venice on the other, the subject being the necessity of closing the war with the City of Ferara.

Petrus Carmelianus, the editor of these letters, is noticed by Mr. Gairdner, in his preface to the "Memorials of King Henry the Seventh," published in 1858, for the Master of the Rolls, as having been in England from the time of Edward the Fourth. He may, therefore, have personally employed Caxton to print his "Sex Epistolæ." The title "Brixiensis" sometimes attached to his name shows that he was a native of the town of Brescia. He seems to have taken an interest in educational matters, as verses by him to John Anwykyl and to William Waynflete, Bishop of Winchester, are prefixed to the "Compendium totius grammaticæ," printed at Oxford about 1482-83. Some more of his poetry is printed in the Oxford "Phalaris" of 1485. Tanner assigns to Carmelianus the following promotions—Rector of St. George's, Southwark, 1490; Prebend of York, 1498; Archdeacon of Gloucester, 1511; Prebend of London, 1519. Being in such favour, no wonder that he waxed rich, and that when, in 1522, "an annual grant was made by the Spirituality for the King's personal expenses in France for the recovery of the Crown," the name of "Mr. Petrus Carmelianus" appears among the "Spiritual Persons" for the handsome sum of £333 6*s* 8*d*. In the Calendar of State Papers, where he is called "Latin Secretary of King Henry the Seventh," mention is made of a letter sent to him from Ferdinand and Isabella of Spain, thanking him for his services, and promising him favour and reward. On the projected marriage of Prince Charles of Castile with the Princess Mary of England he wrote a poem in Latin, printed by Pynson about 1514, of which a unique copy is in the Grenville Library (see *Archæologia*, vol. xviii). In the same library is a manuscript poem on the birth of the Prince of Wales (1486), another copy, beautifully illuminated, being among the royal MSS. in the British Museum. Both are evidently in the handwriting of Carmelianus, the latter being his presentation copy to the king. The argument of this poem is so characteristic of the age that it is worth noting. Almighty God, compassionating the miserable state of England lacerated with civil war, convoked a meeting of the Saints in Heaven to ask their opinions as to how the long standing dispute between the Houses of York and Lancaster might be composed. The saints reply that, if the Omniscient Deity cared for any of their counsels, no one was better qualified to state how the wars might be terminated than King Henry the Sixth (already in heaven), who knew the country and the causes of dissension, and they recommended that he should be appealed to. Henry is accordingly called upon to reply to the Supreme Being, and proposes that the two houses should be united so as to be one house, for which an opportunity then offered by the marriage of the Earl of Richmond with the Princess Elizabeth. The Deity approves and decrees its execution, the marriage takes place, and the poem terminates with an exhortation to England to rejoice on account of the prince's birth. Carmelianus died August 18th, 1527; John de Giglis, Bishop of Worcester, in 1497, his contemporary and countryman, also employed Caxton to print Indulgences.

A manuscript, "Carmen de Vere,"* in the British Museum, which is dedicated to Edward Prince of Wales (afterwards Edward V), dated April 1482, affords some information from the pen of Carmelian himself. He says that for the previous ten years he had been travelling about the world, having very lately arrived in England, with the intention of proceeding to Germany and Switzerland; but, captivated by the pleasantness of the country, he had been unable to leave

* Reg. 12 A xxix, the particulars of which were kindly communicated by Mr. Bond, keeper of the MSS.

it. He adds that his poem was written to gain the favour of the prince. Whence his dignity of Poeta laureatus was obtained is not known.

The only copy known of this tract was discovered in the year 1874 by Dr. G. Könnecke, archivist of Marburg, in an old volume of seventeenth century divinity, in the Hecht-Heinean Library at Halberstadt. It was described in the "Neuer Anzeiger" of Dr. Julius Petzholdt for October 1874; also in the Athenæum for February 27th, 1875.

No. 53.—CONFESSIO AMANTIS. *Large Folio. "Enprynted at Westmestre by me Willyam Caxton the ij day of Septembre / a thousand / CCCC lxxxxiij (a typographical error for lxxxiij).*

COLLATION.—A 4^n, signed ij, iij, iiij, the first and eighth leaves being blank, followed by a 4^n, signed on the second leaf only 1 2, the first leaf being blank; then b c d e f g h i k l m n o p q r s t u x y z & A B all 4^{ns}; C a 3^n, with the sixth leaf blank. In all 222 leaves, of which four are blank.

TYPOGRAPHICAL PARTICULARS.—There is no title-page. Type No. 4 is used for sigs. 1 to x; sigs. & to C, as well as the introductory matter, are in type No. 4*, while sigs. y and z are partly in one and partly in the other. Where type No. 4 is used there are 46 lines to a column, and 44 lines of type No. 4*. On sig. z iiij recto the two types appear in the same page, the first column being in No. 4 and the second in No. 4*. Without catchwords or folios. Space left for inserting 2 to 6-line initials, with director. The signatures at the beginning of the volume are irregularly printed, and show the want of a settled plan in the printer's mind. The first 4^n, which, as it includes the index, must have been printed last, is properly signed; but, on beginning the book, it appears as if the compositor thought there could be no use for signatures if every leaf had a printed folio, and accordingly they were omitted except on the second sheet, which is signed in Arabic numerals only. The inconvenience of this being seen, the folios were omitted, and the signatures printed in the second 4^n, b;

while in sig. c both plans are united, and we have signatures and folios too to the end of the book—the latter, however, with continual errors. The introductory 4^{n} is not included in the enumeration of the folios. Note that sig. b 4 is printed 2 4, and that from sig. p to the end the Arabic numerals used in the signatures give place to Roman numerals. The book is in double column throughout. The date in the colophon is printed a thousand CCCC lxxxxiij, a typographical error, which would have led to some confusion had not the regnal year, "the first year of the reign of King Richard the third," been also added, fixing the right date as 1483.

Commencing with a blank leaf, the paragraph title and table follow on sig. ij, space being left for a 3-line initial, with director.

The Text begins thus:—

t His book is intituled confes‖sio amantis / that is to saye ‖ in englysshe the confessyon of‖ the louer maad and com= pyled by ‖ Johan Gower squyer borne in walys ‖ how the world was first of golde / &‖ after alwey werse & werse folio vj

Thus endeth the prologue

The Text ends on the verso of sig. C 5, Folio CCxj with colophon in first column,

Enprynted at westmestre by me ‖ Wyllyam Caxton and fynysshed the ij ‖ day of Septembre the fyrst yere of the ‖ regne of Kyng Richard the thyrd / the ‖ yere of our lord a thousand / CCCC / lxxxxiij /

Remarks.—The life and poetical writings of the "moral Gower" have received frequent illustrations from modern critics. His chief work, the "Confessio Amantis," appears to have been begun about 1386 and completed in 1392-3. It was originally dedicated to Richard II, but, on the wane of that monarch's power, Gower suited himself to the changing times, and recast his prologue. The copies made after this version are termed Lancastrian. The Latin verses and the marginal index are in some manuscripts, as in Caxton's printed edition, included in the text. They were, Dr. Pauli believes, the original composition of Gower, abounding, like his other poetry, in instances of false prosody and even bad grammar. The verses are imitations in the manner of Boethius, but often unintelligible.

Seventeen copies are extant. British Museum (3); Cambridge; Pembroke College, Cambridge; Hereford Cathedral; Lambeth; Queen's College and All Souls, Oxford; and eight in private libraries.

No. 54.—THE BOOK WHICH THE KNIGHT OF THE TOWER MADE TO THE "ENSEYGNEMENT" AND TEACHING OF HIS DAUGHTERS. *Folio.* "*Emprynted at Westmynstre the laste day of Januer the fyrst yere of the regne of Kynge Rychard the thyrd.*" (*i.e.* 1484.)

COLLATION.—A 2^n, signed on second leaf only **a j**; **a b c d e f g h i k l m** are 4^{ns}; **n** a 3^n, with the last two leaves blank. In all 106 leaves, of which two are blank.

Note—sig. **c iiij** is wrongly printed **d iiij**, and the first leaf of **d** is without any signature.

TYPOGRAPHICAL PARTICULARS.—There is no title-page. The type, as far as sig. **f**, is No. 4, and forty lines, each $4\frac{7}{8}$ inches long, make a full page. From sig. **f j** to the end the type is No. 4*, with 38 lines, each $4\frac{5}{8}$ inches long, to the page. The lines are fully spaced out. Without folios or catchwords. Space is left for 3, 4, and 6-line initials, with directors.

Commencing a blank, the prologue follows on an unsigned leaf, with space for a 3-line initial **A**,

Lle vertuouse doctryne & techynge had & lerned of
a **suche | as haue endeuoured them to leue for a remem=**
braunce

On sig. a j recto,

Here begynneth the book whiche the knyght of the toure made/And speketh of many fayre ensamples and thensygnementys and techyng of his doughters

The Text ends on the fourth verso of sig. n,

Here fynysshed the booke / whiche the knyght of the Toure ma ‖ de to the ensEygnement and techyng of his doughters trans ‖ lated oute of Frenssh in to our maternall Englysshe tongue by ‖ me William Caxton / whiche book was ended & fynysshed the ‖ fyrst day of Juyn / the yere of oure lord M CCCC lxxxiij
And enprynted at westmynstre the last day of Janyuer the fyrst yere of the regne of kynge Rychard the thyrd

Remarks.—In the department of "Maine et Loire," between Chollet and Vezins, may still be seen the ruins of an ancient château, called "Latour-Landry." Archæologists ascribe the structure to the twelfth century. The place originally bore the name of "La Tour" only, the old family name of the owners being "Landry;" but eventually the two were combined, and "De la Tour Landry," became the patronymic of a long race of knights. The earliest instance of the double name is found in a document dated 1200. Passing over the history of the family, we will confine ourselves to Geoffrey and his book, "pour l'enseignment de ses filles." The date of neither his birth nor death is known. He was at the seige of Aiguillon in 1346, when he must be supposed to be at least of the age of twenty years. He tells us he wrote his book in 1371, which would make him, at the youngest, 45 years old, though he was probably older. In all the illuminated copies of his work he is represented as discoursing with his three daughters, for whose instruction in their journey through life it was written, as the knight himself in a preface informs us. But he had also sons, as we learn that a similar work had previously been undertaken for their instruction, "as hit is reherced in the booke of my two sonnes, and also in an Euangely." (See Caxton's edition, sig. n 4.) Neither of these compositions of the knight are known now to exist. We also learn that in the compilation of this work he called to his aid two priests, who read to him the Bible, the "Gesta," and various chronicles of France, England, and other countries. To this may, perhaps, be attributed the predominance of the ecclesiastical element in this book. The knight originally intended to write the whole work in verse, but finding that method necessitated a less concise narration, he soon changed his composition into prose. In the original French, however, a considerable portion of the introduction, though prose to the eye, will be found to have retained its metrical form. Several writers have denounced the work as obscene, and more fitted for the corruption than the instruction of youth, while others, taking into consideration the manners of that age, have arrived at the very opposite conclusion. At any rate, it is plain our Caxton thought highly of it: he says in his preface, "I advise every gentleman or woman having children, desiring them to be virtuously brought forth, to get and have this book, to the end that they may learn to govern them virtuously in this present life." He tells us also the occasion of his translating and printing it, which was "at the request of a noble lady which hath brought forth many noble and fair daughters, which be virtuously nourished." (See an article in the *Retrospective Review:* New Series, 1827; vol. i, part ii, page 177. Also, *Le Livre du Chevalier de la Tour Landry,* par M. Anatole de Montaiglon. 12mo. Paris, 1854.)

We must here notice that, although the anonymous English translation (*Harl.* 1764) preceded that by Caxton, a comparison of the two versions makes it evident that our printer owed nothing to his predecessor. M. Montaiglon, indeed, gives a decided preference to the earlier text. The following amusing extract is suggestive of Shakspere's "Taming of the Shrew." Act V, Scene II.

CAXTON, 1484.

How a woman sprange vpon the table · Capitulo xviij.

J N a tyme it happed that Marchauntes of Fraunce cam from certayn Fayres / where as they sought Draperye / and as they cam with Marchaundyse fro Roan / that one of them said / it is a moche fayre thynge a man to haue a wif obeysaunt in alle thynges to her husbond / Verayly sayde that one / my wyf obeyeth me well / And the second said. J trowe / that my wyf obeye me better / ye sayd the thyrd / lete laye a wager / that whiche wyf of vs thre that obeyeth best her husbond / and doeth sonnest his commaundement that he wynne the wager / wherupon they waged a Jewele / and accorded al thre to the same / & sworen that none shold aduertyse his wyf of this bargayn / sauf only to saye to her / doo that whiche J shall commaunde what soeuer it be / After when they cam to the first mans hows / he sayd to his wyf Sprynge in to this bacyne / and she answerd / wherfore or what nede is it. And he said by cause it playsyth me so / and J wyll that thou do so / Truly said she J shall knowe fyrst wherfor J shall sprynge / And soo she wold not doo it · And her husbond waxe moche angry and felle / and gafe her a buffet / After thys they cam to the second marchauntes hows / and he saide to his wyf lyke as that other saide / that she wold doo his commaundement / And it was not long after that he said to her Sprynge in to the basyn / And she demaunded hym wherfore / And at the last ende for ought that he dyde / she dyd it not / wherfore she was beten as that other was / Thenne cam they to the thyrd mans hous And there was the table coucred · and mete set theron And the marchaunt said to thother marchauntes in theyr eres / that after dyner he wold commaunde her to sprynge in to the bacyn / And the husbond said to his wyf / that what someuer he commaunded her she shold do it / his wyf whiche that moche louyd hym and dred hym herd wel the word . And it was so that they bygan to ete / and there was no salt vpon the table / And the goodman sayd to his wyf / Sail sur table

And the good wyf whiche hadde fere to disobeye hym / sprang vpon the table and ouerthrewe table / mete / wyn / and platers to the ground / How said the good man / is this the manere / Cōne ye none other playe but this / are ye mad or oute of youre wyt. Syre said she / J haue done youre commaūdement / haue ye not said that youre commaundement shold be done what someuer it was. Certaynly J haue it done to my power how be it that it is youre harme and hurte as moche as myn. For ye sayd to me that J shold spryge on the table / J said he / J sayd ther lacked salt vpon the table / Jn good feyth J vnderstode said she for to spryng / thene was ther laughter ynouz & al was taken for a bourd and a mocquerye / Thenne the other two Marchauntes said it was no nede to late her sprynge in the basȳn / For she had done ynough / And that her husband had wonne the wager . . . And thus ought euery good woman to fere and obeye her lord & husbonde and to do his commaundement is hit right or wrong / yf the commaundement be not ouer outrageous / And yf ther be vyce therin / she is not to blame / but the blame abydeth vppon her lord and husbonde.

There are two copies in the British Museum, one at Cambridge, one at Oxford, and two in private libraries.

No. 55.—Caton. *Folio. Without Printer's Name, Place, or Date. "Translated . . . by William Caxton in thabbey of Westmynstre the yere of our lord M CCCC lxxxiij."* (1484 ?)

Collation.—The prologues and table a 3[n], signed ij and iij on the second and third rectos, the first and last leaves being blank: then a b c d e f g h are 4[ns]; i a 5[n]; a j and i 10 being blank. In all eighty leaves, of which four are blank.

Typographical Particulars.—There is no title-page. Two sizes of type are used: No. 2 for the Latin headings, and No. 4* for the Text. The lines, which are fully spaced out, measure $4\frac{5}{8}$ inches, and there are 38 to a full page. Without folios or catchwords. Space is left for the insertion of 3-line initials, sometimes with and sometimes without directors. Commencing with a blank leaf, Caxton's short prologue and his dedication to the City of London follow on sig. ij.

The Text begins thus:—

¶ Here begynneth the prologue or prohemye of the book callid || Caton / whiche booke hath ben translated in to Englysshe by || Mayster Benet Burgh / late Archedeken of Colchestre and || hye chanon of saint stephens at westmestre/ which ful craftly || hath made it in balade ryal for the erudicion of my lord Bou || sher/Sone & heyr at that tyme to my lord the erle of Estsex || And by cause of late cam to my hand a book of the said Caton || in Frensshe / whiche reherceth many a fayr lernynge and nota || ble ensamples / I haue translated it oute of frensshe in to En || glysshe/ as al along here after shalle appiere / whiche I presente unto the Cyte of london /

Unto the noble auncyent and renomed Cyte/the
b Cyte || of london in Englond / I William Caxton
Cytezeyn || & coniurye of the same / & of the fraternyte and felauship || of the mercerye owe of ryght my seruyse & good wyll / and of

The table follows, making, with the introductory matter, eight printed pages, the whole concluding on the fifth verso, with the sixth blank leaf. After another blank is the Gloss, headed by a quotation of seven lines of Latin in type No. 3, with a ij for the signature.

The Text ends on the ninth recto of sig. i, the tenth leaf being blank,

thynge men may intytule this lytell book the myrour of the re || gyme & gouernement of the body and of the sowle /

Here fynyssheth this present book whiche is sayd or called || Cathon translated oute of Frensshe in to Englysshe by Will || iam Caxton in thabbey of westmynstre the yere of oure lord || M CCCC lxxxiij / And the fyrst yere of the regne of kynge || Rychard the thyrd the xxiij day of decembre

In his prologue Caxton says, "To the end that the histories and examples that be contained in this little book may be lightly found . . . they shall be set and entitled by manner of Rubrics . . . and they shall be signed as that followeth of the number of leaves where they shall be written." Accordingly the numbers given in the table agree with their proper folios, but these folios are not inserted, either in print or manuscript, in the body of the work, rendering the table almost useless.

Caxton says in his preface that he translated from a French copy, "which rehearsed many a fair learning and notable example;" and some portions of his own introductory matter suggest also a French original. Were a manuscript to be found, its title would probably agree with Caxton's concluding description of the work—"the mirror of the regime, and government of the body and of the soul."

The year 1483 is usually assigned to the printing of this book; but, as the translation was not ended till December 23rd, it seems improbable that it was printed till 1484.

As already noticed, this "Caton" is a very different work from the composition known as "Catho Magnus," the distichs of which serve here only as a text whereon to hang an extensive gloss. A short notice of "Mayster Benet Burgh" has already been given.

There are copies in the British Museum, Cambridge, Glasgow, Oxford, Exeter College, Oxford, and seven in private hands.

No. 56.—The Golden Legend. *Largest Folio. First Edition. "Fynysshed at westmestre the twenty day of nouembre / the yere of our lord M / CCCC / lxxxiij / By me Wyllyam Caxton."* (1484?)

Collation.—An unsigned 3^{n}, with first and sixth leaves blank; a b c d e f g h i k l m n o p q r s t u x y z & are 4^{ns}; 9 a 3^{n}; A B C D E F G H I K L M N O P Q R S T V are 4^{ns}; X a 3^{n}; Y is a single sheet, followed by a single leaf, the back edge of which is sometimes returned round Y, and sometimes sewn separately; aa bb cc 𝔡𝔡 𝔢𝔢 𝔣𝔣 are 4os; 𝔤𝔤 a 3^{n}; 𝔥𝔥 𝔦𝔦 4os; 𝔨𝔨 a 3^{n}, 𝔨𝔨 6 being blank. In all 449 leaves, of which three are blank.

TYPOGRAPHICAL PARTICULARS.—There is no title-page. There are two sizes of type, No. 3 being used for head-lines and headings to chapters, while No. 4* is used for the text. The whole is in double columns, and the lines, which are fully spaced out, measure three inches; 55 lines in a column, and 110 to a full page. There are folios throughout, but numbered very irregularly. Space is left for the insertion of 3 to 6-line initials, with directors. There are no catchwords. Woodcuts are used throughout, apparently from the hand of the same artist who engraved the cuts for the second edition of the "Chess Book."

The first edition is principally distinguished by the use of Type No. 3 for head-lines, &c., and also by a variation in the signatures 𝔛 and 𝔜. Both this and the second edition are printed upon very large sheets of paper, larger indeed than Caxton ever used before or after. The edition of 1493 is upon the usual size.

The first leaf is blank; on the second recto is a large woodcut of Saints, 9 × 6½ inches, under which the Text begins thus, making a full page:—

(Woodcut of Saints).

𝔥𝔢 𝔥𝔬𝔩𝔶 & 𝔟𝔩𝔢𝔰𝔰𝔢𝔡 t 𝔡𝔬𝔠𝔱𝔬𝔲𝔯 ‖ 𝔰𝔞𝔶𝔫𝔱 𝔍𝔢𝔯𝔬𝔪 𝔰𝔞𝔶𝔱𝔥 𝔱𝔥𝔶𝔰 𝔞𝔲𝔠𝔱𝔬 ‖ 𝔯𝔶𝔱𝔢 / 𝔡𝔬 𝔞𝔩𝔴𝔢𝔶𝔢 𝔰𝔬𝔪𝔪𝔢 𝔤𝔬𝔬𝔡 ‖ 𝔴𝔢𝔯𝔨𝔢 / 𝔱𝔬 𝔱𝔥𝔢𝔫𝔡𝔢 𝔱𝔥𝔞𝔱 𝔱𝔥𝔢 𝔡𝔢𝔲𝔶𝔩 𝔣𝔶𝔫𝔡𝔢 ‖ 𝔱𝔥𝔢 𝔫𝔬𝔱 𝔶𝔡𝔩𝔢 / 𝔄𝔫𝔡 𝔱𝔥𝔢 𝔥𝔬𝔩𝔶 𝔡𝔬𝔠𝔱𝔬𝔲𝔯 ‖ 𝔰𝔞𝔶𝔫𝔱 𝔞𝔲𝔰𝔱𝔶𝔫 𝔰𝔞𝔶𝔱𝔥 𝔦𝔫 𝔱𝔥𝔢 𝔟𝔬𝔬𝔨 𝔬𝔣 𝔱𝔥𝔢 ‖ 𝔩𝔞𝔟𝔬𝔲𝔯 𝔬𝔣 𝔪𝔬𝔫𝔨𝔢𝔰 / 𝔱𝔥𝔞𝔱 𝔫𝔬 𝔪𝔞𝔫 𝔰𝔱𝔯𝔬𝔫𝔤𝔢 ‖ 𝔬𝔯 𝔪𝔶𝔤𝔥𝔱𝔶 𝔱𝔬 𝔩𝔞𝔟𝔬𝔲𝔯𝔢 𝔬𝔲𝔤𝔥𝔱 𝔱𝔬 𝔟𝔢 𝔶𝔡𝔩𝔢 ‖ 𝔣𝔬𝔯 𝔴𝔥𝔦𝔠𝔥 𝔠𝔞𝔲𝔰𝔢 𝔴𝔥𝔢𝔫 𝔍 𝔥𝔞𝔡 𝔭𝔞𝔯𝔣𝔬𝔲𝔯= ‖ 𝔪𝔢𝔡 & 𝔞𝔠𝔠𝔬𝔪𝔭𝔩𝔦𝔰𝔰𝔥𝔢𝔡 𝔡𝔶𝔲𝔢𝔯𝔰𝔢 𝔴𝔢𝔯𝔨𝔶𝔰 ‖ & 𝔥𝔶𝔰𝔱𝔬𝔯𝔶𝔢𝔰 𝔱𝔯𝔞𝔫𝔰= 𝔩𝔞𝔱𝔢𝔡 𝔬𝔲𝔱 𝔬𝔣 𝔣𝔯𝔢𝔫𝔰𝔰𝔥𝔢 ‖ 𝔦𝔫 𝔱𝔬 𝔢𝔫𝔤𝔩𝔶𝔰𝔰𝔥𝔢 𝔞𝔱 𝔱𝔥𝔢 𝔯𝔢𝔮𝔲𝔢𝔰𝔱𝔢 𝔬𝔣 𝔠𝔢𝔯= ‖ 𝔱𝔢𝔶𝔫 𝔩𝔬𝔯𝔡𝔢𝔰 / 𝔩𝔞𝔡𝔶𝔢𝔰 𝔞𝔫𝔡 𝔤𝔢𝔫𝔱𝔶𝔩𝔪𝔢𝔫 / ‖ 𝔞𝔰 𝔱𝔥𝔶= 𝔰𝔱𝔬𝔯𝔶𝔢 𝔬𝔣 𝔱𝔥𝔢 𝔯𝔢𝔠𝔲𝔶𝔢𝔩 𝔬𝔣 𝔗𝔯𝔬𝔶𝔢 / ‖ 𝔱𝔥𝔢 𝔟𝔬𝔬𝔨 𝔬𝔣 𝔱𝔥𝔢 𝔠𝔥𝔢𝔰𝔰𝔢 / 𝔱𝔥𝔢 𝔥𝔶𝔰𝔱𝔬𝔯𝔶𝔢 𝔬𝔣 ‖ 𝔍𝔞= 𝔰𝔬𝔫 / 𝔗𝔥𝔢 𝔥𝔶𝔰𝔱𝔬𝔯𝔶𝔢 𝔬𝔣 𝔱𝔥𝔢 𝔪𝔶𝔯𝔯𝔬𝔲𝔯 ‖ 𝔬𝔣 𝔱𝔥𝔢 𝔴𝔬𝔯𝔩𝔡 / 𝔱𝔥𝔢 𝔵𝔳 𝔟𝔬𝔬𝔨𝔢𝔰 𝔬𝔣 𝔐𝔢𝔱𝔞= ‖ 𝔪𝔬𝔯= 𝔭𝔥𝔢𝔰𝔢𝔬𝔰 𝔦𝔫 𝔴𝔥𝔶𝔠𝔥𝔢 𝔟𝔢𝔢𝔫 𝔠𝔬𝔫= 𝔱𝔢𝔶𝔫𝔢𝔡 ‖

This prologue finishes, half-way down the second column, on the verso of the same leaf. On the third recto is another woodcut, 8 × 4½ inches, of a horse galloping past a tree, bearing a lable, **My Truste Js** (see a facsimile in Dibdin's *Typ. Ant.*, vol. i, page 186). Underneath this commences Caxton's own prologue, with space for a 3-line initial **A**,

> Nd for as moche as this ‖ sayd werke was grete & ouer ‖ charge= able to me taccomplisshe ‖ J feryd me in the begynnyng of the ‖ also haue enprynted it in the moost best ‖ Wyse that J haue coude or myght / and ‖ presente this sayd boook to his good & ‖ noble lordshyp / as chyef causer of the ‖

This occupies the whole page. On the third verso the table is begun, ending on the sixth recto, with sixteen lines in the first column, the rest of the page being blank. The last line is—

> Yues folio CCCC xxvij
> Explicit

On sig. a j the original Text is begun, space being left for a 6-line **T**,

> He tyme of thaduent or comyng of our lord in to this world quysshid of ygnorance & Jmpuissaunce / ‖ to ye yf he had so come to fore / pauen= ture ‖ man myght saye yt by his owne merites ‖

The Text ends on **kk** 5 recto, half-way down the second column,

> afore is made mencyon / Whiche werke ‖ J haue accomplisshed at the com= maun=‖demente and requeste of the noble and ‖ puyssaunte erle / and my special good ‖ lord Wyllyam erle of aron= del / & haue ‖ fynysshed it at

westmestre the twenty || day
of nouembre / the yere of our
lord || M / CCCC / lxxxiij /
& the fyrst yere || of the regne
of Kyng Rychard the || thyrd

By me wyllyam Caxton

In the latter half of the thirteenth century, Jacobus de Voragine, Archbishop of Genoa, who died in 1298, compiled a book called "Legenda Aurea," in which the lives and miracles of numerous saints were narrated. This was found very useful to the priests in their sermons, and soon become so popular that it was translated into nearly every European language. The Latin text of "Voragine" has been reprinted from an early manuscript, and edited by Dr. Th. Graesse, 8vo, Lipsiæ, 1840. It has also received a modern French dress under the title "La Légende dorée, par Jacques de Voragine, traduit du Latin, par M. G. B., 8vo, Paris, 1843." In the early part of the fourteenth century, Jean Belet, an author but little known to modern bibliographers, though often quoted by the writers of his age, translated the Latin of Jacobus into French, not, however, without embellishing it with many new additions. Shortly after the production of Belet, Jehan de Vignay, who has been already noticed as translating the Book of Chess, undertook a new version in French of "La Légende dorée," which he accomplished before 1380, as he dedicated it to "Jeane, royne de France." His translation, however, was founded on the previous labours of Belet, which he amplified, adding about 44 new legends. About the middle of the fifteenth century, certain "worthy Clerks and Doctors of Divinity" compiled a "Book of the Life of Saints," which they describe as "drawn into English after the tenor of the Latin." These worthy Clerks and Doctors, however, would have given a much more true account of their labours had they stated that, with the exception of some additional fables not traceable in the original Latin, they owed the whole of their compilation to "La Légende dorée" of Jehan de Vignay.

It is probable that in Caxton's time the English version here noticed was well known; indeed we may infer this from the account given by our Printer of the origin of his own text: "Against me here might some persons say, that this Legend hath been translated tofore, and truth it is; but forasmuch as I had by me a Legend in French, another in Latin, and the third in English, which varied in many and diverse places; and also many histories were comprised in the two other books which were not in the English book, therefore I have written one out of the said three books." Caxton, with his Latin, French, and English copies before him, found a prologue ready to his hand in the version by Jehan de Vignay. This, as was his wont, he translated literally, merely changing two or three of the inapplicable proper names, and adding some personal observations of his own. The bulk of his text comes also from the same source, being nearly identical with that of the English manuscript already noticed; although to Caxton may be given this praise, that in several places where the "worthy doctours of divinite" had inserted in their English version some stories more incredible or more filthy than usual, he very discreetly considerably modified or altogether omitted them. The reader curious in this matter may compare the tales about Nero in the "Life of St. Peter," as narrated in *Harl.* 630, with folio 202 in Caxton. How much he took from the Latin is impossible to say; nor have I been able to trace to their origin the curious explanatory derivations of the name of each saint, which form the first paragraph in every "Life." As in "The Festial," many saints in the "Golden Legend" have their lives illustrated or interwoven with tales from the "Gesta Romanorum."

This work may be considered the most laborious, as well as the most extensive, of all Caxton's literary and typographical labours. The compilation of the text only must have been a most arduous task, and the very extensive use of woodcuts must have been extremely expensive and troublesome. Caxton, indeed, confesses that he was "in a manner half desperate to have left it," when the Earl of Arundel, who apparently suggested the undertaking, sent John Stanney to him, promising the Printer a small annuity, and to take a "reasonable quantity" of copies when completed. The annuity was to be a buck in summer and a doe in winter; but it is not improbable that these presents were commuted into a fixed sum of money, as was certainly the practice with the Gifts of Wine, which, in the fourteenth and fifteenth centuries, were so frequently bestowed as rewards for services rendered. As a memorial of the Earls connection with the work, Caxton placed the Arundel device "My truste is" after the preface.

Although, from the numerous copies still extant, it is evident that this edition must have been larger than usual, no perfect copy has yet been discovered. The Legend of St. Thomas of Canterbury has been a special object of destruction, being, in nearly every instance, torn out of the volume.

This is one of the most common of the productions of Caxton's press, and probably a larger number than usual was printed. Of the thirty known copies sixteen are divided between the British Museum, Cambridge, Corpus and Pembroke, Cambridge, Oxford, Glasgow, Logonian Philadelphia, King's College, Aberdeen, Lincoln, Hereford and Bath Cathedrals, Rawlett's Library, Tamworth, and the others in private libraries.

While making every allowance for the rudeness of the age and the plain speaking then customary, the tendency of many of the "Lives" here narrated is so immoral, that many persons have doubted whether these legends were really read to congregations of men and women. But the legacy of several copies of this work to the parish church of St. Margaret's, as already noticed (p. 159), and the following extract from the will of Queen Margaret, prove that the "Golden Legend" was reckoned among the Church Service Books:—"Item, I will that mine executors purvey a complete Legend in one book, and an Antiphony in another book; which books I will be given to abide there in the said church to the worship of God as long as they may endure. (Norf. and Norwich Arch. Soc., Dec. 1850, fol. 163.)

Plate XI.

Portion of the "Death-bed Prayers," 1484. *Caxton's Type, No. 3, and Type, No. 4.*

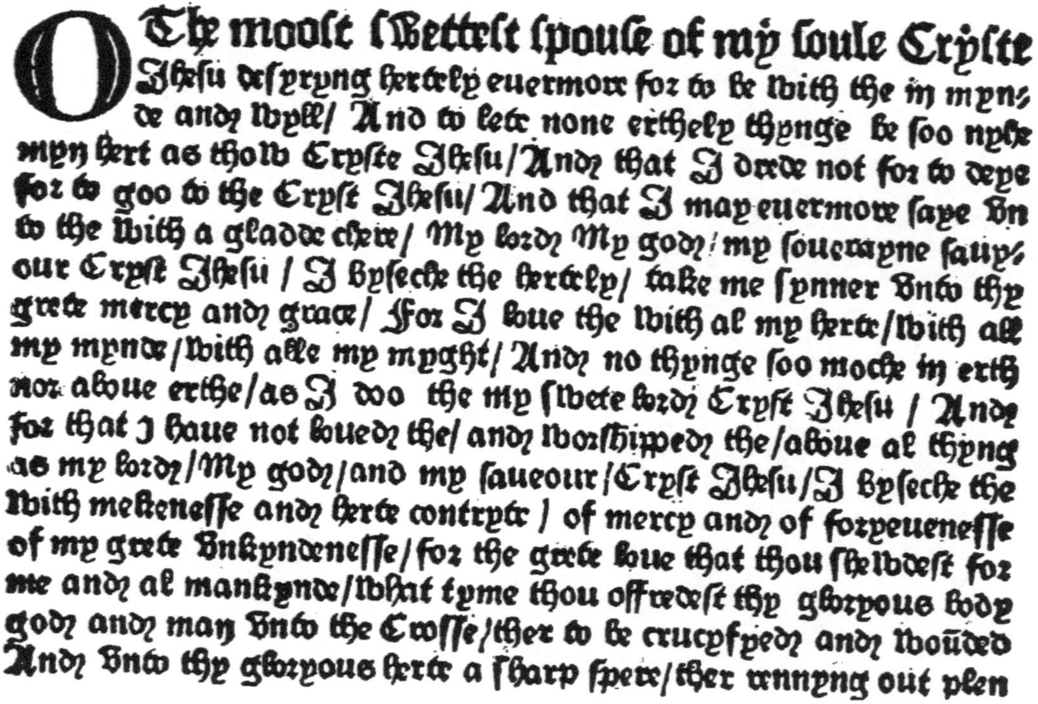

O The moost swettest spouse of my soule Cryste
Ihesu desyryng hertely euermore for to be with the in mynde and wyll/ And to lete none erthely thynge be soo nyhe
myn hert as thow Cryste Ihesu/ And that I drede not for to deye
for to goo to the Cryst Ihesu/ And that I may euermore saye vn
to the with a gladde chere/ My lord My god/ my souerayne sauy-
our Cryst Ihesu / I byseche the hertely/ take me synner vnto thy
grete mercy and grace/ For I loue the with al my herte/ with all
my mynde/ with alle my myght/ And no thynge soo moche in erth
nor aboue erthe/ as I doo the my swete lord Cryst Ihesu / And
for that I haue not loued the/ and worshipped the/ aboue al thyng
as my lord/ My god/ and my saueour/ Cryst Ihesu/ I byseche the
with mekenesse and herte contryte / of mercy and of forgeuenesse
of my grete vnkyndenesse/ for the grete loue that thou shewdest for
me and al mankynde/ what tyme thou offredest thy gloryous body
god and man vnto the Crosse/ ther to be crucyfyed and woũded
And vnto thy gloryous herte a sharp spere/ ther rennyng out plen

No. 57.—Death-bed Prayers. *A Folio Broadside.* (1484?)

Typographical Particulars.—Types No. 3 and 4* are used. The lines are spaced to an even length. It is half a sheet of paper printed on one side only.

From the language of these prayers it is evident that they were intended for use by the death-bed. They were probably printed in this portable form for priests, and others, to carry about with them.

Although short their interest is great, and the reader may not be displeased to read them in the following more modern dress than that of the original.

O glorious Jesu! O meekest Jehu! O most sweetest Jesu! I pray thee that I may have true confession, contrition, and satisfaction ere I die; and that I may see and receive thy holy body, God and man, Saviour of all mankind, Christ Jesu without sin. And that thou wilt my Lord God forgive me all my sins, for thy glorious wounds and passion. And that I may end my life in the true faith of all holy church, and in perfect love and charity with my even* Christians as thy creature. And I commend my soul into thy holy hands through the glorious help of thy blessed mother of mercy, our lady Saint Mary, and all the holy company of heaven. Amen. ¶ The holy body of Christ Jesu be my salvation of body and soul. Amen. The glorious blood of Christ Jesu bring my soul and body into the everlasting bliss. Amen. I cry God, mercy! I cry God, mercy! I cry God, mercy! Welcome my Maker! Welcome my Redeemer! Welcome my Saviour! I cry thee mercy with heart contrite of my great unkindness that I have had unto thee.

O thou most sweet spouse of my soul, Christ Jesu, desiring heartily evermore for to be with thee in mind and will, and to let none earthly thing be so nigh my heart as thou, Christ Jesu; and that I dread not for to die for to go to thee, Christ Jesu; and that I may evermore say unto thee with a glad cheer, my Lord, my God, my sovereign Saviour Christ Jesu,

* "Even" = "fellow." The gravedigger in *Hamlet*, act v, sc. 1, uses the same phrase "even Christian."

I beseech thee heartily take me, sinner, unto thy great mercy and grace, for I love thee with all my heart, with all my mind, with all my might, and nothing so much in earth nor above earth as I do thee, my sweet Lord, Christ Jesu. And for that I have not loved thee, and worshipped thee above all things as my Lord, my God, and my Saviour, Christ Jesu, I beseech thee with meekness and heart contrite, of mercy and of forgiveness of my great unkindness, for the great love that thou showedst for me and all mankind, what time thou offerdst thy glorious body, God and man, unto the Cross; there to be crucified and wounded, and unto thy glorious heart a sharp spear, there running out plenteously blood and water for the redemption and salvation of me and all mankind. And thus having remembrance steadfastly in my heart of thee, my Saviour Christ Jesu, I doubt not but thou wilt be full nigh me, and comfort me both bodily and ghostly with thy glorious presence, and at the last bring me unto thy everlasting bliss, the which shall never have end. Amen.

The only Existing Copy known is in the library of Earl Spencer, where it is bound up in a copy of Caxton's "Pilgrimage of the Soul." It is in perfect condition, and measures 11 × 8 inches.

No. 58.—The Fables of Æsop; of Avian; of Alfonse; and of Poge, the Florentine. *Folio.* "*Emprynted by me William Caxton at Westmynstre . . the xxvj daye of Marche the yere of oure lord M CCCC lxxxiiij.*"

Collation.—a b c d e f g h i k l m n o p q r s are 4os, the last two leaves of s being blank. In all 144 leaves, of which two are blank.

Note.—The first leaf of a is not signed, being printed only on the verso.

Typographical Particulars.—There is no title-page, unless we call the great cut of Æsop by that name. The type is of two sorts. No. 3 used in three places at the beginning of the work for headings, and No. 4*, in which is the whole text and the head-lines. The lines, which measure 4⅝ inches, are fully spaced out, and in those few pages where there is no woodcut there are 37 or 38 lines. There are head-lines and folios throughout, except in sig. n, which has folios only. Woodcut initials are used throughout, and on the verso of sig. a ij is a large floriated A, afterwards used in the "Order of Chivalry."

The first recto of sig. a is blank. Upon the verso is a large woodcut ($4\frac{5}{8} \times 6\frac{3}{4}$ inches), of Æsop, surrounded by the subjects of his fables, with the word ESOPVS at the top. On the second recto, which is signed a ij, the book commences with the following title, in large type, No. 3—

¶ Folio ijo

¶ Here begynneth the book of the subtyl hystoryes and Fables of Esope whiche were translated out of Frensshe in to Englysshe by wylliam Caxton at westmynstre In the yere of oure Lorde . M . . CCCC . lxxxiij .

First begynneth the lyf of Esope with alle his fortune how he was subtyll / wyse / and borne in Grece / not ferre fro Troye the graunt in a Towne named Amoneo / whiche was amonge other dyfformed and evylle shapen / For

The whole is finished by an epilogue, written by Caxton himself, which begins on the recto, and concludes on the verso of sig. s 6.

swere of a good preest and an honest / And here with I fynysshe this book / translated & emprynted by me William Cax=‖ton at westmynstre in thabbay / And fynysshed the xxvj daye ‖ of Marche the yere of oure lord M CCCC lxxxiiij / And the ‖ fyrst yere of the regne of kyng Rychard the thyrdde

The woodcuts by their treatment evidently came from the hands of the artist who had previously illustrated the "Game of Chess." It is perhaps impossible to decide whether they are of Flemish or English origin. The following represents Æsop beaten by his master.

Caxton himself tells us at the beginning of the book that

ÆSOP BEATEN BY HIS MASTER.

it was a translation of his own from the French. It is rather remarkable that although the fables of Æsop, in French, were found in all the great libraries of the fourteenth and fifteenth centuries, and as many as three or four different copies in some, yet none apparently have descended to our time. No trace of an English translation previous to that of Caxton has been discovered, and he must therefore have the credit of introducing these fables to his countrymen in the English tongue. They were reprinted in London, with scarcely any alteration, for nearly two centuries. Whether translated from a manuscript, or an early French printed edition, it is now impossible to say.

This is a very rare book, the only perfect copy known was devised by Mr. Hewett, of Ipswich, to King George III, and is now in the Royal Library, Windsor. Imperfect copies are in the British Museum and at Oxford.

No. 59.—The Order of Chivalry. *Quarto. Without Printer's Name, Place, or Date. Translated by Caxton and presented to Richard III.* (1483–5).

Collation.—a b c d e f are 4os, aj being blank; g a 2°, with the last leaf blank; in all 52 leaves, of which two are blank.

Typographical Particulars.—There is no title-page. The type is No, 4*, but two headings at the beginning of the work are in type No. 3. The lines, which measure 3⅛ inches, and of which there are 26 to a full page, are fully spaced out. Without folios or catchwords. Initial letters cut in wood are used.

Commencing with a blank leaf the work opens with a short preface, on sig. a ij, the first four lines being in type No. 3. The Text begins thus :—

¶ Here begynneth the Table of
this present booke Intytled the
Booke of the ordre of chyualry
or knyghthode

The Text ends:—

> vertuouse dede / And I shalle pray almy3=
> ty god for his long lyf & prosperous wel=
> fare / & that he may haue victory of al his
> enemyes / and after this short & transitory
> lyf to haue euerlastyng lyf in heuen / whe=
> re as is Joye and blysse world without
> ende Amen /

The date of printing, which was in the reign of Richard III, must have been between June 26th, 1483, and August 22nd, 1495. The "Order of Chivalry" has no connection with "L'ordene de chevalerie." Dibdin, in the *Typ. Ant.*, and Moule in *Bib. Herald*, both err in this matter.

Two copies are in the British Museum, and two in private libraries: no others are known.

No. 60.—Chaucer's Canterbury Tales. *Folio. Second Edition, with Woodcuts. "By Wylliam Caxton." Without Place or Date.* (1484?)

Collation.—a b c d e f g h i k l m n o p q r s t are 4ns, with a j blank; v a 3n; aa bb cc dd ee ff gg hh are 4ns; ii a 3n; A B C D E F G H I K are 4ns; L a 2n. In all 312 leaves, of which one is blank.

Typographical Particulars.—There is no title-page. The type of the Text is No. 4*, the heads being all in No. 2*. The lines in the prose portion are spaced to an even length, and measure $4\frac{5}{8}$ inches. 38 lines to a page. Without catch-words or folios, and almost without punctuation.

This second edition, Caxton tells us, was printed six years after the first. Having fixed the year 1477-8 as about the date of the first, that will give about 1484 for this.

Commencing with a blank leaf, the prohemye follows on a ij.

Prohemye

Rete thankes lawde and honour / ought to be gy=
uen vnto the clerkes / poetes / and historiographs
g that haue wreton many noble bokes of wysedom
of the lyues / passios / & myracles of holy sayntes
of hystoryes / of noble and famous Actes / and
faittes / And of the cronycles sith the begynnyng
of the creacion of the world / vnto thys present tyme / by whyche

The proheme, which is an excellent and indubitable specimen of Caxton's own composition, and reflects as much credit upon his disposition as upon his literary abilities, finishes on the verso of sig. a ij—

after thys short and transitorye lyf we may come to euer=
lastyng ‖ lyf in heuen / Amen
By Wylliam Caxton

On sig. a iij recto, with room for a 4-line initial,

Han that Apryll wyth hys shouris sote
w The droughte of marche hath percyd the rote
And bathyd euery veyne in suche lycour
Of whyche vertue engendryd is the flour
Whanne Zepherus eke wyth hys sote breth

The Parson's Tale finishes on sig. L iij verso, and is followed by the Retraction.

The Text ends with seven lines on sig. L 4 recto,

be one of hem at the day of dome that shal be sauyd / Qui
cum ‖ patre et spiritu sancto viuit et regnat deus / Per omnia
secula ‖ seculorum AMEN /

The verso is blank.

The wood-cut illustrations appear to be by the same artist that was engaged upon Æsop. The wife of Bath is represented thus:—

"THE WIFE OF BATH."
FROM THE SECOND EDITION OF CHAUCER'S "CANTERBURY TALES."

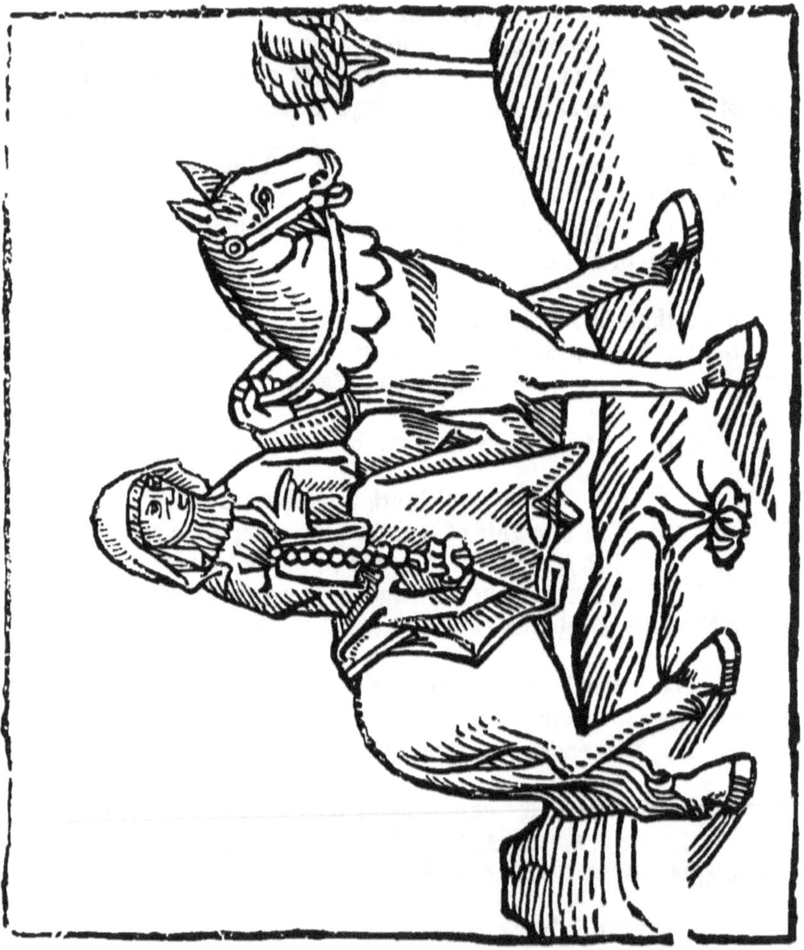

Two copies are in the British Museum, and one in each of the following libraries—Magdalen and Pepysian, Cambridge; St. John's, Oxford; Royal Society, London; Earl of Ashburnham, and Earl Spencer. In the year 1858 I discovered a copy in the Library of the French Protestant Church, in a torn and dirty state, having been used for some time to light the vestry fire. I drew attention to its great value and interest, and it was doubtless saved from further mutilation. Some time afterwards it disappeared from the library altogether, and no one now knows what has become of it. For identification the following particulars are here given:—it wants all before sig. h 5; p 7; t 8 and v ij; bb ij and dd 8; A j; B iij and 4; and all after E 8. In the original binding. Torn, dirty, and ill used. Measurement, 10⅝ × 7¾. Autograph "· · Rawlinson A° 1717." Also, "Ex dono · · · Bateman Bibliopola."

No. 61.—The Book of Fame. *Folio.* "*Emprynted by wylliam Caxton.*" *Without Place or Date.* (1484?)

Collation.—a b c are 4^{ns}, a j being blank; d a 3^{n}, d 6 being blank = 30 leaves, of which two are blank.

Typographical Particulars.—There is no title-page. The type is entirely No. 4*. In the epilogue, which is the only prose part, the lines are fully spaced out, and measure 4⅞ inches. 38 lines to a page. Without folios or catchwords. Space left for the insertion of 2 or 3-line initials, with directors.

Commencing with a blank leaf, the Text follows on sig. a ij recto,

The book of Fame made by Gefferey Chaucer

Od torne vs euery dreme to good
g For it is wonder thyng by the rood
To my wyt / what causyth sweuenys
On the morowe / or on euenys

The poem ends on sig. d 5 recto,

Thus in dremyng and in game
Endeth thys lytyl book of Fame

Explicit

The epilogue immediately follows, the Text ending,

I humbly beseche & praye yow / emonge your prayers / to remem=‖bre hys soule / on whyche / and on alle crysten soulis / I beseche al=‖myghty god to haue mercy Amen

Emprynted by wylliam Caxton

The epilogue has considerable interest, as showing Caxton's opinion of Chaucer, and is here given verbatim.

"J fynde nomore of this werke to fore sayd / For as fer as I can vnnderstōde / This noble man Gefferey Chaucer fynysshyd at the sayd conclusion of the metyng of lesyng and sothsawe / where as yet they ben chekked and maye not departe / whyche werke as me semeth is craftyly made / and dygne to be wreton & knowen / For he towchyth in it ryght grete wysdom & subtyll vnderstondyng / And so in alle hys werkys he excellyth in myn oppyny / on alle other wryters in in our Englyssh / For he wrytteth no voyde wordes / but alle hys mater is ful of hye and quycke sentence / to whom ought to be gyuen laude and preysyng for hys noble makyng and wrytyng / For of hym alle other haue borowed syth and taken / in alle theyr wel sayeing and wrytyng / And I humbly beseche & praye yow / emonge your prayers to remembre hys soule / on whyche and on alle crysten soulis I beseche almyghty god to haue mercy Amen"

As will be seen by the list of Existing Copies, the printed text of Caxton is almost as rare as manuscript; so is the reprint by Pynson in 1526. Manuscripts of this poem were, probably, even in our printer's time, difficult to obtain. The copy used by him was certainly very imperfect. Many lines are altogether omitted, and in the last page Caxton was evidently in a great strait, for his copy was deficient 66 lines, probably occupying one leaf in the original. We know from his own writings the great reverence in which our printer held the "noble poete," and we can imagine his consternation when the choice had to be made, either to follow his copy and print nonsense, from the break of idea caused by the deficient verses, or to step into Chaucer's shoes and supply the missing links from his own brain. He chose the latter course, and thus instead of the original 66 lines, we have two of the printer's own, which enable the reader to reach the end of the poem without a break down. These lines are in the following quotation printed in italics; the entire extract being the first six lines of the last page:—

> They were a chekked bothe two
> And neyther of hym myght out goo
> *And wyth the noyse of themwo* *Caxton*
> *J Sodeynly awoke anon tho*
> And remembryd what I had seen
> And how hye and ferre I had been

It should be noticed that Caxton has here placed his name in the margin to make known his responsibility to his readers. The "out" not having been hitherto noticed, the position of his name there has been a puzzle to the bibliographers, until explained by Mr. Bradshaw.

Copies are in the British Museum; Cambridge; Imperial Library, Vienna, and Althorpe.

No. 62.—The Curial. "*Translated thus in Englysshe by wylliam Caxton.*" *Without Printer's Name, Place, or Date.* (1484?)

Collation.—A 3^n, signed j, ij, and iij, without any blanks. In all six leaves.

Typographical Particulars.—There is no title-page. The type is entirely No. 4*. The lines, which are spaced to an even length, measure 4⅞ inches, and there are 38 to a full page. Without catchwords or folios.

The Text begins on sig. j recto,

Here foloweth the copye of a lettre whyche maistre Alayn ‖ Charetier wrote to hys brother / whyche desired to

come dwelle in ‖ Court / in whyche he reherseth many my-
seryes & wretchydnesses ‖

The "Curial" finishes on the sixth recto,

to god I comande the by thys wrytyng whyche gyue the hys
gra ‖ ce / Amen

Thus endeth the Curial made by maystre Alain
Charretier ‖ Translated thus in Englyssh by wylliam
Caxton

On the verso Caxton has given us his translation of a ballad, written by Alain Chartier, consisting of 28 lines. It has a burthen:—"Ne chyer but of a man Joyous," and commences thus:—

Ther ne is dangyer / but of a vylayn
Ne pryde / but of a poure man enryched

The Text ends on same page, with Caxton's name at foot,

Ther is no speche / but it be curtoys
Ne preysyng of men / but after theyr lyf
Ne chyer but of a man Joyous
Caxton

Remarks.—Caxton translated the Curial from the French, "for a noble and virtuous Erle" probably Lord Rivers, who was beheaded at Pomfret, on June 13th, 1483.

Alain Chartier, born in Normandy about 1386, earned for himself the appellation of "excellent orateur, noble poëte, et très-renommé rhétoricien." He held the office of "Secretaire de la Maison" to both Charles VI and Charles VII. He died about 1457. The most complete editions of his works are those by Galiot du Pré, 16mo, Paris, 1529; and by Duchesne, 4to, Paris, 1617. In the former, however, is an error which has led to some confusion, as "Livre de l'Esperance" is there entitled "Le Curial," the real Curial being a much shorter piece, and totally different in design. By the "Curial" being addressed to his brother it is supposed to have been written by Alain to Jean Chartier, known as the author of "Histoire de Charles VII." As an instance of the great repute, in which the writings of Chartier were held in his age, it is reported that Margaret, the wife of the Dauphin of France, afterwards Louis XI, finding him one day asleep in his chair, kissed his lips to the great astonishment of her attendants. "Je ne baise pas la personne mais la bouche dont estoient sortes tant de beux discours," she exclaimed. There is a painting in Add. M.S. 15300, vividly depicting this scene.

Of the only two known copies, one is in the British Museum, and the other at Althorpe.

No. 63.—TROYLUS AND CRESIDE. *Folio. Without Printer's Name, Place, or Date.* (1484?)

COLLATION.—a b c d e f g are 4ns, the first leaf of a being blank; h a 5n; i k l m n o are 4ns; p a 3n, with the last two leaves blank. In all 120 leaves, of which 3 are blank.

TYPOGRAPHICAL PARTICULARS.—There is no title-page. The type throughout is No. 4*. Each page contains five stanzas of seven lines each, with a blank line between each stanza. Without folios or catchwords.

Commencing with a blank leaf, the poem follows on sig. a ij recto, beginning thus:—

t He double sorow of Troylus to telle
Kyng Pryamus sone of Troye
In louyng / how hys auentures felle
From woo to wele / and after out of Joye
My purpos is / or that I parte froye

Book I ends on sig. b 8 verso; Book II on f j recto; Book III on h 10 recto; Book IV on m j recto; Book V on p 4 recto. On sig. p 4 recto is also Chaucer's dedicatory stanza to the "Moral Gower."

The Text ends on the same page,

So make vs Jhesu for thy mercy dygne
For loue of mayden / & moder thyn benygne
Here endeth Troylus / as touchyng Cresede
Explicit per Caxton

REMARKS.—A good account of the source of this poem, and a comparison between it and Shakspere's "Troilus and Creside," with which, however, it appears to have had little connection, will be found in Bell's edition of Chaucer's works.

Two copies are in the British Museum, one at St. John's, Oxford, and one at Althorp.

No. 64.—THE LIFE OF OUR LADY.—*Folio.* "*Emprynted by Wyllyam Caxton.*" *Without Place or Date.* (1484 ?)

COLLATION.—Two unsigned leaves; a b c d e f g h i k l are 4^{ns}; m a 3^{n}, the last leaf being blank. In all 96 leaves, of which one is blank.

TYPOGRAPHICAL PARTICULARS.—There is no title-page. The type is entirely No. 4*. A page has five stanzas of seven lines each, the space of one line being left between each stanza. The lines in the prose part measure almost 5 inches. Without catchwords or folios. Space left for the insertion of initials of one to three lines deep, with directors.

The Text begins, with a space for a 3-line initial, on the recto of the first leaf,

t Hhis book was compyled by dan John lydgate monke of burye / at the excitacion and styryng of the noble and victoryous prynce / Kyng harry the fyfthe / in thonoure glorye & reuerence of the byrthe of our moste blessyd lady / mayde ‖ wyf / and moder of our lord Jhesu cryst / chapytred as foloweth ‖ by this table

The table follows immediately, finishing with nine lines on the verso of the second leaf.

The poem commences on sig. a j recto, with space for a 2-line initial,

o Thougtful herte plungyd in distresse
With slo'bre of slouth this long wynters nyght

On the lower half of the fourth verso of sig. m,

Here endeth the book of the lyf of our lady
made by dan John lydgate monke of bury /
at thynstaunce of the moste crysten kynge /
kyng harry the fyfth

Goo lityl book and submytte the
Unto al them / that the shal rede
Or here / prayeng hem for charite
To pardon me of the rudehede
Of myn enpryntyng / not takyng hede
And yf ought be doon to theyr plesyng
Say they thyse balades folowyng

The Text ends on the fifth recto of sig. m, the whole page being as follows:—

Blessid be the swettest name of our lord
Jhesu crist / and most glorious marie
His blessyd moder / with eternal accord
More than euer / tendure in glorye
And with hir meke sone for memorye
Blesse vs marie / the most holy virgyne
That we regne in heuen with the ordres nyne

Enpryntyd by Wyllyam Caxton

"The Lyf of our Ladye" appears to have enjoyed, for a long period, a considerable popularity. It was composed, as the mauuscripts and printed edition both tell us, by John Lydgate, at the excitation of King Henry V. The envoy commencing, "Goo lytyl booke," is doubtless a specimen of Caxton's own powers of versification, as perhaps are also the two ballads which follow it. Although the division of the poem into chapters by Caxton does not agree with any of the above manuscripts, yet he probably had a copy so divided, for, as we have seen, the original poem was not chaptered at all, and later scribes would divide it after their own judgment.

It would have surprised our worthy printer could he have foreseen the grave charges of carelessness to be brought against him in future ages, with reference to this production. Ames gives a very slight account of "The Lyf of oure Ladye," but so far as it goes, it is correct. Herbert enlarged Ames's article, but unfortunately wrote his description from a copy deficient eight leaves in the middle of the poem, an imperfection which, notwithstanding the consequent irregularity of signature, he ascribes to carelessness on the part of Caxton; and, worse still, makes Caxton himself confess that he was aware of the blunder he had made before the conclusion of the printing, but thought that to ask the reader's pardon was sufficient reparation; a conclusion drawn from the deprecatory stanzas quoted above, beginning, "Goo lityl book"—a style of "envoy" very common to all Writers of that age. Then follows Dr. Dibdin, who, as usual, did not make an independent examination, but was content with reprinting his predecessor's remarks. The paragraph reads thus:—"This [the omission of several chapters] must be attributed to carelessness, which Mr. Caxton himself ingenuously acknowledges in one of the concluding stanzas.—*Typ. Ant.* vol. i, page 340, and *Bib. Spenc.* vol. iv, page 333.

Both Herbert and Dibdin give the heads of all the chapters in this poem, excepting, of course, those contained in the eight missing leaves of their copy. These are, therefore, supplied here from the table, which differs slightly from the heads in the body of the work.

How the chyef temple of rome fyl the nyght of crystes
byrthe / and other wonderful tokenes capitulo L
How the nyght of cristes byrthe a welle in rome
ranne oyle capitulo Lj
How the senatours of rome wolden haue holden Octauyan
theyr emperour as for her god capitulo Lij Liij
How the romayns whan they had domynacion ouer alle
the world made an ymage & callyd hit theyr god capitulo Liiij
How wyse sybyle tolde to the senate of rome
the byrthe of cryst capitulo Lv
How the prophetes prophecyed the byrthe
of cryst capitulo Lvi
A questyon assoyled whiche is worthyest of kyng
wyne or woman capitulo Lvij

Existing Copies:—British Museum, Bodleian, Exeter College, Oxford, Glasgow, and four in private hands.

No. 65.—THE LIFE OF THE HOLY AND BLESSED VIRGIN SAINT WINIFRED. *Folio. Without Printer's Name, Date or Place. "Reduced in to Englysshe by me William Caxton."* (1485?)

COLLATION.—a and b are 4[ms] = 16 leaves, of which the first is blank.

TYPOGRAPHICAL PARTICULARS.—There is no title-page. The type is entirely No. 4*. There are 38 or 39 lines to a full page, and they are spaced to an even length. Without folios or catchwords.

Commencing with a blank leaf, the Text follows on sig. a ij,

¶ Here begynneth the lyf of the holy & blessid vyrgyn saynt || Wenefryde /

On sig. b 6 recto,

¶ Thus endeth the decollacion / the lyf after / and the transla= || cion of saynte Wenefrede virgyn and martir / whiche was rey || sed after that her hede had be smyton of the space of xv yere || reduced in to Englysshe by me William Caxton /

The Text ends, with ten lines on the recto of sig. b 8, the verso being blank,

celebramus translacionem / cunctorum adipisci mereamur pec= || catorum remissionem / Per dominum nostrum / et cetera /

REMARKS.—Caxton's translation gives all the particulars of the birth, parentage, dedication to God, decollation by Prince Caradoc, restoration to life "after her head had been smyton off the space of xv year," and subsequent canonisation of St. Winifred; followed by the service in Latin for her "commemoration."

The earliest existing notice of this saint is found in Cotton MS. Claud. A. v, which begins "Incipit Vita sancte Wenefrede virginis et martyris." The character of the writing is of the twelfth century, but the Holy Well in Flintshire, dedicated to her as well as the existence of chapels and other places in

Wales bearing her name, prove her fame to have been spread for some centuries earlier. The Cotton MS. itself was probably copied from a much older original. Historians have therefore agreed to consider her as having lived in the seventh century. Being a Welsh saint, her name does not at first seem to have been received with any great veneration outside her own country, and this may account for the entire absence of all notice of her in the early historians. The Cotton MS. has a memorandum in a more modern hand, stating it to be the composition of St. Elerius. For this, however, there appears to be no other reason than the mention of this saint as St. Winifred's confessor. It has, however, been adopted by Leland, Bale, Pits, and other writers. A second life of St. Winifred was undertaken in the year 1140 by Robert, a Welsh monk of Shrewsbury, who compiled his account from MSS. then extant, with the addition of all the floating details which, in the course of centuries, the legend had developed. The fame of the saint at that time was rapidly increasing, partly owing to the grand ceremonial with which her relics had been, in 1138, translated to the Benedictine Abbey in Shrewsbury. The variation in these two accounts, especially as to the length of time she lived after her decollation, has induced a belief that they are independent productions. Had the second history been shorter and less miraculous than the first, there might be some reason for the opinion.

In "Liber Festivalis," and in the "Golden Legend," both printed by Caxton, are short notices of St. Winifred; but in 1484 Caxton himself set about "reducing into English" her Life. It is unfortunate that he makes no mention of the language in which his original was written. There is no reason to suppose that Caxton understood Welsh, or else doubtless he could have obtained several MSS.* Again, it is very improbable that Caxton translated from his usual source, the French, as the saint was unknown across the Channel. It is therefore most probable that the Latin account of Robert, already noticed, was Caxton's original, a probability we are

* Llwydh, in his Catalogue of Welsh MSS., mentions two.

not able to verify by collation, as no manuscript appears to be known.

Caxton's edition has the Latin commemoration of the saint at the end, which was ordained with great ceremony by Arundel, Archbishop of Canterbury, in 1391, who, at the same time, removed the day from June 24th to November 3rd. This shows how the fame of St. Winifred had increased. All the old legends state that on the spot where Prince Caradoc decapitated the Virgin, there immediately sprung up an impetuous stream of healing water. The famous Holy Well is on this spot, and thence flows "St. Wenefrede's Stream," which empties itself at the mouth of the Dee. The fame of wonderful cures effected by these waters spread all over England, and greatly enhanced the shrine of St. Winifred. Holywell became the most favoured goal of pilgrims to the north. Caxton could not perhaps have chosen a more popular life when he undertook his translation. Henry VII built an octagonal well over the source of the stream, with conveniences for using the waters, and over this a beautiful chapel.

The shrine was plundered at the dissolution of the monasteries, and a portion of the ruins was, in 1811, and is proprobably still used as a free grammar school.

In Caxton's "Polycronicon," in the metrical account of Wales, there are twenty-two lines of curious matter concerning the Holy Well, and the awful fate which befel the descendants of Prince Caradoc.

Only three copies of this edition are known. There is a fair specimen in the King's Library, British Museum, a poor one at Lambeth, and a good one at Ham House, Surrey.

No. 66.—The noble Histories of King Arthur and of certain of his Knights. *Folio.* "*Emprynted in thabbey of westmestre, the last day of Juyl the yere of our lord M CCCC lxxxv.*"

Collation.—The prologue and table take up a 4^{n} and 5^{n}; the first leaf in the 4^{n} is blank, the next 3 are signed ij, iij, iiij; the first four leaves only of the 5ⁿ are signed b, bj, bij, biij; a b c d e f g h i k l m n o p q r s t u x y z & A B C D E F G H I K L M N O P Q R S T U X Y Z aa bb cc dd are 4ⁿˢ; ee is a 3ⁿ. In all 432 leaves, of which one is blank.

Note.—Sig. S iij is printed R iij, and T ij is printed S ij.

Typographical Particulars.—There is no title-page. The type throughout is No. 4*. The lines are spaced out to an even length of 4⅝ inches, and 38 make a full page. Without folios, head-lines, or catchwords. Initials in wood of three to five lines in depth.

Commencing with a blank leaf, Caxton's prologue follows on sig. ij, with a 3-line initial in wood. The Text begins thus:—

AFter that I had accomplysshed and fynysshed dyuers hystoryes as wel of contemplacyon as of other hysto ryal and worldly actes of grete conquerours & pryn ces / and also certeyn bookes of ensaumples and doctryne /

The Text ends on the recto of the sixth leaf of sig. ee, the verso being blank.

¶ Thus endeth thys noble and Joyous book entytled le morte ‖ Darthur / Notwythstondyng it treateth of the byrth / lyf / and ‖ actes of the sayd kyng Arthur / of his noble knyghtes of the ‖ rounde table / theyr meruayllous enquestes and aduentures / ‖ thachyeuyng of the sangreal / & in thende the dolorous deth & ‖ departyng out of thys world of them al / whiche book was re ‖ duced in to englysshe by syr Thomas Malory knyght as afore ‖ is sayd / and by me deuyded in to xxj bookes chapytred and enprynted / and fynysshed in thabbey westmestre the last day ‖ of Juyl the yere of our lord / M / CCCC / lxxxv /

¶ Caxton me fieri fecit

Remarks.—There does not appear to be any trace in the collections of the British Museum, or elsewhere, of a manuscript of Sir Thomas Malory's text. Of Sir Thomas himself, all we know is contained in the last sentence of his own book: "This book was ended the ninth year of the reign of King Edward the fourth by Sir Thomas Malory, Knight;" that is about 1470. Caxton tells us in his prologue, that Sir Thomas had "reduced it from certain books in French." These books, judging from the conduct of the story, were the celebrated romances of Merlin, Launcelot, Tristram, the Quest du S. Graal, and Mort Artus, on the origin of which romances very little appears to be known, though much has been written. Manuscript copies of all of them are in the British Museum. Caxton's edition was reprinted several times, the last being the well-known 4to. volume, edited by Robert Southey, who has prefixed a learned dissertation on the rise and development of the story. A very interesting essay upon the character, epoch, and authors of the various romances of the Round Table is contained in *Les Msc. Franç.*, par M. Paris, vol. i, page 160. See also the introduction of Thomas Wright to his reprint of the 1634 edition, entitled *The History of King Arthur*, 3 vols. London, 1858. Also *Les Romans de la Table Ronde et les Contes des anciens Bretons*, par M. le Vicomte Hersart de la Villemarqué. 8vo. Paris, 1860.

The only perfect copy known is in the library of Earl of Jersey; Earl Spencer has a copy, and a fragment is in the British Museum. There is not a copy at Lichfield, as stated by Mr. Botfield.

No. 67.—The Life of the noble and Christian Prince, Charles the Great. *Folio.* "*Explicit per William Caxton.*" *Without Place.* "*Enprynted the fyrst day of decembre / M CCCC lxxxv.*"

Collation.—a b c d e f g h i k l m are 4os. In all 96 leaves, of which a j and m 8 appear to have been blank. The last leaf, however, may have had the device.

Typographical Particulars.—There is no title-page. The type is all No. 4*. The pages have two columns, with 39 lines to a column. The lines, which are spaced to one length, measure 2⅝ inches. Without folios or catchwords. Woodcut initials three lines deep.

Commencing with a blank leaf, the prologue of the French translator follows, on sig a ij, with a 3-line printed initial. The Text begins thus :—

Saynt Poul doctour of veryte sayth to vs that al thynges that ben reduced by wrytyng / ben wryton ‖ somme werkes haultayne doon ‖ & compsed by their grete strength ‖ & ryght ardaunt courage / to the ‖ exaltacyon of the crysten fayth

* * * * * * * * * *

This preface finishes with five lines down the first column of the verso, and is followed by Caxton's prologue, in the same column, which is finished on the 26th line of the opposite column.

Thenne / for as moche I late had fynysshed in enpryntyе the book of the noble & ‖ vyctoryous kyng Arthur fyrst ‖

The Text ends with the following colophon,

Whyche werke was fynysshed ‖ in the reducyng of hit in to en ‖ glysshe the xviij day of Juyn the ‖ second yere of kyng Rychard ‖ the thyrd / And the yere of our ‖ lord M CCCC lxxxv / And ‖ enprynted the fyrst day of de= ‖ cembre the same yere of our lord ‖ & the fyrst yere of kyng Harry ‖ the seuenth /‖

¶ Explicit p william Caxton

Remarks.—Histories and romances of "Karlemaine," in French and in Latin, in prose and in verse, existed so early as the twelfth and thirteenth centuries. These became incorporated later in the general histories, such as the "Speculum Historiale," the "Fleur des Histoires," &c. The compilation of the romance under notice is recounted by the anonymous Author himself in his preface and envoye. From these we learn that Henry Bolomyer, Canon of Lausaune, regretting the existence of several "disjoined" accounts of Charles the Great, "excited" our anonymous Author to compile a continuous history of the first Christian King of France. This he did, and the sources of his narration, as well as the contents, cannot be described better than in his own words, thus translated by Caxton (sig. m, 7 recto), "it is so that at the requeste of the sayd venerable man to fore named Maister henry bolonnyer chanonne of lausaune J haue been Incyted to translate & reduce into Frensshe the mater tofore reduced. As moche as toucheth the fyrst & the thyrd book / J haue taken & drawen oute of a book named myrrour hystoryal for the moost parte / & the second book J haue onely reduced it out of an olde romaũce in frensshe."

On comparing the first and last books of the text under notice with the chapters devoted to Charlemagne, in Verard's edition of the *Speculum Historiale* (vol. iv, book 25), it is evident that the compiler did not confine himself to the account of Vincent de Beauvais. The Second Book, he tells us, was taken from an old romance in French; perhaps the same as is still extant in *Royal MS.* 4 C. XI. 10, or the manuscript in the Imperial Library, Paris, No. 6795.

It is the French compilation of Henry Bolomyer which Caxton was requested by "some persons of noble estate and degree"—"my good singular lords and special masters" as he calls them—to reduce into English. Among these his good friend Master William Daubeny, treasurer of the king's jewels, who is the only one mentioned by name, seems to have most influenced him.

The only EXISTING COPY at present known is in the British Museum, King's Library (C. 10. b. 9). It is *perfect*, and in excellent preservation. Measurement, 10¾ × 7¾ inches.

No. 68.—THE KNIGHT PARIS AND THE FAIR VIENNE. *Folio.* "*Explicit per Caxton. Westminster. December* 19*th*, 1485."

COLLATION.—a b c are 4^ns, d and e 3^ns = 36 leaves, of which the last only is blank.

Note.—d j is misprinted c i.

TYPOGRAPICAL PARTICULARS.—There is no title-page. The type is all No. 4*; in double column, the lines being spaced to an even length, and measuring $2\frac{3}{8}$ inches; 39 lines to a column. Without folios or catchwords. Woodcut initials.

The Text begins on sig. a j recto,

¶ Here begynneth thystorye of ‖ the noble ryght valyaunt & wor= ‖ thy knyght Parys / and of the ‖ fayr Vyene / the daulphyns dou= ‖ ghter of vyennoys / the whyche ‖ suffred many aduersytees by= ‖ cause of theyr true loue or they ‖ coude enioye the effect therof of ‖ eche other / may or ought to haue / The sayd ‖ daulphyn thenne and this noble ‖ lady dyane were viij yere to gy= ‖ dre wythoute yssue that moche ‖ they de= syred to haue / and prayed ‖ our lord bothe nyght & day that ‖ they myght haue chyl= dren play ‖ saunt and redy to hys deuyne ‖ seruyce / and our lord thorugh ‖

The Text ends thus, on sig. e 5 recto, with sixteen lines in the first column,

may accompanye them in the per ‖ durable glorye of heuen Amen /

¶ Thus endeth thystorye of the ‖ noble and valyaunt knyght pa= ‖ rys / and the fayr vyenne dough ‖ ter of the doulphyn of Vyen= ‖ noys / translated out of frensshe ‖ in to englysshe by wylliam Cax= ‖ ton at westmestre fynysshed the ‖ last day of

August the yere of ‖ our lord M CCCC lxxxv / and ‖ enprynted the xix day of decem= ‖ bre the same yere / and the fyrst ‖ yere of the regne of kyng Harry ‖ the seuenth /

¶ Explicit p Caxton

REMARKS.—Although frequently copied in manuscript, and often printed in the fifteenth and sixteenth centuries, there are few romances so rare as "Paris and Vienne." Translated into the "langage provençal," from the original composition, which was in "Catalane," it was turned into Latin, French, Italian, Flemish, and English. The French, which was the translation Caxton used, was accomplished about the beginning of the fifteenth century, by Pierre de la Sippade, of Marseilles. The first printed edition was in Italian, at Trévise, 1482; the second, Caxton's, 1485. G. Leeu, at Antwerp, 1487, brought out two impressions, one in German and one in French. Wynken de Worde made an early reprint of Caxton's edition. The admiration which Jean de Pins, Bishop of Rieux, one of the most elegant scholars of his age, conceived for this romance, induced him to turn it into Latin, for the instruction of the children of his friend the Chancellor Duprat. It was printed in 1516. The Jesuit Charron, in his Memoirs of Jean de Pins (*Avignon*, 8vo, 1748), speaks thus of this romance: "As for children, it would be impossible to find a work more fitted to imbue the mind with correct taste and elegance of style, to influence their characters by the wisdom of its reflections, or to forearm their hearts against those assaults of passion which blindly precipitate the young into the abysses of misery. The work is truly admirable. The situations are so interesting and the *dénoûment* so happy, that their conception would reflect honour on the best writers of the most renowned ages." (See *Histoire du Chevalier Paris, et de la belle Vienne*, 8vo, Paris, 1835).

The only EXISTING COPY is in the British Museum. It

was formerly in Ames's possession, but after the issue of "The Typographical Antiquities," passed into the library of Sir Hans Sloane, and thence into the King's Library, St. James's.

No. 69.—The Golden Legend. *Largest Folio. Second Edition. Small Head-lines.* (1487?)

Collation.—The same exactly as the first edition, with the exception of sigs. X and Y, in which appears the following variation:—

FIRST EDITION.		SECOND EDITION.
sig. X, 6 leaves	= 9 leaves	sig. X = 8 leaves.
sig. Y, 2 „		signed to X iiij, and followed
unsigned 1 „		by sig. aa.

In order to get the matter of the two signatures into one, the sixteen pages of X in the second edition are all made a line longer than in the first. This arrangement was evidently considered as an improvement, and therefore was later in point of time than the edition in which it does not occur.

Typographical Particulars.—These in the main are identical with the edition already described, the chief peculiarity being that the head-lines of the pages and the head-lines of the various lives, which in the first edition are all in type No. 3, are in the second edition all in type No. 5. We must also notice that in places (*e.g.* sig. X j recto) the large capital letters, used in type No. 6, make an accidental appearance in the head-lines, where they were occasionally used instead of quadrats. This evinces a much later period for the impression than the first edition.

Remarks.—The absence of any complete copy, or indeed of any copy having prologues or colophon, suggests the idea that certain sheets only may, for some reason, have been reprinted to supply deficiencies; if so, the reprint is so extensive, that, for the sake of accuracy, it is better to look upon it as a separate edition.

Existing Copies.—British Museum, Cambridge, Oxford, Duke of Devonshire.

A

DESCRIPTION OF BOOKS PRINTED

IN

TYPE No. 5.

BOOKS PRINTED IN TYPE No. 5.

70. Good Manners	May 11th, 1487
71. Speculum. First Edition	1487 ?
72. Directorium. First Edition	1487 ?
73. Horæ. Third Edition	1488 ?
74. Royal	1488 ?
75. Image of Pity	1489 ?
76. Doctrinal	May 7th, 1489 ?
77. Speculum. Second Edition	1490 ?
78. Commemoratio	1491 ?
79. Transfiguratione	1491 ?
80. Horæ	1491 ?

Plate XII.

Caxton's Type, No. 5.

¶ Fynysshed and translated out of frensshe in to englysshe the viij day of Juyn the yere of our lord M iiij C lxxxvj / and the first yere of the regne of kyng harry the vij / And enprynted the xj day of Maye after / etc.

Laus Deo

¶ Thus endeth the doctrinal of sapyence the whyche is ryght vtile and proufytable to alle crysten men / whyche is translated out of Frensshe in to englysshe by wyllyam Caxton at westmester fynysshed the . vij . day of may the yere of our lord / M / cccc lxxx ix

Caxton me fieri fecit

No. 70.—THE BOOK OF GOOD MANNERS. *Folio.* "*Explicit et hic est finis per Caxton.*" *Without Place.* "*Enprynted the xj day of Maye*" *the year of our Lord* 1487.

COLLATION.—a b c d e f g are 4os; h a 5° = 66 leaves (no blanks).

TYPOGRAPHICAL PARTICULARS.—There is no title-page. The type throughout is No. 5. The lines are spaced to an even length, and measure 4⅝ inches. A page has 33 lines. Without catchwords or folios. Woodcut initials of two to three lines in depth.

The Text begins on sig. a j recto,

WHan I consydere the condycions & maners of the comyn ‖ people whiche without enformacion & lernyng ben rude ‖ and not manerd lyke vnto beestis brute acordyng to an olde ‖

making a full page. On the verso, with 2-line wood initial,

HEre begynneth the table of a book named & Intytuled the ‖ book of good maners the which was made & composed ‖ by the venerable & dyscrete persone Frere Jaques le graunt ly ‖ cencyat in Theologye relygyous of the ordre of saynt augustyn ‖ of the conuent of parys .

and ends on tenth recto of sig. h, the verso blank,

¶ Explicit / et hic est finis / per Caxton &c

¶ Fynysshed and translated out of frensshe in to englysshe the ‖ viij day of Juyn the yere of our lord M iiij C lxxxvj / and ‖ the first yere of the regne of kyng harry the vij / And enpryn= ‖ ted the xj day of Maye after / &c

Laus deo

Jacques Legrand was an Augustin friar, and is stated by several writers (though upon what authority does not appear) to have been a native of Toledo, in Spain, confessor to Charles VII, and to have refused a bishopric. He is known to have been the author of the "Sophologium," originally written in Latin, and translated by himself into French for the Duke of Orleans, son of Charles V. He also was the author of "Le livre des bonnes meurs," which he dedicated to the Duke de Berri.

In an interesting prologue appended by Caxton to his English translation of this work (see Vol. I, page 186), we are informed that he undertook the task at the desire of William Praat, a fellow mercer. The terms in which Caxton speaks of Praat as "an honest man" and "a singular friend of old knowledge," whose death-bed request it was that the book which had pleased and instructed his own mind should have greater currency among the people by means of his friend's new Art of Printing, prove the close amity which must have existed between the two Mercers. Caxton, according to his friend's wish, translated and printed it "for the amendment of manners and the increase of virtuous living."

Only three copies are known—one at Cambridge, one at the Royal Library, Copenhagen, and one at Lambeth.

No. 71.—SPECULUM VITÆ CHRISTI. *Folio. "Emprynted by wyllyam Caxton." Without Place or Date. Edition A.* (1487?)

COLLATION.—**a b c d e f g h i k l m n o p q r s** are 4^{ns}, with the first leaf of sig. **a** blank; **t** a 2^{n}, with the fourth leaf blank. In all 148 leaves, of which two are blank.

TYPOGRAPHICAL PARTICULARS.—Without title-page. The type throughout is No. 5. The lines are spaced to an even length, and measure 4⅝ inches. A page has 33 lines, exclusive of the head lines, and one line space between. Without folios or catchwords. There are side notes throughout the volume, a rare practice with Caxton, who, however, probably followed his copy in this particular, as side notes appear in nearly all the manuscript versions. An initial, cut on wood, begins every chapter.

Commencing with a blank leaf, the Text begins thus on sig. a ij recto:—

¶ Incipit Speculum vite Cristi .

AT the begynnynge of the prohemy of the booke that is cleped the myrroure of the blessyd lyf of Jhesu Cryste the fyrst parte for the monedaye / ¶ A deuoute medy= tacion of the grete counceyll in heuene for the restorynge of man ‖ and hys sauacyon . Capitulum primum . ¶ Of the manere

At the head of sig. b ij recto,

Die lune ¶ Prima pars ca j .

dome all the Courte of heune wondrynge and commendyng the soueraygne wysedome assented wel here to / but ferther= more ‖

At the head of sig. f 6 verso,

¶ Ca / xv ¶ Die Mercurij ¶ Tercia pars

parauentur there with a fewe smal fysshes that oure lady had ‖ ordeyned theme as god wold / & soo therwith the Aungels co= ‖

The "Speculum" ends at foot of sig. s i recto,

lord ihesu and his moder Mary now and euer withoute ende ame

¶ Explicit speculum vite Cristi .

On the verso begins a treatise on the Sacrament of Christ's body,

¶ A shorte treatyce of the hyhest and most worthy sacra= mente ‖ of crystes blessid body . and the merueylles therof .

which finishes on sig. t 3 recto with the following imprint:—

There appear to have been two, if not more, original works on the "Life of Christ" in the libraries of the fifteenth century. One by Father Ludolphe, or Rudolphe (*Addit.* 16609), was translated, as already noticed, into French, and thence into English; but this is an entirely different work to that printed by Caxton. St. Bonaventure, in 1410, wrote "The Life of Christ" in Latin (*Royal* 17, D. XVII), which became very popular, and was translated several times into French, with amplifications more or less. In the early part of the fifteenth century Jean de Gallopes, already noticed as the translator of "The Pilgrimage of the Soul" (*ante* page 259), made a French prose translation of Bonaventure's Latin work (*Royal* 20, B. IV). This bears a close resemblance to the English text as printed by Caxton, was dedicated by Gallopes to Henry V, and probably had considerable currency among the English, to whom Gallopes, if not an Englishman himself, was well known from his connection with the Duke of Bedford. The author of Caxton's English text is unknown, but he professes to have borrowed largely from the Latin of Bonaventure.

Of the "Speculum vitæ Christi" two distinct editions were issued, both printed with the same types, page for page, line for line (with few exceptions), and nearly letter for letter. The typographical minutiæ do not enable us with facility to determine which edition has the better claim to priority of workmanship. The greatest variations will be found in the head-lines, where, from sig. k to the end of the volume, there is a difference in every page; one edition (A) using the word **Ca** in the heads, while the other (B) has the full word **Capi-tulum.** In the University Library, Cambridge, there is a copy of each edition.

There is a curious transposition of pages in the copy belonging to W. E. Watkyn Wynne, Esq., proving that even so late as 1489, the practice of printing one page at a time was retained. This is shown by the verso of sig. e iiij being printed on the recto of sig. e 6, and *vice versâ*. In sig. e there are several instances of the side notes having been blocked out in the printing. Pressmen call it "a bite."

EXISTING COPIES.—British Museum (2); Cambridge (2); Hunterian Museum, Glasgow; Lambeth, and six in private libraries. One of the copies in the British Museum is on vellum, and has quite a romantic history.

No. 72.—DIRECTORIUM SACERDOTUM, UNA CUM DEFENSORIO EJUSDEM; ITEM TRACTATUS QUI DICITUR CREDE MIHI. *Folio. Second Version, First Edition. Per William Caxton apud westmonesteriu. Without Date.* (1487?)

COLLATION.—Kalendar a 3^{n}, signed j ij iij; a b c d e f g h i k l m n o p q are 4^{ns}; r a 5^{n}; s t are 4^{ns}. In all 160 leaves. In the only copy known the whole of the kalendar is inserted between the first and second leaves of sig. a, making a j appear as the first leaf in the book.

Note.—The signature to e j is not printed.

TYPOGRAPHICAL PARTICULARS.—Without title-page. The type is all No. 5. The lines, which are fully spaced out, measure 4⅝ inches. Exclusive of head-lines there are 33 to the page. Without folios or catchwords. A few 2-line woodcut initials.

The work commences with a kalendar of the months, a month to a page, each being headed by a Latin couplet on unlucky days, and a woodcut KL.

The Text begins on sig. j recto,

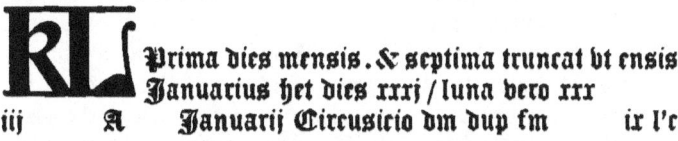

KL Prima dies mensis . & septima truncat vt ensis
Januarius het dies xxxj / luna vero xxx
iij A Januarij Circusicio dm dup fm ix l'c

The Text ends on sig. t 8 verso,

de michi / Na qui predcas regulas memoriter tenet vir poterit errare in seruicio diuino / Deo gras /

¶ Caxton me fieri fecit

The engraving, which is really on sig. a j verso, is here transposed, very naturally, to precede the Kalendar, which at first misleads one to believe that it does not belong to the volume. It measures 9 × 5¾ inches, and occupies the entire page, being thus described by Herbert—"In the middle part Christ is seen naked, half length, as at a window, with his arms across and his head inclined, showing the wounds on his hands and under the right breast; a spear erect on the right and a sponge on the left; over his head is a tablet with INRI. On a tablet beneath the window the title appears evidently to have been printed, but from this copy has been indiscreetly cut out. About this middle part are 28 square divisions, each containing some symbol of the passion, forming a kind of border." An engraving similar in design was used for the "Horæ," described at page 318 *post*.

There was another edition of this work printed in 1489 (see page 341), but the present edition, from the type being earlier, and from the absence of the almanac at the beginning, appears to have been the first. In both the Latin is printed with many contractions. In the various editions of "Typographical Antiquities," the two editions being treated as one has led to several errors.

The numerous and constantly varying alterations in the daily order of Church Service must have rendered, in all ages, a book of directions most necessary to all officiating priests. But the introduction of new Feasts and Commemorations would, in course of time, render any such book incorrect. Thus it happened that Clement Maydestone, a monk of the order of St. Bridget, and a priest, finding, as he tells us in his prologue, that one of the most important festivals in the year, that of Corpus Christi, with its Octave, was, according to the written directions, celebrated *cum regimine chori*, while the admitted and general custom of the Salisbury rule was to celebrate that festival *sine regimine chori;* finding also several necessary things omitted altogether, and a wrong disposition made of others, determined, by the consent of his superiors, to correct and supply all defects. When Clement Maydestone had thus reformed and renewed the Pica, he gave his work the now recognised title of "Directorium Sacerdotum." This is the text as printed by Caxton.

Clement Maydestone appears to have been the son of Thomas Maydestone (probably of Hounslow, Middlesex), and flourished in the reign of Henry V. An account of the martyrdom of Archbishop Scroop is also ascribed to him.

In the latter half of the fifteenth century the reformed Pica of Maydestone was again collated with the true "Sarum Ordinale," by one Clarke, a singing man of King's College, Cambridge, by order of the University, which at this period evidently followed the Salisbury use. A notice of Clarke's work may be seen in the prologue appended by Pynson to his "Directorium" of 1497. In the copy of this edition, lately purchased of Mr. Maskell for the British Museum, are numerous notes in the autograph of Bishop Wagstaffe, the nonjuror, which have supplied material for some of the above remarks.

The only EXISTING COPY at present known is that in the King's Library, British Museum (C. 10. b. 16), which is *perfect*, in fair condition, and measures $10\frac{1}{2} \times 7\frac{1}{2}$ inches. On a fly-leaf is the autograph "W. Bayntun, Gray's Inn, bought of a man introduced by Doctor Nugent." This copy, which is catalogued by Dr. Middleton as being in the University Library, Cambridge, was stolen thence between 1772 and 1778. Before 1787 it was purchased by W. Bayntun—and probably (though, of course, in ignorance) from the thief himself.

No. 73.—HORÆ—A FRAGMENT. *Third Edition.* *8vo.* *Sine ullâ notâ.* (1488?)

The COLLATION cannot be given, eight leaves, or the whole of sig. m being all that is known at present.

TYPOGRAPHICAL PARTICULARS.—The type is No. 5 only. The lines, of which there are seventeen to the page, are fully spaced out and in length measure $2\frac{5}{8}$ inches. Large full-faced capital letters are used.

On sig. m j recto the Text begins,

Non fecisti

The first words on the recto of each leaf is—1, **non**; 2, **perhanc**; 3, **habitabile**; 4, **A Doro**; 5 (injured); 6, woodcut; 7, **Domine**; 8, **siones**; the last word on the eighth verso, **cospui**.

The woodcut on **m** 6 recto is an "Image of Pity," very similar in treatment to that noticed on page 316. It occupies only the depth of ten lines of text, and beneath, in six lines, is the following:—

To them that before * * * * yma
ge ofpyte deuoutly sey . v . P'r
noster / v . Aues & a * * * * py=
teously beholdyng * * * * * * of
Xp's passyon ar graunted * * * *
M / vij . C & . lv / yeres of pardon

These unique leaves, which have evidently been rescued from the binding of an old book, were presented, in 1858, by Mr. Maskell to the British Museum (C. 35. a). Measurement $5\frac{1}{4} \times 4$ inches. They are in the same binding as the fragments of another Horæ described at p. 328.

No. 74.—The Royal Book or Book for a King. *Folio. Without Printer's Name, Place, or Date. "Translated out of frensshe into englysshe by me wyllyam Caxton / whiche translacion was fynysshed the xiij day of septembre in the yere of our lord M / CCCC . lxxxiiij."* (1488?)

Collation.—**a b c d e f g h i k l m n o p q r s t** are 4^ns^, the first leaf of **a** being blank; **u** a 5^n^, with the last leaf blank. In all 162 leaves, of which two are blank.

Note.—**m iij** is wrongly signed **m ij**; and **n j** is wrongly signed **n iiij**.

Typographical Particulars.—There is no title-page. The type is entirely No. 5. The lines are fully spaced out, and measure $4\frac{5}{8}$ inches, 33 forming a full page. Without folios or catchwords. 2-line initials in wood are used at the commencement of the chapters. There are six small vignette illustrations in wood, all of which, however, except the first, which appeared in the "Golden Legend," are from the "Speculum" just described, where they are suited to the text, and not, as here, used without any reference to fitness.

Commencing with a blank leaf, the prologue follows on a ij recto, with a 2-line initial.

The Text begins thus:—

Whan I remembre and take hede of the conuersacion of || vs that lyue in this wretched lyf. in which is no surete || ne stable abydyng. And also the contynuel besynes of euery

The Text ends, with a full page, on sig. u 9 recto,

This book was compyled & made atte requeste of kyng Phelyp of Fraunce in the yere of thyncarnacyon of our lord / M. CC · lxxix. & translated or reduced out of frensshe in || to englysshe by me wyllyam Caxton. atte requeste of a wor= || shipful marchaunt & mercer of london. whiche Instauntly re=

* * * * * * *

to be called Ryall / as tofore is sayd. whiche translacion or re= || ducyng oute of frensshe in to englysshe was achyeued. fynys || shed & accomplysshed the xiij day of Septembre in the yere of thyncarnacyon of our lord. M / CCCC. lxxxiiij / And in the || second yere of the Regne of Kyng Rychard the thyrd /

In Caxton's printed epilogue (*ante* vol. i, page 187) we thus read:—"Which book is called in French "Le livre Royal," that is to say the royal book, or a book of a king; for the Holy Scripture calleth every man a king which wisely and perfectly can govern and direct himself after virtue." But "Le livre Royal" was by no means the title by which Caxton's contemporaries knew this work. The most common name is that found in *Royal MS.* 19 C. II "Le livre des Vices et des Vertus;" although it was sometimes entitled "La Somme de Roi," or "La Somme des Vices et des Vertus." By whatever name known it was for centuries a favourite book, as is proved by the numerous copies still extant. Its author is said to be "Frere Laurent de l'ordre des predicateurs et confesseur de Phillippe le Hardi" (*Les Msc. Franç.* t. iii, page 388), but his name does not appear in any of the above-mentioned manuscripts of the work. Very soon after its appearance it was favourably received in England, where, in the year 1340, it was translated by a priest of Kent, for the purpose of being read to the people in their own dialect. This was called "The Ayenbite of Inwit," and was printed from the Arundel MS. (No. 57) in the British Museum, in 1855, for the Roxburghe Club. Another and purer translation into English (*Addit.* 17013) was also made in the fourteenth century.

Existing copies—Bedfordshire General Library, British Museum, Cambridge (2), and four in private collections.

No. 75.—Image of Pity. *Quarto Broadside. Sine ullâ notâ.* (1489 ?).

This is a woodcut measuring $5\frac{1}{2} \times 3\frac{5}{8}$ inches, printed on one side of a quarto. Like the folio woodcut described at page 315, and the 8vo cut described at page 318, there is a central figure of our Saviour upon the Cross, surrounded by eighteen small compartments, each having some reference to the Passion. Beneath the central figure the block has been cut, and the following sentence inserted in type No. 5:—

To them that before
this ymage of pyte de
uoutly saye v Pr nr
v Aues & a Credo py=
teuously beholdyng these
ar of Xps . passio ar
grauted xxxij . M . vij . C
& lv . yeres of pardon ·

No. 76.—The Doctrinal of Sapience. *Folio. "Caxton me fieri fecit." Without Place or Date. Translated May 7th*, 1489.

Collation.—A B C D E F G H I are 4^{ns}; K and L 5^{ns}. In all 92 leaves. No blanks.

TYPOGRAPHICAL PARTICULARS.—There is no title-page. The type throughout is No. 5. The lines, which are spaced to an even length, measure 4⅝ inches, and there are 33 to a page. Without folios or catchwords. There are side-notes, which, however, never exceed the three letters **Exa**, which are placed in the margin whenever an "Example" occurs in the Text. Two woodcuts and printed initials.

The Text begins on sig. **A j** recto, with a 3-line initial,

This that is writen in this lytyl boke ought the prestres to lerne and teche to theyr paryssħes : And also it is ne= cessary for symple prestes that vnderstode not the scrip

This prologue is followed by the table, which commences on the bottom line of sig. **A j** verso, and finishes at foot of **A iij** recto; and on the verso, with a woodcut down the side of the type, and a 2-line initial **E**, is the commencement of the work.

Woodcut from "Speculum," of Jesus in the Temple.

EUery crysten man & woman ought to bi leue fermely the xij artys= cles of the cristen feith .

On **B j** is another woodcut, the Crucifixion, also from the "Speculum." On the verso of sig. **I ij**, the 64th chapter is thus dismissed:—

¶ Of the neclygences of the masse and of the remedyes I pas‖se ouer for it apperteyneth to prestes & not to laie men . C . lxiiij

The Text ends on the tenth recto of sig. **L**,

god his grace graunte for to gouuerne vs in suche wyse and ‖ lyue in thys short lyf that we may come to hys blysse for to ly ‖ ue and regne there wythout ende in secula secu= lorum Amen

¶ Thus endeth the doctrinal of sapyence the whyche is ryght ‖ vtile and prouffytable to alle crysten men / whyche

is translated || oute of Frenshe in to englysshe by wyllyam Caxton at westme || ster fynysshed the . vij . day of may the yere of our lord / M / cccc ||lxxx ix

Caxton me fieri fecit

On the verso is Caxton's large device.

REMARKS.—The "Manipulus Curatorum," compiled in the early part of the fourteenth, was printed frequently in the fifteenth century. Greswell mentions—"Savilliani anno 1470; Aug. Vindel 1471, Gering at Paris 1478;" and several times later. In these, as in all the early French editions, the authorship is ascribed to Guy, Archbishop of Sens, who died 1409. This has been adopted by the compilers of the Harleian Catalogue (III. 1552), and from them by all subsequent bibliographers. That it is, nevertheless, erroneous, appears from the extracts given above. In no manuscript copy is the authorship attributed to Guy de Roye: in fact, it was well known before his time, for it was "envoié à Paris," by Blanche, Queen of France, who died in 1370. The archbishop was, nevertheless, the cause of its being circulated in the French language; for about the year 1388 he employed several doctors of divinity to translate it from the original Latin, and promoted its use by the clergy in all the parishes of his diocese. Further than this he appears to have had no direct connection with it.

It was known in France under the titles of "Livre de Sapience" and "Doctrinal de la foy catholique," but most commonly as "Le Doctrinal au simples gens."

The following remark of Mr. Douce is written in his copy of the "Doctrinal." "The Sermons of Vitriaco," or some other of his works, much quoted in "Scala Cœli," seem to have been used in the "Doctrinal."

EXISTING COPIES.—Cambridge and Oxford (2), and seven in private libraries. The copy at Windsor Castle is so interesting that a special description is necessary. It is printed on vellum, and has a chapter on "Negligences happing in the Mass," which does not appear in any other known copy. The parchment used is very coarse, discoloured, uneven in substance, and disfigured with holes. Dr. Dibdin could never have seen it, or he would not have written in terms of admiration. A slip of paper at the beginning states, "This book was presented to the Royal Library by Mr. Bryant," which was doubtless the reason why it was (together with the Æsop) retained when that splendid collection became national property. It is not known how Bryant obtained it, but it is curious to note in these days, when every leaf of a Caxton represents a bank-note, how Bryant demurred at giving the exorbitant price of four guineas for this vellum copy, and then only after mature consideration with "old Pain," the celebrated bookbinder.

The unique chapter at the end of this copy occupies three leaves, unsigned, and begins thus:—

¶ Of the necligences happyng in the masse . and of the reme= ‖ dyes Capitulo · lxiiij°

Lyke as we haue seyd that thys is made especyally for the symple peple · and for the symple prestes . whiche understond not latin / bycause that he is not so suffy= saut ‖ but that somtyme for necligence or other wyse he may faylle

The whole of this chapter is very curious, and is occupied with what the officiating priest is to do—if, after the consecration of the wine, he remembers that no water had been mingled with it; or finds that he has consecrated water only; or remembers that he has eaten ought since midnight; or finds a fly, a "loppe," or a venomous beast in the chalice; whether, if a small piece of meat abide in the teeth, and be swallowed during the celebration, it incapacitates the priest from singing Mass; what is to be done when the priest lets fall any portion of the consecrated elements, or meets with a similar accident.

On the third verso the chapter ends.

And yf the body of Jhesu crist or ony piece fylle vpon the palle of the aulter or vpon ony of the ‖ vestymentes that ben blessyd · the piece ought not to be cutte || of on whyche it is fallen . but it ought right wel to be wasshen || And the wasshyng to be gyuen to the mynistres for to drinke / || or ellys drynke it hym self / This chapitre to fore I durst not sette in the boke by cause it is not conuenyent ne aparteynyng that euery laye man sholde || knowe it Et cetera /

No. 77.—Speculum Vitæ Christi. *Folio.* "*Emprynted by wyllyam Caxton.*" *Without Place or Date. Edition B.* (1488?)

Collation the same as No. 71.

Typographical Particulars the same as No. 71.

Commencing with a blank leaf, the Text begins thus on sig. a ij recto:—

¶ Incipit Speculum vite Cristi .

AT the begynnynge of the prohemye of the booke that is cleped the myrroure of the blessyd lyf of Jhesu Cryste the fyrst parte for the monedaye / ¶ A deuoute medytacion of the grete counceyll in heuene for the restorynge of man || and hys sauacyon . Capitulum primum . ¶ Of the manere ||

At the head of sig. b ij recto,

Die lune ¶ Prima pars Capitulo j

dome all the Courte of heuene wondrynge and commendynge the souerayne wysedome assented wel here to . but forthermore ||

At the head of sig. f 6 verso,

¶ Die mercurij ¶ Tercia pars Capitulum xv /

parauenture ther with a few smale fisshes that oure lady had || ordeyned thenne as god wold . & soo therwyth the aungels co= ||

The "Speculum" ends at foot of sig. s i recto,

hys moder Marye now and euer wythout end Amen
¶ Explicit speculum vite Cristi .

On the verso begins a treatise on the Sacrament of Christ's body,

¶ A shorte treatyce of the hyhest and most worthy sacra= mente ‖ of crystes blessid body . and the merueylles therof /

which finishes on sig. t 3 recto with the following imprint :—

¶ Emprynted by wyllyam caxton

Some prayers follow, and on the verso of the same leaf the Text ends,

¶ Jhesu lord thy blessyd lyf / helpe and comforte oure wret ‖ chid lyf · Amen · soo mote it be
Explycit speculum vite Cristi complete /
¶ In omni tribulacione / temptacione · necessitate & an= gustya ‖ succurre nobis pijssima virgo maria Amen .

The recto of sig. t 4 is blank, and the verso occupied with Caxton's device.

No. 78.—Commemoratio Lamentationis sive Compassionis beatæ Mariæ in morte filii. *Quarto. Without Name, Place, or Date.* (1491 ?).

Collation.—a b c d are 4[ns], signed on the first and third leaves only. Altogether 32 pages. If a sheet is printed in 4to, a signature on the first page is sufficient guide for the binder; and two sheets so printed, and the second inserted after folding inside the first, would give signatures as in this copy, and, as in the "Servitium," No. 79, which has Caxton's imprint. This method, however, points to a late period of Caxton's career, and the date 1491 has therefore been affixed.

Typographical Particulars.—There is no title-page. Type No. 5 only. The lines are evenly spaced, and 24 to a full page. Without folios or catchwords. One small woodcut is on the first page.

The Text begins on a j recto,

> **Comemoraco Lametacois sine copassiois bte Marie i morte filij & dr Comemoraco bte ma= rie pietatis vl' 9memoraco pietatis q celebrari debet feria sexta imediate pcedete domica i passi one p eo q) ipo die legit' i eccl'ia de resuscitacoe lazari etc**

The Commemoration ends on sig. d 8 verso.

This particular Commemoration seems quite unknown to all bibliographers; and of the edition printed by Caxton, the only copy known is preserved in the Public Library at Ghent. It was first recognised as a Caxton by Mr. M. F. A. G. Campbell, chief librarian of the Royal Library, The Hague.

No. 79.—SERVITIUM DE TRANSFIGURATIONE JHESU CHRISTI. *Quarto. Caxton me fieri fecit. Without Place or Date.* (1491 ?).

COLLATION.—Sig. a consists of a sheet folded in quarto, having a half-sheet inside; the first recto of the sheet is unsigned, but upon the first recto of the half-sheet, which is the third recto in the book, is the sig. a ij. Sig. b is a whole sheet, signed only on the first recto, b j. There are altogether ten leaves and no blanks.

TYPOGRAPHICAL PARTICULARS.—There is no title-page. The type is No. 5 only. The lines are spaced to an even length, and measure 3⅝ inches. 24 lines to a full page. Without folios or catchwords. One small woodcut of the transfiguration on the first recto. The initial letter in wood, with many rubrics, are printed in red, not as noticed in "Quatre deremnieres choses," by the same pull of the press, but by a separate operation.

The Text begins on an unsigned leaf, in red ink,

> **¶ Octauo Jd9 Augusti fiat seruic' / de tnsfigu**

The Text ends on sig. b 4 verso,

> **sci dc9 . Per oia scl'a seculoru amen**
> **¶ Caxton me fieri fecit /**

REMARKS.—This little tract has considerable interest for the bibliographer, for although Caxton had already printed several service books before this was undertaken, such as the two (if not three) editions of the "Horæ" (pages 189 and 240 *ante*), the Psalter with Service for the Dead (page 105 *ante*), and the "Servitium de Visitatione" (page 264 *ante*), not to mention the service books for the priests, such as "The Festial" and the three editions of "Directorium," yet this can certainly claim a unique distinction in two particulars, for it is the only *perfect* service book in the types of Caxton, and it is the only one known to have his imprint.

The observations concerning the printing of the "Horæ," last noticed, might be repeated here. This also has every appearance of being a very late issue. No other book from the same press was signed in a similar way. The first sheet was evidently, like sig. b, printed four pages at once, in which case it would be only necessary to sign the *first* page, so as to show the binder how to fold it. As in the first sheet the red ink title and the woodcut would answer that purpose we find no signature at all; but the first page of the half-sheet, which is the *third* leaf in the tract, is signed a ij. This is very systematic, and according to the same plan the second sheet is signed b j on the first recto only; but it is an advance in the art, beyond the usual practice of Caxton.

This service is one of the numerous additions made to the "Church Calendar" in the fifteenth century, and, being newly ordained by the Church, would not be found in the old manuscript "Service Books." To supply this deficiency it was, therefore, printed separately.

The only EXISTING COPY was purchased many years ago in a volume of theological tracts by Joshua Wilson, Esq., of Tunbridge Wells. When, in 1831, Mr. Wilson presented a large portion of his collection to the Congregational Library, Blomfield Street, London, this volume was among the number. Here it was first noticed, in 1860, as containing a Caxton, by Mr. Cowper, who sent an account of the volume to *Notes and Queries*. It was determined shortly after to dispose of it, and, in July 1862, it came under the hammer of Mr. Puttick, when it fetched the high price of £200, and added another curiosity to the Caxtonian treasures of the British Museum. The volume is in its original binding, somewhat dilapidated, of oak boards covered with stamped leather, and contains besides four other black-letter tracts.

No. 80.—HORÆ—A FRAGMENT. *Fourth Edition. 8vo. Sine ullâ notâ.* (1490?).

The COLLATION cannot be given, as four leaves only, signed **d j, d ij, d iij, d iiij**, are known.

TYPOGRAPHICAL PARTICULARS.—The type is No. 5 only. The lines, of which there are seventeen to a page, are fully spaced out, and measure 2⅝ inches. Large full-faced Lombardic capitals are plentifully used, and printed in red ink separately, as are also such words as *Psalmus* and *Versicle.* This points to quite a late production in the career of Caxton, probably after he had resigned the management of the practical part to his successor, Wynken de Worde.

The Text of sig. **d j** recto begins thus, with a 2-line capital **O** in red ink.

O Gloriosa femina exel=
la p'rper sidera qui te cre=
auit prouide lactasti sacro vbere

The first words on the succeeding recto are—2, **rum libe=rati**; 3, **dominum**; 4, **Deus**.

These unique leaves, which have evidently been used as binder's waste to form the covers of a book, were presented to the British Museum, in 1858, by Mr. Maskell (C. 35. A.). Measurement 5¼ × 4 inches.

A

DESCRIPTION OF BOOKS PRINTED

IN

TYPE No. 6.

BOOKS PRINTED IN TYPE No. 6.

81.	Fayts	1489
82.	Statutes	1489
83.	Governal	1489
84.	Reynard. Second Edition	1489 ?
85.	Blanchardyn	1489 ?
86.	Four Sons of Aymon	1489 ?
87.	Directorium Sacerdotum	1489 ?
88.	Eneydos	1490
89.	Dictes. Third Edition	1490 ?
90.	Mirror. Second Edition	1490 ?
91.	Divers Ghostly	1491 ?
92.	Fifteen Oes	1491 ?
93.	Art and Craft	1491 ?
94.	Courtesy. Second Edition	1491 ?
95.	Festial. Second Edition	1491 ?
96.	Four Sermons. Second Edition	1491 ?
97.	Ars moriendi	1491 ?
98.	Chastising	1491 ?
99.	Treatise of Love	1491 ?

No. 81.—THE FAYTS OF ARMS AND OF CHIVALRY. *Folio. "Per Caxton." Without Place. Printed the* 14*th day of July, the fourth year of the reign of K. Henry VII., or* 1489.

COLLATION.—Two unsigned leaves of table; A B C D E F G H I K L M N O P Q R all 4^ns^; S a 3^n^, with the last leaf blank. In all 144 leaves, of which one is blank.

TYPOGRAPHICAL PARTICULARS.—There is no title-page. The whole book is in one type only, No. 6. The lines, which are fully spaced out, measure 4¾ inches, and there are 31 to a full page. Without folios or catchwords. Woodcut initial letters.

The Text begins, with a 3-line initial,

Here begynneth the table of the rubrysshys of the boke of the fayt of armes and of Chyualrye whiche sayd boke is departyd in to foure partyes /
¶ The fyrst partye deuyseth the manere that kynges and

On sig. A j recto,

Here begynneth the book of fayttes of armes & of Chyualrye / and the first chappytre is the prologue / in whiche xprystyne of pyse excuseth hir self to haue dar enterpryse to speke || of so hye matere as is conteyned in this sayd book

The Text ends on the verso of the same leaf,

remayne alleway vyctoryous / And dayly encreace fro uertu to vertue & fro better to better to his laude & honour in this || present lyf / that after thys short & transitorye lyf / he may at= || teyne to euerlastyng lyf in heuen / Whiche god graunte to || hym and to alle hys lyege peple AMEN /

Per Caxton

REMARKS.—There is a MS. in the British Museum (*Roy*, 15 E vi) containing the original French text of Christine de Pisan. It agrees very accurately with Caxton's English version, and has the introductory chapter, in which Christine excuses herself, and explains her reasons for writing a work on chivalry. This manuscript is also interesting from having been written for the celebrated John Talbot, Earl of Shrewsbury, who died in 1453, and by whom it was presented to Queen Margaret. A still greater degree of interest would invest the volume if we suppose it to be the identical manuscript from which Caxton made his translation. This is certainly not improbable, as the original from the Royal Library was entrusted to our printer, for the purpose of translation and printing, by King Henry VII of England, as we learn from the prologue:—"which book, being in French, was delivered to me, William Caxton, by the most christian king, my natural sovereign lord, King Henry VII, in his Palace of Westminster, and desired me to translate this said book, and to put it in print."

Many French bibliographers (*Les Msc. Franç.* t. v, page 94), ascribe the composition of "Faits d'Armes et de Chevalerie" to Jean le Meun, so well known from his connection with "Le Roman de le Rose." The sole reason for this appears to have been the fact that Jean le Meun translated into French the celebrated work of Vegetius "De re militari," written in 1284, a work often quoted in the "Faits d'Armes;" but since the writings of Christine have become better known, no one has ventured to claim for the thirteenth, a work containing references and facts applicable only to the fifteenth century. That a book on the "Rules of War" should in any age have been written by a woman, is sufficiently improbable to require a critical examination; and, therefore, as the claims of Christine to the authorship of "Les Faits d'Armes" are still denied by some writers, it may not be inappropriate to state both sides of the argument.

Among the manuscripts in the British Museum is one entitled "The Boke of Noblesse" (*Royal* 18, B. XXII). This, for the first time, was printed in 1860, for the members of the Roxburghe Club. The author is entirely unknown, and the only reason for mentioning this at all is that the name of Christine frequently appears in its pages as an authority upon military matters, but is always referred to as "Dame Cristyn in hir booke of Tree of Batailes," or some military phrase. But "L'Arbre des Battailes" is the well-known compilation of Honore Bonet, of which copies may be seen in *Royal* 20 C. VIII, and *Addit.* 22768. Now, what is the natural conclusion from this erroneous ascription? Evidently that the unknown writer of the "Book of Noblesse," quoting probably from a copy of "L'Arbre des Battailes," which had neither prologue nor epilogue; and having in his mind the great fame of Christine as the writer of a book on a similar subject, made the not unpardonable mistake of misquoting the author's name, and attributing to Christine, the compiler of "Les Faits d'Armes," all the quotations drawn from Bonet's "L'Arbre de Battailes." Not so, argues Mr. John Gough Nichols, in his interesting preface to the Roxburghe impression. "Christina de Pisan," he urges, "was a Poetess;" and it is not likely that she had more to do with the "Faits d'Armes" than the "dame Christine" of "The Book of Noblesse" had with the "Arbre des Battailes." In support of this opinion is quoted a marginal note in "The Boke of Noblesse," in an old hand-writing, but more modern than the original manuscript, to the following effect:—

"*L'Arbre des Battailles compose par Honore Bonet Prieur de Sallon en Prouuence.*"

"Note y^t in some Authors this Booke is termed Dame Christine of ye tree of Battayles, not that she made yt; But bicause she was a notable Benefactour to Learned men and perchance to ye autor of this Booke And therefore diverse of them sette furthe their Bookes under her name."

The author of this note was evidently unacquainted with the particulars of the life, or the character of the writings, of Christine—the "virilis fœmina" of her eminent contemporary, Gerson—and "La grant sagesse" of her editor, Jean Marot. The assertion that authors set forth their books under her name is unsupported by a single known instance; while her early tuition, political life, and numerous writings, would both enable and incline her to compose such a work.

Christine expressly states in the preface that she wrote the work; and although Verard, in his printed edition of 1488, omits the prefatory address, it appears in numerous manuscripts, and may be read in Caxton's translation. "Because," says Christine, "men of arms are not clerks, nor instructed in the science of language, I have assembled and gathered together diverse books to produce this work. And because that this is a thing not accustomed and out of usage to women / which commonly do not intermit but to spin on the distaff and occupy them in things of household. I supplicate humbly * * to have nor take it for no evil if I a woman charge myself to treat of so high a matter."

No one doubts that Dame Juliana Berners wrote the well-known "Treatise on Hunting and Hawking," and the evidence that Christine de Pisan wrote "The Fayts of Arms" is equally strong.

Christine was no common poetess whose strength was in the prettiness of her amatory verses. The short account of her already given (see *ante* page 193), will show the energetic and comprehensive character of her mind. Educated by her father in the whole course of literature at that time in vogue, she had, while yet young, made herself mistress of the Latin language, and stored her mind by the perusal of the most celebrated writings, as well Pagan as Christian. Living in the midst of wars and preparations for war, many of her acknowledged writings teem with warlike allusions. In politics her opinion had great weight; she was consulted by the highest nobles of France; and many years of her life were spent in the endeavour to raise the political and moral tone of the country. The celebrated Jean le Meun found in her no weak opponent, and the equally celebrated Chancellor Gerson a most potent ally.

There are 21 copies of this work known, of which eleven are in private libraries.

No. 82.—Statutes of Henry VII. *Folio. Sine ullâ notâ.* (1489?)

Collation.—a b c d are 4^{ns}, with the first leaf of a blank; e a 5^{n}, with the last blank. Total 42 leaves, of which two are blank.

Note.—The signature is omitted on a ij. The third and fifth leaves of e are erroneously signed d iij and d b.

Typographical Particulars.—There is no title-page. The type is all No. 6. The lines, which are spaced to an even length, measure 4⅝ inches, and there are 31 (in three instances 33 lines) to a full page. Without folios or catchwords. Only one 2-line woodcut initial is used.

After a blank leaf, the work commences on the second recto of sig. a.

The Text begins thus—

¶ The kynge our souereyn lorde henry the seuenth after the conquest by the grace of god kyng of Englond & of Fraunce and lorde of Irlonde at his parlyamet holden at west=

The Text ends on sig. e 9 verso, the whole page being as follows—

pleysure / Whether he wylle after the fourme conteyned & ordei ‖ ned in and by this acte / or after the maner & fourme afore ti ‖ me used /

Remarks.—This is the earliest known volume of printed statutes, and is further remarkable as being in English. It contains some very curious and interesting legislation on political, trade, and domestic matters.

The British Museum copy was purchased from Mr. Lilly, who, a few days before, had bought it at Hodgson's for £2 10s. It was then bound up with some other law tracts and year-books, mostly from the press of Machlinia, one of which, being unique, was catalogued by Mr. Lilly at 100 guineas. There is also a perfect copy in the National Library, Paris, and the Inner Temple, London, with one copy only in private hands.

No. 83.—The Governal of Health.—The Medicina Stomachi. *Quarto. Sine ullâ notâ.* (1489 ?).

Collation.—The "Governal," 𝔄 and 𝔅 4^ns; the "Medicina," two unsigned leaves = eighteen leaves.

Typographical Particulars.—Without title-page. Only one type, No. 6, is used throughout. The lines, which are of an even length, and measure 2⅝ inches, excepting 𝔅 7 verso, which has 24, have all 23 lines to a page. Wood-cut initials to chapters. Without folios or catchwords.

The Text begins on sig. 𝔄 j recto,

> In this tretyse that is cleped Go
> uernayle of helthe : What is to
> be sayd wyth crystis helpe of so=
> me thynges that longen to bodi
> ly helthe / habbe and to be kept or
> to bodily helthe . lost and to be recouered / and

and ends,

> This receyte boughte is of no potycarye
> Of mayster antony ne of mayster hughe
> To all indyfferent it is rychest dyetarye
>
> Explicit medicina stomachi :

Remarks.—The "Governal" was originally written in Latin, and soon after translated into English, but no trace of the translator's name is left. The date of the original composition is unknown; we can only gather from the non-existence of manuscripts of a later date than the latter half of the fourteenth century that it was composed about that period.

The name of the author or compiler is doubtful. From *Sloane* 989 one would say that John de Burdeux wrote it for the good of a "frende," but *Sloane* 3149 attributes it to another writer, "Explicit tractatus Bartholomei." John de Burdeux was the author of several tracts on medicine, and flourished in the latter half of the fourteenth century. Bartholomeus was rather a prolific writer of the fourteenth and

Plate XIII.

Caxton's Type, No. 6.

In this tretyse that is cleped Go
uernayle of helthe: What is to
be sayd wyth crystis helpe of some thynges that longen to bodi
ly helthe/hadde and to be kept or
to bodily helthe lost and to be recouered/ and
is departed in viij. chapytures/that is to saye
In the fyrste chapytre of the profyte of goode
Gouernayle of helth/In the ij. chapytre what
is first on morowe to be don/In the iij. chapitre
of bodyly excersyce/ that is to saye. besynes &
his profyte; In the fourth chapytre of spyces
of excersice/In the fyfthe chapiytre howe a mā
sholde haue hym in mete. in etyng his metes :
In the vj. chapitre how a man shold haue hym
in drynkyng of his drynkes/In the vij. chap
ytre what sholde be done after mete/In the viij
chapytre of the noyse of euyll gouernaunce

IT nedyth hym that woll haue longe
lyff to knowe the crafte of holsome gouernayle. And so for to kepe contynuelly the
helthe of his body/ for els he maye not com to

fifteenth centuries, but the "Governal" is not found among the works generally attributed to him. Whoever may have been the author, the work possesses small claims to originality, being a compilation from the medical works of the Arabian and Greek physicians, and quoting largely from the "Regimen Sanitatis Salernitanum." The "Medicina Stomachi" is contained in most collections of Lydgate's poetry, and in *Harl.* 116 is directly attributed to him.

Both tracts were reprinted by Wynken de Worde, *sine anno*, who repeats all the blunders of the first edition. These editions are equally rare, the only copy of the second being in the Public Library, Cambridge. An annotated reprint of Caxton's text was issued privately by the editor of this work in 1858. On no other occasion does this interesting treatise, which was the earliest medical book printed in the English language, appear to have passed through the press.

A good copy is in the old library of the Earls of Dysart, at Ham House, Surrey, and another in the Bodleian.

No. 84.—THE HISTORY OF REYNARD THE FOX. *Second Edition. Folio. Sine ullâ notâ.* (1489 ?)

COLLATION.—An unsigned sheet of introductory matter; sigs. a b c d e f g h are 4^{ns}; i is a 3^{n}. No blank leaves. In all seventy leaves.

TYPOGRAPHICAL PARTICULARS.—There is no title-page. The type throughout is No. 6. The lines, which are fully spaced out, measure 5⅝ inches, and there are 31 (sometimes 32) to a page. Woodcut initials are used. On the first recto is Caxton's device, underneath which is the following line only:—

¶ This is the table of the historye of Reynart the foxe/

On the verso commences the table, which ends seven lines down the second recto, underneath which is,

¶ Hyer begynneth hystorye of reynard the foxe.

The preface finishes the page. The second verso is blank.

On sig. a j,

¶ How the lyon kynge of alle bestys sent oute hys maude‖mentys that alle beestys sholde come to hys feest and court/

¶ Capitulo Primo

The conclusion of the text cannot be given, no perfect copy being at present known. For an account of the first edition of this celebrated allegory see *ante* page 227.

The only EXISTING COPY is in the Pepysian Library, Cambridge. It unfortunately wants the last two leaves, containing the epilogue of Caxton, and ends on sig. i 4 verso, with these words,

And her wyth wil I leue fforw hat haue I to wryte of thyse mysdedis I haue ynowh to doo

It is in good condition, but cropped, measuring 9 × 6¾ inches. Pepys's arms on the binding, and his book-plate inside. The wanting leaves are supplied in manuscript of seventeenth century.

No. 85.—THE HISTORY OF BLANCHARDIN AND EGLANTINE. *Folio. Sine ullâ notâ.* (1489 ?)

COLLATION.—Imperfectly known. The introductory matter makes a 3ⁿ, signed i, ii, iij, the sixth leaf being blank. A B C D E F G H I K L M are 4ⁿˢ, and there were probably several other additional signatures.

TYPOGRAPHICAL PARTICULARS.—Without title. The type is all No. 6. The lines, which are all of one length, measure 4⅝ inches, and there are 31 to a full page. Woodcut initials. Without folios or catchwords.

The Text begins on sig. j recto, with a prologue by Caxton,

UNto the right noble puyssaut & excellet pryncesse my redoubted lady my lady margarete duchesse of Somercete/moder vnto our naturel & souerayn lord and most

and finishes on the verso of the same leaf,

Ioyes desirs in thys present lyff: ¶ And after this short and transytorye lyff. euerlastynge lyff in heuen Amen/

The table follows on sig. ij, with a 2-line initial,

Here begynneth the table of the victoryous prynce Blanchardyn / sone of the noble kyng of Fryse

and finishes on the 5th recto, which, however, in the only copy known, is unfortunately, in manuscript. This appears to have been copied from the very rare reprint by Wynken de Worde, the last four lines being—"How Blanchardin wedded his love the proude | pucelle in amours: And of the grete ioye that | was made there . and of the Kynge of Fryse deth capl° liiij°"

The sixth leaf is blank. On sig. A j recto the first chapter commences as follows:—

¶ The first chapitre of this present boke conteyneth how Blanchardyn departed out of the court of his fader kynge of fryse / Capitulo primo.

That tyme when the Right happy . wele of

All the text after sig. M iiij is wanting in the only known copy.

REMARKS.—The prologue to Caxton's translation of this romance is fortunately preserved, from which we learn that Margaret, Duchess of Somerset, brought to Caxton the French version of this romance (which she had "long before" purchased of him), with her commands that he should translate it into English. Having made the translation, he presented it to Her Grace, probably as a manuscript, as he says nothing of any command to print it. It was, however, soon after put to press, perhaps at Caxton's own risk, as a trade speculation. As to the date, there are only the typographical particulars to guide us, which, however, all point to about the year 1489.

The only known EXISTING COPY is in the library of Earl Spencer. It is, unfortunately, imperfect.

No. 86.—THE FOUR SONS OF AYMON. *Folio. Sine ullâ notâ.* (1489?)

The COLLATION cannot be given accurately, as no perfect copy is known. A B C D E F G H I K L M N O

P Q R S T V X Y Z aa bb cc dd ee ff gg hh ii kk ll are all 4[ns], mm being a 3[n], with the sixth leaf, probably, blank. This makes a total of 278 leaves; but it is more than likely that some introductory matter preceded sig. A.

Typographical Particulars.—Only one type, No. 6, is used. The lines, which are all of an even length, measure 4⅝ inches, and there are 31 to a full page. Without folios or catchwords. Woodcut initials throughout.

The only known copy of this edition begins on sig. b iij, in the middle of a sentence,

Reynawde one of the sones of Aymon / wherof specyally tre

The Text ends on the fifth verso of sig. mm, with the following sentence:—

My fayr lordes thenne that this present boke shal rede or here. we shall praye god & the gloryous sayntc Reynaude the marter / that he gyue vs grace to perseuere / and ‖ contynue our liff in good werkes. by the whiche we may ha ‖ ue at our endynge the liff that euer shall laste /

AMEN.

Remarks.—Manuscripts of this favourite romance, concerning the original of which little appears to be known, mount up to the thirteenth century, and references to it are found in manuscripts of a still earlier date; but all these are rythmical romances, and Caxton's translation (if we may give him the credit of it) was evidently made from a French prose text, perhaps that printed at Lyons, about 1480, under the title "Les quatre filz Aymon."

Before the discovery of the volume under review, the earliest printed English text of "The four sons of Aymon" was the 1554 edition of R. Copland, to which was appended the following colophon:—

" ¶ Here finishith the hystory of the | noble and valiaunt knyght Reynawde | of Mountawban, and his three bre- | thern ¶ Imprinted at London, by | Wynken de Worde, the . viij. daye of | Maye. and y[e] yere of

our lorde . M , C | CCCC iiii . at the request and com- | maundement of the noble and puis- | saunt erle, the Erle of Oxenforde, | And now Emprinted in the yere of | our Lord . M . CCCCC . l iiii . the | vi daye of Maye, By wylliam Cop- | land, for Thomas Petet."

From Copland's colophon we learn that an edition was issued in 1504 by Wynken de Worde, although, unfortunately, not a single copy is now known to exist. He, of course, reprinted from the text under review; and, indeed, the first portion of the colophon above quoted, so far as it concerns Wynken de Worde, is quite in Caxton's style, and recalls the numerous instances already noticed, in which Wynken de Worde, by altering the printer's name and the date, has falsified both typographical and historical truth. That in this case he used Caxton's colophon, with alterations, is rendered almost certain when the prologue to Copland's edition is perused. Here we have all the peculiarities of our first printer's style, and his very diction.

No manuscript or printed copy of Caxton's life of Robert, Earl of Oxford, is known.

The only known EXISTING COPY of Caxton's edition is in the library of Earl Spencer. It is imperfect, wanting all before sig. 𝔅iij; 𝔇 8, and 𝔑 8.

No. 87.—DIRECTORIUM SACERDOTUM, UNA CUM DEFENSORIO EJUSDEM; ITEM TRACTATUS QUI DICITUR CREDE MIHI. *Folio. Second Version. Second Edition.* "*Impressum per Willelmu Caxton apud westmonasteriu prope London!*" *Without Date.* (1489?)

COLLATION.—A preliminary 4[n], signed only on the fourth recto with the figure 4; 𝔞 𝔟 𝔠 𝔡 𝔢 𝔣 𝔤 𝔥 𝔦 𝔨 𝔩 𝔪 𝔫 𝔬 𝔭 𝔮 𝔯 𝔰 𝔱 𝔲 𝔵 𝔶 are all 4[ns]; ʒ is a 5[n]. Total 194 leaves. No blanks.

TYPOGRAPHICAL PARTICULARS.—There is no title-page. The type is all No. 6. The lines, which are spaced to an even length, measure 4⅝ inches. Exclusive of head-lines there are 31 to a page. A few 2-line woodcut initials. Without folios or catchwords.

The "Kalendar," which has the same woodcut KL as in the first edition, commences on the first recto, thus:—

KL Prima dies mensis et septima trucat vt ensis
Januarius habet dies xxxj / luna vero xxx

The Text ends on sig. ȝ 10 verso,

vix poterit errare : in seruicio diuino Deo Gracias

¶ Caxton me fieri fecit .

REMARKS.—From the fact of the Printer beginning his table for finding the Golden and Dominical Letters at the year 1489, we may safely assume that year to be the date of printing, as to print back years would be useless. The combination of red and black figures, the black form being first printed, and the red form secondly and separately, shows a great advance in workmanship over other books by Caxton.

Like the first edition there is only one EXISTING COPY known of this, which is in the Bodleian Library. It is, with "The Art and Craft to know well to die" by the same printer, still in the original parchment wrapper, as issued from Caxton's workshop. It is perfect, and in good condition.

No. 88.—ENEYDOS. *Folio. Without Printer's Name, Place, or Date. "Translated by me wyllyam Caxton," June 22nd,* 1490.

COLLATION.—Sig. A a 3^{n}, with the first leaf blank; B C D E F G H I K L are 4^{ns}, with L 8 blank. In all 86 leaves, of which two are blank.

Dr. Dibdin erroneously ascribes only four leaves to sig. A.

Note.—Sig. a is very irregular: the first leaf, which is blank, is not reckoned in the signatures, the second and third leaves being signed respectively A j, and A ij. The fourth leaf, which, to agree with the others, should have been signed A iij, has no signature at all; while the omitted signature, A iij, appears on the sixth or last leaf of the 3^{n}.

TYPOGRAPHICAL PARTICULARS.—There is no title-page. The type is all No. 6. The lines are spaced to an even length, and measure 4¾ inches. There are 31 lines to a full page. Woodcut initials of two, three, and six lines in depth.

After a blank leaf the prologue begins on the second recto, signed A j,

After dyuerse werkes made / translated and achieued / hauyng noo werke in hande. I sittyng in my studye where as laye many dyuerse paunflettis and bookys. happened that

The Text ends on sig. L 7 recto, with the following colophon:—

HERE fynysshed the boke yf Eneydos / compyled by Vyr ‖ gyle / whiche hathe be translated oute of latyne in to frenshe / ‖ And oute of frenshe reduced in to Englysshe by me wyllm ‖ Caxton / the xxij. daye of Iuyn. the yere of our lorde. M. iiij ‖ C lxxxx. The fythe yere of the Regne of kynge Henry ‖ the seuenth

Caxton's device on the verso. The eighth leaf is a blank.

Remarks.—The "lytyl booke in frenshe, named Eneydos," which happened to come under our Printer's notice while sitting in his study surrounded with many divers pamphlets, is a free paraphrase of portions of "The Æneid," by Virgil. Had Gawin Douglas, who, in 1553, issued a Scotch metrical version of "The Æneid," read Caxton's preface, he would have seen that Caxton does not pretend to give a translation of the Latin poem, and might have spared himself the trouble of some hundreds of lines in abuse thereof. The "Eneydos" was issued only as a romance compiled from Virgil's "Æneid" and Bocace's "Fall of Princes;" and, with little merit, it seems to have gained little favour, even with the lovers of such compilations, for it never reached a second edition. It would appear, however, that a good sale was expected, and an impression more numerous than usual struck off, as few of Caxton's books are so common as "Eneydos."

Existing Copies.—British Museum (3); Cambridge; Trinity College, Cambridge; Oxford (3); St. John's, Oxford; Hunterian, Glasgow; and 8 in private libraries.

No. 89.—The Dictes and Sayings of the Philosophers. *Third Edition. Folio. Westminster. The year* 1477 *erroneously reprinted, the real date being about* 1490.

Collation.—The device and prologue occupy two unsigned leaves; then, 𝔄 𝔅 ℭ 𝔇 𝔈 𝔉 𝔊 are 4^{ns}; ℌ and ℑ 3^{ns}, the sixth leaf of ℑ being blank. In all 70 leaves, of which the last is blank. Dr. Dibdin erroneously states "It contains only 66 leaves."

There is no title-page. The only type used is No. 6. The lines which are fully spaced out measure $4\frac{5}{8}$ inches. There are 30 and 32 lines to a page, but mostly 31. Without folios or catchwords. 2 and 3-line woodcut initials.

Caxton's device is in the centre of the first recto, the prologue commencing on the verso with a 2-line wood initial,

WHere it is so that euery creature by the suffraunce of our lord god is born and ordeyned to be subgette and thrall vnto the stormes of fortune . And so in diuerse and

SEdechias was the first. Philosophir by whom through the wyl and pleaser of our lord god. Sapience was vnderstande and lawes resceyued. whiche. Sedechias saide that euery creature of good beleue

The Text ends at foot of fifth recto of sig. ℑ,

Whom I beseche Almyghty god tencreee and to continue in his vertuous disposicion in this world . And after this lyf to lyue euer lastingly in heuen . Amen .

¶ Caxton me fieri fecit .

The verso and final leaf are blank.

Remarks.—This is another instance of the original date and imprint of a book being reproduced in subsequent editions. All the typographical particulars prove it to have been about 1490; and the presence of signatures, printed initials, and evenly spaced lines, give direct testimony against the date 1477, at which time none of these had been adopted at Westminster.

For literary particulars, see the first edition, page 186, *ante*.

EXISTING COPIES.—Cambridge: St. John's College, Cambridge; Oxford, and Lambeth Palace. Three copies are in private libraries.

No. 90.—THE MIRROUR OF THE WORLD. *Second Edition. Folio. The Name, Place, and Date of the First Edition reprinted; but about* 1490.

COLLATION.—a b c d e f g h i k l are 4os, the last leaf occupied with the device only. In all 88 leaves.

TYPOGRAPHICAL PARTICULARS.—There is no title-page. The type is all No. 6. The lines, which are spaced to an even length, measure 4⅝ inches, and a full page contains 31. Without folios or catchwords. 2 and 3-line initials in wood.

Commencing with a blank leaf, the table follows on the second recto, signed, however, a j.

The Text begins on a j recto,

Here begynneth ye table of the rubrices of this presente volume named the myrrour of the world or thymage of the same/

The Text ends on the seventh verso of sig. l,

and transportye lyf he brynge hym and vs in to his celestyal blysse in heuene AMEN/

¶ Caxton me fieri fecit.

On the eighth verso is the device, the recto being blank.

REMARKS.—Although this book bears the same dates as the first edition, it is very evident from the type, from the device, from the use of a woodcut to head Chapter II, which had been used shortly before in the "Royal Book," and from many other more minute evidences, that it really was not printed till about 1490.

It would seem that the proper cut for Chapter II, viz. a figure of a philosopher with the globe in his hand, having been injured or lost, that the workman chose the first which offered itself, and thus, in this edition, we have the very inappropriate illustration of Christ's transfiguration, as head to the chapter, "Why God made and created the World."

EXISTING COPIES.—Cambridge: Pepysian, Cambridge; Exeter College, Oxford; Hunterian, Glasgow; Baptist College, Bristol; and seven in private hands.

No. 91.—A BOOK OF DIVERS GHOSTLY MATTERS, CONTAINING:—THE SEVEN POINTS OF TRUE LOVE AND EVERLASTING WISDOM, OR OROLOGIUM SAPIENTIÆ: THE TWELVE PROFITS OF TRIBULATION;—THE RULE OF ST. BENET. *Quarto. Wyllelmu Caxton. "Emprynted westmynstre." Without Date.* (1490?)

COLLATION.—The "Seven points of True Wisdom" has A B C D E F G H J K L M all 4ns, or 96 leaves.

The "Twelve profits of Tribulation" has A B C D all 4ns, or 32 leaves.

The "Rule of St. Benet" has a b 4ns and c a 2n, or 20 leaves.

Total of the three tracts, 148 leaves, all printed.

Note.—The signatures to the third tract are unusual, viz. a is signed aa, a ij, aa iij, a iiij; b is signed bb b ij, b iij, b iiij; c is signed cc, c ij.

TYPOGRAPHICAL PARTICULARS.—Without title-page. The type throughout is No. 6. The lines, which are spaced to an even length, measure 3⅝ inches, and 24 make a full page. Without folios or catchwords.

The Text of "The Seven points of True Wisdom" begin on sig. A j:—

> Ttese ben the chapitres of thys tretyse of ye seuen poyntes of trewe loue and euerlastyng wysdom drawen oute of ye booke yt is writen in latyn and cleped Orologium sapiencie /

The tract ends thus, on sig. M 8 verso,

> ¶ Thus endith the treatyse of the vij poyntes of true loue & euerlastyng wysdom /

drawen of of the boke that is wryten in laten na
med Orologiu sapiecie .

¶ Emprynted at westmynstre

¶ Qui legit emendet / pressorem non repre
hendat

¶ Wyllelmu Caxton . Cui de⁹ alta tradat

The "Rule of St. Benet" ends on verso of sig. c 4,

¶ Emprynted at westmynstre by desiryng
of certeyn worshipfull persones : .

Remarks.—Little is known of Jehan de Soushavie, or Souaube, as a French copy has it. Bibliographers generally call him Henry de Suso, probably after the example of Echard, in his "Script. ordin. Prædicat." The English version printed by Caxton is correctly described, not as a translation, but as "drawen oute of" a book named "Orologium Sapientiæ." The printed text is not equal in extent to one-half of the original. Was it this induced Caxton to end the tract with "Qui legit emendet, *pressorem* nor reprehendat?"—a parody of the phrase often seen in manuscripts "Qui legit emendet *scriptorem* non reprehendat." Caxton says of the "Rule of St. Benet," which is a translation from the Latin, that he was employed to print it "by desire of certain worshipful persons."

The signatures given by the Printer to these three tracts suggest the probability that they were intended to be issued separately: but as in all the known copies they appear bound together, and as they have hitherto been described under the general head of "Divers Ghostly matters," it has been deemed advisable to retain that arrangement.

Existing Copies.—Cambridge, Durham Cathedral; and four in private libraries.

No. 92.—The Fifteen Oes, and other Prayers. *Quarto. Printed by commandment of the Princess Elizabeth, Queen of England, and the Princess Margaret, Mother unto our sovereign lord the King, by their most humble subject and servant William Caxton. Without Place or Date.* (1491?)

Collation.—a b are 4^{ns}; c is a 3^{n} = 22 leaves.

Typographical Particulars.—There is no title. The type is all No. 6. The lines, which are spaced to an even length, measure 3¼ inches, and there are 21 to a full page. Without folios or head-lines. Woodcut initials. A woodcut border, in four separate pieces, is placed round each page. This border was used later, for an undated but very early edition of "Horæ," by Wynken de Worde. The wood engraving of the Crucifixion, which appears upon the verso of the first leaf, has considerable artistic merit. It appears to have been a favourite, having been used at a later period, by Wynken de Worde, in several publications.

The recto of the first leaf is blank, but the verso is occupied with the woodcut of the Crucifixion, already noticed.

Upon the second recto (not signed, unless the signature has been cut away in binding) the Text begins with a 5-line initial in wood,—

> O Jhesu endles swetnes of
> louyng soules / O Jhesu
> gostly ioye passing & ex=
> cedyng all gladnes and
> desires. O Jhesu helthe &
> tendre louer of al repentaut sinners that

and on the verso of c 6, ends thus:—

> ¶ Thiese prayers tofore wreton ben en
> prited by the comaudementes of the mos
> te hye & vertuous pryncesse our liege la
> di Elizabeth by the grace of god Quene
> of Englonde & of Fraunce. & also of the

right hye & most noble pryncesse Marga rete Moder vnto our souerayn lorde the kyng / &c

¶ By their most humble subget and seruaunt William Caxton

REMARKS.—The fifteen prayers, named from the fact of their all commencing with the letter O, "the fifteen Oes," are commonly found in the manuscript Horæ of the fifteenth century, in their original Latin. They were frequently printed both in that language and in English, Caxton's version of the latter being possibly the earliest. All these prayers breathe a spirit of earnest devotion, and as an example the following is laid before the reader.

"O Jhesu heuenly leche haue mynde of thy langour and blewnes of thy woũdes & sorowe that thou suffredest in the heyght of the crosse / when thou were lifte vp fro the erthe / that thou were all to torne in all thy limmes / soo that there was noo limme abydynge in his right ioynte / soo that noo sorowe was like to thyne fro the sole of thy fote to the toppe of thy hede there was no hole place / And yet forgetying in maner all those greuous paynes / thou preydest deuoutly & charitably to thy fader for thine enmyes sayeng thus / Fader foryeue it theim / for they wyte not what they done / For this blessed charytable mercy that thou shewdest to thyne enemyes. and for mynde of thyse bytter paynes / graunte me / that the mynde of this bytter passion be to me plenar remyssion & foryeuenes of my sinnis Amen / ¶ Pater noster Aue maria"

Another prayer commences thus:—

"O blessid Jhesu swetnes of hertes and gostli hony of soules. I beseche the for the bytternes of the aysel and galle that thou tasted" &c.

The "Rex Henricus" of the Prayer on c iiij verso, was Saint Henry, surnamed the Pious and the Lame. He was son of Henry Duke of Bavaria, and was born in the year 972; crowned King of Germany, at Mentz, in 1002; died 14th July 1024; and was canonised by Pope Eugenius III in 1152.

Preceding a printed Latin version of the "Fifteen Oes" in the British Museum (C. 23. b. 24), is the following paragraph in English:—"These be the . xv. oos the whyche the holy virgyn saint brygitta was wonte to saye dayly before the holy rode in saint Paules chyrche at rome: who so saye this a hole yere he shall deleuer . xv. soules out of purgatory of hys nexte kyndred . and conuerte other . xv. synners to gode lyf and other . xv. ryghtuouse men of hys kynde shall perseuer in gode lyfe."

In *Harl. MS.* 2255 is a paraphrase of the "Fifteen Oes," by John Lydgate, beginning—"O blessyd lord my lord, O Christ Jesu."

The only EXISTING COPY known is in the British Museum (C. 25. c), and is bound with several tracts printed by Wynken de Worde. It is *perfect* and in good preservation, although a good deal cropped in the binding. Measurement, $6\frac{3}{8} \times 5$ inches. Purchased in 1851.

No. 93.—THE ART AND CRAFT TO KNOW WELL TO DIE. *Folio. Translated by Caxton in* 1490 *Without Printer's Name, Place, or Date.* (1491?)

COLLATION.—𝔄 a 4ⁿ; 𝔅 a 2ⁿ; then a single leaf improperly signed 𝔅 iij, which was, probably, followed by a blank. Total, thirteen printed leaves.

TYPOGRAPHICAL PARTICULARS.—There is no title-page. The only type used is No. 6. The lines, which measure $4\frac{5}{8}$ inches, are spaced to an even length, and there are 31 to a page. Without catchwords or folios. Several 2 and 3-line initials in wood.

The Text begins on sig. 𝔄 j recto,

¶ Here begynneth a lityll treatise shorte and abredged spekynge of the arte & craft to knowe well to dye

WHan it ys soo that what a man maketh or doeth / it is made to come to some ende / And yf the thynge be goode and well made / it muste nedes come to goode ede . Thenne by better & gretter reason / euery man oughte to

The Text ends on a single leaf, signed **b** iij,

> **Thus endeth the traytyse abredged of the arte to lerne well to deye / translated oute of frensshe in to englysshe . by willm Caxton the xv . day of Juyn / the yere of our lord a M iiij Clxxx x .**

REMARKS.—Manuscripts of this work are usually known as "The Art and Craft to live well and die well." This was often printed. A Latin edition was issued by Guy Marchand, at Paris, in 1483, and French editions by Verard, at Paris, and Colard Mansion, at Bruges. From the latter it seems very probable that our Caxton, as he says in the colophon, "abredged" his text.

An English version of the full work was made early in the sixteenth century by Andrew Chertsey, and printed by Wynken de Worde in 1506.

Copies are in the British Museum, Oxford, and National Library, Paris.

No. 94.—THE BOOK OF COURTESY.—*Quarto. Second Edition. "Emprynted at westmoster." Without Name or Date.* (1491 ?)

COLLATION.—This little piece probably consisted, like Caxton's early editions, of a 4° and a 3°, making fourteen leaves, all printed—a conclusion gathered from the only fragment known.

TYPOGRAPHICAL PARTICULARS.—The fragment, from which alone we know that such an edition was printed, consists of two quarto pages only, printed upon one side of a half-sheet, the other side being blank. One of the pages is signed **bb**, which, as already seen in "The Rule of St. Benet," was used for **b** j. Here then we have the first recto of the outermost sheet of the second signature, and, by folding the half-sheet with the unprinted part inside, we see directly that the opposing page must be the last of that signature, and, in all probability, the last of the tract.

The type is all No. 6, but the appearance of the small

device, which was probably never used in Caxton's lifetime, points out a late date for its execution.

The last lines, underneath which are the imprint and the small device, are as follows:—

a Thraue of thresshers a Lyeng of pdoners
a Lasshe of carters a Pastynes of cookes

¶ Here endeth a lytyll treatyse called
the booke of curtesye or lytyll John .
Enprynted atte westmoster .

The small "W. C." Device up-side-down.

As this edition, like the first and second, has three stanzas to the page, it would, although in a somewhat smaller type, take up the same number of leaves. The early editions had a blank leaf at the end, which here we find filled up with the curious epithets noticed above.

The *fragment* is in the Douce collection at the Bodleian, having apparently been rescued from the cover of a book. Measurement, $6\frac{3}{4} \times 5\frac{1}{4}$ inches. The reversal of the device, and the blank side of the paper, suggest the idea that this fragment was a *first proof*, although, from the numerous blunders in most of Caxton's pages, it is difficult to believe that corrections were ever made after the matter was once set up.

No. 95.—The Festial (Liber Festivalis). *Folio. Second Edition. "Caxton me fieri fecit." Without Place or Date.* (1491 ?)

Collation.—a b c d e f g h i k l m n o p are 4^{ns}, with the first leaf of a blank; q has but one printed sheet, or two leaves; R a 4^{n}; s a 3^{n}, with device on s 6. In all 136 leaves, of which one is blank.

TYPOGRAPHICAL PARTICULARS.—There is no title-page. The type consists of two sizes, Nos. 6 and 7, the latter being that in which Wynken de Worde printed many of his early books. The lines are in double column, and measure only 2⅝ inches. They are spaced to an even length, and there are 33 to a column. Without folios or catchwords. Plain initials, cut in wood, of the depth of 2, 3, or 5 lines are used. There is a small rude woodcut on sig. f 6 verso.

Commencing with a blank leaf, the prologue follows, in double column, on sig. a ij, the Text beginning—

¶ The helpe and grace of al=‖myghty god thrugh the besechyn‖ge of his blessed moder saynt ma‖ of all the hie festis of the yere. I ‖ wyll & praye that it be called fes=‖tiuall / the whiche begineth at the ‖

The Text ends on the fifth verso of sig. s, three-fourths of the way down the second column,

the rather by the helpe of his bles‖sid moder mary / & his holy spow=‖sesse saynt brygytte / and all sayn‖tes. AMEN

Caxton me fieri fecit

The next recto is a blank page, the verso having the large device.

REMARKS.—From the use of No. 7 type, which was Wynken de Worde's, it is very probable that this book was printed by him immediately after his master's death. This edition too is not an exact reprint of Caxton's, issued in 1483. Every Festival has the prefix "Gode men and wymmen," or "Good frendis," and every tale is preceded by the word "Narracio." Several stories not in the first edition have been added, while the Pardon of Corpus Christi, in Latin and English, which follows Trinity Sunday in first edition, is here entirely omitted.

Copies are in the British Museum, Cambridge, Oxford; and three private libraries.

No. 96.—FOUR SERMONS. *Folio. Second Edition. Sine ullâ notâ.* (1491 ?)

COLLATION.—A B C are 4ns; D is a 5n = 34 leaves.

TYPOGRAPHICAL PARTICULARS.—There is no title. The type is all No. 6. In double column. The lines measure 2½ inches, being a very little shorter than the "Festial," and are spaced to an even length. 33 lines to a column. Without folios or catchwords.

The Text begins on sig. A j, with a 3-line woodcut initial:—

The maygster of sentence in the seconde boke · and the fyrst dystynction / sa=‖yth that the soueraygn cause / whi ‖ god made all creatures in heuen ‖ se myn owne soule . ne yours / I ‖ purpose me by his leue hoomly ‖ thus to shew it and rede it to you ‖ in the boke / for to your lernynge ‖ it is as good thus as wythout ‖

The Text ends half-way down the second column of the ninth verso of sig. D, with the collect "Absolve quesumus," the last three lines being—

gloria inter sanctos et electos tuos ressussitati respirent / Per ‖ xpm dmn nostrum Amen / ‖

On the recto of the tenth leaf is the device of Caxton, the verso being blank.

For REMARKS, see the first edition, page 263.

Copies are in the British Museum, Cambridge, and three private libraries.

No. 97.—ARS MORIENDI; THAT IS TO SAY, THE CRAFT FOR TO DIE FOR THE HEALTH OF MAN'S SOUL. *Quarto. Without Printer's Name, Date or Place.* (1491 ?)

COLLATION.—A a 4n = 8 leaves, all printed.

TYPOGRAPHICAL PARTCULARS.—No title-page. The type of the text is No. 6, but the four lines of heading at the beginning, and some head-lines at the end, are in Wynken de Worde's No. 1 type. The lines are spaced very evenly, except on four pages at the end, and there are 24 to a page. Woodcut initials to chapters. Without folios or catchwords. With the exception of the use of Wynken de Worde's type, this tract agrees in all particulars with No. 83, "The Gouvernal of Helthe."

The Text begins on sig. A j recto,

> ¶ Here begynneth a lytyll treatyse schortely compyled and called ars moriendi / that is to saye the craft for to deye for the helthe of mannes sowle.

> When ony of lykly hode shal deye / thenne is moste necessarye to haue a specyall

The tract ends on A 8 verso, with a full page:—

> For suche right here ad-uersite or oni tribulacon
> To that ye chirche techeth ye put ful credulyte.
>
> That god hath purpaced trust it well withou defallacyon.
>
> In hope abydyng his reward and euerlastyng glorie. Amen Explicit.

Remarks.—This short tract appears to be a translation from the Latin, and doubtless by Caxton himself. No other copy, however, manuscript or printed, in Latin or any other language, appears to be known.

This unique specimen is in the middle of a volume of black-letter tracts in the Bodleian Library.

No. 98.—The Chastising of God's Children. *Folio. Sine ullâ notâ.* (1491?)

Collation.—An unsigned sheet (two leaves), containing table and prologue; A B C D E F G are 8vo; H a 2°. In all 48 leaves, and no blanks.

Typographical Particulars.—In this book we meet with the first approach to a title-page, which consists of a

3-line paragraph printed in the centre of the first recto. The types are No. 6 for the Text, No. 7 being found on the first page only. Double column—the lines measuring 2⅝ inches, and being fully spaced out. 36 lines to a column. Without folios or catchwords. Initials in wood 3 and 4 lines deep.

The Text begins with the following 3 lines in the centre of the first recto,

¶ The prouffytable boke for manes soule / And right comfor=‖table to the body / and specyally in aduersitee & trybulacyon / whiche ‖ boke is called The Chastysing of goddes Chyldern

On the verso, with a floriated 5-line initial, and in double column, the first two lines being in type No. 7,

IN drede of almigh=
ty ‖ god Relygyous
sus= ‖ ter a short
pistle I sen ‖ de
you of the mater of ‖ temp=
tacons / whiche pystle as
me ‖

The causes considered . and
many ‖ other skylfully . I
may drede to wri ‖ te of this
chastysing But askyng ‖
helpe of god almyghty / by
whoos ‖ might the asse had
speche to the pro ‖

The Text ends on the recto of sig. h 4, with the verso blank,

not denye to the alone that
prayest ‖ her soo besely / Yet
ouer all this ‖ whan thou art
harde tempted . and ‖
* * * * *

to ful Joye & blisse / Now
god gra ‖ unt that it myghte
so be . that euer is lastyng
in Trinyte /

REMARKS.—The use of a title-page, a practice unknown to Caxton, the appearance of type No. 7, and the adoption of signatures having three sheets only—all point to Wynken de Worde, rather than to Caxton, as the printer of this book, which was probably executed about 1491. The original writer of the work is unknown, and there seems but little reason for attributing its composition to Caxton.

EXISTING COPIES.—British Museum; Cambridge, University Library (2); Pepysian, and Sydney Sussex College; Hunterian, Glasgow; Lincoln Cathedral; Sion College, London; and three copies in private hands.

No. 99.—A TREATISE OF LOVE. *Folio. Translated in* 1493.
Without Printer's Name, Place, or Date. (1493?)

COLLATION.—A B C D E F G H are all 3^{ns} = 48 leaves, all printed.

TYPOGRAPHICAL PARTICULARS.—Without title. The type is No. 6 for the Text, but on the first page is a line in type No. 7, the first of Wynken de Worde's founts. The whole is in double column.

The Text begins on sig. A j recto,

¶ This tretyse is of loue
and spe || kyth of iiij of the
most specyall lo || uys that
ben in the worlde and she
* * * * *
whiche tretyse was
translatid out of frenshe
Into en = || glyshe / the yere
of our lord M cccc || lxxxxiij /
by a persone that is vnper ||
fight insuche werke wherfor
he hu || bly byseche the lernyd
reders wyth || pacyens to cor=
recte it where they || fynde
nede. And they & alle other ||
redders of their charyte to
pray for || the soule of the
sayde translatour ||

The Text ends on the second column of the sixth recto of sig. H,

Whiche boke was lately
transla= || ted outeof frensh
in to englisshe || by a Right

well dysposed persone/ ‖ for
by cause the sayd persone
thoug ‖ hte it necessary to al
deuoute peple ‖ to rede / or to
here it redde / And also ‖
caused the sayd boke to be
enpryn= ‖ ted /

Underneath this is the small device. The reverse is blank.

REMARKS.—This is evidently an issue from the press of Wynken de Worde, whose earliest type is seen in the first page, and who was accustomed to make up his books in 8^{ns} instead of 4^{ns}, as was the plan during Caxton's life. The tract does not appear to have been translated till 1493, and may have gone to press the succeeding year: now Caxton died in 1491. The non-occurrence of the small device in any other book attributed to Caxton is another reason for supposing it to be in reality the workmanship of Wynken de Worde, who frequently used this shaped device in his early publications. At a later period he added his own name to the design.

Although not the work of Caxton, "A Treatise of Love" has been included in this chapter, because "A List of Books printed in Type No. 6" would be imperfect without it.

Copies are at Cambridge; Hunterian, Glasgow; and two private libraries.

Plate XIV.

*From Caxton's "Order of Chivalry." Type 4**

¶ Here after foloweth the mater and tenour of this said Booke. And the Fyrst chappyter saith how the good Heremyte deuysed to the Esquyer the Rule & ordre of chyualrye

[A] Contrey ther was in which it happed that a wyse knyght which longe had mayntened the ordre of chyualrye And that by the force & noblesse of his hyghe courage and wysedom and in auenturyng his body had mayntened warres Justes & tornoyes / & in many batailles had had many noble vyctoryes & glorious / & by cause he sawe & thought in his corage that he myght not long lyue / as he which by long tyme had ben by cours of nature nyghe vnto his ende / chaas to hym an hermytage / For nature faylled in hym by age / And hadde no power ne vertu to vse

Plate XV.

Woodcuts from Caxton's "Speculum vitæ Christi."

Plate XVI.

The earliest instance of a Title-page in any English Book;
Printed about 1491.

¶ The prouffytable boke for mannes soule/ And right comfor-
table to the body/ and specyally in aduersitee & trybulacyon/ which
boke is called The Chastysing of goddes Chyldern

Plate XVII.

WOODCUT INITIALS FROM CAXTON'S BOOKS.

Plate XVIII.

CAXTON'S DEVICE.

A

LIST OF BOOKS

NOT PRINTED BY

WILLIAM CAXTON,

BUT HAVING SOME

CONNECTION WITH HIS TYPES;

ALSO OF

DOUBTFUL WORKS,

AND

BOOKS ERRONEOUSLY ASCRIBED TO HIS PRESS.

No. 100.—THE LIFE OF SAINT KATHERINE.—THE REVELATIONS OF SAINT ELIZABETH OF HUNGARY. *Folio. Sine ullâ notâ.* (1493?)

COLLATION.—a is a 4^{n}; b c d e f g h i k l m n o p are 8^{ns}; q is a 2^{n}. Total 96 leaves, all printed.

TYPOGRAPHICAL PARTICULARS.—There is no title-page. The type for some of the headings is No. 7, the same as that already noticed in "Chastising" and "Festial;" but the type for the body of the work is a partial re-casting of No. 4*, with many new additions, and on a rather smaller body, being evidently a different fount from any known to have been used by Caxton. For a more full account of these see the chapter on type No. 4. The pages are in double column, and have 43 and 44 lines to a page. Full lines measure 2$\frac{7}{8}$ inches. Without folios or catchwords.

This book, like some already mentioned, was in all probability the workmanship of Wynken de Worde, shortly after Caxton's death. This opinion is borne out by the types used, by the signatures being in 8^{ns} instead of 4^{ns}; by very long pages, and by wood initials, identical with those used in the early books of Wynken de Worde.

No. 101.—THE GOLDEN LEGEND. *Third Edition. Folio. "Fynysshed at westmestre . . The year of our lord M CCCC lxxxxiij / . . ¶ By me wyllyam Caxton."*

COLLATION.—Table and prologue a 2^{n}; a b c d e are 4^{ns}; ff a single sheet; f g h i k l m n o p q r s t v x y z & 9 are

4^{ns}; e a 2^{n}, signed to e iij; A B C D E F G H I K L M N O P Q R S T V X Y are 4^{ns}; aa bb cc dd ee are 4^{ns}; ff a 3^{n}, signed to ff iiij; and gg a 2^{n}, signed to gg iij. Total 436 leaves, all printed.

TYPOGRAPHICAL PARTICULARS.—Without title-page. The types are No. 7, and the re-casting of type No. 4*, noticed in the preceding work, which fount is only known to have been used for these two books. The work is in double column, and the lines, of which there are 44 to a column, measure 2⅞ inches. Without folios or catchwords. Many woodcuts and woodcut initials.

Caxton died two years before the date of printing.

No. 102.—THE SIEGE OF RHODES. *Folio. Sine ullâ notâ.*

COLLATION.—Four unsigned 3^{ns}, or 24 leaves all printed.

TYPOGRAPHICAL PARTICULARS.—Without title of any sort. The type is very rude and uneven, being a different fount to that used for the "St. Katherine" and "Golden Legend" just noticed. Some of the letters are the same as Caxton's No. 4*, but many rude additions have been made. There is a space between each line, probably made by the use of "reglets," the unevenness of which is very apparent. The lines are spaced to an even length, and there are 26 to a page, except the first and second, which have, respectively, 30 and 31. They measure in length 4½ inches, the depth of 26 lines varying from 7 to 7⅛ inches. Without signatures, folios, catchwords, or printed initials.

No. 103.—MISSALE AD USUM SARUM.—EXARATUM PARISIUS IMPENSA OPTIMI VIRI GUILLERMI CAXTON. *Folio. Paris, 4th Dec.* 1487.

The type is the usual church text used for service books. In double column, with head-lines.

As connected with Caxton, the whole of the interest centres in the colophon.

Missale ad usum Sar' cun ctitenctis dei dono / magno conamine elaboratum finis feliciter. Exaratum Parisius impensa optimi viri Guillermi Caxton. Arte vero et industria Magistri Guillermi Maynyal. Anno domini M.CCCC.lxxxvii. iiij Decembris.

This is on the recto of the last leaf, and upon the verso is Caxton's large device.

Remarks.—Passing by the great interest which this missal has in being five years earlier in date than the celebrated Rouen edition, dated October 1st, 1492, hitherto considered as the *editio princeps*, we have to elucidate it in relation to Caxton.

It has not, until the discovery of this volume, been supposed that Caxton employed foreign printers to help him, although it is well known that his successors did so. In this case he used the services of a printer at Paris, whose name very seldom appears in typographical annals. Little is known of William Maynyal, who is erroneously called, by Panzu, George. In 1480, working in conjunction with Ulric Gering, the first printer at Paris, he produced "Speculum aureum," as well as "Sumina de virtutibus cardinalibus," both in Roman types. Afterwards, he worked alone. In 1487, Caxton, not having appropriate types of his own, sent instructions to Maynyal, of Paris, to print for him the Salisbury Missal. The commission was executed, and Caxton, desirous of associating his press more directly with this issue than by the colophon only, which many people might overlook, probably designed his "mark" for the purpose of attracting attention. It is certainly the earliest date at which it has yet been found; and the state of the block, which has fewer breakages than any other known example, confirms the priority of this in a most interesting manner. Since 1484 Caxton had not used woodcuts; but just at this time, 1487, he appears to have found some one for the purpose, and the "Royal Book" and the "Speculum" appeared with numerous cuts. The same artist was probably employed to design and engrave the new "trade mark."

The only known copy is in the possession of W. J. Legh, Esq., M.P., and was first made known in the *Athenæum*, March 21st, 1874.

Bartholomeus de Proprietatibus Rerum.

This work is supposed to have been printed by Caxton, at Cologne, on the strength of a statement by Wynken de Worde. As, however, this printer has perpetrated the most curious contradictions and mis-statements in many of his prologues and colophons, it seems more than probable that he blundered here also, as no connection whatever can be traced between the typographical customs of Caxton and those of the Cologne school; nor does any copy of "Bartholomeus" exist which can, with any show of reason, be attributed to Caxton's press.

For further remarks on this subject, see page 64.

The Metamorphoses of Ovid.

In the Pepysian library, Cambridge (2124) is an English manuscript of the fifteenth century, not improbably Caxton's autograph, and consisting of the Tenth, Eleventh, Twelfth, Thirteenth, Fourteenth, and Fifteenth Books of Ovid's Metamorphoses. Each book in the manuscript begins with a red-ink title, the first being:—

"Here followeth the || xth booke of Ouyde · || wherof the first fa || ble is of the mari || age of Orpheus || and Erudice his lo || ue . Cap° p'm°."

For an imitation of this paragraph see Dibdin's *Typ. Ant.*, vol. i, page 14. At the end of the volume is the following colophon:—

"Translated and fynysshed by me William Caxton at Westmestre the xxij day of Apryll / the yere of our lord m . iiij^{c} iiij^{xx} And the xx yere of the Regne of kyng Edward the fourth."

Now Caxton, from what we know of his disposition, would never have begun a translation in the middle of a book. He therefore, no doubt, translated the former nine books also. But all Caxton's translations, and especially in the busy time of 1480, were made for the press. There seems, therefore, good reason to believe that the Metamorphoses were printed also by Caxton, although unfortunately no fragment of such a work is at present known.

It seems not unlikely that the Pepysian MS. is in Caxton's own autograph.

The Life and Miracles of Robert Earl of Oxford.

In the preface to "The Four Sons of Aymon," Caxton says, "Therefore late at the request and commandment of the right noble and virtuous Earl, John, Earl of Oxford, my good singular and especial lord I reduced and translated out of French into our maternal and English tongue the life of one of his predecessors named Robert Earl of Oxford tofore said, with divers and many great miracles which god showed for him as well in his life as after his death as is showed all along in his said book."

Having translated this Life, it is not improbable that Caxton also printed it.

A Ballad.

The "small fragment of an unknown work," preserved among some old ballads in the British Museum (643. m.) and described by Sir Henry Ellis, and Dr. Dibdin in *Typ. Ant.*, vol. i, page 359, is a portion of the "Cook's Tale," from Caxton's first edition of Chaucer's "Canterbury Tales."

Several works, such as "Statuta" (probably Machlinia's) "Lyndewode's Constitutiones," "The Lucidary," "An Accidence," and others, have been by various writers included among the books issued by Caxton, but in all cases erroneously.

THE COMPARATIVE RARITY OF BOOKS PRINTED BY CAXTON,

SHOWING THE NUMBER OF COPIES OF EACH WORK KNOWN TO EXIST.

Quanta fuisti si tanta sunt Reliquiæ.

	No. of Copies known.
Book of Courtesy, 2nd edit.	*frag.*
Directorium Sacerdotum, 4to.	*frag.*
Horæ, 1st edition	*frag.*
Ditto, 2nd ditto	*frag.*
Ditto, 3rd ditto	*frag.*
Indulgence—Sixtus IV	*frag.*
Anelida and Arcyte	1
Ars moriendi	1
Aymon, Four Sons of	1
Blanchardin and Eglantine	1
Book of Courtesy, 1st edition	1
Catho, Parvus et Magnus, 1st edition, 4to	1
Ditto, ditto, 2nd edition, 4to	1
Charles the Great	1
Chorle and the Bird, 1st edit.	1
Ditto ditto 2nd ditto	1
Commemoracio beatæ Mariæ	1
Death-Bed Prayers	1
Directorium Sacerdotum, folio, 1st edition	1
Ditto ditto ditto 2nd ditto	1
Fifteen Oes	1
Glass, Temple of	1
Gouvernal of Health	1
Horse, Sheep, and Goose, 1st edit.	1
Ditto ditto 2nd ditto	1½
Image of Pity	1
Infancia Salvatoris	1
Indulgence—Sixtus IV	1

	No. of Copies known.
Another, different	1
Meditacions sur les sept Pseaulmes	1
Paris and Vienne	1
Psalterium	1
Quatre derrenieres Choses	1
Reynard the Fox, 2nd edition	1
Servitium de Transfiguratione	1
Sex Litteræ	1
Visitatio Mariæ Virginis	1
Brass, Temple of	1½
Advertisement, An	2
• Arthur, Life of King	2
Propositio Johannis Russell	2
Saona, Gul. de	2
Stans Puer	2
Æsop, Fables of	3
Art and Craft	3
Catho, Parvus et Magnus, folio, 3rd edition	3
Curia Sapientiæ	3
Curial, The	3
Dictes and Sayings, 2nd edition	3
Good Manners, Book of	3
Jason, Les fais du	3
Moral Proverbs	3
Rhodes, Siege of	3
Saint Winifred, Life of	3
Book of Fame	4
Chivalry, Order of	4

	No. of Copies known.
Festial, The, 1st edition	4
Treatise of Love	4
Troilus and Creside	4
Vocabulary	4
Golden Legend, 2nd edition	5
Pilgrimage of the Soul	5
Four Sermons, 2nd edition	5
Divers Ghostly Matters	6
Festial, The, 2nd edition	6
Knight of the Tower	6
Recueil, Le	6
Reynard the Fox, 1st edition	6
Statutes of Henry VII	6
Chronicles of England, 2nd edit.	7
Dictes and Sayings, 3rd edition	7
Jason, The Life of	7
Chastising of God's Children	8
Four Sermons, 1st edition	8
Life of our Lady	8
Royal Book	8
Canterbury Tales, 1st edition	9
Ditto 2nd ditto	9
Chess, Game and Play of, 2nd edit.	9
Doctrinal of Sapience	9
Golden Legend, 3rd edition	9

	No. of Copies known.
Chess, Game and Play of, 1st ed.	10
Chronicles of England, 1480	10
Cordial	10
Description of Britain	10
Godfrey of Boloyn	10
Katherine, Life of St.	10
Speculum Vitæ Christi	11
Caton	12
Mirrour of the World, 2nd edit.	12
Dictes and Sayings, 1st edition	15
Mirrour of the World, 1st edit.	15
Boethius	16
Confessio Amantis	16
Recuyell, The	16
Eneydos	18
Fayts of Arms	21
Tully of Old Age, &c.	23
Polycronicon	25
Golden Legend, 1st edition	31

The reader who examines this list may well be astonished at the number here given of *unique* Caxtons. Out of 99 works above enumerated, no less than 38 are known to us by single copies, or by fragments only. The fact is almost incredible even to those most conversant with the rarities of the Westminster Press; and the question naturally arises—If about one-third of Caxton's issue has been *nearly* destroyed, how numerous may have been the editions of which we shall never learn the existence? A glance at the titles of the *uniques* will show that the books most liable to destruction, probably owing in part to their being much used, and in part to the destructiveness of religious sectarianism, are those, directly or indirectly, of an ecclesiastical character—such as "Horæ," "Psalters," "Meditacions," &c. .School books also, such as the "Stans Puer," "Catho," &c., are always difficult of preservation. On the other hand, there seems no especial reason for the almost total destruction of such works as the romances of "King Arthur," "The Four Sons of Aymon," "Blanchardin," "Charles the Great," the second edition of "Reynard," or the various short poems in quarto.

The greatest number of copies ever brought together is 81, being the number now in the British Museum; but of these 25 are duplicates, leaving the number of works 56, of which three are mere fragments. The Caxtons in Earl Spencer's Library, although numerically less than those of the National Library, make nevertheless a more complete collection, and embrace 57 separate works. Other Libraries come far behind these two. The Public Library, Cambridge, has 38 separate works, a total considerably augmented by the numerous unique pieces of poetry in quarto. The Bodleian has 28 separate works, and the Duke of Devonshire 25.

INDEX.

www.ingramcontent.com/pod-product-compliance
Lightning Source LLC
Chambersburg PA
CBHW021332110726
47900CB00005B/1432
* 9 7 8 3 3 3 7 0 3 0 8 6 5 *